What People Are Saying About
Teen Ink™ *Written in the Dirt ...*

"As a parent and storyteller, I find great hope for the future based on the depth of feeling and creativity in this unique book."

George Lucas
filmmaker

"*Teen Ink* is a forum for young people's voices."

Amazon.com

"It's thrilling to me to read these pieces by teen writers—not only because of the dozens and dozens of new ideas, but because of the passion for writing these teens bring to their work."

R. L. Stine
author, *Fear Street* and *Goosebumps* series

"*Teen Ink* is a great tool for the classroom or for those who wish to establish a connection with young people and events/feelings in their lives. . . . A must purchase."

KLIATT

"This book is the answer to anyone who complains that American teens don't express their ideas very well or that they don't have many ideas worth expressing. The stories, poetry and art in these pages let us see things through fresh and unspoiled eyes."

Charles Osgood
television and radio commentator,
host of *CBS Sunday Morning*

"Today's young people have so much to say to one another. I applaud *Teen Ink* for providing a forum for their voices."

Lois Lowry
author, *The Giver*

"*Teen Ink* is solid, lively and extremely candid. The writing is first-rate and fills an important need."

Jonathan Kozol
author, *Amazing Grace*

"Teens looking for more substantial fare than music videos, mall sales and fashion magazines should check out *Teen Ink*. Adults, too, will gain insight into adolescent concerns."

U.S. Airways *Attaché* magazine

"You don't need to be a teenager to benefit from the passion and intelligence flowing from these prose, poetry and artwork in this inspiring collection."

Parenting Today's Teens.com

"This title is sure to be popular with fans of the series and useful for teachers looking for strong examples of student writing."

School Library Journal, 2003

"The *Teen Ink* books are the best out there for teenagers. Because all the fiction, poetry and artwork is created by teens, readers get the chance to see the world through the eyes of their contemporaries. In a world dominated by adult literature, *Teen Ink* is a breath of fresh air."

Rosy Hilliard, age 17

"Teens will read the book cover-to-cover in one sitting because they won't be able to put it down. I recommend it to parents and teachers as a mightily effective way to recapture a vision of the world from a teen perspective."

Sara Hoaglund Hunter
parent and author, *The Unbreakable Code*

"*Teen Ink* invites young authors to write down and share their ideas, beliefs, feelings and aspirations. At a time of technological upheaval, this seemingly traditional practice may constitute the most radical innovation."

Howard Gardner
author and professor, Harvard University
Graduate School of Education

"My name is Candace Coleman, and I recently read one of the *Teen Ink* books, and I loved it because it was something I could relate to as a young person."

Candace Coleman, age 17

"Most of the adults think that we are brats, a group of annoying "mocking-adults." However, there is someone who really cares about us and takes us seriously. It even generously giving us a wide space to voice our own ideas. What else? It must be *Teen Ink*!"

Coral Eng-Yuh Lean, age 19

"*Teen Ink* lets kids show their creativity."

Lakeland (FL) Ledger

"There is a story for everyone, but I loved every single one, and I am sure you will too!"

Liz Murphy, age 19

"The stories here show that teenagers aren't lifeless, careless, thoughtless and heartless pieces of humans, who do nothing but whine, moan, complain, fight and scream. That we, too, can express ourselves not through yelling, but through the art of the word. *Teen Ink* is my number-one choice for teenage literature."

Mark Christmas, age 13

Written in the Dirt

Fiction by Teens

A collection of
Short Stories
Poetry
Art
Photography

Edited by
Stephanie H. Meyer
John Meyer

Health Communications, Inc.
Deerfield Beach, Florida

www.hcibooks.com
www.TeenInk.com

The following pieces were originally published by The Young Authors Foundation, Inc. (©1989–2004) in *The 21st Century/Teen Ink* magazine. We gratefully acknowledge the many individuals who granted us permission to reprint the cited material.

"Marbles in Hands." Reprinted by permission of Torey Bocast. ©2002 Torey Bocast.

"Written in the Dirt." Reprinted by permission of Timothy Cahill. ©1997 Timothy Cahill.

"Eggplant Parm." Reprinted by permission of Melissa Sowin. ©2001 Melissa Sowin.

"Even the Devil Waits in Line." Reprinted by permission of Axel Arth. ©2003 Axel Arth.

"Iron Fence." Reprinted by permission of Gretchen Loye. ©2002 Gretchen Loye.

"Speak to Me." Reprinted by permission of Joyce Sun. ©1999 Joyce Sun.

"Looking over Gaza." Reprinted by permission of Kerry E. McIntosh. ©2003 Kerry E. McIntosh.

(continued on page 390)

Library of Congress Cataloging-in-Publication Data

Teen ink : written in the dirt— / edited by Stephanie H. Meyer, John Meyer.
   p. cm.
  Stories originally published in the 21st Century/Teen Ink magazine, 1989–2004.
  Summary: A collection of poetry, fiction, photography, and art by teenagers, exploring their versions and experiences of what it means to be a teenager.
  ISBN 0-7573-0050-2
  1. Teenagers—Literary collections. 2. Teenagers' writings, American. 3. Teenage artists—United States. [1. Teenagers—Literary collections. 2. Youths' writings. 3. Youths' art.] I. Meyer, Stephanie H., date. II. Meyer, John, date.

PZ5.T294975 2004
810.8'09283'09049—dc22

2003068587

Publisher: Health Communications, Inc.
           3201 S.W. 15th Street
           Deerfield Beach, FL 33442-8190

Cover illustration and design by Larissa Hise Henoch
Inside book design by Lawna Patterson Oldfield

"Fiction is fact's elder sister."

—RUDYARD KIPLING

"Poetry is life distilled."

—GWENDOLYN BROOKS

For Matty, the newest light of our lives
And for all our future readers!

Contents

2. Learning to Live: Family Pieces

3. Bales of Comfort: Creative Works

4. A Forced Eruption: Challenging Tales

5. The Visitor: And More from Other Worlds

6. I'll Call You: Love and Friends Explored

7. Dragon: Fairy Tales Redux

Preface

by Jason Drake

Everyone expects me to be able to do this. They've all told me what a great writer I am. Being asked to write the preface is supposed to be a great honor, and a lot of people have a lot of faith that I can do it.

To be honest, I don't have the first idea where to start.

This book, as I understand it, is supposed to be for teens, by teens. It should be simple, then, expounding on that concept. All I need to say is, "Hey, you. Yes, you, the one reading the preface. This is a book for teens, by teens. You should probably buy it, you know, if you're interested in teens and stuff."

If only things were so easy.

The problem is that I haven't the faintest clue as to just what a "teen" is. I've always considered myself more than a little detached from my generation, and I have a hard time understanding my peers. Who are they? What drives them? Just what is this creature, this teenager, anyway?

The conventional answer, of course, is that a teenager is someone who falls between the ages of twelve and twenty, probably attends a school of some sort, and generally overreacts to life's problems. This definition isn't entirely unreasonable, and, in fact, most people are

entirely content to let the issue end there. For our pur-
poses, however, this answer is also entirely unsatisfac-
tory. So where do we go from here? Whom do we ask?

Here's what I think, or rather, what I *don't* think: I
don't think there is any one person you can ask who can
give you a definitive answer. There *is* no definitive
answer. Instead, you have a multitude of voices crying
out, saying, "*This* is what it is to be a teenager. *This* is
what it's about." You'd have to listen to them all, piece
them together, figure out how they relate to one another,
and maybe then you'd have an answer.

That's what this book is truly about—over 150 teenage
voices, struggling to be heard above the din. These are
their stories, *their* experiences and *their* versions of what
it means to be a teenager told in poetry, fiction, photography and art. Read them. Look at them. Think them
over. Compare them with each other, and yours, and
then maybe we can all be one step closer to understanding just what it is to be a human being. Or at least
a teenager.

*Jason Drake, still very much a teen, created his imagi-
native piece, "So Long-a in Uganda" (page 139), which
first appeared in* Teen Ink *magazine.*

Preface

by Juliet Lamb

It was one of those days that just wasn't meant to be.

I overslept my alarm by almost a half-hour, making me late for work. The Red Sox lost. My computer shut down unexpectedly, swallowing several pages of an essay, and my family's only response was an unsympathetic, "You should have saved it." It rained. My friend was out of town.

Alone, these small annoyances might be laughed off, but taken together, they drove me deeper into a black mood. The only retreat was my bedroom. I wanted to sit and glower at the world without anyone suggesting that, compared to Africa's starving children, my problems weren't that bad.

After several minutes of self-pity, I picked up a notebook. *Perhaps,* I thought, *the day won't seem as rotten if I write about it.* I found a pen, smoothed out the first page and scribbled, "It is April 22nd."

No—April sounded too pretty. Self-pity didn't fit with blooming daffodils and spring rains; the month ought to be as miserable as I was. Replacing "April" with "February," I devoted the next few sentences to gleefully describing February's awfulness. Only when a priest appeared in my second paragraph did I realize I was no longer writing about me. This was someone else's story; all we had in common was an awful day. Strangely, I didn't mind.

I wrote for hours, getting up only to turn on the light. When I emerged, eight pages of nearly illegible writing later, my terrible mood was gone. The retreat into my characters and their fictional world had cured the misery of my bad day.

Being a teenager inevitably involves more than its share of such awful days. Adults have trouble understanding the unique trials of these years without trivializing them; we often find their sympathy tempered by a feeling, on some level, that our difficulties can't possibly compare with those of the "real world." Conversely, we often lack an outlet for our ecstasy over inconsequential victories. Adolescence is all about emotion. When no audience can fully appreciate our triumphs and sorrows, we turn to music, drama, sports and, like the authors of these pages, writing.

Each piece here represents the tip of an iceberg: drawers stuffed with loose-leaf pages, cramped wrists, pencils sharpened down to nothing. Behind them are years of reading, hours spent searching for the perfect word, nights accompanied by the clicking of a keyboard. They represent successes and failures, touchdowns and strike-outs, compliments and jeers. Some of us have lived through horrible experiences, while others, like me, have suffered only the occasional bad day. Yet we all share the trait that when our lives seem out of hand, we turn to writing. We don't do it for recognition (although that's certainly nice). We do it because we *have* to.

So, as you enjoy these stories and poems, take time to consider and appreciate the voices behind them. And keep in mind that the next time you hear someone say "I'm having a terrible day," listen! Who knows what you might be missing?

Juliet Lamb, now in college, penned her engaging tale "Hollow" (page 36), which depicts a priest in turmoil, while she was in high school.

Introduction

Have you ever seen a *Teen Ink* book? If you haven't, welcome to the world of teen expression. This book is truly unique because everything in these pages is created entirely by teenagers.

You may wonder how this book came about. Well, it all started fifteen years ago when our children were teenagers. We had the idea that it would be good to give all teens the chance to be heard, so we began to publish a magazine filled with their words. Unlike a high-school newspaper that reports school events and is created by a few lucky kids, *Teen Ink* was a safe, open place to chronicle the highs and the lows of the teen experience. Whether from Utah, California, Maine or France, all teenagers were encouraged to submit and began sending us their creations in droves. Before we knew it, we had more pieces than we could use—and that has continued since our first issue back in 1989, before some of you were born!

A few years ago, after publishing 20,000 teens, we realized that we wanted to share some of these amazing pieces with a much larger audience—including you. And so the *Teen Ink* book series was born! The first five books are available in bookstores nationwide and on the

Web: *Teen Ink: Our Voices, Our Visions; Teen Ink 2: More Voices, More Visions; Teen Ink: Friends and Family; Teen Ink: Love and Relationships* and *Teen Ink: What Matters.* All these books are collections of some of the most stunning pieces and poems we've seen. Teens and adults alike grabbed over 200,000 books, which is quite a feat! Then we realized that none of them showcased enough fiction and poetry.

So here is the sixth book, filled with creativity in its purest form: fiction and poetry (as well as art and photographs). The stories run the gamut from fairy tales to science fiction to stories that feel so real you'll think they could be happening to you. And the poems—some so beautiful, some funny and others poignant—all touch the essence of teens' experiences.

So open these pages and read! And if you are a teen, you are invited to join the thousands of other young people who have seen their names in our magazines and books by sending your work to us.

Stephanie and John Meyer
publishers of Teen Ink *magazine*

Welcome

This is your book! All the words and images on these pages were created by teens just like you and gathered from pieces that appeared in *Teen Ink* magazine during the past fourteen years.

Did you know that this is the sixth book in the *Teen Ink* series? The first five *(Teen Ink: Our Voices, Our Visions; Teen Ink 2: More Voices, More Visions; Teen Ink: Friends and Family; Teen Ink: Love and Relationships* and *Teen Ink: What Matters)* are all available in bookstores nationwide and on the Web.

You can join these teenage authors and artists by sending us *your* stories, poems, art and photography to be considered for the monthly *Teen Ink* magazine and future books in this series.

If you want to participate, see the submission guidelines on page 363. You can send your submissions through our Web site: *www.TeenInk.com,* e-mail us at *Submissions@TeenInk.com,* or through the mail to Teen Ink, Box 97, Newton, MA 02461.

To learn more about the magazine and to request a free sample copy, see our Web site at *www.TeenInk.com.*

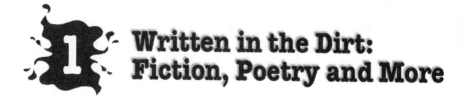

Written in the Dirt:
Fiction, Poetry and More

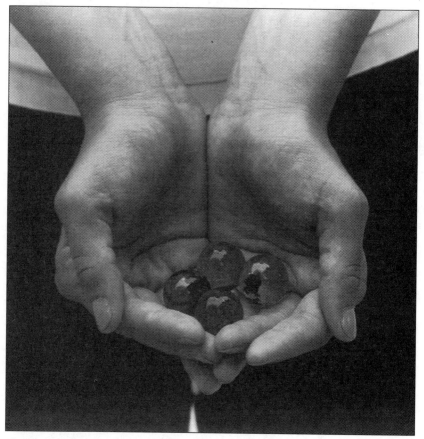

Photo by Torey Bocast

Written in the Dirt

by Timothy Cahill

T he light grew brighter, filling my eyes until I could see nothing of my surroundings. Giving my horse a gentle tug, I brought her to a halt and reached down for my canteen. I gulped a mouthful and noticed there was hardly any water remaining. I had never grown used to the infernal heat that permeated everything—heat that stung your eyes, pierced your skin, spurred every sweat pore on your body into overdrive. It was enough to damage a man's wits and destroy his will, which was, of course, exactly the point.

I blinked my eyes hard until the white blur began to dissipate and my vision came back into focus. As I had come to expect, there was not really anything to see; the light-brown dirt stretched on for miles, creating a panoramic spectacle daunting enough to inspire second thoughts about even bothering to survive. Heaving a deep sigh, I glanced down at my empty canteen and swore. I had filled it only a few hours after sunrise, yet had only taken four gulps during the day to finish it. There was evidently a leak. *Nothing to panic about,* I reminded myself, removing the brown broad-rimmed hat from my head and wiping my brow. According to the directions the fellow at that post office gave me, I should reach a settlement by dark and restock my supplies. I could certainly afford some new equipment. Heading out here was the best business decision I'd ever made.

With this thought, I reached into my saddlebag to pull out the earnings from my stay in the last settlement. Not bad for a single day's work. And one buffoon had even given me what looked like a gold Spanish medallion. I didn't know much about its worth, but, from what I'd heard, they can fetch a pretty penny at a pawn shop. That old sap hadn't been able to see much farther than his nose. He must have judged by the size that it was an ordinary quarter. I admiringly tilted the gold coin in my hand and rolled my eyes over the strange engravings.

"Pardon, mister?" My daydreaming was cut short by what I suspected was an apparition. As the figure on horseback drew nearer, it became apparent that he was quite real.

"Why, mister, you're a doctor, perhaps?"

"Mighty perceptive of you," I allowed, casually slipping the money back into the saddlebag. "How'd you figure that one?"

"Praise God in heaven!" the other rider exclaimed, his eyes wide and his demeanor somewhat manic. "Why, I saw that black bag, looked like the one the doctor back home carries with him, and I just knew! It's nothing short of a miracle, finding you way out here . . ." The man caught himself from rambling and took a deep swallow. "I've got a serious problem, mister. My li'l girl's so sick I'm afraid she ain't gonna make it another few days."

"Fortunate that I came along when I did," I noted with

a curt nod, allowing my instincts to return. This, after all, was business. "Whereabouts is she right now?"

"We sure weren't about to push on all the way to the settlement at Oak Creek, so I put up camp just over them hills," he jerked his head to the south. "It's been three days now, and we're mighty low on food, but if we push on, she ain't got a chance. Please, mister?"

I looked him in the eye and nodded grimly. "No guarantees, sir, but I'll do what I can." I gave him an encouraging nod, at which point the man spurred his horse, leading me at a speedy gait to the camp.

When we arrived, I noticed that the flaps of the tent were drawn closed. Dismounting with great urgency, the man held his hand out in a halting gesture. "Better let me go first, mister. In this state, she's liable to scream if she sees a strange face." He rushed inside, and I could hear him murmuring reassurance in the universal tone parents use to comfort sick children.

I slipped off my own horse, lifted my sleek black bag off its back and stole a glance at the tent. I quickly pulled the sack open and scoured through it until the appropriate vial was on top. *This sell should be simpler than most,* I told myself confidently.

"She's feeling a littler calmer now, mister," the man noted, leaning out of the tent. "You can come in."

I gripped the bag firmly in my hand and walked in, ducking under the propped-up flap. It was fairly dark inside, the only light coming from a freshly lit candle. The dwelling was plain, with a small blanket doubled over on the ground to serve as a bed. On it rested an angelic little girl, no more than six or seven. Her face looked pale, and I could hear rough, guttural wheezing with every breath. The poor thing was lying on her back, staring forlornly at the top of the tent, her eyes open but her expression blank. She grasped a rather large, tattered shirt that was serving as a blanket, and she occasionally shivered. The sight was almost enough to bring a tear to my eye. Almost.

"This been going on for long?" I asked the father, with a professional edge to my voice. "Days? Weeks?"

"Well, we been stopped here just a little while . . . couple a days," he replied hesitantly. "She hadn't been doing very well early on either, but it just got worse," he added.

I nodded confidently and placed my hand on her forehead. Drawing it back quickly, I proceeded to lean over the young girl and peered deeply into her eyes. She appeared to be conscious of her surroundings, but seemed confused by her condition. Needless to say, so was I. Not that it really mattered. "Well, sir, these are less than ideal circumstances for a complete diagnosis, but I'd be inclined to call it an advanced case of Dutch Fever."

"Is it . . . serious?" he asked, gulping. His eyes were wide and full of hope. *Gotta love the easy jobs,* I told myself with an inward grin. Most of 'em are buying things they won't ever need: boot clips, glove strings, saddle cream, and so on. But if they need it, well, there isn't even a challenge. Truthfully, you could fool most of the people I do business with by telling them the word "gullible" was written in the dirt.

"I won't lie to you, sir," I said, my mouth locked in a solemn line and my eyebrows narrowing. "It's a tough illness to fight off, but I've got something here that's had some success over in Cireves County." I reached into the black bag, careful not to open it all the way, and pulled out the vial of purple liquid. "Now, hers is a pretty tough case, so I'm gonna give you this whole vial. You give her a mouthful every two to three hours, and I bet she starts clearin' up in a few days."

He clasped his hands around the container of home-made cough syrup and looked up at me with intense gratitude. "Oh, thank you, mister. You truly are a god-send!" He blinked hard and gulped once more. "We ain't got much money. How much do I owe you for this?"

"It's a pretty costly bit of medicine," I remarked with a frown, subtly eyeing the humble surroundings, "but I wouldn't want to drive you broke now. How much can you afford?" Always let the poor give what they can. If they've got it, they'll hand over more than the rich will ever consider.

"Why, I left my money out in my saddlebag!" he exclaimed. "Was 'fraid the camp would be robbed while I was looking for help. Hang on there." As he scurried out of the cabin, I looked down one last time at the young girl. Placing my hand on her forehead again, I couldn't help but hope the darn cough syrup did some-thing to help. Her body seemed to have stabilized a bit since I had first come in; the wheezing had disappeared entirely. Perhaps she had drifted to sleep.

"Here you are, mister," the man said, clasping my hand against his to pass over the coins in his palm. I smiled graciously and slipped them into my pocket. Noble men don't count their earnings in front of others.

"It's a pleasure I was able to help someone way out

here," I said, patting the fellow's shoulder. "It's a good thing I came along when I did." I let out a contented sigh to signify that my work was complete, nodded to the concerned father and strode quickly back to my horse. Taking a glance at the sun, I smiled at the thought that I might yet reach the settlement by nightfall.

* * *

"Pretty shabby canteen you're carrying there, fella." The comment was made by a street merchant as I dismounted in front of the local inn. "I could sell you a nicer one for a quarter," he added enticingly, handing me his product.

The price was a tad steep, but I needed the canteen. "Sure," I agreed with a nod. "Just picked myself up some cash." I reached into my pocket and groped around for a quarter. Finding one, I handed it to the peddler and wrapped the canteen strap around my neck. "Good day, sir."

"Now, hold on there," he demanded, pulling my shoulder back with a jerk. "I ain't never seen any money like this. This ain't no good."

Giving him a scowl, I snatched the quarter back and held it up to the light. *What the . . . ?* In my hand I held a gold Spanish medallion. "Now hold on," I said aloud, confused. "This was from my saddlebag when . . ." I stopped in mid-sentence as the realization struck me like a rock between the eyes. I didn't even need to check my saddlebag to know that it was empty.

Noble men don't count their earnings in front of other men, but I had been counting my money that afternoon, and there had been someone watching. It had all been perfect. Too perfect. The man entered the tent first. He went outside to get his money. A sick little girl who wasn't too sick after all.

There was no use going back to the camp. Con men move quickly. I should know. One thing's for sure, though: I'm not ever again telling anyone that the word "gullible" is written in the dirt. ▣

Eggplant Parm

by Melissa Sowin

On the night of the blizzard,
I'm locked in my house
with my mother and her boyfriend.
I used to cry at the sight of his curly brown hair,
but now I am making dinner with a man for the first time:

Just me and him—
My smile real as we cook eggplant parmesan:
First, protecting sliced eggplant
with a coat of flour.
Then, letting the slices sizzle in oil
until they are golden brown on the bottom.

I flip the eggplant over, looking at it as if it
were just born.
Next, he and I spread tomato sauce together,
forming a comfortable padding for freshly
sprinkled parmesan cheese.

When dinner's out of the oven, we sit:
a candlelit table set for three,
garlic bread made by mother,
salad, pasta and the main dish made by us.
Outside: two feet of snow.
Inside: three friends with napkins on our laps,
passing the salad, twirling separate spaghetti strands into
a bond around our steel forks.

Even the Devil Waits in Line

by Axel Arth

I stood in line, waiting for my pizza. It was yet another Saturday night, and I was, as usual, alone. And let me tell you, it wasn't for lack of trying. It was more for lack of someone else trying back.

And it didn't really help that I knew almost all the people who worked at the pizza shop. Whenever I'd made it to the counter, I'd have to put up with the jeers of my fellow jerks from behind the counter. For some reason, I never brought up the fact that they were the ones working on a Saturday night, and I was the one who could be doing something—if I had a life to be doing something with, that is.

But tonight, something different happened. Due to a large storm on its way, everyone was wanting a pizza to kick back with, throwing off my time frame. That, and a party had come in and taken up residence—a party of ten yelling children.

The line was now fifteen minutes long, and the building was getting hot. The sound of screaming children didn't help my mood. It was shaping up to be a night I was going to have to hurt someone, and that someone would most likely be me.

I was almost to the point of choking one of those damn rugrats if they touched me one more time, when I began to mutter to myself, *Damn kids, going to break something. Jesus, if only they'd shut their little mouths . . .*

And it was then that the stranger in front of me, the one in the ominous trench coat and black fedora, decided to speak to me.

"You know, I don't think He'd be the best person to help you right now," he said, over his shoulder.

I stood silently, not knowing who he was talking about. He turned to face me and continued. "Jesus, I mean. He loved children. I've never been able to figure out why, though. Pesky little brats. But, hello and, you are?" he said, extending his hand.

"I'm Axel," I said, caught off guard by his up-front attitude. This was getting very weird, very fast. "And you?"

"Well, I have many names. You can call me Lucy."

"That's an interesting name," I said, not really wanting to bring up the fact that I knew a kid with that nickname, and he wasn't exactly someone you'd want to be compared to.

He took off his hat, but his short red hair didn't even move. He reached up with one of his gloved hands and stroked his short beard. I began to blush, remembering the small piece of peach fuzz I had growing beneath my chin. And something I'll never forget—his eyes were like black pits, sucking in the light.

He continued, "You know, there's an easy way out of all of this."

I braced myself for the worst. This guy was going to start selling me some piece of junk, and I was going to be stuck listening to him until I got my pizza. Trying not to let this show, I said, "Really? What's that?"

"Simple. Find an exit," he said with a stupid grin. I let out an uncontrollable laugh, not expecting anything even half as stupid. When everyone in the store stopped looking at me, he continued.

"But, seriously, I can help you out. And for a reasonable price, too."

Here comes the sale, I thought. "What can you do? And how much will it cost me?"

"Look over there," he said, pointing to the parking lot.

My internal monologue continued its rant. *A car salesman? Car wax?* But I saw something I never expected.

It was another pizza place, just like this one, only different. There I was, sitting in a booth. A girl I had been chasing after was sitting on the other side. We were sharing a pizza. And it looked like we might be sharing a little more than that later. It was amazing. It was exactly what I had been looking for.

My eyes glued to the image, Lucy continued, "That's just the beginning. It can all be yours. Money, fame, all you have to do is ask."

This wasn't any jerk trying to sell me car wax. This was Satan. And he was offering me a deal.

"And the price?" I asked, trying to concentrate, but not succeeding. The vision in front of me was filling my brain, making it hard to think.

Lucy let out a big sigh. "Honestly, you're not a stupid kid. What do you think it is? It's your soul." I could tell that wasn't the question he'd expected me to ask. "Sometimes I ask myself why I even bother with you mortals . . ." he muttered.

"So, I give you my soul, and I get everything?"

"Yes, that's the deal."

The image of the pizza place disappeared, and I felt empty, like I had to have that again.

"How do I seal the deal?" I asked, ready to get this over with.

"Right here," he said, pulling a contract and a pen from his coat.

I bent down, ready to sign. This was the life I wanted. This was how it should be. It's all I would ever need.

But a thought popped into my head: *What fun would that be? Half the fun is the chase. It'd be a lot easier, but not nearly as much fun. Let life come as it may.* I straightened. "I'm sorry, Lucy, but I think I'll pass."

His grin grew even wider. "Good. You're the kind of guy I like to see get away from me. And besides, The Man Upstairs has plans for you."

I stood, shocked. "Plans? Like what?"

His grin continued to grow. "If you had sold your soul to me, you'd know by now."

The rest of the wait passed in silence. Lucy was leaving with his order, when I stopped him. "Hey, you've been nice about this whole 'soul' thing. Do you mind if I ask one more question?"

"Not at all. What is it?"

"Why did you wait in line? It's not like anything was stopping you from getting what you wanted."

"It's like you said. It's not fun if it's just handed to you.

That, and like tonight, I can sometimes get a soul out of it. Now hurry, your pizza's getting cold." With that, he turned and walked out the door.

I stood there, staring, not quite believing what had just happened. The jeers from my friends brought me back to reality, and my life was normal once more. For a while, anyway. ▣

Photo by Gretchen Loye

Speak to Me

by Joyce Sun

speak to me i want you to touch me
and i want you to touch your hand to mine
and lay them, palm to palm, i want to
relive that night on Broadway again,
(night on Broadway, yes, your hand in mine
i could hear your heart beating amidst the neon lights),
i want this to be that summer again, i want

i want
i want so many things
i want to be famous. i want to be rich.
i want to go down in history, i want
millions to look at me and say, she is
all that i aspire and yearn to be, she is the
embodiment of my desires, i want to be
just like her.
i want to be a god to millions. i want to
live forever, and i,

i

i just want you
to speak to me.

Looking over Gaza

by Kerry E. McIntosh

"I look at the sky; I look at the people."

—*Arien Ahmed, Palestinian, would-be suicide bomber,*
upon deciding not to detonate her explosives
(Newsweek, *June 2002*)

I gaze out the window at my tiny view of the world. People are walking down the road that skirts the sea. The sun, deep red in the evening sky, is slowly lowering itself over the horizon of lapping waves. I look at the sky. I look at the people. In my mind I can still see, with vivid detail, all the people at the coffee shop this morning, and I wonder what would have happened to them had all gone as planned. The pregnant woman quietly sipping the cappuccino; the group of students talking and joking; the stressed clerk with the oversized uniform; the little girl holding the juice.

Amid the faces flashing in front of me when I close my eyes, I see the little girl's the clearest—as if her exact image is etched deep inside my mind. Her olive skin and flowing chestnut hair. Her hazel eyes, afire with life as she tilts her face back, peels of laughter resonating from her youthful, ebullient grin that only falters momentarily when her juice bottle crashes to the ground. Where would she be right now had my mission succeeded? And what about the many others waiting in line for coffee that morning?

Dead. All of them, dead. The bustling scene I had walked in on this morning would have ceased to exist had one more second gone by. The windows would have been shattered, the tables overturned and the unused coffee cups stacked beside the counter would have all been frozen in time like the pottery in the picture of the ruins of Pompeii I had seen in a history book. I remember looking at that picture as the missile came through the roof of the school. As the white dust rained down over our heads, I remember closing the book and huddling under my desk, fearing I would soon be living the picture on the page. But that day, I had gone to al-Aqsa instead.

A pit was forming in my stomach. I realized that I would have made the people in the coffee shop live the picture on that page had I acted in accordance with my prescribed fate. What if the girl who dropped her juice bottle were my little sister? What if one of the young men standing in line were my husband-to-be? Or worse yet, what if the lady sipping the cappuccino were me, five years from now, pregnant with my first child and unaware that an attack had been planned against me?

Crazy scenarios popped into my head like swiftly falling raindrops on a tin roof. Situations, some incredibly far-fetched, some realistic, about the lives of the people I would have killed, invaded my thoughts faster than I could stop them. I had been tormented with fear ever since a bomb had fallen on my neighbor's home the first year I'd lived in Jabaliya, so what kind of fears would the young clerk have felt if a bomb had gone off at her workplace?

The easy part about being a martyr is that I never would have had to handle thoughts like these, I realize, reminding myself that I, too, would be as nonexistent now as the people at the Starbucks. Guerrillas and snipers must be hardened, able to kill and then suppress all remorse for their actions until such feelings become extinct, and they can go on and kill again. Yet, martyrs need not suppress their remorse over the lives of those they have taken. Yes, to be a guerrilla or a sniper took a certain type of person, but anyone could be a martyr. A martyr could have been me.

Depending, of course, on the martyr's mission suc-ceeding. If it fails, and she gets the chance to reflect on what she's done, all is rapidly negated. I never should have been apprehended this morning, I told myself. It was a fluke that the soldiers were patrolling the Community Square. I sighed, feeling that the mere hic-cup in the system that allowed the soldiers' presence was hardly the real reason I had not completed my mission.

Knowing I could not continue this frail half-truth, I finally allowed myself to admit the real reason I had been caught: I never should have paused to look at the people, especially after being told countless times that a martyr must never stop and look. Yes, due to my mistake, due to looking, my destiny suddenly wasn't my destiny anymore. Because I had looked, suddenly my destiny, and that of the others at the Starbucks that morning, was altered. My moment had not come this morning, as I had assumed, but instead was now undetermined.

Leaning against the sandy plaster wall of my cell and gazing out at the sunset, I find myself questioning more than I ever have. I wonder what will become of me. The Israeli Defense Forces do not treat would-be martyrs kindly, I am sure. Because I am young and a woman, I am hoping the tribunal will be less harsh, but my hopes may be in vain.

Back in Jabaliya, I've heard all kinds of stories about what they do to Palestinians in interrogation rooms, and I know it is wishful thinking to hope that they will not do the same, or worse, to me. And for my family—I shudder to think what the soldiers will do to my family. My family knew nothing of my decision to join al-Aqsa. I told no one. I believed I was destined to be a martyr, yet now, as I stand here in my cell, I know that I had lied to myself.

I should get used to this cell; I'll be spending a lot of time in cells. I wonder if I'll ever be allowed to return to Jabaliya. Probably not. Yet if I do, I think hopefully, if I ever return to my people, I won't go back to al-Aqsa. Martyrdom is not my destiny. Even if the soldiers invade again, even if life is miserable and my family again has no money, I won't take another chance at martyrdom. I will not try it again and succeed the next time, for even if I weren't alive to feel the remorse for my actions—oh, I shudder to think of the consequences anyway.

Sometimes our decisions may seem like what is best— our destinies seem set in stone—yet these same decisions may seem foolish, if not ghastly, in retrospect. The little girl with the juice, the young men laughing in line, the clerk who typed my name, Najat Rashaad,* into the database, and the slim guard who exposed my false destiny with the words "By the order of the Israeli Defense Forces of the Territories, you are under arrest"—I, too, could live like them. Like the child who dropped her juice, I, too, could learn to laugh off the bad times, recover from life's messes and go on another day.

I look out my cell window, knowing that the small view of the road and the dunes and the water meeting the horizon is the only view of the world I'll have for several days, at least. It is all I need to see to remind myself that, yes, the world is turning, and, yes, life is ever-renewing, and each sunset is both the beginning and the end of good and bad days.

I look to my future, and although it may seem bleak, I know I have one. And as the sun sets over Gaza this evening, my destiny is as open and broad as the sea in the distance. I'm looking toward tomorrow, a tomorrow that this morning I never expected to see. ▣

---

*Najat is an Arabic name meaning salvation; Rashaad comes from the Arabic verb rashada, meaning to go the right way.

Hunger

by Leslie D. Johnson

A hungry wolf is tearing at my gut.
He growls with restlessness
Circles in me three times,
Plops his heavy firmness down
To slumber, until
He wakes and growls again.

I think of how he got inside.
Ironically, this has nothing to do
With what I ate,
But what I did not eat.
I swallowed this beast with the regrets
Of the lunch I sorely missed.

We wait until supper, agonizingly delayed.
Temptations dwell in the air; corn and roast meats.
Wolf gives a leap, thunder rumbles in me;
He wags his tail, beating heavily against my insides,
Whines and begs, paws the pit of my stomach.
We sit, licking our chops.

Anxiously, he bolts
Devouring the very essence of his destruction
For when he eats, he grows smaller,
Satisfied to be put to rest.
Still he greedily aches for more—
Ravenous!

"Don't wolf your food," says my father.

Like Raspberries with Milk in the Summer

by Leah Multer Filbrich

The can was cold under her fingers. They were pressed up against it by his hand, entwined with hers. She drove the car easily with one hand; it was a trick best learned through practice, and he liked it, so she practiced. Occasionally she pulled her hand out of his to steer around turns or through intersections, and he would frown, but she just kept staring ahead. The road was illuminated by her headlights, and the moon shone over the hills. The night sky was not black, only a very full blue, a canvas for the silhouettes of the tall pines they passed. Snow banked the sides of the roads, mixed with pieces of dead grass and dirt. The little lights on the dashboard blinked red and green, casting a ghastly glow on her hand as she raised it to steer around a curve. He frowned and turned to look out the window. After a moment, he took a sip of his soda and sighed.

"Coke is my favorite kind of soda," he said, turning to her. "What do you like best?"

She had been about to put her hand back down, but when she opened her mouth to answer his question, she shut it abruptly and, startled, dropped her hand to her lap and looked perplexedly at the road ahead, as if it were some kind of giant maze and she could not discover how to get out. After a few minutes of silence, he looked out the window again, and she raised her hand to grip the steering wheel tightly. She tipped her head to one side and smiled slightly.

"You want to know what I like best?" she asked. "Well, then, I'll tell you." He looked over at her and started smiling, then, chuckling to himself, he reached for her hand. The headlights caught a sign on the side of the road, and, grinning almost maliciously, she flicked on her blinker and slammed on the brakes. He jerked his hand back as the car flew around a corner.

"Where are you going?" he asked. The skin on her knuckles was white. "Stick to the main roads. You'll never make it back home before nine."

"I'll go fast," she said as the car sped along. Pieces of newspaper scattered from the road. The moonlight shone directly on her face now, and she looked thoughtful for a moment, then very intent as she stared at the road.

"What I like best is at the end of the day when I'm tired and thoughts stream meaninglessly through my head. I'm all ready for bed, and I go in my dark room and close the door. One of the best things in the world is closing the door on a darkened room. I like the way my long white nightgown flows over my body. I like how it touches me only in a few places. I like to raise my arms above my head and sway and dance rhythmically in the dark, like I'm dancing to slow African drums. I like to collapse on my bed and look out the window. I like

to see the stars, the moon's tears, and they taste like raspberries with milk in the summer. I love to see the moon
cry. I love the taste of solitude. I like the dark, and I like
myself."

They drove the rest of the way in silence, both staring
ahead. They passed a little house with the lights on, and
inside she saw a little girl playing the piano and a man
giving a little boy a piggyback ride.

"I never liked soda very much anyway," she said. "I've
always preferred a warm cup of tea." One tear fell from
her eye, rolled down her cheek and under her shirt. He
said nothing. When they pulled into his driveway, she
threw the car into park.

"Well, I'd better be going," he said. "I do love you." He
leaned over and kissed her gently on the cheek, seeming
not to notice the dampness.

"Yeah, well, that happens sometimes," she said.

"Good night," he said, getting out of the car.

"Bye," she said. He shut the door, and she put the car
in reverse. She watched his back as he walked up to his
house. A dog barked. As she turned to check the road, a
stray curl fell in her face and she brushed it away absent-
mindedly. The car sped down the road, and she was
alone. The moon and its tears shone brightly over the
hills, and her headlights illuminated the road ahead. ▣

The Other Side

by A. G. McDermott

If I told you
that I miss my station wagon most
when I think of the evening
steaming in summer city traffic
with a pouting now ex-boyfriend when
I suddenly realized that
it had long been too dark for
  sunglasses
and, clipping an ear, snatched them from my nose and
flung them over my shoulder, then
in the rearview mirror
watched them crack and crumple and
slide down the window glass
all the way at the back

or that I never considered religion until
I was sent to Catholic school and,
obliged to cross myself and hypocritically
intone an "Our Father" each morning,
promptly identified myself as an implicit
  atheist
and with a sixth-grader's self-assurance
unlocked the closet door but crouched inside

amid my armory of arguments,
"confessing" only to the curious;
and that even after breaking through the suicidal crisis
   I was
powerless to reason my way out of that spiritual
   quicksand until
I grasped a rope in a book on quantum physics

or that the other day in homeroom when
some guy I only vaguely recognized
called across the room wanting to know
first my position in the class then
my GPA and SAT scores
and though he and his friends were
rather rowdily impressed and suggested I should
strut down the hall with a "number one" index finger held
   high
I just wanted them to shut up before
gravity and the rushing wash of emotion defeated
surface tension and my eyelashes
for control of a certain stinging salty solution—

would I be more human
or stranger still?

READER/CUSTOMER CARE SURVEY

We care about your opinions. Please take a moment to fill out this Reader Survey card and mail it back to us.
As a special "thank you" we'll send you exciting news about interesting books and a valuable **Gift Certificate.**

Please PRINT using ALL CAPS

	First Name		MI.	Last Name

Address

City _____ ST ☐☐ Zip ☐☐☐☐☐ - ☐☐☐☐

Phone # (☐☐☐) ☐☐☐ - ☐☐☐☐   Fax # (☐☐☐) ☐☐☐ - ☐☐☐☐

Email

(1) Gender:
_____ Female   _____ Male

(2) Age:
_____ 8 or younger   _____ 17-20
_____ 9-12   _____ 21-30
_____ 13-16   _____ 31+

(3) What attracts you most to a book?
(Please rank 1-4 in order of preference.)

	1 2 3 4
3) Title	○ ○ ○ ○
4) Cover Design	○ ○ ○ ○
5) Author	○ ○ ○ ○
6) Content	○ ○ ○ ○

(7) Other than school books, how many books do you read a month?
_____ 1   _____ 3
_____ 2   _____ 4

(8) How did you find out about this book?
Please fill in ONE.
1) _____ Friend
2) _____ School (Teacher, Library, etc.)
3) _____ Parent
4) _____ Store Display
5) _____ Teen Magazine
6) _____ Interview/Review (TV, Radio, Print)

(9) Where do you usually buy books?
Please fill in your top TWO choices.
1) _____ Bookstore
2) _____ Religious Bookstore
3) _____ Online
4) _____ Book Club/Mail Order
5) _____ Price Club (Costco, Sam's Club, etc.)
6) _____ Retail Store (Target, Wal-Mart, etc.)

(11) Did you receive this book as a gift?
_____ Yes   _____ No

(12) What do you like to read? *(Please check all that apply)*

Magazines:
12) _____ Teen People
13) _____ Seventeen
14) _____ YM
15) _____ Cosmo Girl
16) _____ Rolling Stone
17) _____ Teen Ink
18) _____ Christian Magazines

Books:
19) _____ Fiction
20) _____ Self/Help Books
21) _____ Reality Stories/Memoirs
22) _____ Sports
23) _____ Series Books (Chicken Soup, Fearless, etc.)

TAPE IN MIDDLE; DO NOT STAPLE

BUSINESS REPLY MAIL
FIRST-CLASS MAIL PERMIT NO 45 DEERFIELD BEACH, FL

POSTAGE WILL BE PAID BY ADDRESSEE

TEEN INK™
3201 SW 15TH STREET
DEERFIELD BEACH FL 33442-9875

FOLD HERE

(24) Do you prefer to read books written by:
1) ____ Teen Authors?
2) ____ Adult Authors?
3) ____ No Preference

Comments:

That Slight, Slight Noise

by Kristopher Dukes

Ring. *Ring.*

I flushed, washed my hands and dashed into my room to catch the phone on its fourth ring.

"Hello?"

"Hey, Mary, it's Mommy."

"Oh, hey. How are you?"

There was a near inaudible sigh. "I'm fine. How are you?"

"I'm good. So, how's everything going?"

That slight, slight sigh again. "Oh, it's okay. I was calling you because I got an e-mail address. You can send me a message, I won't be able to reply, but you can e-mail me telling me to call you or something." Her words nearly slurred, but the thought that she might be drinking faded quickly because I wanted it to.

"Oh, okay, cool."

"All right." I jotted the information on one of the pink Post-its that decorated my desk. "Okay, got it."

"If you have time tonight, e-mail me, and I'll call you later to tell you if I got the message. I'm not sure how it's supposed to work."

"Sure, I'll e-mail you. So, how are Uncle Paul's kids?"

My mom babysat for her brother's two elementary-school children.

"Oh, they're good." There was another slight sound in the background. I could hear, or maybe I just imagined, her molars grinding or her lips smacking. "Shelly and Jacob brought home their report cards today."

"Oh, yeah? How's the weather? Is it cold yet?"

Those slight, slight pauses. "Yeah, well, it was thirty degrees this morning."

"Oh, wow," I said, knowing I was the patronizing California daughter. Thirty degrees did sound cold, but so did a lot of things. "Did you know Grandma and Grandpa Snyder came to visit?" I wanted to suck my words back in as quickly as I said them. It was hardly a big deal that my dad's parents came to visit—they often did—but Mom had been wanting to see us lately.

"Oh, yeah, Steve told me. Are they still there?"

"No, they left Tuesday."

"So, are you guys still trying to come out during winter break?"

"Oh, I think so. We're still trying, but we have to start paying for car insurance soon. And then, I went to take my driver's license test, but they told me I need driver's training since I'm under eighteen, so now we have to sign up for classes and it's more than a hundred bucks for each of us."

"Yeah." I heard what annoyed me, but what I liked to pay attention to: those slight, slight personal noises.

"Well, I'd really like to see you guys."

"Yeah, me, too. I'd really like to go down there soon."

"I'd like to visit you guys in California."

"Yeah," I said, almost uncomfortable. There was what was best for everyone, and then there was what meant a couple of weeks of smiles between welcoming and departing tears.

"Oh, yeah, I wanted to tell you guys, with my disability, you should be able to apply for more grants. I was trying to work it out for Steven, but with you it'd be easier if you just listed me as your parent. Because with Dad and Christine's salaries . . ."

"It's too much for scholarships!" I interrupted with a laugh, and then wondered if I shouldn't wish to suck back that comment and laughter, too.

"Yeah. 'Cause I'm not getting anything. Someone should get something outta my disability."

I giggled again, pretending her comment was a joke. My laughter covered those slight noises.

"So anyway, could you remind Daddy to get my Section Eight application? I left him a message but . . ."

"Yeah, sure."

"You know what, maybe you could get it. Just call up the welfare office and ask for housing authority."

I scribbled on a pink Post-it as my eyes let me know they'd enjoy tears spilling out. "Okay," I said, thinking I controlled my voice.

"All right, honey." She yawned in the background. "I'm going to let you go now; I need to get to bed."

"Yeah, it's late over there, huh?" I tried to steady my wobbling voice as shady, transparent thoughts of my mother's, not just lost potential, but wasted and solid talent was so apparent in this phone call.

"Yeah. I need to wake up at six."

"Well, all right, Mommy."

"Good night, honey. I love you."

"I love you, too. Good night! Take care."

"All right."

I hung up and went back to the bathroom to take my shower. I looked in the mirror as my face began to scrunch, trying to squeeze out the tears. Ridiculous black tears trickled down my cheeks. Earlier that night I had reveled in perfecting my Halloween makeup.

I got in the shower and sobbed, hardly weeping, though. My face continued to scrunch in sobs and laughter as I thought cynically about my little moment. My pitiful mother, my pitiful mother, it's so sad, all that could have been her life. I know lots of people with such wasted potential, but this is my mother. *You're a lucky girl if your biggest problem is being sad about your mother* . . . Yes, lucky, thank you, Lord. I know so many people have it worse than me, but stop crying, oh, now you're laughing, yes?

My face convulsed again as I realized how uncommitted I was to this moment, this being one of the very few times I cried and wanted to let "it" all out. *Let what all out?* my mind demanded. *Where is this crying getting you? How is this not just a big distraction (oh, the evils of the word!) from all the things you'd like to accomplish?*

I knew I'd write this down, and I laughed, but what might have been audible was drowned by the shower. *I bet you're just clinging to this moment because you just want something to write about,* my mind insisted. I laughed and sobbed again.

I got out of the shower and brushed my teeth. I

smudged the mist on the mirror so I could see my face. I was always interested in how my face looked before, during and after a good cry. I liked my wrinkled brow and ruddy complexion against the white, white bathroom walls.

I went into my room and saw my computer waiting for me, waiting for me to process my little conversation-turned-moment into neat black words.

Oh, but my curling hair couldn't wait. Before I blow-dried it, I tried to reflect more on my mom's misfortune, but I'd already mentally and emotionally filed that experience under "Not-Really-a-Big-Deal." I was disappointed in, but proud of, myself. *My, what large emotional defenses you have,* I thought. I grinned at my still-wrinkled brow and still-pink face. It contrasted nicely with the beige, beige walls of my bedroom. ▣

Click Three Times

by Sarah Nerboso

The smell of exhaust fumes and echoes of flat wind lashed against her back. Facing the deserted farm, something inside her twinged, tugging her toward the house. The last time she was here, Aunt Em had still been alive, although even then shades of decay were spreading.

She walked off the dirt road and passed through the gate. It slammed behind her with a sudden bite. A guilty gust blew the front door open in apology. Two steps and she stood in the threshold. Gray dust carpeted the floors, wall, cabinets, lamps. Brown light seeped in the windows. *No place like home.* Stepping gingerly, trying not to disturb the cobwebs, she entered her bedroom. Aunt Em had made it into a guest room, and her crisp, sparse touch still stained it. Devoid of doggie smell, shed hair, with a made bed, the room somehow remained her own. The window was wide open, allowing the same sun and air from her childhood to fill her. At the foot of the bed was the wooden chest Uncle Henry had made for her, now warped with time. She sprung the chest open, using spontaneous impulses long left idle. Beside several boxes, on top of winter underwear, her old blue and white checkered pinafore lay. It was slightly frayed at the ends, but still bright, still her favorite. Her cheeks flushed with a rush of memories as she lifted it. Standing in front of the long mirror, she draped the dress and whirled, phantom braids catching the wind.

Her knee-length skirt didn't really provide enough leg room to spin in, and she staggered to a halt. Her hand lingered on her chestnut hair. She had shucked it off three years ago; now it was barely long enough to touch the back of her neck. With furtive glances about her, as if the crows were peeking in, she pulled the blinds down, one hand closing the door on her way. Now, truly alone, she kicked off her pumps and wriggled out of her skirt. The pinafore required tugging to fit over her white blouse, and it was a bit snug. As her head peeked over the neckline, a faded green shoebox in the chest caught her eye. She hungrily seized the box and tore it open.

The flash of red momentarily blinded her. Eyes squeezed closed, shoe shapes danced across her lids. Blinking, she moved the shoes out of the sun, hesitating to put them on. Had they always been so gaudy, so bright? Her stomach twisted. They looked like showgirl heels, a cheap showgirl at that. How could she ever have mistaken those sequins for rubies? These hand-me-downs, her inheritance from a fluke accident, why had she even kept them? She must have had a reason. Forehead furrowed, she struggled to remember. Someone had even tried to kill her for them. Why hadn't she just given them away? And there were witches. A blond witch tearing them off a dead woman, giving them to her. Something happened, two sisters ended up . . . dead? Murder? She shook away these flashes of the forgotten with two violent flicks of hair. Enough of that; it wasn't her fault. Her eyes refocused on the shoes in her hand. She tightened her grip. No one would see if she slipped them on, just for a little while. Reverently, she lifted the precious, garish shoes.

Perfect fit like always; no toes or heels had to be severed to pry the beauties on. Over her dark nylons, the shoes shimmered happily. Eyes on her feet, she rose and let the dress swoosh about. She grinned, thinking how she must look exactly like she had when she first wore these shoes, minus a couple of inches of hair. She hoped she had a bit more of an experienced air than her younger self, that clean, naive thing whose veins practically burst with American idealism.

Laughing, she confidently turned to look in the mirror once more. But the reflection that met her gaze wasn't dressed in blue and white. The ghost in the glass had such assurance it bordered on arrogance. Her pointy chin was stuck out, matching her equally sharp nose and hat. Beneath her black frock, ruby slippers peeked out. Eyes locked on both sides of the mirror, viewer met reflection. Slowly, with terrifying realization, the woman in the room went ashen as the reflection's olive complexion went from vivid green to a pale, sour shade. Murderer regarded her forgotten victim, two mouths forming a single "O" . . .

Dorothy's scream rose, only to be swallowed by the twists of dead air that circle over Kansas. ▣

Photo by Thalia Demakes

Hollow

by Juliet Lamb

It is February 22nd again. The wind blows small, dazed snowflakes through the sky, bitter with clinging winter. The ground is hard, the gutters filled with the discolored slush that is neither snow nor mud, but the worst elements of both. Church Street is stained with salt in wave-crest patterns. The sky, gray as old stones, dulls the ordinary noise of life to a choked whisper.

It is appropriate, thinks Father Wyckham, staring out his frost-filled window. It is appropriate that mourning marks only February, that the glories of the other eleven months remain untarnished and pure. February requests mourning, exudes mourning, becomes mourning. Father Wyckham supports his chin on his fingertips, feeling his age far more acutely than usual. *See these hands, bony beneath loose leather skin, flecked with brown? These are my hands.*

He watches the school bus wheeze to a stop on the corner. There is little daylight left; evening is already encroaching upon the slate sky. The children who file off are subdued, their motions labored. A few wave mittened hands half-heartedly in the direction of his window, and Father Wyckham waves back with matching languor. He wonders if they are surprised to see him there, but realizes that is hardly likely. Children, in his experience, view the comings and goings of adults with the same incomprehension as one views ants swarming about a disturbed anthill. If there is anything out of the ordinary about Father Wyckham's presence at his window at four o'clock in the afternoon, it is nothing so unusual that it has not happened before and will not happen again.

And yet, it is unusual. Father Wyckham fills his days with motion without necessarily intending to. In fact, it might be more accurate to say that his days are filled with motion. He does not know why they come, but they come, drifting in and out with the regularity of the mail plane. The stories are the same: "Father, I was just . . . heard you could . . . felt badly . . . just dropping in, but . . . really needed someone to . . . hope you don't . . . you see, there's this . . . don't know what to . . . thank you for . . . someone who listens . . . been a real help . . ." There is something about him that draws them: the wisdom in his lined skin, the softness of his gaze, the nostalgic warmth of his parlor. And he sees them, soothes and listens, fills the need that draws them in. Every day but one.

"Playing God again, are you, Edward?" laughs Reverend Howes of the Methodist church, who cannot explain why he stops by every Thursday evening to have a cup of tea in Father Wyckham's parlor on the other side of town. The Father smiles, sitting in the same chair where he entertained the town socialite and the town drunk, a Methodist minister and an atheist poet.

Reverend Howes' face becomes serious.

"They don't know you're human," he says softly. "They think you're immortal. What are you to them? A pair of ears and a few comforting words, and they're out the door. It's hollow, Edward."

Father Wyckham sits alone now, remembering these words. Perhaps it is hollow. But one might dream one does some good. And yet he can do no one any good today. He watches several of the children approach his door. The bell jangles loudly, jarring though expected, and Frances is there in an instant. Ordinarily, she would usher them in, and the parlor would be filled with stomping boots and laughing salutations, hair shaken free of clinging snow. Frances would serve cocoa as the chattering voices competed to relive the day's events for the old father. But today he watches as she sends them away with uncharacteristic brusqueness, her face drawn and her movements short. The children troop off, slump-shouldered, into the gathering dusk. Father Wyckham realizes he has been clenching his fists and releases them slowly, relief overcoming his momentary guilt. He could not face their lively stories today.

Frances appears at the door. Her face softens as she looks at him, small in the huge armchair. Her fingers dust and smooth unconsciously as she speaks, "I'm going out for groceries. I won't be long. Don't bother opening the door. I'll leave a note in case anyone comes by." Trailing off, she awaits a response. Father Wyckham nods, and Frances is out the door in a rush of motion. He watches as she hurries down the front steps, walking briskly over a small film of snow and out to Church Street.

The shadows in the room have begun to mesh, and darkness will soon arrive with winter's characteristic suddenness. Father Wyckham does not turn on the lamp. Instead, he leans back and holds his fingers to his temples. Outside, a car's headlights approach, filling the room with an intensifying light. Just as Father Wyckham wonders if it can possibly get any brighter, the car sweeps past, leaving the room dim. *They don't know you're human. See this hand? This is my hand. See this heart? This is my heart.*

When the telephone rings, Father Wyckham feels almost as though he has been expecting it. Smoothly, he reaches over to answer it.

"Father Edward Wyckham. May I help you?"

The voice on the other end is distant. "I'm calling from County General. There's a man here asking for a priest, and your name is in our records. He doesn't have much longer, I'm afraid."

Father Wyckham does not hesitate. "Thank you. I'll be right there . . . what is your . . ."

"Emily."

"I'll be right there then, Emily. Thank you."

"Thank you."

Father Wyckham pauses to leave a note for Frances, then retrieves his scarf and jacket from the peg in the kitchen. It is odd how little he hesitates about making this call, how eager he suddenly feels to hear the patient's story. Shrugging into his coat, he opens the garage door and starts his car, his breath puffing smoke into the winter air. The snow is still twirling lamely, no harder than before, barely frosting the stiff grass around the rectory.

As he pulls out, the headlights skim over the headstones of the cemetery across the street. Father Wyckham catches his breath and turns left toward County General.

The drive passes as if he's in a dream. He is conscious of each snowflake, of the deer whose wide eyes follow his car from the roadside, and yet he is surprised to arrive at the hospital without remembering exactly how he got there. He heads through the dusk to the fluorescent-lit building, walking in and out of the bright pools of light spilled by street lamps, his shadow contracting and stretching to meet them. The door opens before him, pulling him in, and he wonders if this was what it was like being a king or queen before the wonder of automatic doors opened with ease to the common man.

Emily meets him, small and pale amid the sterile angularity of the waiting room. Startled, she peers into his pained face, probably wondering if his needs or the patient's are more pressing. He smiles at her concern, reassuring her with a quick, "Don't worry, I'm fine. Where will I find the patient?"

"Room 113, second door on the left down that corridor," she gestures. "He's expecting you."

Father Wyckham thanks her and finds the door. At first, he is afraid he has arrived too late. The man is lying on his back, his gaze fixed on the ceiling. He is webbed in by lines and tubes, with racks of bags suspended above his head like a colony of sleeping bats, yet his face and neck are untouched. Near his head, on the windowsill, is a carefully arranged bouquet of flowers in brilliant reds and blues and purples. Father Wyckham clears his throat and steps closer. Slowly, the patient turns his head. Catching the priest's eye, he murmurs something and struggles to hold up a hand.

Father Wyckham is beside the bed in a moment. He takes the thin hand in his own. "I'm Father Edward Wyckham. Is there something you needed to say?"

"Father," rasps the patient, his eyes suddenly afraid. "Father, I'm dying."

Father Wyckham looks into those eyes. He feels the fear slip away, the muscles relax, and he waits for the man to continue. Gently, kindly, he strokes the hand that holds his. Finally, when he has just begun to think that the patient will not talk, the man speaks again.

"Father, forgive me. Please, forgive me."

Outside, the winter world is silent. Darkness has settled behind the windows, squeezing against the lighted room. There is no moon, and the stars are concealed behind banked clouds. Father Wyckham thinks of the other darkness that deepens the night, the darkness that awaits this man, the darkness that will eternally cloud this day.

"I am not God, my child. God will forgive. I will listen." *But are you talking to me, really? Are any of them talking to me? Or are they crying out to another father, an inaccessible father of which I am only a shadow?*

"I have killed a woman."

Tree branches scrape hollowly against the window. The night grows darker, closer. Father Wyckham breathes deeply, realizing he has been forgetting to do so.

"She was so young, maybe eighteen, and beautiful. I didn't mean to, Father. I was scared. I ran away. I kept expecting the police, someone, but nobody came. Nobody knew. I didn't even know her name."

Father Wyckham feels the hand clutch his. For some reason, the room is amazingly, feverishly clear and sharp. The man's voice has grown stronger with emotion. His eyes are speaking, pleading, crying out the words his voice cannot form. *See this hand? This is my hand. See this hand? This is . . .*

"I thought so many times that I should turn myself in, but I was a coward. And then I got married, and I was protecting my wife. Then we had a child, and I was protecting my daughter. There was always something. But, Father, I never was the man they thought I was. I lied every day. And my daughter grew up, and each day I thought of that girl and her family, and what I had done to them. Erin is that same age now, and she's so beautiful, and she loves me. But, oh, God," the man weeps silently, "I can only imagine losing her. I feel such incredible pain, and I know I'm never going to see her graduate and get married, and to think . . . to think I took that from someone else's father . . ."

The man's fragile body is shaking with sobs. Father Wyckham is desperate, searching, flailing in his mind. He should be in control. He should know the necessary things to say. Hasn't he prepared for this? Yet now, in the moment, he is as lost as the man in the bed. *They don't know you're human. See this hand? Hollow, hollow, all hollow.*

Outside, the knife-edged winter wind thrashes the trees, merciless and angry, crashing branch on branch and flinging glittering snow at the window. Father Wyckham clutches the hand, unsure whether he is anchoring the man or himself against that wind.

The man is whispering. "Every day, I am torn apart. Every day . . . for twenty-three years . . ."

Impeded by tears, Father Wyckham's tongue stumbles in his haste to speak. "He . . . forgives . . . son." His voice is unexpectedly forceful. "Trust Him."

Then the room is silent, and the two men weep. The storm is subsiding, the branches swaying but not crashing. Father Wyckham has fallen to his knees. He is not aware of the moment when the hand slips from his, nor that he is sobbing alone. Believing the man crumpled on the floor to be a distraught family member, an orderly leads him gently to the reception area as staff members remove the body and begin cleaning the room.

Father Wyckham opens his eyes to find himself in a chair. He stands slowly, weakly. The snow outside the door is gentle again, the wind calmer.

An orderly brushes by, cradling a bouquet of flowers. He recognizes them as the ones from the windowsill. "Miss . . . miss?" The woman turns. It is Emily, who called him earlier. "Where are you taking those flowers?"

"To the Dumpster. Do you want them?"

Father Wyckham accepts the bouquet, mutely nodding his thanks. She touches his hand for a moment, her eyes filled with pity. "Do you need any help?"

"Thank you, no. I'm fine." The words strike him as ironic, yet oddly true.

He returns to his car, placing the bouquet gingerly on the passenger seat. Despite his loose scarf and unbuttoned coat, he does not feel the wind. The car flies back over snow-frosted roads, the windshield dotted by the occasional snowflake. He turns onto Church Street feeling as though he has come home from far away. Frances is back, and lights blaze in the first-floor windows. He backs into the driveway and sits for a moment in thought. The hollowness has gone, the hollowness he never really acknowledged. *They don't know you're human.* He takes off his driving gloves and stares at his hands, then slowly picks up the flowers.

The sound of the car door closing is muffled in the still air. Holding the bouquet like a child, he crosses the street and opens the cemetery gate. The paths of packed dirt are white aisles of fine snow. He walks to the end, turns, and passes by the first stone. He knows it by heart: *Theresa Snow Wyckham, Beloved Wife of Edward, Born July 12, 1927, Died February 6, 1949.* It is the next stone he kneels before, laying the flowers gently atop the fresh snow. He does not read the words, but whispers them to himself: *Anna Elizabeth Wyckham, Beloved Daughter of Edward and Theresa, Born February 6, 1949, Died February 22, 1967.* Twenty-three years.

Behind him, the snow has stopped. The wind still blows, but its edge has softened, its bitterness dulled, and in it is the promise of spring. ▣

The Geometry Lesson

by Stephen D'Evelyn

I saw the sea of geometry.
Its bright, lucid waters sparkled at me.
Equipped with a few theorems, I plunged
Believing it all obvious, I lunged
Into—surprise!—deep fathoms of space.
I swam downward, my bubbles a fine shining lace:
A link to above. Yet down I went still,
For, though a challenge, it was also a thrill.
I saw danger and beauty like never before,
Poisonous diversions, garish on the sea floor.
But I swam geometry's depths until finally, at last,
I saw an overgrown wreck with one still-erect mast.
And there I found treasure, not sea-greened silver bars,
But glistening understanding, order of the stars.
And, so, with my loot I began to ascend
Through the dark that seemed to have no end,
And then I broke out into liquid sunshine,
Tears of laughter mixed with this brine.
A little knowledge is dangerous, for
It showed me uncertainty I'd never known before.
Yet it brought me back up, and now I know
That bright skies hide fathom-blues below.

Kody

by Arielle Mark

The other guys there that night will tell you they saw it all. They saw Kody smile and wave, then go over the edge, hearing the squeal of car tires as he hit bottom. They'll say they saw his face, meek and pathetic, and almost thought he was going to jump before he did it. But they'd be lying.

It's not something I'm proud of. It's not a story I'd go and barter to all the kids in town for baseball cards and bubble gum. But I wouldn't trade it for all the baseball cards in the world. I saw Kody Thomas, a normal kid, jump onto the Mississippi Interstate.

Some people ask me how it happened, but I don't like to talk about it. The other guys there that night—Bobby Kelley, Eric Smith and Evan Simmons—they're always eager to tell you what they think they know. But all they saw, or heard, was the silence that passed between us after they found out Kody wasn't with us on the bridge anymore.

"Matt," Kody said to me that night, eyes narrowed to slits and voice slurred by alcohol. "You think . . . that if I fell onto that highway right now, that I would be . . . missed?" He grinned sheepishly, teetering back and forth ever so slightly on the railing that it made my heart hitch.

I grinned back, humoring him, feeling the effects of alcohol surging to my brain. "Ya think anyone would even notice?" He started laughing then, cackling. He threw back his head, his arms outstretched, right hand still holding the empty bottle, his left jeans pocket holding the keys to his Cadillac.

It was then that I started to get nervous. "O' course people'll notice," I slurred, whipping back my head to chug more beer into my system, absolutely entertained by the blinking lights of midnight traffic and the other guys—Bobby hunching over the railing and throwing up a perfectly good dinner, and Evan and Eric offering him a drink when he was done.

"What about your parents, Kode? Ain't they gonna notice you're gone?"

He laughed again, the horrible cackle that seemed to wake even the sleepiest nerve in my body. Kind of made you want to keep guys like Kody Thomas sad all the time, so he wouldn't laugh, especially when you were around.

But to keep a guy like Kody silent was a crime, a crime against all nature and the pretty girls up in Jackson. Kody was a sweet talker. He could always get himself or any one of us out of a jam, telling our mothers we were studying at his house, all of us knowing that they wouldn't bother to call his house and disturb his parents any more than they were already. Got his car from sweet-talking; talked the salesman down $300 and into a free oil change. He could have been a car salesman himself, the way he sweet-talked his way in and out of everything. But I guess the dear Lord had something else planned for Kody than working at some old lot.

"Doubt that, man," he said, looking out toward the sky from the bridge that held our small part of Western Avenue over the busy interstate. "They're too busy bitchin' and fightin' to even know I'm still alive." He went to take a swig from his bottle, but it was empty. He tossed it to the side, watching it shatter, its wet glassy shards twinkling from the street lamps. He looked at the broken bottle, mesmerized at the shining light bouncing off the glass. I never knew what was going on in his head, but later, I could have sworn to God and heaven above he was wondering if he, like the streetlight, could easily bounce right off and shine.

"Matt," he said, his hand digging into his pocket, searching for the only thing he ever leaves there.

His hand returned with his keys. The Cadillac, a legend in our select group, was the wonder of all cars, a luxury not many of us small-town Southerners could afford. Kody was the only one our age to have a car, and he knew it was special. With that car, he was somebody special. He never misused it or treated it badly. It was his baby.

Now, I wonder if he had used that time talking things out with his parents or spending that car money on some girl if he might've felt better that night, and he wouldn't have wanted to dig into that pocket and pull out his keys, reluctantly passing them to me.

"I want you to take care of that car," he said, pointing to the ivory beauty illegally parked on the bridge. "Treat it nice. Only the expensive gas, you hear me?" He smiled, and I wondered then if he had become delirious from the beer.

"What the hell you talkin' about, Kody?" I asked, my open palm holding the keys. "I can't take your car. It's yours. You worked hard for this, man—"

But Kody's stare and slight smile made me stop. "Okay," I admitted, "you didn't do jack for the car. But it's yours, man. You're special with this car. You're somebody in this town with that car. You know that."

He sighed, looking up into the black night, the faint sounds of bottles tinkling and soft laughter next to me reminding me that the other guys were still there.

"Am I really, Matt? Am I really special with that car?" He paused for a second, and in that second I could swear Kody Thomas shed a tear. I knew Kody had cried before; he had cried every day in Sunday school when the big bullies would push him into the baptism pool. He had cried all the time in his little tree house as a child, hearing the screams and occasional crack of furniture breaking inside his house. He cried all the time. But I had never seen him just cry. There was always a reason, a big one. Now, he just cried. He blinked back tears and muffled a sob in front of me, for no reason. He was crying just because.

"Kody, I . . ." I didn't know what to say. I had never been philosophical, never been the guy to talk to when you're feeling down, never the guy who was good with words. That was Kody's job. And right now, he was the one who needed the talking.

"I don't got nothin', Matt," he said, his voice warbling for a very different reason than alcohol. "Nothin'."

"Kody, you've got a lot," I said, his words sobering me completely. "You've got your car. You've got your family. You've got us."

He exploded, his face twisting into a sneer. I never knew what he was going to do, and I don't think he knew. "I don't got nothin'!" he said again. "I don't got no reason for anything, man! I don't got no reason to do well on tests, 'cause no one's gonna see it! I don't got no reason to drink. I just remember every damn thing in my screwed-up life anyway!" He swung his legs around then, quietly, slowly, almost playfully, and moved his body across the bridge's railing. "I don't got no reason not to just jump off this here bridge . . ."

I tried to stop him, but I never knew what to say. "Kody, you ain't gonna jump off that bridge, are ya?" I asked slowly, standing up, inching my way toward him. The other guys didn't know what the hell was going on; later they pieced it all together from what they read in the paper, just like everyone else. They just made it sound nicer.

Kody was smiling, looking down at the steady stream of cars passing under him. His feet bumped against the side of the bridge in time with the cars, one, two, three. He was counting. I didn't know what he was counting up to or why the hell he was counting the cars with his feet.

He got up to twenty when he looked back at me again, calling over his shoulder, "You keep good care of that car, Matt," he said, his voice small against the blare of horns shouting at him to get off the damned bridge. I guess if I had done that, just told him to get off that damned bridge, that his mother would worry sick about him (although she really wouldn't), he might have listened. Or he might have gotten off the bridge and done it some other way, one so he wouldn't get in the papers. Or he might have just kept on counting.

"I'm counting on you, man."

And with that, a little smile and a small wave, Kody Thomas let his legs fall out from under him, and there it was: the blaring horns, the screaming tires and my voice screaming his name, so loud and so long I didn't even know it was my voice anymore.

"What the . . . oh my God!" I heard Evan shout, his voice slow and slurred. There were lots of sounds after that; the other guys screaming, shouting, crying like they never had before. The honking horns and frightened people below. The siren of Cooksville's only police car. But I couldn't hear it. All I heard was the silence, the silence of the world without Kody Thomas's evil cackle, the silence of life without the sweet talker, the silence of his Cadillac that won't ever purr the same again. The other guys cried, but I couldn't move a muscle, save my hand tightening around the car keys. My best friend had just flung himself onto the Mississippi Interstate, and I didn't do a damn thing before, during or after. Kody Thomas was dead, and I didn't feel nothing.

* * *

Squeak. I heard it before I saw it, and that was how it always was. Kody was here. Kody came around.

Throwing off the covers my mother had painstakingly tucked around me, I rushed over to the window, eager to see my best friend.

"Kody!" I whispered, hoping he would hear me.

Kody looked down at my back gate, moving it back and forth, creating the most horrible screeches imaginable. "Your old door needs some oil, Matt," he said nonchalantly, as he always did when he came through the back gate. That's how he was; always with the sweet talk.

"What happened this time?" I asked solemnly. I knew Kody didn't come around my house at one o'clock at night just to oil my back gate. I knew something had happened with his parents, or he wouldn't be here.

Kody looked down again, not meeting my gaze. "They're just fighting, I guess," he said. The boy so known for his liquid words was having difficulty talking. "They're throwing stuff again, and I didn't want to be in there now." I knew the next question. He had asked it many times before. He was going to ask it long after tonight, and he was going to ask it now.

"Can I sleep at your place tonight?"

I smiled, waving him in. He had already disappeared through the back door. As I knew the question, Kody knew the answer.

"Sure, Kode," I said, as I had said so many times before.

* * *

I thought I heard it that night. The back gate squeak. I knew it could have been a million and one things besides him. A stray dog. A bum. The wind. But none registered in my mind. Neither did the fact that Kody hadn't come for the night since we were thirteen. I only knew that squeaks meant visitors, Kody or not. I didn't even fathom the fact that less than three hours before Kody had died on the Interstate.

I raced to the window, everything in the room the same as always. I hoped, prayed, wanted Kody to be nonchalantly swinging that gate, creating sounds as grating and evil as his laughter. But somehow, I already knew he wasn't there—that Kody wasn't gonna come around no more.

"Kody?" I asked, hoping against hope that the familiar voice would tell me to oil that damn gate. But there was just silence. Horrible silence, the silence that haunts you at night, when you know something must be going on somewhere, but you can't hear it. I felt defenseless, knowing I could have said something, could have tried to get him to stop, and at any moment, the rest of my world could be gone, too. That silence sounded deathly that night, worse than all the other nights I had been half-asleep, waiting for any sign of a squeak.

* * *

"But I'm not gonna go that way, Mama," I argued, knowing full well that when I was up against Mary Laumont, I was not going to win. "I'll just take Sotheby Drive. It's quicker—"

"Oh, hogwash, Matthew," she said, shaking a finger at me. "It'll take you twenty minutes more if you take Sotheby. Besides, I need you to go to the other side of town and get some groceries." So that was her deal. She wanted me to go there. But I couldn't. And she damn well knew that.

"Can't I just get them near here?" I asked uselessly. She shook her head deliberately, to make her point. Finally, I gave up beating around the bush, "I'm not going to Western Avenue, Mama," I said. "I'm not a little boy anymore, an' you can't tell me where t' go—"

"Everyone's going to be there, Matthew," she interrupted. "It's been a year. You've got to mourn. You've got to be there with them."

"I know you mean well, Mama, but I just can't. I don't get off on that broken glass and crosses like Kody did . . ." At the sound of his name, even coming from my own mouth, I closed my eyes tightly and held back a sob. If I didn't go there, then it wouldn't be true . . .

"Now, boy, I didn't want to get tough with you, but I'm going to," I heard my mother say, her distinctive Cajun accent turning more and more into a Southern drawl every day. "He was your best friend. Now you take that car of yours and drive on down to that bridge and pay your damn respects, you hear me?"

I heard her, all right, but I only heard her say one thing. *Take your car down to the bridge.* My car. "But it's not *my* car, Mama," I whispered, not caring if she heard me. "It's Kody's. I'm just takin' care of it while he's gone."

Mama took me by the shoulders, her hands firm yet gentle, as she looked me in the eye and spoke words I could only believe were nonsense.

"Go to the bridge, Matthew, and mourn," she said. "Everyone else is going to be there. I never wanted to force you, but enough is enough. You can't keep denying that Kody's gone. You're gonna have to face reality some time, and that time is now."

I looked at my palm, the metal glinting in the sun.

* * *

"Well, well, well, Matthew Laumont. Nice of you to grace us with your presence today." I didn't look at Evan

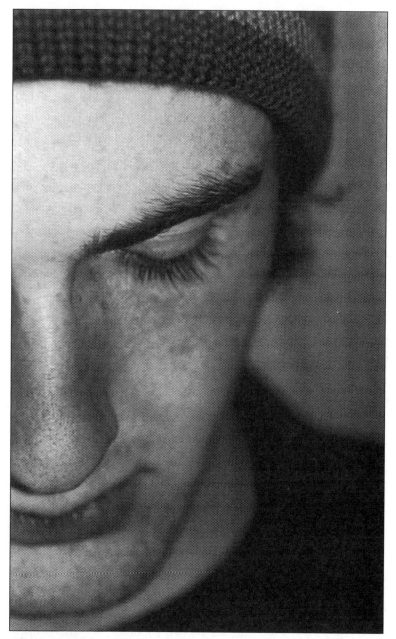

Photo by Alex Koplow

while he spoke mockingly. I could already tell, before even getting out of the car, that Evan and the boys had taken a couple more than a few 45s before I got there. I hadn't seen them for more than five minutes since last year, and after this, I wasn't planning on seeing them again. They had changed since Kody died. We had all changed.

"Shut the f––– up, Simmons," I said, making sure not to slam the door. Didn't want to scratch that damn nice car. My eyes narrowed behind mirrored sunglasses as I approached the ones I used to call my best friends, even though I knew there was only one best friend in my world, and there would be only one forever. "Just hand me a bottle, will ya?"

"Well, look at you," he said with the Southern-trash accent he would never shake, reluctantly handing me a beer. I swung my head back, letting the alcohol run through my system. Lord, if I was gonna be on that bridge that day, I needed to be good and drunk.

"Looks like y'all just came from California with those sunglasses and that damn Cadillac of yours—" I opened my mouth, ready to protest, but someone spoke for me.

"It ain't his Cadillac," a rough voice said. I looked up to see Eric, a cigarette dangling from his mouth and a bottle neck between his fingers. His eyes were bloodshot and red, and he looked like he hadn't shaved in days. He looked the worst of all of us. This year must've been hell for him. "It was Kody's."

I gazed down, not wanting to look into any of their accusing eyes, the sunglasses hiding any trace of tears. "I'm just keepin' it for him," I muttered, my shoe pushing around an old piece of glass. "He told me t' take care of it, and that's what I'm doin'."

"Maybe," Eric countered, "but ain't none of us ever heard Kody say anything to you about it that night. Maybe you just fancied that car, and you knew the police would believe your story—"

"Are you saying I did this? What the hell are you tryin' to accuse me of? Kody Thomas was my best friend, and you don't got any right to accuse me of anything!" I blew up at Eric. What was he trying to pull? Did he actually think I could have done that? "Y'all didn't even have the right to say what you did to the papers! Y'all didn't see nothing that night, and you had no right to say that you did! What makes you think—"

"That's . . . that's enough." Bobby Kelley finally spoke up, his small frame coming between me and Eric. He had always been the quietest of the group, and Kody had spoken up for him more than he did for any of us. It felt odd for Bobby to be the voice of reason. Maybe he just felt like someone had to take Kody's place. "We don't need to fight here. Kody wouldn't have wanted us to fight. He would've wanted us to get along. So let's just get along today . . . for Kody's sake?"

I backed off, the sound of Kody's name reverberating in my head. My eyes darted across the desolate avenue, my vision blurred by my tears as I saw the fake flower cross littering the way. "Who the hell put that there?" I asked, not thinking anyone was gonna answer me.

"Kody's parents." My head snapped back, my mouth open in amazement. Did he just say that Kody's parents took time from their busy self-hatred to see what had happened to their son? "His mother was cryin' and s———, sayin' how much the Lord must love her boy, and his father just kept askin' how they went wrong." Evan chuckled, and if it had been a year ago, I guess I would have, too. I would have laughed out loud at that irony, but now, it was just sad. I didn't feel an obligation to be there. I had to go and get some milk for my mama.

"Oh." We stood there in silence for a few minutes, looking out across the avenue, hearing the occasional honking of a horn. I could see the pieces of glass from when Kody dropped the bottle. I didn't even know if that was the same glass, but in my mind, it was. I took another swig as I remembered every word Kody had said the day he decided he didn't have any reason to live. It wasn't gonna do me any good to cry in front of these guys. I didn't want to cry, anyway.

"Is anyone gonna say anythin'?" Evan asked in a small voice. None of us knew what to say.

As if he was some kind of mind reader at a county fair, Bobby spoke for us. "Kody would've known what to say," he said quietly.

We said nothing, but we all knew he was right. We were all lost without Kody, and now, he'd never know. I snapped out of the trance the silence had put us all in. I had to get out of there. I should've stopped him from jumping. I would never stop blaming myself, and I couldn't just go there, have a drink with three guys I didn't know anymore and be all right with it. It just wasn't going to happen.

"Hey, look guys, I've gotta go," I said, already halfway to the Cadillac. There were no objections. "I . . . have to get some groceries for my mama."

Bobby's voice broke the silence. "You gonna be here next year?" he asked, his voice on the verge of hopeful. But he had to know I wouldn't be there. Like I said, the broken glass and crosses didn't do anything good for me. It did a heck of a lot to me, but none good.

"Nope." And with that, I opened the door to the car, put my—Kody's—keys into the ignition, and roared off.

That was the last time I ever set foot or tire on the Western Avenue bridge, and I haven't spoken to Bobby, Evan or Eric since. Haven't seen them around town, either. Maybe that's just dumb luck. Or maybe we're all trying to avoid each other.

I still listen for that familiar squeak on my back gate, even now that it's been such a long time. Because, just maybe, Kody'll come around. I miss him. I miss his evil-sounding cackle, his sweet talking; I miss the Cadillac when I knew it was his Cadillac. I miss Kody. Oh, Lord, he's gotta know that his best friend ain't doin' all that well with this silence he's brought. He's gotta know that he's gotta come down again, back to Earth on his little cloud Cadillac from heaven he got from the Lord by sweet talkin' and come to my back gate.

And I just want him to know that I'll be here whenever he wants to come around again. ▣

Day After Christmas

by Tarilyn M. Tanice

I stood by the sink, my hand covered in thick red blood.
A glass lay shattered in a pan of soapy, red dishwater.

I tried to call your name.

Maybe it was shock. The tears caught in my throat,
but the only words out of my mouth were "Oh God,
   oh God."

Such words spoken by a nonbeliever.
Which God was I asking to help me?

You were upstairs, straightening up the room,
calling over and over, "What happened?"

You jumped over the banister onto the bottom stair,
only to become wide-eyed, pale-skinned
at the sight of your girlfriend's blood.

And for the first time in two years, I realized
that these scars would forever be a reminder of the time
you couldn't hold me and tell me not to cry.
For while my blood fell on your mother's white kitchen tiles,
while my skin came apart,
so did you.

Supernova

by Gabrielle Haber

He had to be certain, even though you couldn't ever be certain of something like this, and so he went searching through the tiny galaxy of his apartment that revolved around a sun about to supernova, and he looked under the bed and through the pile of dirty clothes in the corner, and as talking heads floated across the television screen, he adjusted the antenna to even the balance of the axis of his world, and when the talking heads told him that maybe he ought to try looking in the refrigerator, he did, but all he found there were a few jars of formaldehyde and a strange smell that crawled down his throat and wrapped around his gut in a tight fist, and he recalled that he hadn't eaten that day, or the day before, or, judging by the boniness of his wrist and the loose skin, in the many days preceding that, but he wasn't really hungry and hunger didn't seem to matter because all that mattered was that he would figure out once and for all what he'd been suspecting for a long time now, ever since his room- mate moved out anyway, or ever since he found the note behind the radiator, or, no, it was ever since the black hole appeared in his living room, yes, that was it, and when the tree started growing in the hole he was almost sure, and when the tree sprouted buds and flowered and fireflies flew out of the blossoms and nested in his cupboards, laying eggs that eventually hatched into tiny alligators that he flushed down the toilet, and that would somehow make their way back to his plumbing system someday but when they did he would be ready for them with the flame-thrower that he had misplaced a few days ago after dealing with the termites, though he hadn't caught them in time and they had managed to eat away at the entire outer wall so that the city could now watch him bathe, assuming that he did occasionally bathe, which he didn't do very often for fear that a few alligators would mature early and climb up through the drain to pull him down into it, yanking him into their dimension and away from the sweet ticking of the clocks lining the walls, which were now out of sync and needed to be fixed soon, because within a few hours of this arrhythmic ticking his heart would get confused and stop, which he didn't suspect would be a good thing because he really wanted to be certain before it was his time to disappear, and he was so close he could taste it with the tip of his tongue as he periodically licked at the air, and just now he thought he could taste a slight difference in the vicinity of the bedroom and so he ambled toward the pile of trash and dug with his foot until he felt it with his toes, and before he bent down to pick it up and find out for sure if he was right or not, as he happened to glance out the window, the sun exploded. ▣

Vegetables

by Katherine S. Assef

Nothing fancy.
Just peas, sweet corn and carrots.
Mother bought them from the
freezer aisle
while I lingered hopefully
by the ice-cream bars.
At home, I helped her unload
the groceries, striving to impress
her by carrying the bulkiest bags.
Take it easy, *she said.* That's heavy.

When I had a morning headache
she laid me down on her queen-sized bed,
placed a bag of frozen peas on my forehead
and let me sleep five more minutes.
Then she said, It's time to go to school.

Not long ago
she helped me plant a vegetable garden.
Nothing fancy,
just peas, sweet corn and carrots.
Give it time, *she says,*
kissing my troubled forehead
as I crouch by the garden,
searching for sprouts.
It will . . .

2 Learning to Live: Family Pieces

Photo by Anna W. Butterworth

Learning to Live

by Maria Carboni

Sitting in the fuzzy blue chair in the intensive care waiting room, head in her hands, Eve closes her eyes and wonders if a person who has spent her life among the dying can ever really learn to live. Images of oxygen tanks and tubes swirl before her in a distorted surrealism, and the sterile smells of antibacterial soap and urine burn her nostrils.

The nurses often tease that she has grown up in the hospital, yet Eve can remember the first time she ventured through its doors and into the world of the ill. She had pestered her mom forever, wanting to accompany the fair-haired lady in pale green scrubs to work. But when she begged, Mom set her jaw, causing her mouth to form the thin line that meant the topic was closed to discussion.

Then when Eve was five years old, Mom dressed her in a brand-new jumpsuit and put her in their peeling Volvo. As they headed toward the hospital, the young girl decided she was undeniably grown up. This was not the only time she was wrong.

Once inside, Eve's mom told her to follow quietly and not touch anything. Perhaps it was the bloody stump of the man with the amputated leg or the woman with a surgical camera inserted down her throat that made the child vomit. Or maybe it was the stench of the overcooked liver casserole combined with the smell of the unbathed lady with the deficient bladder. Either way, Mom simply smiled wryly at her daughter's mess, cleaned it up and said, "You'll get used to it, kid." And she did. Later, Mom explained there was a certain numbness required to work in medicine, and if Eve could gain this without losing her sympathy, she would make a great doctor.

With a start, Eve, still slouched in the blue chair, opens her eyes. She is now aware of two teenagers giggling over magazines nearby. She listens for a moment to their discussion of a family picnic and watches them through her curtain of blonde hair.

Footsteps echo from the corridor outside, and a powerful-looking woman with good posture strides by wearing gloves. She reminds her of Mom, but it can't be. Eve thinks of her mother, who is at home packing, and will probably be on her way soon.

Smoothing her candy-striper uniform, Eve brushes past the cheerful adolescents and out the door. As she wanders the halls, she takes in the pictures on the walls, the marble floor, the stagnant air, the familiar names of the doctors being paged. She wonders how much of this she will miss and how much she'll remember.

She passes a clock. It's almost time to leave. Eve can feel her tuna salad churning in her. There must be someone she forgot to say good-bye to.

Maybe her father will be angry that Eve is leaving and that he is the last to know. Or maybe he will be glad that he gets to spend more time with his latest girlfriend, Suzanne, the redhead who likes to cluck her tongue at

Eve through her fuchsia lipstick as she pretends she is Eve's mother. Eve knows her father's reaction will depend on how much he has had to drink.

It doesn't really matter. Her departure means leaving behind her lifelong dream of being a doctor. She already knows her father will refuse to pay for college if she abandons him. Maybe he will be sad she is gone.

Outside it is sunny, and Eve hears The Supremes blaring from Mom's radio. When she climbs into the dilapidated convertible, she notices that the hot seats are crammed with overflowing duffel bags.

Looking at the sky, Eve sees a cluster of gray clouds she had not noticed before. She then watches the large hospital until it is out of sight, and a bitter taste forms in her mouth.

Mom is saying something about Chinese food for dinner and how Eve must watch the maps and direct her to California. As if she knew the way. Eve had never been out of the state, much less halfway across the country. The determined look in Mom's eyes tells Eve not to bring that up.

Eve rests her head against the seat, and, for some reason, pictures an old lady who died in the hospital years ago. The woman is handing her a large sunflower. She grasps it, then runs through a meadow. Where is she going?

Eve is surprised when the car stops. She looks at her mother, who commands impatiently, "Go write your father a note."

When she walks across the lawn to the cheerful yellow house, Eve realizes that the clump of clouds has gotten darker and larger.

Inside, she sits at the kitchen table with a notebook and thick marker, staring at the lines on the paper. She will never be a doctor. The lines seem to jut out at her, and she feels hot and dizzy. She holds her head and rocks back and forth in the wicker chair.

She is still rocking when her mom comes in, smelling like coconut lotion, with leopard-print sunglasses perched on her head. "Come on," Mom says.

"Not yet . . . I didn't write a note."

"Don't worry. We'll call him from the road."

"No . . . I'm not ready . . . I forgot something . . . I didn't finish the note."

Mom is pulling on Eve's sleeve. "Come on."

The rocking stops, and Eve looks up at her mother. Her mouth, for the first time, is set in the same line as the woman standing above her. "No."

Her mother takes a few steps backward. "No?" She steps back again and is pressed against the window. This is when Eve sees the rain, pouring from the sky in bursts, into the convertible with the top down.

Her mother runs outside, closes the car and removes her daughter's luggage, all the while giving instructions about this and that.

Eve stands in the rain on the front stoop of the cheerful yellow house she and her father share. She observes her mother scampering about, but she is not really listening to her. Then, in a cloud of coconut lotion, The Supremes and a wet, green convertible, her mother is gone. And Eve is standing in the rain. 回

Cycle

by Valerie Bandura

When she was young and firm-chested
My mother sat up one morning
Cold, stone-like, petrified.
She was lost somewhere
Between falling in love
And a mathematics college.
So she traded herself in
For two kids and a husband,
And a systematic disease
Came rushing through her blood and zeal.

In her tired skin,
In her porous cells
She pushed me out
In a claustrophobic nightmare.
I got caught in her genes,
—all suited up
With the burden of her resurrection
Embodied in my fear of being standard.

Now she looks at me across
The dinner table.
Serious, presumptuous.

Expecting me to follow up
As if it's as easy as peeling an orange,
Finding the fruit inside sweet.
Looking at me, she, I, in my skin
Keep turning
By accident, then by choice.

Drawing by Katie Stuart

Lilac Mist

by Rebecca Olsen Snyder

The vinyl bus seat clung to my thighs, and the sharp cracks jabbed my skin. Raising my legs, I rearranged the navy skirt and felt the collection of sweat along the creases of polyester fabric.

I remember when I found this skirt last summer. It was a muggy afternoon, and my mother had dragged me to her monthly hair lightening appointment. While approaching Curls 'R Us, I noticed a Salvation Army store.

"Mom," I stuttered, interrupting her hip-swinging walk through the crowded parking lot. Stopping, but not responding, she waited for me to continue.

"Mom, tomorrow is the first day of sixth grade, and I still don't have a uniform," I said quickly, sensing her impatience.

"Damnit, Misty," she muttered, reaching for her purse. My heart lifted as her skinny fingers and sleek red nails groped in her leather handbag. I hadn't actually expected her to acknowledge my need for a uniform, even though it was required.

Handing me a crumpled five-dollar bill, my mother grumbled something about wishing she'd left me home.

"Spend this wisely. It's all you're getting." With that she swiveled her spandex-bound hips 180 degrees and clicked her magenta pumps across the asphalt.

Elated, I gripped the money and skipped into the secondhand clothing store. I remember the moment I laid eyes on the skirt in a "Two for Ten" bin. Ignoring the wrinkles and price, I tried it on and admired how the waist clung to my middle and hung so nicely right above my knees. In the cracked mirror, I pranced around, falling in love from all angles. I imagined I was Mary Ellis, or one of her perfectly dressed friends. I giggled and laughed, spinning in quick little circles. The boys liked me, and I liked them, and we sipped Clearly Canadians all afternoon at each other's houses.

I was walking on clouds when I entered the beauty parlor with my new-to-me skirt tight in my hands. I clenched it even harder when I noticed the look in my mother's eyes. She and her yellow-haired beautician laughed about their children's stupidity, but once we were alone in the car, my mother reminded me what was what. I had to go to school the next day dressed in my new prized possession, a stained white shirt and a black eye. I did not giggle or dance, and Mary Ellis continued to drink her Clearly Canadians, oblivious to my longing stares.

I took a deep breath, slowly sucking in the thick diesel air. I pretended the stench was a light lilac fragrance, a perfume Mrs. Engerly, my teacher, wore every day.

Breathe it all in, I thought. *Breathe it in until you are there.* And then I was not on the yellow bus, but next to my teacher in her log cabin on Lake Ariel. Her husband and house were my father and home. We all loved each other dearly, and Mama and Daddy had recently told me I would have a baby brother. It was just us and our playful golden retriever named Skip, so I was ecstatic for the addition to our loving home. It was perfect now, and in a few months it was going to be even more perfect.

But the diesel aroma this afternoon was almost too foul to be transformed into Lilac Mist, and the squealing giggles around me interrupted my thoughts.

It is my birthday today, I remembered. I am twelve years old, and not one single person on this bus knows. My mother hadn't even remembered. She did the day before (when I asked her if she would bring birthday cupcakes to my classroom). Vanilla sprinkled ones and Kool-Aid like the other kids' denim-clothed mothers brought. It had been a good day for her, which is why I dared ask. But the question had caught her off-guard, and with a moment's thought, she said something about me being too old for that type of thing. I had never had classroom birthday treats, even when I was younger, but I didn't mention that. I only shifted my eyes to the soap opera she was watching and desperately prayed she would forget my request. She did.

With the screeching halt of the bus's tires and the opening of the door, I stood up. Waiting to regain my balance, I began to walk down the narrow aisle. The cruel remarks and revolting gestures thrown at me made my stomach churn and my cafeteria lunch creep up my esophagus.

The walk home from the stop was long, but a peaceful release from the school day. I used to tell myself it was my opportunity for my mind and thoughts to embrace solace, but I have since realized that my lack of social interaction already allowed endless hours of silence for thoughts.

The daffodils were in full bloom that week. That's how I always knew my birthday is coming. Without them, I am afraid I might forget. Before walking up the five flights of stairs to our apartment, I picked a couple into a bouquet for my mother. She loved daffodils, and she loved surprises. I knew they would brighten her if her day weren't going well.

She'd had a job interview that morning at the bakery department in a supermarket. Before leaving for school, I had watched her fret over her outfit, hairstyle and jewelry. This job offered benefits, she told me, very nice benefits and security, too. I liked the security part, so I let my ears make music out of the sound of every syllable.

But I knew how things worked. Employers didn't like my mother's look.

"They're just jealous of me," I heard her say once after a failed interview. And maybe that was the truth. So I nodded and dished out whatever compliments made her downturned face smile. I loved it when she smiled. It brought me back to the days when we lived with Grandma Pam in North Carolina, and I loved going to school. It was only pre-school, but I still soaked in every bit of information my teachers shared with me. Hand in hand, my grandma would walk me home from Tree House School, and I would spend the rest of the day eating warm goodies and watching "Winnie the Pooh." When my mother came home at night, her face would light up like the sun, and she would run to me with open arms, squealing, laughing and showering my face with kisses. Every night I would go to sleep to the soft voices of my grandma and mother in the other room, the constancy of their tones taking me into a dream world. Those perfect days and nights with Grandma made my mother's bad days appear not as awful as they were. I knew I was safe when Grandma was there.

But Grandma died, and we moved away. Mother said she didn't even want to think about Grandma or North Carolina anymore, so we drove for days, maybe even weeks. That's when the smiles left. Every now and then when they do resurface, even if just for a moment, I take a huge breath. I concentrate on sucking it all in and keeping it inside me for as long as possible. I can almost feel the smiles inside my lungs, pumping my heart so I can live. I keep them there, mentally documenting their arrival and gestation, and bury them deep within me so they cannot escape.

The living room that afternoon was as cluttered as usual, so I carefully held the flowers in my left hand and picked up empty chip bags and clothes with my right. The TV was frozen in black, and I knew my mother was not back. She always had the TV on.

Reaching for the power button, I pressed the box back to life. Sound filled the room, and I headed for the kitchen. Finding a cup in the sink, I filled it with water and placed the daffodils in it.

I pictured my mother's face as she noticed the beautiful yellow flowers.

"Oh, Misty!" I imagined her exclaiming, tears welling up in her eyes. "You are the most thoughtful daughter in the world!" And then she would hug me and tell me about her wonderful job interview. "I start tomorrow, and the manager says if I am a hard worker, I might have a shot at a management position!"

But my mother did not come home that night. I made dinner when she didn't show up by eight, but her macaroni and cheese congealed after an hour on the coffee table. The next morning I went to school as usual and came home as usual. But the house was empty, and the television set was still silent from when I had turned it off that morning.

When I came home from school the day after that, the door was open. My heart beat wildly as I peered through the narrow crack and called out to my mother. Nobody answered, but when I entered the family room, I saw her, passed out on the carpet, both eyes black and swollen.

"Mommy . . ." my voice quivered as I gently lifted her head. The revolting smell of alcohol was thick in the air. Her eyes were puffed as large as golf balls, and her lips were cracked and bloody. Draping her wobbly head over my shoulder, I stood up and carried her into her bedroom. Her sleeping body remained motionless as I removed the torn blouse she had so meticulously picked out three mornings before.

A warm washcloth easily melted the dried blood from her swollen face and the stench that surrounded her. I made sure she was covered with blankets and safely on her bed.

I retrieved the almost-wilted daffodils, placing them on her nightstand. I sat next to her and pictured the flowers as they had been when I first arranged them.

"These flowers are for you, Mother," I said softly, knowing she was too far away to hear or understand my words. "I know how much you love daffodils. I saw them and thought of you."

This would make her smile. I knew it would. Her pearly teeth would appear, all twenty-four perfectly in a row. And I would smile, too, because she smiled. And then I would breathe, one large, deep breath that could take it all in: the yellow daffodils, my mother and me, and our smiles. ▣

Frying Wontons
by Diane Lowe

I watch my mother scoop
the pork mixture with
nimble chopsticks
And wrap the wontons
in sheets of dough
Into the hot oil they go

I try, but my chopsticks
aren't so nimble
And the wontons don't
look so neatly wrapped
in my clumsy
sheets of dough

The kitchen is filled with
such quiet memories
of making wontons
and egg-drop soup
and moon cakes
All wrapped in awkward
sheets of dough

Raspberries

by Adam Kirshner

Brittle bushes thrash my young skin,
thorns prickle the cuticles on my right fingers.
I hold in my left hand a tiny basket,
filled with raspberries.

My father
helps me
escape the bushes
a forest only as tall as his arms, and my mother
puts those ruby berries in a place
not even my longest finger
could reach:
the top of the refrigerator.
My lips smacked shut, closed out my tongue
from serenading the last berry.

When my father enters,
his hands are dirty from the outside,
and with those dirty hands he picks me up, and
carries me to the white sink so we both wash
earth from our juice-smelling hands.

I kick off my shoes and always find a thorn
stuck to my sweaty white sock,
never understanding how it got there.
My mother pulls it out, always saying
that she warned me to watch where I was walking.

Now crystal tap water cleans the raspberries,
my teeth squeeze the tip of one
and juice splatters onto my chin, not needing a napkin:
My tongue cleans the spot.

I have to eat this berry,
biting into its concave center
and slowly disposing of it down my throat asking for more.
And more,
until there are no more.
I ate them all.
No more,
Not until next year.

The Legacy

by Nicole K. Press

It was the first time the coat seemed necessary. He died in early spring, and after his possessions had been divided among greedy family members, they were distributed to already-established households and ignored—until I woke today and realized the cold of six inches of snow would chill me through my canvas jacket.

After my father died, my sister dealt with her grief by drowning herself in my mother's jewelry. Uncle Bruce took my grandfather's car, something the two brothers had always fought over. Bruce deserved the car; he'd dreamt about owning it when he was younger, but it was left to my father, who couldn't appreciate something so troublesome. Out of spite, my father kept it and taunted Bruce. I didn't agree with that, but it was his, and he could do as he chose. Because of this, Bruce always hated my father and me, too, since I was given the privilege of driving it. After Bruce got the car, he bragged, telling me it was worth more than the house. He knew how much I missed my father and had to get his last dig in. He couldn't have cared less—he had his car.

I expected him to drive by my house every day, showing me my loss, but for some reason, I never saw him behind the wheel, except sitting in the garage.

My grandfather was an old-fashioned man. He believed the oldest son should inherit his father's property, which is how my father ended up with the car. It's also how I rid myself of my sweaty apartment in Arizona and became the sixth owner of my family's three-story house in Vermont. I remember the house being full of the souvenirs that gave the appearance that my father traveled the world when actually he had bought them at tag sales and through catalogs. Now it seemed bare, although to the unknowing eye, it looked like a well-furnished home. It comfortably held couches, coffee tables and armchairs, but someone who knew my father would wonder why you could see the backs of bookshelves, why his gold penholder wasn't on his desk and why his musket wasn't delicately placed on its ivory hooks over the fireplace.

Although the house seemed bare to me, it was still full of treasures.

So the morning I woke up to six inches of snow, I opened the closet in the master bedroom and took out my father's favorite wool coat. It was a single-breasted, ankle-length, black nightmare. But because I had only been in the house two days shy of a month and was used to the weather of Arizona, I wore it with the same pride my father had.

I hadn't seen snow since I was a child and visited my grandparents in this house. Outside, the wind chilled me, and I thrust my hands deep into the pockets that still smelled like my father. My hand felt the metal of a key. I pulled it out, held it in my hand, smiled, then dropped it, letting it disappear beneath the snow. ▣

Despair

by Brad Mann

I haven't quite gotten over the fact that
My father tried to hang himself when
His life seemed too much to bear
When his veins finally got the best of him.
I hope he realized when the knot slipped
And his improperly wound noose unraveled,
That he was stronger than what he brought
Himself to become, stronger than what he is

I can see Chinese sailboats not quite faring
In foreign waters, with black sails flying
Upon rotting masts that could be stabbed with
The bluntest of pipes, or the sharpest of swords
But don't bother, there is no use anymore

There are only sore throats here
Rope burns on necks, sore jugular veins
Voice boxes scratchy and rusted from the din
Of anguish and something that felt like heartbreak
That collapse of the soul, the empowerment once
Felt deep in the confines, in the ruins as they now lay.

I have viewed the fall of an empire
Something much worse than merely Rome or the Ottoman
I figure he is a nomad now, a roaming migrant who
Will only give time to what might matter to him,
The people who will wish him the best with his endeavors
Whatever they may be, wherever they might lead him
I trust he has found the direction that has been missing
For oh so long, all those drowsy days and sleepless nights
Obliterated from memory banks that ran dry of currency
When the market crashed on that fateful day.

Photo by Stephen Siperstein

Holes

by Julsa Flum

I sit on the dock alone, my legs hanging off the edge. The water laps at my feet like a hungry dog, like it is trying to pull me into its gaping black mouth. I am strong, although I always was the stubborn one, like a piece too big to swallow, refusing to go down. It's the first time I've come back home since my mother's death. I figured it would be too painful. I was right. I half expected my mother to be here, sitting on the dock, staring into the glossy water. Everything is empty, though, lonely and badly in need of repair. I feel isolated, but safe, here on the dock. Maybe that's how she was feeling all those years. I realize I never knew my mother, and as I gaze into the silvery water, my childhood stares back. I taste salt in my mouth. I am crying. I realize how many holes there were in my mother's heart. I realize how much she needed my love and how I could never give it. I realize today, years later, when I returned home, and everything is flooding back to me. I'm drowning in my grief like she was, without me even noticing.

My father was like a train. You always heard him coming long before he arrived—felt the ground tremble, felt the excitement. My father was a large man. He wasn't fat, but he was tall. Standing at six feet, five inches, I never had trouble finding him in a crowd. I'll never forget my father's smell. It was a mixture of soil, the dark brown, rich kind, sweat and Juicyfruit gum. I never did know what he did for work; all I remember is his coming home. The doorway was smaller than he was, so he would always duck his head into the hallway, like he was peeking into a doll house. He'd sit in the green plaid armchair, and I'd curl up in his lap, my arms around his neck, and I'd listen to his chest rumble as he spoke. My mother would come prancing in, with coffee and the newspaper. She'd sit on the leg opposite me and kiss him passionately until, giggling, I'd push them apart. My parents were in love, and they were equals in the game of marriage.

On Friday nights we'd have company, little parties, and I'd sneak out when I was supposed to be in bed. I would be lightly scolded, but I always ended up entertaining the guests, reciting a poem or singing "The Sailor and the Sea," my father's favorite song. Then I'd fall asleep on the couch and would be carried to bed. They worked in the garden on Saturdays or did projects trying to make my mother's dream house, they said. On Sundays we took trips, zipping through the country in my father's periwinkle Studebaker.

I loved the routine of things, the comfort and security. One day my father didn't come home. I waited for his voice at the front door, and I waited on the porch swing staring down the empty road until dusk settled in. I waited in the kitchen where I watched my normally disorganized mother fold and refold our napkins. I watched her dust the seashells we had collected on the beach, lining them up from largest to smallest. The phone rang at last, piercing the awkward silence that hung between us—silence that pushed on my ears and made me want to scream. She dashed to the phone. "Ed?" she practically screamed. She grasped the receiver with hopeful hands. I could hear the mumbling of a man's voice on the other end. For a moment I thought it was my father, delayed at work, but my mother's face fell. She dropped the phone and sank to the floor. The day my father died, my life turned black and white. It has never returned to color.

I always thought therapy was a waste of money and time. When I was seventeen, right after my mother died, the children's house I was living in sent me to a therapist. They said it would be good to have someone to talk to after such a traumatic experience. I tried to tell her my mother died ten years ago, along with my father. She didn't understand. Instead, two times a week I sat in her air-conditioned room and listened to her tell me about my grief. The woman's words were as fake as her plastic red nails. When I got older, I went through one rocky relationship after another, and my friends referred me to their therapists whom they claimed turned their lives around.

"Just give them a try," they whined, and I did. They were all the same. They pretended to know too much about you without you telling. They hid behind their diplomas and big words.

When my mother died, I watched her go. Drowned, the police said, no questions asked. I knew better. I had walked to the beach that morning. She was there just as she had been every day since my father's funeral. It was as if she had given up on me, stopped caring. I was afraid of her. The children at my school called her crazy. She was. At night she would run up and down the stairway calling "Ed, Ed, Ed," as if expecting him to answer. Then she would fall sobbing on one of the steps, tearing her nightgown with trembling fingers. I would stand on the balcony, watching her for hours. During the day she would stomp around the house, wailing or moaning. She covered the windows with blankets so no light could enter. She smashed all the mirrors, each time shrieking, "Here is to seven more years." Actually, it was really, "Here is to f——ing seven more years."

It was a month after my father's death that she started going down to the dock. My father built it on a Saturday. He'd sanded it for hours, "Until it was smooth as a baby's bottom," he'd said, and laughed his deep, throaty laugh. I helped him stain it a deep mahogany. When it was dry, the two of us sat on the end. He held me and I felt as if nothing would ever hurt me. You know that safe, perfect feeling you get when you're in your father's arms. My mother joined us, and we watched the sun set. I remember the colors were vibrant that evening, reflected in the water, like the sky was a canvas and the colors were painted in long, sweeping brushstrokes. My mother claimed the dock as her own. Each day in the morning she would do yoga on a blanket spread over the boards. Salute to the sun, she called it, and she was beautiful. But when my father was gone, the yoga stopped. Instead she sat staring blandly into the distance. I would call her name, but she never heard me. I would have to walk down and touch her shoulder. The nanny we hired was paid for with Social Security checks; she took care of me. She made me meals and tucked me in at night, but there was no love there. I began to call my mother by her first name. She wasn't Mommy anymore, just a woman who slept in my house at night and sat on the dock in the day. There was no anger in her, no sadness. Her face was blank and unfeeling—dead. Soon her existence became part of my daily routine, like brushing my teeth. There, but automatic.

Ten years after my father's death, I was seventeen. I went to school, got good grades and had a few friends. One day at lunch I went down to the dock to call for her to come up. She turned to me, and I saw a light in her face I hadn't seen for years. She took my hands and smiled.

"I'll tell your father you said hello," she breathed. Taking off her nightgown, she slipped into the water. Confused, I waited for her to come up, but all I could make out in the murky depths was my own reflection. I waited by the water for two days, long after emergency crews had left, expecting her to surface. I waited until a social worker came and led me away.

My toes are getting numb, and it's getting dark. My past I had tried so hard to forget has engulfed me completely. "Good-bye, Mommy," I say and walk up the path to my childhood home. I never realized how many holes my mother had in her heart and how many she passed on to me. ▣

Breaking the Surface

by Brandon R. Wilke

I remember fishing with
my grandfather in Ontario where

the crystal blue waters of Eagle Lake
stretched for miles. Red boats lined up

like soldiers glinting in
the sunlight. Grizzled old men smelling

of fish and worms stampeded
toward the dock, leaving my grandfather and me

coughing in a cloud of dust. We
ambled down to our boat.

The motor
sputtered and finally grew

to a thunderous roar, and we
sped off. The water, white and frothy from

the blurred revolutions of the motor,
splashed up in my face and stung my cheeks.

Hours later after absolutely
no activity, a slight tug

jerked my grandfather's pole.
He sprang into action,

leaning back with all
his might, pulling

the end of the line. Ten minutes
later, with sweat beads dripping

down his forehead and
burning his eyes,

a twig surfaced, then
a bigger branch, then

the whole trunk. Dejected, my grandfather
pulled his hat down tighter, turned

his back to me, and I just stared
at the back of his head,

imagining his embarrassment and
trying to hide my laughter.

On with the Tomboy

by Ashley Belanger

've had this idea. Ever since I was a little boy. Except I never was a little boy. I get confused sometimes because my father always wanted me to be one.

And so I'd romp and wrestle with him. Roll in the dirt and skip the showers my mother learned to decree a necessity in order to get dessert. All just to know he loved me.

Not that I doubted he loved my sisters. They were girls. All four of them. He brought them presents, little dolls and chocolate kisses. I usually got a slap on the back and some licorice. I hated licorice. But I choked it down. Because I loved him.

Psychologists might claim this is unhealthy, but I think I have more authority with a degree of expertise than their books give them. I grew up a boy and still I am a woman. I call this the law of genderality. That would be my own private term to encompass gender and sexuality. Although Mrs. Arace, my high-school anthropology teacher, hammered deep into my brain the grave difference between the two, I also saw that one depended heavily on the other. But which one is the dependent, and which one is being depended on?

You see, my father was a good man and my mother a good woman. They just never had any sons, and a man could go crazy in that girlish prison of American Girl dolls and tea parties. I see myself a martyr, losing out on my girlhood days in order to ensure that my father remained sane enough to keep a steady job and pay the bills. Mission accomplished.

My father was massive. His chest and shoulders seemed immeasurable. I couldn't see all of him in one look. And so I'd have to view him in parts. For example, first I'd zone in on the funny way he used to part his hair until my mother, fed up with his faltering fashion sense, suggested he change his look. Or the way he curled his toes when he was about to make a cutting remark.

My favorite part of him was his belly: rotund and gelatinous—it was his definitive weak spot whether we were wrestling, boxing or just arguing. My sisters used to bounce on it, the roughest he ever got with them. It was also a place of comfort, often a pillow while he read *Cinderella* or *Rapunzel.* I always liked the story of Rapunzel, but I never admitted it to him. Quietly, I would press my ear up to the door to listen as his voice raised and his pace quickened to liven up the part when the witch discovers Rapunzel's lover. I wished my hair were long and silky, but I never allowed my mother to braid it.

This is not to insinuate that my father held me back from a frivolous need to play with hair. That would be like suggesting God forced Adam and Eve to eat those apples. This was a decision all my own. I wouldn't trade our games and gallivanting for anything, not even an elegant, swirling braid.

There was this one time—wow, my father and I got those awful neighborhood boys good! They were pelting our precious cocker spaniel, Buddy, with rocks and then depositing the rocks in our pool. My father, always adventurous, knew just how to handle the situation, even in times of livid anger, which I saw on his face that day and still makes my knees knock and the tears well up. He sent me out alone—the decoy—and my assignment was to distract the ringleader.

I thought about my older sister then, and how her girly magazines dictated the proper ways to drive a boy crazy and how she'd probably bat her lashes and use her sexuality to lure him away. I, however, was only eight years old and had never read those magazines. So I started throwing rocks at the biggest boy, which caused him to chase me, but I was an expert. He was in my territory, and I led him into the shed where I armed myself with rope. I'll never forgive myself for what I did to that poor boy, but I'm positive not many eight-year-old girls would have dreamed up the torturous plot I unleashed on him in the confines of that tiny shack. I will tell you I learned it from the Teenage Mutant Ninja Turtles.

Anyway, my father, realizing the army would collapse once its leader had fallen, lashed out with water balloons and took the whole lot of them out. He was such a good shot and threw so hard at just the right angle that he never failed to burst them. He was my hero.

Anthropologist W. H. Haviland defines gender as the elaborations and meanings cultures assign to the biological differentiation of the sexes. *Elaborations and meanings.* My father simply elaborated the more male aspects of my life, such as my inclination to go hiking in the woods over my sisters' inherent desire to accompany my mother to the grocery store. There is nothing unhealthy about that. In fact, I believe such girls are so numerous that there is even a label for the phenomenon: tomboy.

Someone once told me that the term tomboy originated from *The Adventures of Tom Sawyer.* Although I'd never read the book, I automatically thought that obviously Tom Sawyer must have some very feminine characteristics. If a boyish girl is a tomboy, then Tom Sawyer must be very in touch with his feminine side. It also got me started thinking about the original tomboy and why we weren't named for her sake and not some fictitious misrepresentation of a boy found in *Tom Sawyer.* That's when I also decided that somebody male had definitely coined the term.

But anyway, this tale isn't about who decided to call a manly girl a tomboy. This is about my utter adoration for a respectable male. My father. I believe praise ought to be issued where praise is due, and this man sacrificed so much to keep his children happy. What an impossibility! After all, we ranged in age with eleven years between the oldest and the youngest.

I looked up the word "praise" once. The dictionary told me it was the exaltation of a hero. The exaltation of a hero? My then ten-year-old mind couldn't grasp the meaning and what I had to do to demonstrate my appreciation. How could I express this to the man who'd devoted ten years of his life to my existence and, more important, to my happiness? I thumbed through the pages until I discovered the meaning of exaltation. Do you want to know what that maze-like, irritating source informed me? That exaltation was "to glorify, to honor, or . . . to praise." I was back where I began.

I remember once, when fathers were plentiful, the wind in my hair, gritty sand beneath my nails and love on my tongue as he whirled me on a rusty merry-go-round. This was one toy I didn't have to fight my sisters for because they were too prim and proper. There hung a rusted bell that rang of liberty with each swooping turn. Freedom from the expectations of this world, of what a girl is, what a boy is, and why I was lost somewhere in-between, it cried to me. "Faster! Faster!" He pushed and panted. I cackled and chanted. "Faster! Faster!" I rose and wrapped my legs securely around the posts, lifting my arms and swaying as the ride, raucous and jerky, led me in a desperate tango. I stared up at the treetops and painted them with my happiness.

Around the time I turned twelve, my father's appearance began to strike me as abnormal. The shirts that used to hug his belly snugly, the ones that made his cavernous belly button impossible to hide, now hung loosely, alarmingly resembling king-sized sheets flung carelessly over a clothesline. I hid my concern like a twelve-year-old boy might by pretending everything was fine. I dragged him outside to build a snow fort with me. It was a tradition that with the first snow we would reap the benefits of a snowplow's hard work and convert it into a hideaway.

What I didn't realize was that I was draining him. He used to be as big as the ocean, and I'd reduced him to a meager pool that was constantly being absorbed by the sunlight in my sisters' eyes and my constant splishing and splashing. The less water that remained, the less time he spent with me, and the less I felt his influence. I found myself spending afternoons engaged by Zack and Screech from *Saved by the Bell*. Laughing merrily, I'd join my sisters in decorating Christmas cookies and running tinsel through my hair.

Then something remarkable happened. I came home from school one day, and there on my pillow was a mound of Hershey Kisses, each and every one for me, and a piece of paper on which he'd scrawled MGR. We always wrote everything in code to ensure my sisters' spying eyes could not invade our private escapades. I was thirteen. I ran for the merry-go-round in high anticipation.

That was the day the wind whispered the news. My father's strength had waned; he wasn't coming out to play. The bell was imposing in its silence as I inwardly begged for it to jangle noisily and create some distraction. I began to cry because our founding fathers had promised liberty but not life. Late autumn maples rained overhead. My beaten sneakers dangled in a puddle of dry leaves. I dismounted. Silly games. Silly fun. Silly fathers.

At my father's funeral, I wore a long, cascading black skirt that swooshed around my ankles in a foreign manner. I felt like I was betraying him as I awkwardly stood among my sisters, hiding my tears for more private times when he'd taught me it would be acceptable to shed them. As if from the grave, he was watching us and saying his good-byes, only he couldn't recognize me, couldn't discern me from the crowds because this wasn't who I was.

So I paid a special tribute to him myself. I found a way

to give thanks to the man who made my ascension into womanhood a possibility. My father, always selfless, had seemingly given himself so that I could become a person. So that I could accept my true gender. So that I could blur the lines between boy and girl, and with that knowledge evolve into an even greater woman.

When I was fourteen, I had my first kiss. He was nervous, and his palms were sweaty. Mine were, too. Are girls supposed to admit that? I had no idea, but it helped to ease the moment. Right then I was him and he was me, and we were both insecure. I found my immature, boyish humor helped in this case.

I went to the prom my junior year. My dress was blue and had an awful, itchy lining. My skirt irritated me the whole night, but I had to grin and bear it. I was such a girl! My date showed up at the door, all dorky in his tuxedo. From his awkward movements I could tell he was uncomfortable. He was such a sport, and he forced a smile; it reminded me of how I felt at my father's funeral. So out of place.

Another year brought me to graduation. It's amazing how in that sea of faces—where everyone wears the same cap, same gown, same broad grins—gender and sex lose significance. We were collectively happy, male or female, boy or girl, woman or man. I felt so at home in that sanctuary from gender designation.

My mom bought me a cat as my graduation present. It was a beautiful, light-colored Persian. That night it lay curled up on my stomach. It spoke its discontent when I tried to rub its belly (must've been a sensitive spot), and I was reminded of my father and how his voice used to rise when the witch discovered the lover in the tower. I called the cat Rapunzel.

This all brings me back to the laws of genderality and how, sooner or later, every person whose gender is culturally assigned by their biologically determined sex at birth learns to embrace that gender. Lies and lives and loves, they all make a person who he or she is. But who is she? Who is he? Are life and love about gender, or are they about the experiences that lead up to the way gender is handled?

I dealt with my gender the best way I knew how, and my father was not an impediment to my bloom. He weeded out the troubled times so that my garden wouldn't be marred with roses, and so when I finally blossomed into the woman I am today, I didn't have to feel smothered by the beauty surrounding me, but rather felt more beautiful for having kept the world waiting, for having spent a greater portion than most as a weed. After all, who wants to disturb the late-blooming flower? Its beauty comes with time, and time was what my father afforded me. Today I am a joyful girl.

And so I've had this idea, ever since I was a little boy, about how to offer praise. Regardless of the dictionary's suggestions, praise isn't about the smiles, isn't about the presents, isn't even about the gestures. Praise wasn't the exaltation of a hero; praise was the unwavering admiration one person holds for another who has altered his or her life.

Has my life been altered by my father? In so many ways that counting would be trivial. And so I thank him for the silly games, the silly fun, my silly father. Praise fathers. Praise fathers long gone. Praise fathers for the moments that make us who we are and remind us of who they were and show us how, although the two are entirely separate concepts, like sex and gender, one still depends heavily on the other. ◙

Photo by Ed Jaffe

To What Was and What Will Never Be Again

by Kathleen McCarney

I used to love her room
the vibrant faces
lining the wall
ceiling to floor
the comfy couch
with patches over worn spots
a hug for everyone
who smiled in the door
the music loud
and meaningful
and the hostess
full of energy
pulsing through the room
but when the sun set
and the winter tones
started blowing
her room began to scare me
the posters stare back
lifeless and yellowed
with tobacco and pain
the couch looks sullen

and covered
in cigarette bruises and puncture wounds
now each knock on the door
is met with a guarded
"who are you"
and frequently turned away
there is no music now
just the lull of commercials
and Sally Jesse Raphael's
speaking to a nodding audience
she just lies on her bed
ashtray at her side
eyes slipping in and out of focus
as her cigarette burns
and the ashes cling
to the deathstick
like her streaky, dirty hair
to her pale and abused body

My Mom Fought the Club and the Club Won

by Matt Denno

In the smoke-filled living room,
My shopping mother stands.
She likes to view Home Shopping Club,
And buy from distant lands.
Sweat stands out upon her brow,
While she thinks nothing would be nicer
Than to jump right up and buy
One of Home Shopping's kitchen slicers.
No! *She screams inside her head,*
Although she feels the urge,
I will not drive my family broke,
Because I like to splurge.
But in the end she will break down,
She'll throw her family's welfare down,
Pick up the phone and go to town.
Every day now we expect
Another guy from U.P.S.
And from his brown truck he's brought
The merchandise my mother got.
Then she runs a marathon,
Back to where the TV's on.
She'll shop and squander, and splurge and spend.
Then she'll shop some more again.

If Things Could Be Salvaged

by Jennifer McMenemy

I try not to steal things people give me, but I can't help it. Until now I have spent all my time throwing rocks and gluing bits of glass together. That's how I ended up here. But well, I'm not exactly from humble beginnings and . . . how should I put it? I won't miss Auntie Junie. In fact, I know that because of her, I stole and salvaged. But to you, it would seem like all I did was cause trouble and misbehave. How can I explain that I'm not all I seem to be? Instead of being the one who steals, I am the one from whom others have stolen.

Mom used to tell me, "You're never broke if you have some change in your pocket, Bridge. If you can be glued back together at the jagged edges, you can be fixed." She said a lot of stuff with double meanings, probably because she knew she wasn't going to live long enough to teach me all of life's little lessons.

I throw stones at a rich white house. I live with my Auntie Junie, who is always in a state of euphoria due to some new drug that stimulates her already too-swollen head. She and my mother thought it would be best not to tell my father about me. He left my mother not knowing I would be born, which, according to my aunt, was about the best thing my mom ever had happen to her. I throw stones at a rich white house down the block because Auntie Junie tells me my father lives in a big white house. She wants me to hate.

I wonder how my dad could have left Mom. He lives in ignorance. I consider him one of those people who would deny my existence even if he had watched me being born. I throw stones at that rich white house because a happy family lives there, and it's not mine.

I am not full of hate, although sometimes I wish I could hate my mother for not telling my father about me. I wish I could hate Auntie Junie for not caring about me. I wish I could hate the happy family who lives in the rich white house. But I can't hate! I can't hate any more than I can love, because I can't feel. I can't. My Auntie Junie, with all her hate, has stolen all my emotions. I only know that life is short, so very short that there is no time for any emotion more demanding than vague acceptance.

You probably want to know how I came to think like this. What turned me into such a doubting, lackluster child? Where is the magic cure? That great fabled antidote? Who can save this disillusioned child?

I don't know.

As I sit here by Auntie Junie's pond among the broken bottles, I long for a tube of Instant Krazy Glue. When I was little, gluing was my hobby. I made a string of broken Christmas lights into a swarm of bumblebees. I made a flock of geese out of Auntie Junie's broken wine bottles. Out of old-fashioned soda bottles I made turtles. I always made animals that were headed home when the bad weather came, because my home was the center of bad weather. I live in the Snow Queen's ice palace. I'm the child stolen from her parents, only to be imprisoned in a palace of ice. But I want out. I've glued enough figures together out of sharp ice. I wonder if the cave of wonders I've fashioned will ever be valuable enough to buy my way out of this prison.

Overexposure to ice can do more than numb you; it can freeze your soul. Auntie Junie was always all smiles on the outside, but she destroyed her soul to hide her loss. She stuck tea bags under her eyes to stop the swelling. One night after way too much medicine from the long-necked bottle, she put the tea bags on her eyes. She fell asleep and woke up with two yellow circles under her eyes. She looked like a hoot owl. From that day on, I never liked hoot owls. What do hoot owls have to do with wisdom? With big eyes like that, they look more like dragons on the hunt than benevolent beholders of nighttime truth.

Gee, for a person who didn't want to get all introspective, I've certainly failed. But with a past like mine, can you blame me? This is my last night out in the California Garden of Eden. I'm more than thrilled to leave this paradise behind, snake and all. All I want to do is see snow—to roll and dance and make a snow angel.

I think maybe I need to get away and have a chance to live like a child, not always worrying if a teacher may show up and find Auntie Junie drunk and me burning pasta on the mildew-covered stove.

I've always taken care of things. At the age of five, I took care of my mother. She died anyway. I guess I wasn't good enough at taking care of her. I wasn't a good enough salvager, not yet, at least. Mom contracted AIDS as a result of my birth. She never knew her transfusion was tainted. Even though my mom died when I was young, she left an impression on me. I would have left California a long time ago if it weren't for her.

But I promised her I'd stay and take care of Auntie Junie. I believe Mom thought that if I stayed with her big sissy, then Auntie Junie would have to make her break with the bottle. But Auntie Junie thought it was easier to break walls and bones (mostly mine) than give up her wine.

Here I am, by this calm pond. I have a few of Auntie's bottles. I've even uncorked a few and let their smelly liquor rain into the pond. After I emptied them, I smashed them one by one. I can't stand smashing the bottles. I don't think my problems can be solved by smashing. All my life I've tried to glue the pieces back together, but that hasn't worked either.

I graduated early. I never told Auntie Junie. I was afraid she'd show up drunk. I was the only one without family to cheer me on. I was also the only one with a broken arm. But Auntie Junie can never boast that she's broken my spirit. I won't let her do that.

I was accepted to Parson's Institute and will leave for New York tomorrow. I don't think breaking or hitting or drinking will solve any of my problems. Nor do I think that trying to fix everything will solve all my problems. But I know time will help some.

I am off on my own. I am not like a bird in a flock. Nor am I like a bee buzzing about. I am like a turtle, off on my own. It may take me awhile, but I'll find what I'm looking for. I am persistent. I will find a home. If things could be salvaged, then I'd have salvaged half the world with all my broken-bottle sculptures. But they can't, and I can find only minor solace in gluing together the broken bottles. I will find what I'm looking for, even if it means gluing together all the broken bottles from across the country. 回

Drawing by Lauren Daniels

Visiting the Untouchable

by Renata Silberblatt

They say it's a hospital
but I know better.
Visitors, holding carnation bouquets,
wear brightly colored T-shirts, casual khaki shorts,
but their eyes are all glazed hard with worry,
their smiles are just brightly painted plastic.
The front-desk attendants are chatty and careless, talking
about Sunday plans.
They call it a hospital
but I know better.
He is calm now. The medications tape his pallid
153-pound body together. They kindly allow him to
*   speak, but*
not to hear. They allow him to maintain his wild delusions,
but not to listen to us.
They say it's a hospital
but I know better.
He looks at my mother and says:
"I had twin puppies yesterday.
They took them away from me, though.
They put them in a place where only the Marines could go.
And I tried to go there, but
they caught me. Isn't it nice that

they allow me to have visitors in jail?"
The photographs around him try to create a
chorus of the familiar.
But they just depress me more. Who wants to remember
   that
this man was once a gardener, father, husband? The
   nurses
alone can admire the photograph of his beautiful white
country house.
"Fiona,"
he mumbles at my four-year-old sister, as she pulls herself
closer to my mother's leg.
"Fiona, what a beautiful name for a beautiful child."
They call it saving a man's life
but I know better.

Fireflies

by Eileen J. Kessler

The light glimmered within the depths of the glass. I brought my face close to the jam jar, and my breath clouded it. Had I really captured one? The light winked off, and my breath caught. Did it escape? I felt my throat tighten. Oh! There it was again—my firefly, its yellow-green light floating around my jar as it searched fruitlessly for an escape.

"I got one!" I shrieked. "I got one, Sherry!" There was no answer. Perhaps my sister was in hot pursuit of her own. I ran off to find her, the jar with its treasure clasped tightly in my sweaty little hand.

My feet made small thudding sounds as they pounded the grassless dirt in our backyard. I pushed the forsythia branches out of my way. I burst into the driveway where the adults sat around the grill, baking their faces in the last remnants of heat from the glowing coals. Mommy, Daddy, Aunt Nina . . . no Sherry.

"What, dear?" my mother asked. Twigs were caught in my hair from crouching in the bushes, waiting patiently (and sometimes not so patiently) for the lightning bugs to flash and give themselves away.

"Was that you I heard bawling?" my aunt asked teasingly. "Wailing that you couldn't do it?"

I stuck my tongue out, and the adults laughed. "Sherry showed me how."

"Did you catch one?"

"Uh-huh." I nodded vigorously and proudly held up my jar. "Where's Sherry?"

It was Sherry who had taught me the proper technique of lying in wait, then pouncing and clapping the cap on, her deft eight-year-old fingers twisting it shut, something my chubby fingers could not manage as well. None of the adults answered my wails of frustration, but my sister had put her jar down (a jar with three impressive fireflies trapped inside) and come running over. She had looked at me sympathetically, tears running down my face, the jar hurled in frustration now lying, unbroken, on a patch of moss.

"It's hard, I know," she'd said, patting my back. "Try one more time. I'll show you how."

Now that her strategy had proved successful, I was looking for her to show off my prize. I gazed into the jar, tuning out the adults who were talking about where Sherry had gone. The bug's light turned on, a glow so sparkly, so iridescent, that I was sure I had caught a queen, or a princess at the very least. Status in firefly society is measured by the brightness of its light, Sherry had said. Only royalty live a long time, and they have the very best lights. She had brought her jar over, pointing out an especially large bug. "That's a prince," she'd announced proudly.

"Do you think mine's a princess?" I interrupted the chatter, which had drifted away from Sherry.

"A princess?" My mother looked puzzled, then the

slow light of understanding dawned on her face as she recognized what must be one of Sherry's fantasies. "I don't know, dear, ask Sherry."

I turned to go to the backyard, then remembered my mission. "Where's Sherry?"

"Oh, Larry called her in the house a few minutes before you came up," Aunt Nina said.

"That's right!" my mother exclaimed. "I'd completely forgotten. Why don't you run in and find her, honey?"

I checked to make sure my firefly was still burning. I wanted Sherry to see her at the very brightest, sparkliest, yellow-greenest she could possibly be. I pushed open the screen door, the air in the house just as humid as the summer night outside. Inside, the smell of dirt and coals and dark nights full of stars vanished, giving way to the scent of damp wallpaper paste and narrow, musty hallways. My bare feet left dirty prints on the hardwood floor as I passed through the kitchen.

The house was quiet, the silence broken only by occasional alcohol-mellowed laughter from outside. I was halfway up the stairs, the golden runner carpet prickling my toes, before I heard Uncle Larry's voice.

"Don't tell, Sherry. Auntie Nina would be mad at you. Mommy would be, too."

Some instinct prompted me to stop. I pressed against the blue and white wallpaper. Had Sherry done something wrong? Sherry, who made me tell Mommy the time I threw the potato skin on the floor on purpose so I wouldn't have to eat it? I heard Sherry sniffle. Maybe she'd broken the vase on Mommy's dresser, the one we were forbidden to touch. I sidled up the stairs, wanting to peek into my mother's bedroom to see if I was right.

"I don't want to touch it." Sherry's voice broke with a hiccuping sob. Maybe Uncle Larry was trying to get her to clean up the broken pieces. Mommy told us never to touch broken glass.

"C'mon," came the low and pleading reply from Uncle Larry.

"I don't want to!" Sherry's voice rose, and instantly Uncle Larry's voice broke in, anxious and trying to be reassuring.

"Shh, Sherry, it's okay. You don't have to. Just be quiet, for God's sake!" I heard my sister swallowing her hiccup-sobs. "It's okay, honey. Come sit on my lap, Sherry."

I peered around the door. Uncle Larry pulled my sister onto his lap and cradled her against his meaty chest. He stroked her head, patting at her nose and eyes with tissues until her sobs quieted. He kissed the top of her head, ran his hand over her fine, wispy brown hair and rubbed her back. "There, there."

The vase sat on my mother's dresser, china blue and porcelain white, perfect and smooth.

"Better now?" asked Uncle Larry tenderly. Sherry sniffled and nodded her head against his chest. He rubbed her lower back again, then slid his hand under her bottom. Sherry stiffened.

"Relax, honey, I'm not going to hurt you," murmured Uncle Larry. "You're just so pretty; I can't help myself." He put his hand under her shirt, kissed the top of her head again. "Just so sweet and pretty," he whispered into her hair. He moved his hand back under her bottom and shifted her weight. With a start, I saw his pants were unzipped. He took her hand and pushed it down to the unzipped fly. The light pink paint was chipping off her nails.

I drew away from the door. I backed toward the stairs, my forgotten firefly in the jar clutched tightly in my hand. I hurried on tiptoes down the stairs and out the back door, my throat tight.

I plopped down on the steps, leaned my forehead against my jam jar and closed my eyes, breathing deeply the reassuring summer night smells. An outburst of well-fed, amused grown-ups drifted on the night again. I lifted my head, my throat loosening. Fireflies' lights danced among the quince and forsythia bushes, bright and tempting. I lifted my jar to look at my princess firefly again.

At the bottom of the jar, dark and unlit, the forlorn body of my firefly lay, never to sparkle again. ▣

Alligators in Bangkok

by Amy Tangsuan

n a warm July night, I turned seven. To celebrate this special occasion, my grandparents treated me to a birthday dinner at my favorite Thai restaurant. When we got home, we found my parents waiting with a chocolate cake. I made a wish and blew out the candles before I turned to the pile of presents on the couch. A huge box caught my attention.

"Happy Birthday, from Grandpa" was written on top. I tore away the wrapping paper and opened the box. My grandfather had given me a big, old, stuffed alligator that stood on its hind legs and was half my size. Because I was hoping for a Tigger doll, I was a little disappointed. I tried to hide my feelings, but I could never hide anything from Gramps. "Come here," he said. "I'm going to tell you a bedtime story, okay?" I nodded as he carried me and the alligator to my room.

Gramps put on his serious face and, in a deep quiet voice, began. "One day, many years before you were born, it started to rain and rain in Thailand. The rain kept coming down, and it finally filled all the rivers in the north. There was a big flood—the biggest in Thailand in over fifty years! But the rain still did not stop. It rained and rained, and the northern rivers flowed south with the floodwaters. All the places those rivers passed started to flood, too. Of course, the government got worried because those rivers passed right through Bangkok, the capital of Thailand, where the king and queen lived. The government tried everything they could to keep the floodwaters out of Bangkok. Even the King tried to help, but nothing worked and the rain kept falling.

"In the path of those raging rivers, about 100 miles north of Bangkok, was a very, very big lake. In this lake, there were lots and lots of big, scary alligators . . . like this one!" Gramps held up my stuffed alligator, and we laughed.

"Anyway, the flood was still headed toward Bangkok, and nobody could stop it. In a few days, it passed through that big lake, and the force of the flood took the alligators on a wild ride straight to Bangkok. Almost everyone left. The flood hit Bangkok, destroying homes and businesses.

"Soon, all anyone could see were the rooftops sticking out above the water . . . and it was still raining!"

I stared at Grandpa with wide eyes. "So, what happened?"

"Well, after a few weeks, it finally did stop raining. The sun came out. Very slowly, the floodwaters began to dry up. Eventually, the people returned to their homes, only to get the shock of their lives. There were big, scary alligators everywhere! They were in the street, in houses, on top of cars and even lying on the steps of the Royal Palace! The people were shocked and scared. There were alligators all over Bangkok! Finally, the government came up with a plan to return the alligators to their homes.

They called for brave, strong young men to help get rid of the alligators. Each was armed with a thick, long rope and went around tying up the alligators and dragging them into big trucks that would drive the alligators home. Would you believe your old gramps was one of those men?"

"Really, Gramps? Weren't you scared?"

"Of course not! I got my ropes, threw them over my shoulder and went alligator hunting! Almost immediately, I found a beautiful young woman desperately in need of my help. There was a fat, old alligator lying on the steps of her house. So I told her to stand out of the way. Somehow, I got my rope around the alligator's jaws and tied it tight. You see this scar on my arm? I guess I didn't tie it tight enough. The thing broke the rope and took a bite out of my arm. But I didn't let a little blood stop me! No, sir. I came at the alligator from behind. I stepped on his back so he couldn't move and got the rope around his jaws again. This time, I made sure it was really tight so he couldn't bite me again. I dragged the alligator to the truck and threw him in. My job was finished."

"Wait, what about your arm?"

"Oh, my arm. That's right, I was bleeding. Well, I went back to the house to make sure there were no more alligators. The coast was clear. The young lady saw my arm and cried out; I was dripping blood. I told her it was nothing, but she ordered me into her house and told me to lie down while she sewed up my arm. I needed thirteen stitches. Lucky for me, she was a nurse and knew what she was doing. When she finished and I was as good as new, she thanked me for getting rid of the alligator and invited me to have dinner with her."

"Oh, Gramps. You made that part up, didn't you?"

"Made it up? No, no, no! It's all true . . . just ask your grandmother."

"Why would Grandma know?"

Gramps laughed and winked at me. "Do you know who that lady was? She's sitting in the kitchen with your mom and dad." He laughed at my shocked expression. "How do you think I met your grandmother?"

"Really?"

"Yep. And do you know what day it was when I saved your grandmother from the alligator? It was right on your birthday! I gave this alligator to her on our first date, as a memento of the time we met."

"Wow, that's neat, Grandpa. Thank you for the alligator and the story." I gave him a kiss, reached for my alligator and pulled it under the covers with me.

Gramps smiled as he tucked both of us in and kissed me good night.

Now, years later, the alligator still sits on my dresser, watching over me just as my grandfather always did. ▣

Portrait of My Brother

by Katie M. Weiss

The first time I met him,
I was two years old.
His head was as bare
as the body of a newborn gerbil.
His eyes were big and brown
and stared back up at me;
I thought I was looking
into the eyes of a puppy.
His face was as bright
as the sunrise on a May morning
when the morning mist has cleared,
and I can see olive-green leaves on the sleeping trees.
His miniature hands reached out,
clutching the ends of my chestnut hair,
yanking each strand.
His small fingers and little toes
were still pinkish,
sensitive to the touch of caring hands.
His mouth
made soft gurgling noises,
and little bubbles
formed on the edge of his lips.

Join The Young Authors Foundation and get a monthly subscription to **Teen Ink** magazine.

Foundation Members Receive:
- Ten months of Teen Ink magazine
- Members Newsletter
- Partner in Education Satisfaction – You help thousands of teens succeed.

SUPPORT TEENS' VOICES!

Only $25 per year!

The magazine includes stories, poems and art plus music, book and movie reviews, college essays, sports and more.

☐ **Annual Dues $25* (minimum)**
I want to receive ten monthly issues of Teen Ink magazine and become a member of The Young Authors Foundation!
(Enclose Check or include Credit Card Info. below)

☐ I want to sponsor a monthly class set *(30 issues)* of the magazine for a school near me for only $130. *Please send me more information.*

☐ I want to support the Foundation with a tax-deductible donation for: $_____
(Do not send copies of the magazine)

NAME_____ PHONE _____

STREET_____

CITY/TOWN _____ STATE _____ ZIP _____

EMAIL _____

M/C OR VISA *(CIRCLE ONE)* #_____ EXP. DATE _____/_____

Send a gift subscription to:
NAME_____

STREET _____

CITY/TOWN _____STATE_____ZIP_____

Mail coupon to: Teen Ink • Box 97 • Newton, MA 02461 – Or join online: www.TeenInk.com

If you like **Teen Ink**, then you'll love **Teen Ink** magazine.

Join the Young Authors Foundation with a minimum donation of $25 and you will receive 10 monthly issues of *Teen Ink* magazine.

We will start your monthly subscription when we receive your check or credit card information.

Thanks for your support!

3 Bales of Comfort: Creative Works

Photo by Maria Potocki

Bales of Comfort

by Kathryn Walat

She lay on the bales.
The hay scratched
Her pale, blotched cheek—
The stalks not soft and sickeningly
Sweet like the sugary malt
Of reassuring words
That oozed from her
Parents' mouths.

Bits of hay held firm
To her wool sweater,
And would not be shaken
Like frosty friends,
Who had melted
Like snow in her hand
When she clung to them;
Leaving palms red and raw.

As she beat them,
The bales would not break
And submit to her punches,
But were firm enough
To make her fist sting;
And absorb a little
Of the inner pain
Escaping through her hands.

To Surrender

by Olivia Cerrone

Nikki, you look like you're dead." Jackie Galbert chuckled at the tall figure who strode down the stairway of the high school. Nikki smirked at the obnoxious greeting.

"I'm sorry I didn't say hi to you in the corridor. I've been oblivious to everything today," she called out, nearly tripping on the loose matting that someone had kicked apart.

"Don't worry about it," Jackie said with a shrug. "You were actually kinda funny today. Jimmy and I saw you walk into your locker, like, twice."

"I know," Nikki exclaimed. "It felt like the hallways were closing in all around me. I think I almost blacked out a few times. I didn't get any sleep last night. Or any sleep this whole week, for that matter. It's been fun."

"I can imagine," Jackie said as her lips spread into a mischievous grin. "So, are you ready?"

"Yeah," Nikki said, shifting the heavy backpack on her shoulders. "We should hurry, though. Getting to Boston takes like an hour in this kind of weather."

Jackie glanced over her shoulder at the window. Sheets of rain poured from the dismal sky. The girls walked out to the parking lot along with the rest of the masses who were looking forward to a weekend full of work, clubbing, practices and sleep. *Sleep,* Nikki thought as a sheepish grin crossed her pale face. *What a wonderful idea.* She felt her legs grow weak as her stomach churned, reminding her that she had skipped breakfast and lunch.

She stumbled into the dump of a car she had been driving since she got her license: a gray Chevy Nova whose odometer turned 100,000 long ago. She feebly reached for the door handle.

"So, what do you think?" Jackie asked abruptly.

"About what?"

"About everything I have been talking to you for about the last twenty minutes!" Jackie snorted angrily.

"Oh, sorry, I wasn't listening," Nikki admitted. Jackie never stopped talking, so much so that it was easy to get used to the sound of her voice and not realize she was talking at all. Nikki laughed at herself as she collapsed in the driver's seat. Every muscle in her body throbbed from fatigue, and suddenly sitting only amplified the exhaustion.

"What's so funny?" Jackie demanded as she got into the passenger seat.

"It's just the hysteria coming on," Nikki muttered.

"Listen, I'm sorry, Nikki. You really do look like crap," Jackie said quietly. "Do you want me to drive?"

"Jackie, you only have your permit."

Jackie shrugged, running her hands through the pixie haircut that framed her pretty face. "So? No one would know."

Nikki shook her head and rubbed her eyes as she

started the car, listening to the noisy hum of the engine.

"No, I'm fine," Nikki insisted as she clumsily backed out.

Later, Nikki hardly had any memory of how she made it into Boston without crashing. Every noise around her seemed to intensify and converge into one unending ringing in her skull. She couldn't even see where she was going. The rain was sloshed back and forth by the windshield wipers, making the view look more like a surreal painting than the relentless traffic around them. And in that mess of rain and bleary images, random words formed, words that made Nikki shudder with apprehension. Words like "stop" and "death." In the back of her mind a dreadful suspicion lurked that she would soon be seeing the word "redrum."

"You know what your problem is?" Jackie suddenly and loudly interrupted her thoughts.

"What?" Nikki inquired with a knowing smile.

"You try too hard. I mean, look at you. You beat the crap out of yourself studying, and it's not even like you get straight A's. It's just not worth it. All that stress is such a waste of time."

"I guess I'm just lucky," Nikki laughed. Yet, she didn't understand why she was laughing. Normally Jackie's blunt truthfulness irritated her, especially when it came to the miraculous way that Jackie pulled perfect scores like nobody's business.

Maybe it was the gnawing pain in her stomach or the heaviness she felt when she breathed or the way her fast heartbeat had not slowed since . . .

"Nikki, stop the car! You almost passed J.D.'s!" Jackie cried.

Frantically, Nikki swerved the car into an open space at the curb and came to a sudden halt. For the moment the screech of the brakes shattered the pounding in her brain.

J. D.'s Comics was a small shack of a store imbedded within others clustered around it. Outside, a tall man dressed in a long trench coat waited for them. The figure abruptly elongated several feet into what seemed to be a giant black snake. Nikki rubbed her eyes, and the man was his normal size again. He moved swiftly into the backseat.

"Hey, ladies!" He greeted them warmly as he brushed the hair out of his eyes.

"Hey, Dave!" Nikki said casually.

"Hey, baby!" Jackie cried ecstatically, and leaned over into the backseat for a kiss. Nikki turned her head sharply away and pretended not to look. She didn't mind picking up Jackie's boyfriend from work, even if it was in Boston. It wasn't his fault his car was in the shop and he didn't have a ride to see Jackie for the weekend. It was the episodes of making-out that bugged her. There was only so much that a third wheel could take.

Jackie and Dave rambled on (Dave talked more and louder than Jackie) as Nikki drove over the Tobin Bridge. Something long and black flickered in the corners of her eyes. She cocked her head slightly to the side but saw nothing. Wearily, she shook her head to shake the illusion from her mind. The crackling sound returned, even louder, now accompanied by another noise that came closer from the dark recesses of her mind, close enough that it burned in her ears.

Surrender. Surrender.

Nikki ignored the voice, as well as the growing fear in her gut. But suddenly something caught her attention. She sharply shut her eyes to the rearview mirror to witness something dark and ominous fall from the clouds. It exploded into a ball of a million black tentacles, like an octopus or a squid or even some bizarre remnant of a squashed spider that immediately climbed the thick cables on either side of the bridge. Soon they were crawling next to passing cars, covering them completely until they were simply moving balls of black string. And much to Nikki's dread, her own windows became clouded in the thick black mass. Desperately, Nikki tried to stop the car as a million thoughts raced through her mind, causing a cold sweat to break out. It would be better to crash than to fly blindly off the bridge!

The whispers abruptly became a hundred voices, all talking at the same time in one chaotic tongue. Nikki tried to throw a wild glance at Jackie, but found that her neck couldn't move. Her whole body, it seemed, was paralyzed. She cut her eyes to her hands on the steering wheel. A creeping sensation danced on the underside of her palms. A small black tentacle sprouted from her olive skin, followed by another and then another. Strangely, she felt no pain, only the heat of fear and shock that escalated to an unbearable height. *It is choking me,* she thought deliriously. *It is killing me.*

A crazy thought entered her mind: She had been set up. Somehow, she had been set up by something evil that wanted her to give in. Almost like the way sleep tried to overwhelm her when she knew there was work to be done. She had never given in to sleep. In fact, she had never surrendered to anything, especially to her own weaknesses. How could she now?

Somehow the black tentacles had found a way into the car. They were swarming now, like a sea of little centipedes mingling in and out of the compartments of the car and Nikki until everything was drowned in blackness.

And the crunching noise became one with the choir of dreadful voices, breeding an entirely new and terrifying sound. *It was almost like a piercing scream,* Nikki thought, *a scream from hell.* And that scream, that sound formed coherent words, words that cried, "Nikki, are you all right?"

Nikki opened her eyes to a brilliant light that slowly took the shape of Jackie. She studied Nikki carefully with wide and fearful blue eyes.

"Oh, my God, Nikki, I was so scared. I thought you were going to die or something!"

"Why?" Nikki asked as she shifted her body slowly. She was in a bed, a hospital bed, with an IV hooked up to her arm. "What the . . . what happened, Jackie?"

"You passed out right as you were backing out of the school parking lot," Jackie informed her breathlessly. "I didn't know what had happened. I called the ambulance on my cell phone. The doctor said that your body must've collapsed and gone into shock from all the strain. The EMTs couldn't even revive you. Doesn't that mean anything to you?"

"Of course it—"

"Obviously, it doesn't!" Jackie snapped. There were tears in her eyes. "I already phoned your folks. They're on their way, and knowing them, they're probably more ticked off than I am. You really scared me, you know that? I care about you."

Jackie turned and walked out, leaving a stunned Nikki. She gazed at the ceiling and smiled. At least the worst of it was all just a dream. She propped her head up against the pillow and gazed straight ahead. There, as if waiting for her, was the black mass with its squirming tentacles. She did not know whether it was an illusion, because the moment she shut her eyes, she was out like a light. She had exhausted her will to fight sleep. 回

Fearless Frank

by Terra J. McNary

Have you ever gone over to the big park just outside the town square and laid eyes on that magnificent bronze statue of a dog? Did it happen to cross your mind why the town fathers saw fit to spend all that money puttin' up a great and grand memorial to a dog? Yup, a dog. And yes, I agree with you 100 percent, an ugly dog at that! Well, it seems I'll have to tell that ol' tale again, so make yourself comfortable 'cause it's a doozie.

Well now, most of the older folks 'round these parts would surely remember a man who used to come to town every Saturday to buy what he needed to get through the week. Supplies from Joe's Hardware, meats and cheeses from the butcher shop right around the corner, and every other week or so, he would slip quietly in to see Butch, the barber, for a trim. On occasion he would stop along the way at that beautiful Victorian mansion right there just outside of town and have a few words with Jim. You see, Jim was the only animal doctor for three counties, and the town folk and the country folk all relied on his advice from time to time. Jim always found the time to see the man, too. Well, mostly he felt so doggone bad, so downright shameful over the way he

and everyone else in town had misjudged and n
the man's dog.

His name was Kaiser, and he was a dachshund. In
Germany, where his ancestors came from, the name
means "king." Oh, how people made fun of his la-di-da
name! As a matter of fact, most people just started calling
him "Frank," and that's what stuck.

You gotta understand, Frank was just plain ugly, and I
do mean ugly. Where other dachshunds mostly have a
beautiful shiny coat of black and tan, Frank's was—well,
now, I know you won't believe this, but he was spotted.
Now, I'm not talking about a handsome spotted coat, like
that of a spaniel huntin' dog. I'm tellin' you this dog had
spots and splotches, all mixed up in three shades of
brown. An' dirty! Why, this dog was always covered in
dirt, from snout to paw. His ears were too long, an' his
legs were too short!

On Saturdays when the man came to town, Frank
always trotted a few steps behind. You couldn't exactly
say the man brought the dog to town; it seemed more
like Frank was just a natural part of the man himself. To
be truthful, what with his nondescript dirty color and all,
most people didn't even seem to notice him. But, there
is always a handful of people who seem to think they
need to speak right out about anything and everything.

Like Joe down at the hardware, for example, made it
plain that no nasty, ugly dog was welcome in his store.
Why, the barber would make a point to be out front
sweeping and seemed to enjoy swishing his broom right
in Frank's face. And never once did that butcher ever
think to throw Frank a scrap or a tasty bone. What with

all this nastiness, you'd think Frank might just decide to stay home on Saturdays, but being with the man was Frank's place—good time or bad.

The man had picked Frank out of a litter of puppies from which he was the runt. Jim, the vet, suggested the man might want to choose another as he was planning on taking that little ugly brown one down to the river since he would never amount to much. I suppose this made the man want Frank all the more, although at the time he could not say why. After that day, the man kept Frank with him at all times. When the man had to work, he left Frank just outside the mine entrance, and Frank would faithfully be waitin' there at the end of the shift.

Now, to be perfectly honest about how that sad lookin' dog was treated, I must say that the man had to quit leaving Frank at the front entrance on account of the other men's taunts and kicks. Luckily, the man knew of a second way in. Down around the bottom of the mountain was a secret cave with a narrow tunnel into the mine. This cave was the perfect place for Frank to spend the day. Why, there was even a skinny little crick that ran right by the entrance. Sometimes the man would sneak out on his break to share a tidbit of his lunch with Frank and splash that icy cold water over his face.

(Right here in the story is where that ugly wiener-dog Frank becomes a hero. So, pay attention now!)

The man, well, you might have guessed he was a coal miner, and one dark and dreary day late in October, all of a sudden a great shakin' and tremblin' started up that could be felt for miles around. Now, did Frank go scootin' out of that cave with his tail between his legs?

Lordy, no! He just started diggin'. Ya see, the reason Frank was always so dingy was the dog loved to dig. Why, diggin' was his greatest joy! So, Frank just started in diggin' and diggin' at that narrow little tunnel that led the way to the man.

Well, just picture that! Soon there was as much dirt piled up behind that dog as was left in front—Frank was trapped. With no other thought but the man in his head, he kept on goin' forward. After what seemed like a lengthy amount of time, when ol' Frank had just about worn out his paws from all that rootin' and tearin' and scratchin', why, he finally broke through and stuck his long nose into the mine beyond.

Although it was just as black as tarnation in that there mine shaft, the man was near; Frank could smell him, and lots of other men huddled down in that lowest part of the mountain. Frank could smell fear on these men. It seems that they had given up hope of ever bein' found alive. Although that tenacious dog was just about done in, he somehow found the strength to squeeze on through. The men were packed in that little air pocket so tight that Frank was jostled and stepped on, but he kept on diggin' until he finally reached the man. His man! Hope was renewed among the men when they saw the hole where Frank had broken through. They got out their shovels and picks and started makin' that hole bigger! In short order, the first man was able to crawl through, then another and another.

Up top, at the proper entrance to that mine, why, there was all sorts of sirens goin' off and women wailin' and men shoutin' out and givin' orders. So it's no wonder that no one noticed a long line of dirty men stragglin' up around the back of the mountain 'til they were within the circle of emergency lights. Where had they come from? How did they get out? Why, they said it was that ugly little brown wiener-dog Frank dug 'em out! And where was this hero?

Have you ever gone over to the big park just outside the town square and laid eyes on that magnificent bronze statue of a dog? His name is Kaiser, and he's the town's greatest hero. On that October night long ago, he saved over a hundred men from sure death. He even saved the man. But poor old Kaiser had given it his all.

Yup, that brave, little, ugly, brown-spotted dog, he's a real hero. ▣

Photo by Susan DeBiasio

Yesterday's Catch

by Emily K. Larned

first you
let water boil let burn let bubble
add salt to speed salt to quicken salt to smear in my open
*   cuts*
listening to me scream
listening to the lobsters
singing for their supper
listening

ate at night to whatever fish you may fry
in your wide bed of
tattooed late-night game shows dimly
lighting hibernating spiders alone in corners
tin foil trapped leftovers plastic wrapped
in metal picture frames face down in drawers
you know that i know that there are many that there
*   are many that*
there are so many
other

fish in the sea and you know that you will never have
*   me back*
ever that you that i will not bite again never that i will not

*swallow i will never fall hook line sinker head over tail
ever*

*and so go dip her in butter and covet her white fish flesh
and so go
and later and that
later it is a comfort because
and later she will know i know that she will know*

*that you eat her fleshy
foul-smelling
insides
for breakfast
and hide the bones underneath your bed*

So Long-a in Uganda

by Jason S. Drake

Harry Lynchburg was an American. By this I mean he was a strange and fantastic creature, almost incomprehensible to the likes of you and me. A more cynical person would probably say this meant he was loathsome, even lazy, while jaded members of the international community might say this meant he was greedy or imperialistic. A more optimistic person might take it to mean he was interested in the common good of his fellow man, that he was straightforward and honest, and worked hard for a living.

To Harry Lynchburg, it meant he put a red, white and blue bumper sticker on his car, got off work on the fourth of July, and gave his money to certain people in April. It didn't even concern him that his profession was protected under his country's vaunted First Amendment. Harry was the reason cynical people used words like lazy, loathsome and greedy. To his credit, Harry was not imperialistic, although he probably would have been if he'd known what that particular word really meant.

Something needs clarification: Harry Lynchburg was a war correspondent, hence the reference to our freedom of speech and press. His was in no way a glorious job. There was never an instance of Harry wiring the latest development in some fantastic overseas conflict just in time to be printed in a widely distributed paper with a dynamic name like *The New York Times* or *San Francisco Tribune*. No, Harry worked for a low-end, no-class tabloid, its title the deceptive *State of the Union*. It specialized in government conspiracies, like the supposed Roswell alien sightings and Al Gore. Essentially, Harry's job was to go wherever there was fighting and find "evidence" connecting it to some contrived plot involving the United States.

It would be unfair to suggest, however, that Harry Lynchburg did his job poorly. In fact, he was little short of brilliant when it came to finding new and interesting ways to make the public believe whatever drivel he made up. He was especially talented with the creation and use of fake photographs. His caveat, however, was the fact that he was a horrible journalist. His only training as a reporter had been during his time in Vietnam, where he helped produce the Army paper. He had a tendency to exaggerate events and overly involve himself in his own stories, although when this became apparent, they began refusing his work. When he was discharged on a downplayed charge of theft, he found it difficult to get a job with any major paper. They cited his lack of credentials, objectivity and talent.

For *The State of the Union*, however, Harry Lynchburg was a godsend. A grizzled war veteran who could be trusted for the straight story, drawing on his own experience to understand the situation around him—or so they could tell the public. It was all included in his mini-biography at the end of each of his stories, along with a little picture that was ten years old. They paid him a reasonable salary, and Harry Lynchburg never looked back. In fact, it was a practice of Harry's never to look back, never to regret what he had done, no matter how despicable. Maybe that's why he got that grenade in Uganda, back in '97.

Listen: Harry Lynchburg was a war correspondent for a cheesy conspiracy tabloid. This led him to far-off and terribly uncomfortable places, such as Uganda. There, Sudanese-supported Joseph Kony led the Lord's Resistance Army, a radical group claiming Uganda should be ruled in accordance to the Bible's Ten Commandments. To the Sudanese, he was a means of striking indirectly at their neighbors to the south, who in turn were supporting the Sudan People's Liberation Army to the north. In all it made for a great bloody mess, ripe for the ministrations of Harry Lynchburg's doctored photographs and egocentric reports.

It was an unfortunate turn of events that children should be involved in these proceedings. The LRA regularly kidnapped children from schools and villages, forcing them to serve in their military. Girls were commonly forced to become officers' concubines. Both boys and girls were little more than property to their commanders, with abuse and death likely. It has been estimated that as many as 8,000 children were abducted, forming the backbone of the LRA's military power.

Harry Lynchburg had little concern for this angle, save how it could be used in his story. It presented a certain shock value, as the public loved reading about the misfortunes of children in faraway lands. They would sigh and shake their heads, or perhaps even their fists, and then would take up another article with which they could express indignation and moral outrage. They would never have to face the real thing, and thus could feel justified in their mutterings and letters to the editor, feeling they'd accomplished something just by saying evil shouldn't be.

Harry Lynchburg, however, didn't have such a luxury. He would remember vividly his encounter with one of these child soldiers until the end of his days. It was only a matter of coincidence that that happened to be two minutes after the fact.

It was after a small skirmish near the border with Sudan, and Harry had all of eight minutes left to live, although he didn't know it at the time. He had managed to get wind of the fighting from a source in a nearby village, although he arrived too late to catch any of the actual gunfight. He would report as though he had seen it, though, and arbitrarily decided he'd wire in the battle as a draw. Both sides had been forced to retreat, allowing Harry exclusive access to the battlefield. An old, unused photo of a rebel group in The Democratic Republic of Congo would do for the visuals.

As Harry wandered about where he believed the fighting had taken place, he began formulating his story. He would sometimes mutter parts aloud to get a feel for what they sounded like, putting emphasis on different words and making changes. He was in the middle of what he felt was a spectacular story, wherein U.S. arms were found left behind by the fleeing rebels, when he was distracted by a flash of motion. Reacting quickly, he turned his head in time to catch sight of a large, black bird touching down several feet away. It regarded Harry for a moment, cocking his head and half-heartedly flapping its wings to settle them. Harry immediately recognized it as a vulture, although it was in fact a buzzard. Harry had never bothered to learn the difference. He merely knew they both ate carrion.

Harry was still fumbling for his camera when the buzzard lost interest in him; he was obviously very much alive, and the buzzard had no way of knowing the man would be dead in a mere three minutes. Rather, it waded into a nearby patch of grass and brush. Harry, intent on getting a photo for his article, followed.

The grass was a golden brown, more than waist high, and thick enough to obscure the short, tough shrubs. They had a way of catching Harry's foot, threatening to trip him every few steps, which the war correspondent found infuriating. Harry was ready to give up. Doing so would have considerably extended the two and a half minutes he had left to live. Whether or not it was unfortunate that he decided instead to continue on is a matter of opinion that will not be addressed here.

This is what kept him going: Harry Lynchburg, tired of stumbling about in search of a bird, was beginning to turn around when he heard two sounds. The first was a low gurgling, followed by the high-pitched cry of the buzzard. Both originated from the same location, several yards in front of him. Readying his camera, Harry pressed on.

Harry's years as a war correspondent did little to prepare him for what he saw next, although his utter sense of apathy for the well-being of others did well enough in

a pinch. He had come suddenly upon a clearing dominated by a squat boulder just short enough not to show
through the grass. Next to it was the buzzard, although it
was the bird's next meal that was of interest. A human
skeleton, yet clothed in ebony flesh and drawing breath
in a twisted mockery of life, leaned against the boulder.
Large eyes, more wary than fearful, stared at Harry from
deep caverns, regarding him silently. Ill-fitting fatigues
hung from a frame shriveled by starvation and stunted by
malnutrition, but most important, still small with youth.
It, whatever its gender, was little more than twelve years
old, although if Harry had ventured a guess he would
have said no more than eight.

A small hand, bony, pressed against where a large red
stain was spreading on the child's shirt. The other hand
gripped what might have been a rock. Harry ventured a
few steps closer, but he kept out of arm's reach of the
child. He checked his camera and held it to his eye.

The child removed his hand from his stomach, showing the neat entry hole of a bullet. Feebly, it extended its
arm to Harry, saying something in its native language too
strained to be understood, a pleading look replacing the
wariness in its eyes.

Harry Lynchburg took a picture. He took extra care to
include the buzzard. In his head, he was writing his acceptance speech for the Nobel Prize for photojournalism.

Meanwhile, the child let its arm drop, mumbling inco-
herently as it closed its eyes for the last time. Faint
breaths caused the chest to rise and fall in short gasps,
but to little good—blood now poured freely where the
pressure had been alleviated on the stomach wound. The

buzzard let out a triumphant caw and began to approach the child, but it was shooed away as Harry slowly moved closer for a better look. It is perhaps worth mentioning that the buzzard's cry coincided with the thirty-second countdown to Harry Lynchburg's imminent death.

Harry, curious to see what the child held in its other hand, reached out and grasped its forearm; He could feel the bone beneath the tightly stretched skin. He was studying the child's face, thinking of what he felt would be an award-winning addition to his story, as he tugged on its arm to draw the hand out to where he could get a look at its contents. He heard a faint click and glanced down to see what had produced it.

Harry Lynchburg had five seconds to live.

A small grenade rolled from the child's hand to rest next to Harry's foot. He had just enough time to notice its missing pin.

Harry Lynchburg had three seconds to live.

It was all right, though—Harry Lynchburg had no regrets. ▣

And This World

by Aditi Gupta

And this world that is so beautiful
where plants die so snowmen can grow,
their carrot noses orange in the cold

where the sugary smell of orchards
rises from swollen apples underfoot,
that crawl with drunken bees

where mosaics of green leaves
turn to echoes of crinkly gold,
this world

is so ugly,

with glass rain and flaming mushroom clouds.

Lighthouse to My Childhood

by Meredith Ann Shepard

For supper tonight
we shall have
sprigs of emerald parsley
on white plates with
black rims
and we shall dance
in the long chambers
of our minds
and hear the rain shattering
the glass of our pupils
you are the hand
of the moon
in a white gown of love
and I can see your eyes guiding me
that drafty lighthouse
of my childhood
with the staircase and
missing stair where if I am lucky
I might hit and fall into the
cornfield maze of your heart
and eat a kernel of gold and return

to the purple summer nights
with corn and butter and kickball
that are swaying like smoke
scattered memories behind
the eyes

Photo by Dena Galie

List of One

by Matt Davis

Fifteen! Mark it up!" a proud young voice announced beside me.

I had barely heard the shot and hadn't noticed the scratches of the tally being inscribed on the wall behind me. Toward the edge of my scope, I did see the dust scatter along the ridge where the target fell, but the motion was a blur to me and the sounds faint. Nothing mattered but the intersection of the crosshairs. I was focused on my opponent and determined to get the kill.

* * *

Many years have passed since that moment, and now that I am finally able to look back on the war, I realize I wasn't just determined to kill, I was obsessed. Sniping was a drug, and I couldn't get enough of it. Each hit lessened the craving, but it always returned, stronger than ever. At night I would lie in my bunker and replay the shots in my mind, critiquing and trying to figure out how to get that perfect kill.

I saw every potential victim, every potential scratch on the wall, as a challenge to me and my gun. I used to think there was an understood respect between me and my prey, a pact forged by the war, which set us on opposing sides in this deadly game. Thinking about it now, this competition was not unlike the games of tag and kick-the-can I played as a child. Players scurried, hoping to strike before they were spotted. If they were successful, the honor and bragging rights were theirs, but the price of losing was lethally different. The defeated in children's games may get picked on until they have a chance to redeem themselves, but war is not a game for children. You have one chance, one opportunity to strike. If you fail, there will be no tomorrow.

* * *

The shells hadn't found my target yet, leaving him and me alone, absorbed in our game. Judging by the shadow cast by my helmet peeking over the edge of the trench, I had been waiting longer than usual, but I wasn't about to give up. I'd stay as long as I needed; the game was more fun like that.

"Sixteen!" the same voice called.

"Hey, man, leave some for the rest of us," someone to my left said.

I shifted my position, never removing my gaze from the scope, in an attempt to revive my numb arm. I felt the cool metal crucifix around my neck press against my blistered chest. Amy, my former high-school sweetheart, had given it to me at the train station as her eyes flooded with tears. I'd never really attended church and didn't even believe in God, but that didn't mean I didn't fear Him. In war, one seeks any advantage, and if there is a God, I want Him on my side.

Using the German's sleeve that I could see in a gap in the wall as a reference point, I positioned my rifle where I determined the back of his head to be. Only a couple of feet of dirt and rocks were left as his border between life and death. I visualized my opposition, his torn uniform and worn leather boots caked with blood and earth, leaning against the trench wall and clenching the barrel of his rifle tightly like it was the key to his soul, which, in many ways, it was. I could picture every detail of his uniform, boots and hands, but I left his face blank.

I always left their faces blank. That's how I was taught—to see the targets as nothing more than non-descript shapes, symbols of evil, moving bulls'-eyes. Officer Kruger, with his beady eyes and perpetual look of disgust, preached to us the day we arrived at training camp, "You are not here to kill men. You are here to kill ideas, and the troops in the other trench are the ideas. Every patiently placed shot eats away at those ideas, but they'll eat you, too, if you see the enemy as men."

The sun was already setting, the shadows creeping across the terrain, when one of our mortars landed about ten yards from him. Trying to escape death, he instinctively dove aside, landing face down in the gap. Had I not been stalking him, he would have gone unnoticed. But I wouldn't let that be. I was determined. Dirt and rock erupted in all directions from the blast. After a moment's hesitation, he looked up, face smudged and decorated with scars.

In that split second, with the rifle aimed and my finger taut, when I met his stare, is the reason I'm penning this today, for it has haunted me ever since. The pain and pleading in his eyes were his only defense, and it was mesmerizing. I am unable to express his look, whether because there were no words or my mind was refusing to cooperate, I do not know. The eyes of a man in his final moment, when his soul knows with certainty that it is the last message it will communicate, penetrates one's mind and never exits. Looking into those desperate, defeated eyes, I pulled the trigger.

"Thirty-eight!" I heard.

That was the last "idea" I killed, but the first man. I never recovered from that moment; those eyes never left me. I didn't kill again; I couldn't. After a few weeks of silence from my gun, I was reassigned. I became a victim of shell shock, plagued by insomnia, nightmares, headaches, dizziness and depression. I was sent to a hospital and, because of their efforts, I am here today. In retrospect, their labor was in vain. I would prefer to have died then.

A few months after the war ended—at least the war between the countries—I returned to where my old life had been, but not back to my old life. Before the war, I was a promising, optimistic young man. After, everything fell apart.

When I got home, I thought everything would be like the memories I had held close. I soon realized those days of happiness had died with that shot. I'd seen worse things in the war, sights of pain and agony that could scar the toughest of men, but none had the intensity of that moment. I cared not for that man. I only did what I was instructed to do, and had things been switched he would have done the same. It wasn't the sight of his face that forever imprinted itself in my mind, but the image of death.

All my life I have been fascinated with death. The curiosity began when I was eight, and my aunt Sophie was defeated by cancer. At the funeral, I thought what my death would be like and who would be affected. Using a napkin from the refreshment table, I scrawled a list of who would be touched by my death. It started with the obvious: my mother, my father, brother and sister, aunts and uncles, cousins and other relations. There were thirty-three names. Then I added friends, classmates and others for twenty-one more. Teachers, doctors and neighbors were eleven more. My parents' friends and acquaintances totaled eighteen for a list of eighty-three. Eighty-three people, at least, would be affected by the death of a shy eight-year-old boy.

After returning, still programmed with the war mentality, I no longer saw people walking down the streets, but lists similar to my old one, helplessly and unknowingly caught in the breeze, going through the motions of life willingly and ignorantly, because that's what is expected. Sighting each individual, I inspected them and wondered how long their list was or if anyone would even notice.

Eventually, a few years ago, I cautiously looked at the dead soldiers lying on the battlefields as lists instead of colored shapes. I read in the newspaper that there were 24 million deaths caused by the war. In normal conditions, if everyone had a list like mine, they would affect a total of about two billion people. The conditions, however, were anything but normal. In war your list is immediately shortened to the soldier beside you or the recruit who has to use your corpse as a shield from enemy fire.

It was during this period that I realized how trusting and naive humans are, and I still can't believe I used to be among them, thinking as they do. They confidently swagger into an opening surrounded by trees and buildings, while I can't tear myself from the shadows. They trust doctors to give them the right medicine. They live for the day, while I await death.

There was a time when I tried to enlighten them about the fragile presence of life. I stopped an elderly man on the street and told him the seventeen ways I had seen men die. I approached a housewife hurrying home, her arms full of groceries, and explained her vulnerabilities. My ventures, however, were in vain; people refused to listen. Life's easier that way.

I finally admitted defeat. There was no way they could understand; they hadn't been there. With my knowledge of the truth, I retreated to my state of isolation. I peered out my window at what people consider everyday life and, as the years passed, my list got shorter and shorter.

It's not that I am or was afraid of death, but I want to be in control. That is the reason my old gun is laying loaded beside me as I write this. I will never again fit into society. Thoughts of death and the pain consume my days, and now me.

At first I planned to don my uniform. I put it on and stood in front of the mirror. My reflection was pathetic, and I was reminded too much of the men at the veterans' home who sit around comparing war stories, more made-up than real. Then I thought about wearing my old school uniform, representing a time before I was corrupted. But being ignorant of the horrors of life is hardly better than committing them.

Now I sit here, in my rundown and sparsely furnished apartment, naked as I entered this world, uninfluenced nor educated, free. The darting shadows from the uniforms burning in the trash dance across the bare walls. Looking into the mirror, I'm greeted by a pathetically abused figure with bold, deep rings around his sunken eye sockets. I've seen too much and aged too quickly. The explosion of shells and cries of dying men constantly play in my head. Everything I see and everything I do is forever tainted by that moment. I can never be the same.

The war is finally ending for me. I slide the gritty barrel into my mouth. 回

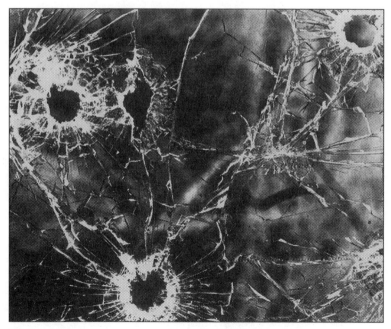

Photo by Mary Amor

Announcement

by Suzanne L. Kolpin

We are selling our red barns in the valley
And all the pastures that do surround,
From the limestone cliff to the brook
Where we played
On blistering summer days
And taught my little sister how to swim.

We are selling the old red barns
That have nestled near the brook
Through 150 spring floods,
And waiting for the river to recede
And calm itself
And flow on to the reservoir,
Past the house and through the woods,
Around the big willow tree
Where we used to swing
In fall, hunting for woolly bears
And countless special leaves
And wondering endlessly
If anyone knew about our place.

We are selling our red barns
And taking a last glance

Around the valley
At the majestic eagles resting on a tree
With brown fuzzy chicks who chirp
Constantly voicing their demands
Of their ever-hunting parents
Across the valley wide
Calling at all hours
From a nest of entwined mud and grass
High in their tree.

We are clearing out from
The old hayloft;
And our family
Shall no longer fear
The old wet hay will start a fire
Of our peaceful home,
Donning heavy leather gloves
And climbing up the haystack
Through cobwebs and huge black spiders
With swallows flying through the rafters,
Pulling down the first bale
And kicking it through the hole
To hear it thump the cold cement floor
To climb again the haystack
And pull down another bale
Till all of them are gone.

Mrs. Johnson, the kind old maid
Whose job always seemed easy
She tended the garden in summer
And cleaned the house through the winter,

Will no longer deliver to us
Wicker baskets of tart juicy apples
And wood for the furnace
Chopped with care to equal size,
And the young boy
Who loved raising chickens,
We always paid him generously,
But he can no longer spare
A dozen eggs for us every Monday,
And fresh milk,
Or a freshly butchered chicken.
We are selling the red barns in the valley
Because Ma'am Paterson,
Who used to help us
With studies for school
In her family room
Is moving to Wyoming
And my mom is traveling for work
And my sister
Has fallen very ill,
And because we can no longer
Stay to watch
And make sure the barn aisles are swept
Or the pastures stay mowed
Or that colonies of mice
Do not decide to live
In the grain bins
As has been the case
Every
Year.

The New Zealand Exit

by Rachel Levine

The license to hope expired today
Yet the subways and the traffic still flow
I point out my faded coat has enough room for me
As I'm aware your umbrella keeps only you dry
My final request, you ask?
Let's depart as if we don't mean anything to anyone
And prove our gift of minutes worthwhile
By not laughing or ruining perfectly good thoughts
Spent on wondering what could've been *if we tried*
There is no trying in life
For I have swallowed my pride before I knew what it was
And battled off my moral side
For the price of being human
We don't owe each other much
And fault is something you realize happened . . .
When you wake up sixty years from now.
I skip through the New Zealand downpour,
And since it feels like I'm floating on air
I don't mind that I've ruined my best shoes

Winter

by Matthew Siegel

Finish one, I told her,
cracking lips pressed
against my teeth.

It must be the cold
that destroys my face.

Cold is an older man, with a chisel
shaping my face to be more like his:
bent, crumpled,

twigs
that are not quite dead
that twist under combat boots.

Aspirin rattles
down the sticky vent of my throat.
I must be catching a cold.

It's like when my dad tossed
me that white white and red baseball,

the one I had thrown out years ago
into the woods.

A Forced Eruption:
Challenging Tales

Art by Cara Lorello

A Forced Eruption

by Amie V. Barbone

The worn, wooden cabinet doors slam open.
Shelves full of colored bags and boxes,
Screaming to me.
Chanting familiar songs,
I'm lured into their trap.
"No. Just shut the cabinet. You can do it this time."
Instead, my mind whirls in all different directions.
My red, bitten hands grab for anything they can reach.
Boxes are torn open, bags are ripped,
Exposing the poison.
I swallow, and swallow,
Not bothering to chew.
My throat is ripped and torn,
But I still manage to choke it down.
More boxes, more bags.
More cookies, more chips.
I look around.
A circle of trash surrounds me,
Like I'm some kind of enemy.
Trapped.
"Here we go again."
I drag myself into the dark bathroom.
The door shrieks.

It's warning me.
All alone.
Kneeling by the toilet,
It's something I now worship.
I toss my head back,
With a fist eagerly formed.
My knuckles already red and blistered,
From the previous gnawing of my teeth.
Fingers thrust down my throat,
Tickling my windpipe.
A human volcano erupts,
Spewing everywhere.
My throat is a raging fire.
Eyes tear.
Hair saturated with toilet water.
I fall onto the tiled floor,
Smashing my head.
With a flush,
It's all over.
With a bite,
It starts all over again.

The Great Escape

by Rachel A. Miller

The journey was unavoidable—things were not right. I had to see for myself. I lazily packed what would fit into my bag, a small travel carry-on that I used for practically everything. I locked my tiny apartment, even though there was nothing worth stealing. I slid into my car and turned the key until it finally started. I drove to the airport in the rain, mesmerized by the darkness, by the tiny glass raindrops splashing, crashing into the windshield.

I was returning home, something I'd sworn I would never do once I'd escaped. I had lived my whole life there, waiting for my eighteenth birthday, the day I could leave and start a new life, far from my parents, who were almost total strangers to me. I grew up listening to their violent arguments, crying myself to sleep almost every night. I was even forced to conceal a few bruises I'd gotten trying to protect my mother. I learned to stand by and pretend everything was okay, normal. I remember feeling so alone, with the exception of my brother, because we were going through the same thing. From the day I learned there was such a thing as escape, I'd saved every cent I earned. Now, after a year and a half on my own, I was finally getting the one thing I'd always dreamed of:

a new life in the city, a nice job and financial stability.

But I'd awoken earlier to the phone ringing. I covered my head with my pillow and tried to ignore it, but after seven and a half minutes of constant ringing, I managed to drag myself to the phone. It was my mother, crying, pleading for me to return home. She said it was urgent I get there as soon as I could. My thoughts immediately turned to my brother. Had something happened to him? No, but I needed to come home. It was only an hour flight, but in that hour, I knew I'd conjure up the craziest story to worry myself about.

The monotonous movement of the windshield wipers made my eyes sore, and I barely remembered to blink. When I finally turned my car into the airport, my eyes were red, my hair was pulled into a messy knot on the back of my head, and my body ached to return to the comfortable bed from which it had been kidnapped.

The heat inside the airport only made me drowsy. Attempting to find Gate 36B was absolute torture, and when I finally did, I slumped into the closest chair and held my purse tightly to my chest. I felt as though my entire world had suddenly come to an abrupt halt. Busy people rushed past, planes were taking off and landing, but I just felt as though my entire world had stopped. A coldness ran through me, a chill from my rain-soaked hair. My mother's sobs kept running through my head. She wouldn't tell me what was wrong; she hadn't even given me a clue.

I sat there dazed for at least half an hour until I heard a man's sharp voice announce my flight. I could feel myself wake up as I walked through the cold tunnel to the plane.

On the plane, I pushed past businessmen and mothers with whining babies to my cramped seat. My whole body was relieved of tension just knowing I had an hour to relax. Immediately, though, I began to imagine the worst. Was my brother in the hospital because of a car crash? Was my father unconscious again after a rowdy bar fight? Or, knowing my mother, had the dog been hit by a car and I was making this trip to attend Muffin's funeral and pay my respects to the dead mutt? I sat like a zombie, dazed, staring out the window at the tiny specks of light against a black, black sheet until I dozed off.

I was awakened by a timid flight attendant softly shaking my arm. I looked up at her through sleepy eyes, forgetting for a moment where I was. She offered me a drink, so I asked for ginger ale, knowing it would calm my upset stomach. It seemed like an eternity before it was announced we were preparing to land.

I searched for my mother's face as soon as I entered the terminal and finally found her in the coffee shop, perched on a stool. I knew she'd be there. Coffee was the answer to everything and the only thing to satisfy my mother's (and my only) addiction to caffeine. As I sat next to her, she got up, so I dutifully followed. There were no hugs, no hello, how was the flight, just mute orders, like it had always been. We walked to the car and silently got in. I could feel her looking over like I'd caught her doing something wrong. I turned to her, and she just smiled and patted my hand. Then she told me: The house burned down.

Wild thoughts rushed through my head. Then she told me it was an accident, set by my father, who had been smoking in bed. "Yes, dear, he's dead," my mother blurted out. "Your father was burnt in the fire. I'm sorry to have to tell you like this. I didn't know how else to do it. I've never been good at this mother job. I'm sorry." Then tears poured down her face. I couldn't understand why. She never loved him. She stayed with him because she thought it was what my brother and I wanted. She never liked living in that terrible house.

"What about my brother?" I asked. My brother, I learned, was gone. Gone, but not dead. He'd run away. He'd finally gotten his chance to escape, too, but now, here I was again.

I knew her next question: "Would it be all right if I live with you for a while? I have nobody else, and I think we need each other." What could I say? I had no choice. I hadn't escaped after all. 回

Photo by Torey Bocast

Blood of the Soul

by Jenny Pirkle

And here you are, hiding again
Maybe this time it will work, right?
This time the disguise is even better
A bright red dress
By drawing attention to your body
You draw it away from your mind
No one thinks to ask you how you feel
No one cares about your dreams, your ideas
They just compliment your camouflage
"Oh, how pretty you look today, Jenny
Red is definitely your color"
A forced smile,
Beautiful to these untrained eyes
Painted lips a shade lighter than the blood from your
    tongue, as you bit it
In order to stay quiet
Stay a lady . . .
Your mouth matches your dress
What are you hiding from today, Jenny?
Oh, it doesn't matter
As long as no one finds you here
The compliments are comforting
You chose well today, Jenny
Now . . .
What shall you wear tomorrow?

Seeing Outside the Lines

by Marnie Kaplan

We are rushing home from Florida
to beat an impending blizzard.
Something obstructing my view fades away,
and flashes through my eyes quickly like the dark green
highway signs
that disappear overhead.
Something else appears before my sleepy eyes like another
approaching sign.
I rub my eyes and peer out the salt-rimmed window
covered with the ghosts of northern snowflakes.
We are driving up I-95,
a dark road lit by giraffe-like streetlights that stretch high
above the charcoal runway as a string of red lights
*   traverse onward.*
Sixty-nine degrees, reads the car thermometer
in fluorescent turquoise as we head east.
I am outside my home,
my world.
Passing a vacant school bus,
I remember when I was one of many buckled into
a dark brown, ripping leather seat, bouncing up and down
with each turn of the road, blending into the blue-shirted
girl next to me as we rounded another curve.

But that was only in the afternoon, since every morning
     my dad shuttled
us to school, even when we reached the heights of junior
     high which was thirty minutes away.
We zoom by the school bus, dull yellow in comparison
with the memory of my first sunshine-bright bus.
I boarded to attend kindergarten as the Journal News
snapped a picture of my brother, my neighbor and me
     dressed in sweatsuits.
I watch my childhood zoom by.
Only three hours before, I was in Miami Beach
at a posh restaurant famous for its stone crabs
which cost more than lobster
($49.40 for the large portion, five crabs)
with two of my mom's siblings and their families
and a rich woman she calls Aunt Lillian,
     although the blood
running through their veins is not the same.
I am brought back to 6:30 P.M.
being led into a full restaurant thanks to my affluent "aunt"
with a jeweled stone crab pin and personal account,
     walking through hordes
of people with empty wine glasses and diamonds
     around their necks.
I'm sitting at Joe's eating $23 chicken that is too dry
and a communal portion of hash browns that sticks to
     the roof of my mouth.
I cut into the white meat with a knife that probably cost
     more than my outfit.
My cousin laughs at me and my brothers and our
     doting mother.
I step into the black slinky shirt of my twenty-three-year-
     old cousin

and see a vision of my family through her amber eyes,
see my mother through those eyes, inside of which is the
   reflection of my image, dwarfed.
I shake my head in the silence of my thoughts.
Cousin Steven, a thirty-five-year-old child, tries to
   beckon a tuxedo-clad waiter
to deliver his new wife another cup of coffee, as I clutch
   my reverence for my mother.
I don't agree, Cousin.
My mother is not at fault.
My father slams a loafer-clad foot on the brakes.
As my body jolts forward, I realize part of me is still in
   the shadows of that bus,
part of me is still in that posh restaurant, seeing outside
   the lines.
But the part of me that is restrained by my gray seat belt
   is smiling.
Sitting next to my mother, I look at her adoringly.
We don't rear-end the Ryder truck in front of us,
and I am no longer seeing outside the lines.
I am seeing my mother, the same mother who placed me
   on that yellow bus,
with the same brown curls that spring in each direction
   yet never move out of place
with the same soothing voice and the same radiating
   warmth.
I am just a child, straying once outside the black line
   with my gray crayon.
I move my chubby hand back, move the crayon inside
   the black confines.
I am not ready yet.

Cold Towels

by Katelyn Stoler

Yesterday I saw a daisy on the side of the road. It stood in bright sunlight, and it was pure and beautiful. The petals reached out to me, begging to be plucked. I picked the daisy for my mother. She was going to love it.

When I reached the door of our house, I looked at the daisy. I must have held on too tightly, for the stem had snapped, and the petals were wilted and gray. I placed the flower on the ground and headed inside. That's okay, Mom wouldn't have wanted the flower anyway. She had no need for flowers. Flowers weren't going to make her better.

Positive thinking. She said that's what we all need.

I'm tired, though. Too tired to think positively. I'm tired of medicine all over the house, and long brown hair in the sink and constantly worried faces. I am standing in the kitchen, missing the days when Mom was around doing chores, like ironing.

As the heap of laundry grows larger in the corner of the room, I sit and try to remember Mom humming soft tunes as she sat by the washer and folded clothes. She always let me lie in the fresh, warm towels as soon as they were done in the dryer. I imagine her warm, brown eyes twinkling, "Edy Lou, would you like to help me fold the laundry, darling?" Of course, I was never any help. I'd snuggle up in the towels and watch her do all the work.

My smile is interrupted by talk of tumors, hospital bills and sickness. All thoughts and feelings seem to melt away, like ice slipping away to nothing. Nothing matters anymore. Since Mom got sick, we all stopped functioning. My family isn't living; it's just existing.

A trip planned for Lake Tahoe, put on hold. I don't know if we'll ever get there. The funny thing is, I don't really care. I thought about getting out of bed this morning. Then I wondered, *What's the use?* The same thing with taking a shower, and changing my dirty clothes, and brushing my hair and teeth. There just doesn't seem to be a point. I would do these things for the sake of normalcy, but things aren't normal.

There's a pile of dirty dishes in the sink. Dinner last night: soggy cereal and milk. It tasted like mud, nothingness. My body is numb and achy. Like when you're sick and everything that touches your skin hurts. Positive thinking wonders if maybe someday I will feel right again, if I'll be the same old Edy. These thoughts dissolve at the sound of a cough and a groan from Mom's room.

I know she's in there, wasting away. And soon, there'll be nothing left. A big gap in the family photo, silence at the dinner table. Out in the living room, I can see Mom's favorite rocking chair. It stands empty, except for the faint imprint of a body smoothed onto the seat. Soon, all the little things, like her toothbrush or her worn bedroom slippers, will stop appearing around the house.

I wonder if I'll cry when she dies. I don't think I will. I don't think I'll be able to realize that crying is what I'm supposed to do. When I hug her, she's like the daisy; I hug too tightly, not wanting to let go. And beneath my warm, unknowing grasp, she is slowly fading away.

I move to the pile of laundry and pick up a towel. It is rough and cold.

Positive thinking. She said that's what I need.

I'll pick another daisy and be more careful with it this time. And Mom will tell me that she loves me and sigh one last sigh. Then, she'll close her eyes, without seeing my flower. That's okay, though. Mom wouldn't have wanted the flower anyway. She has no need for flowers. 🔲

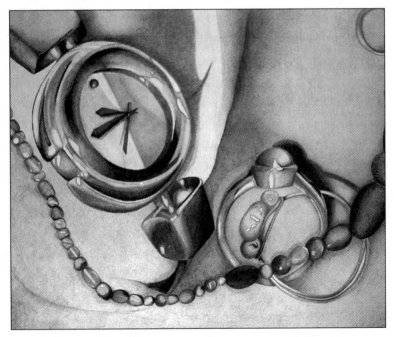

Drawing by Kristen Cupstid

Problem Child

by Jessica Dudziak

Michael,
You don't listen when
your mother tells you to stop.
Instead you go out and
roll your problems into another joint.
To me your actions are a problem
and they burden your mother even more.
See, it is unfair because we can't just
roll you up and smoke you away.
Instead we keep begging and pleading,
but even tears don't make you blink.
I can see straight through you,
straight through your eyes,
and I wish I could erase all the lies
written in bold letters across your forehead,
but you have to do that.
Hello, Michael?
Are you listening to me?
Michael?
You have to come down now.
Michael, please.
Michael?

Endless Song

by Nick Duennes

I screamed into the microphone and slammed down on my guitar.

"Thanks for coming. That was 'Ruby Soho' by our all-time favorite band, Rancid," I said as my band finished our cover song.

"This one's a new one. Bryan just finished it last night, so it might sound like crap," Tim said, as we prepared the largely unrehearsed song.

I played the intro and coughed a few times to get that necessary rasp.

Seeds of revolution now trampled,
your hard-fought riots for nothing,
we watched, we watched,
we watched punk rock die.
We watched, we watched,
we watched punk rock die.

My voice sang out as some flashes came from the crowd. I looked down to see Kirsten with the camera I had given her right before the gig. She was the best thing that had ever happened to me, and I think she knew it.

Your war has been lost.
You fought, but the law won.
You raged on, but anarchy has failed.
Our punk rock days have sailed!

Tim screamed in his deep, scratchy voice. The crowd started to cheer, and Kirsten's camera sent blinding flashes at my eyes. The cloud of cigarette smoke hung over the crowd, and the colored lights illuminated it, providing a perfect effect. The floor that only half an hour ago had been empty was now crowded with possible fans.

We watched, we watched,
we watched punk rock die.
We watched, we watched,
we watched punk rock die.

The crowd echoed the chorus, and as Tim took over singing, I mechanically played as my thoughts drifted to next year. I had dipped into my college fund to pay for my car, my guitar, my amp. I didn't have much left for school, and I was debating whether I should even try to go. I was more concerned with getting the band started and moving away from this town.

Our land's been lost,
God won't save our queen again!

Tim sang, looking at me to start the chorus. I snapped out of my world and was back at the show.

We watched, we watched,
we watched punk rock die.

My voice grew scratchy. I was sick of high school, sick of my parents, and sick of having a prepared life set out before me like a plate of food for an infant: high school, college, a working-class job. Then I'm stuck in a cubicle staring out a tiny window envying the birds.

I've always only been able to watch others flying freely. I needed to break out. My hometown had caged me for too many years, and I started to hate every street, every house and every store that lined its one main road. This town wasn't for me. I was suffocating. My parents rejected the person I had become; they rejected my girlfriend; they rejected my band, my music. Yet it was my life, and they hated it.

You killed, you killed,
you killed our punk rock.
You killed, you killed,
you killed our punk rock.

I sang in defiance. This was the first time I'd actually heard my lyrics, and I could have sworn that bit sounded better the night before when I scribbled it down.

I drifted off again. College? I didn't want to go to college. I wanted to play music and be around Kirsten. I was sick of living up to everyone's expectations. My town didn't know real music, and I didn't fit in. I wanted to stay out on this stage forever and savor each picture that Kirsten could take on a never-ending roll of film in a never-ending song on a never-ending night.

"Go to college. Don't take even a year off because then you'll never go. Listen to me, since no one else in your family has and look at them." The words of my uncle repeated in my head.

"If you take a year off and decide not to go to college, isn't that because you're happy? If you enjoy what you're doing, but didn't go to college, is that so bad? Maybe there's a reason people don't go after they take a year off." I fought his supposedly wise advice.

Your rebellion was crushed,
your riot was squashed,

your revolution was smashed,
we cry as your punk rock dies.

I sang and then faded into my own thoughts again. Choose a college. Choose a major. Choose a job. Choose a wife. Choose a house. Choose posters to hang in my cubicle. Choose paper for my walls. Choose colors for my baby's room. Choose a retirement plan. Choose a retirement home. It all seemed too soon. I wanted time to live. I didn't want to choose. I wanted to drop from this life and seep into the subculture that my music was made for. These suburbs, these parents, these choices . . . I wanted to get away from them all. I was sick of everything.

No more going to the show.
No more let's go.
No more hey ho.

Tim's raspy voice spewed out the words that were scribbled on a napkin from a late-night diner. When I wrote the song it sounded much more satirical than it did here, in front of a live audience, but then again, what the band hears and what the audience hears are always different.

No more going to the show.
No more let's go.
No more hey ho.

I joined in as it dropped to a bass and drums medley. Kirsten was now angled to get better shots of the whole band. Each flash seemed to last an hour. Her purple-tipped blond hair draped over the camera. Her beauty was stunning. She was older by a few years and had not yet gone to college. She lived in a nine-by-nine-foot room she paid for with a six-fifty-an-hour job. It was inspiring.

I admired every aspect of her life. I'd rather live like that than waste away for the price of steady pay: twenty-five dollars an hour, driving my sports car into my large garage attached to my even larger house. My disdain for that lifestyle nauseated me. It's not who I wanted to be.

I jumped into the song with my guitar screaming. Tim joined in shortly after, and the crowd approved. The camera flashed as the four of us did what we felt we were born to do. Pete was a great drummer, and Joe was probably the best bassist Tim and I could ever hope to find in this small town. The band took four months to assemble, let alone learn to play together, yet there we were at our first gig. Who played punk anymore? Who listened to punk anymore? I was up there singing about how it's dead, and yet it felt so alive. It was in my veins, in my blood, in every cell of my body.

So take your patches,
take your pins,
take your CDs,
and burn them all.
They're artifacts
of an ancient sound,
artifacts not meant to be found.

I thought I was going to lose my voice or break a string. This song had been going on for so long, I didn't think both would last. I took in everything I could see. It all became very precious to me.

We watched, we watched,
we watched punk rock die.
We watched, we watched,
we watched punk rock die.

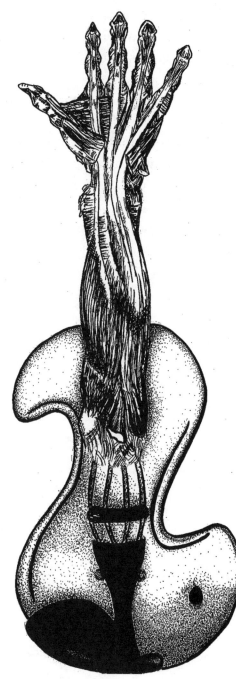

Art by Jalina Colón

The crowd sang in a unified voice. I looked out and saw that even the people in the back were tapping a foot and drumming their fingers to the beat. *How could I ever do anything but this?* I wondered.

Tim and I screamed into the microphones. I continued to play, lost in my endless song and dwelling on thoughts of escaping this planned life. Even if we never became a well-known band, I'd rather keep playing than stare into a computer. Of course, I'd be rejected by my parents and I'd fail them once more, but it was for something I loved. I hoped they'd understand. Tim tapped me, and I noticed I was the only one left playing; the song had ended.

"How long was that song?" I asked as we tuned our guitars.

"You wrote it; you should know. It was three minutes," Tim replied. ▣

Hopeless

by Susan Diehl

The argument in the car was building to a crescendo. Jake was well into his familiar tirade, but it didn't seem to have the usual effect on her. Martha knew it by heart: the same words over and over, the same sneering words with the intent to prick her conscience. She was a bad wife, a bad mother, a horrible cook, unintelligent, undisciplined, ignorant. However, on this blasted August day, the words didn't cut into her. Today, there were no tears or pleading to stop. He noticed.

"What is wrong with you? You deaf or something?" He pulled over to the side of the road. "Answer me!"

Martha slowly opened the car door and stepped out into the sweltering afternoon air. "I don't know if I believe you anymore." Sighing, she closed the door and began walking down the long, winding road. Jake sat in the car for a moment, but then trudged after her. He wasn't really angry with her; it was just what he usually did on a day like this. He slowly followed Martha until he was a step behind her.

"You better come back to the car. We're in the middle of nowhere, so you don't have much of a choice," he murmured softly, then gently laid a hand on Martha's shoulder and pulled her to a halt. She remained facing forward, her back to him, eyes raised to the setting sun.

"I have . . . a choice. I want . . . out." The words came out softly and slowly. She didn't just mean getting back in the car. He knew what she meant. This was her familiar tirade, but Martha never yelled the way he did. It would have made him feel better if she had.

"We don't have time for this." He was getting angry now. He knew their marriage was over. It had been for years, but why change things now? They had lasted this long; why not longer? *God knows Martha wouldn't be able to survive without me,* he thought. He had tried to toughen her up so she could make it in the world. That's why he criticized her and told her what she did wrong. He had always protected her, though, because no matter how hard he tried, she never toughened up. She was so tiny and weak. Especially now, with her back hunched and her arms hugging her body, she seemed so fragile. She was his Martha and, in his own way, although he never told her or showed it, he loved her. A smile danced across his face as his mind recalled the glittering first years of their marriage: the young girl with alabaster skin and raven hair. The dashing young man in his uniform. They moved around a lot, but they had no ties to the world—only each other. France, Italy, Germany, Spain, the most romantic places on Earth. They had seen the world holding hands and enjoyed . . .

Her words broke through his train of thought. "I can't go on with this." His hand moved to pull her to face him. As she turned, he saw the breeze ruffle her limp, charcoal black hair around her ghostly pale skin and sunken eyes.

He looked closer and realized a slow smile had spread across her face. Jake frowned, the tender expression wiped from his face. Her expression bloomed into the first real smile he had seen in years. He was catapulted back to when she was that young, carefree girl again.

"Get in the car." Jake ground the words out, now furious in the face of her happiness.

Her voice grew louder and rang with confidence. "I said I'm not going on." She stood up a little straighter, folded her arms and stared straight into his eyes.

"I heard what you said. Now get in." But the words no longer held force and conviction. They sounded tiny and weak. He knew he had lost her completely, and, in the process, he lost himself. 回

Mockingbird

by Jonah McKenna

You squawk like a mock-crow
in your cardboard cradle,
pacing from corner to corner
through shavings, seeds and excrement.
You carry your left leg crooked,
wings wet with nervous sweat.
You fell into the cold arms
of the pavement,
scuttling over the sidewalk
like a feathered lizard.

When I look at you,
you freeze in place,
peering at me through raisin eyes.
Left alone, you cry out for food
through your paper-thin beak,
squawking too loudly for so small a bird,
no bigger than my fist.

I bear you in your box-home
back to the tree.
You try to fly away,
but cannot break free.

Something invisible holds you there.
All afternoon long, I sit on my porch,
watchful for neighborhood cats.
If I'm too near, your parents won't take you back.

Still your mother swoops down to feed you,
your parents perch atop the cardboard nest,
worms dangling from their beaks like frayed threads.
They feed you till evening: they guard you now,
silent in the branches like pulsing gray statues.

At night, I tie your cardboard nest
to a narrow branch with twine;
the cats should not reach you here,
your parents will be near.
I can only say good night.

In the sunlight of the morning,
the box is still there,
but no chirping, no parents near.
I look inside your empty nest
and choose to believe
you have flown away.

The Tune-Up

by Patrick S. Hallock

You stupid piece of . . . aargh!"

Edgar turned the key again, bearing down on his thumb, and the engine coughed and wheezed. He released the key, slumped back and dragged his hands down his face. When his eyes were uncovered again, they glanced down at the gauges. The gas tank, according to the needle, was to blame for his recent predicament.

"Empty," Edgar sighed. "Figures."

Edgar Dickinson's journey had not been going well. It had all begun with the manuscript that now lay in his backpack, sitting shotgun. He'd put all of his heart and mind into that story and taken it to a publisher in the city. He had been so excited.

Now, ten miles from his hometown, his rusty old Ford died a slow and agonizing death. Reviving it had proven futile, so Edgar now climbed out of the old truck and slammed the door in anger. The thud was followed by a dull clang, which caused Edgar to jump. He looked toward the front of the rust-bucket he called transportation.

The front bumper had fallen off, the dull chrome shining dimly in the summer sun.

A growl passed through Edgar's clenched teeth, his hands grasping handfuls of his black hair. "Stupid . . . son of a . . . aargh!"

Could it get any worse? Edgar wondered as he kicked the hubcap in anger. About four pages into his greatest accomplishment, the balding old editor had shaken his fat head and said, "Sorry, kid, but we don't publish horror genre."

Horror genre? Edgar had nearly screamed at the old geezer. *This story is a tragedy! You got that? A tragic tale of a man cursed with vampirism.*

Seven months of his life had been dedicated to writing that tale, just to have some idiotic editor say, "Sorry, kid."

Edgar muttered the words to himself. "Kid," he repeated. "I'm not a kid. I'm a young adult!" He then sighed, leaning up against the truck and reaching into his breast pocket for a cancer-stick. He groped inside the pack, his fingers searching aimlessly, and found it empty.

"What the . . . ?" Edgar sighed again. "Can it get any worse?"

This poor, trampled, would-be writer climbed back into the truck and pulled out the thick manuscript. He flipped through the pages slowly, glancing over the familiar fictional names and events. A smile slowly came to his face as he read one of the humorous parts involving the vampire's messiest kill.

Memories of writing this wonderful story came back: how excited he'd been as he carefully typed each scene, each character; how a great rush of emotion had circulated through his veins as his friends had read it and said how awesome this scene or that character was. The smile broadened to a humble grin of achievement.

Ever since Edgar Dickinson had been little, he'd created stories. It began in the fourth grade during a writing assignment. As the others told childish tales of their pets and friends, Edgar wrote a story about a zombie stalking the children in his hometown of Winsville. When he had been in junior high, he had learned that Stephen Rice, an author whose books Edgar read religiously, had also been born in Winsville. Edgar always figured that if Stephen could do it, so could he.

As he sat there thinking how his dream had evolved, only to be shattered in a moment, a few cars passed, occasionally peering at his hopeless wreck. Edgar would stare back sadly, then return to the story.

He continued to read it, enthralled with the plot and noticing small errors. Hours passed, the sun slowly set, and Edgar pulled a pen from his pocket. A typo here, a grammatical error there—all were tuned-up by his ballpoint.

Edgar was nearly finished with the seventh chapter when he noticed how dark it had become. He glanced out the windshield, noticing the glorious array of colors the setting sun painted on the horizon, then looked at his watch.

"Eight-forty?" he asked the timepiece. "Oh, man. I gotta get some help here."

When he attempted to wave down a blue Buick, it simply swerved around him and continued. He tried signaling the spotty deal behind it, but received only a horn blare and mocking laughter.

Over the hill, a sleek vehicle appeared, shining bright

in the remaining sunlight. Edgar waved his arms helplessly as the vehicle approached, and he sighed in relief as the vehicle slowed down.

"Finally," he muttered.

The driver's door opened, and a tall man slowly materialized. Dressed in fine casual clothes and a pair of sunglasses, he approached Edgar with a warm smile.

Edgar swore this guy looked familiar. He had most certainly seen this face before.

"Havin' a little car problem, son?" the man asked, placing his hands on his hips. A sigh escaped his lips as he pointed to the bumper that lay in the dirt. "Heck of a problem, I guess."

"Yeah," Edgar answered with a slight chuckle, joining this familiar-looking stranger's glare at the bumper, then looking back at the face. The face was human, Edgar knew, but it seemed almost God-like.

"Well," the man asked, "you got any idea what caused this? I mean, besides rust."

"Outta gas," Edgar replied. "By the way," Edgar added, stretching his hand out toward the man, "I'm Edgar Dickinson."

"Is that a fact?" the man replied, chuckling.

"Yeah, I know. Ironically, I'm even trying to become an author."

"Well, there ain't no irony in that, son. Ya can't *try* 'n be an author; ya gotta be one." That smile seemed permanent, and the man shook Edgar's hand. "I should know."

It hit Edgar fast, so fast that his jaw dropped and his body turned to jelly. The familiar face, that flashy car, the writing tips: It could only mean that—

"Oh, my God, you're Stephen Rice," Edgar proclaimed, to which the man nodded humbly.

"Now, don't you go gettin' all worked up," Stephen laughed as Edgar's face flooded with joy and shock. "I'm no less human than you, son, but I do enjoy meeting fans."

Edgar laughed, a laugh of disoriented glee that flew out of his gaping mouth uncontrollably. "I'm not just a fan, sir. I mean, you're my idol, I swear."

"Please, Edgar," Stephen replied. "Sir, just don't sound right to a hick-town boy like me. Call me Steve."

"Yeah," Edgar replied, the smirk on his face unmanageable. "Sure, Steve."

"Well," Stephen let out a deep rough sigh, "I got to be honest with ya: I ain't gotta clue when it comes to cars. That was my brother's field. But I can give you a lift, no problem."

"Okay, that'd be . . . " Edgar laughed outrageously again. "Oh, that'd be awesome." He started for that shiny automobile, but stopped halfway and turned back toward the truck. "Wait, I gotta get—" Edgar paused midsentence. *I gotta get—my story! My wonderful story that needs—just needs a tune-up by a professional.*

"Mr. Rice—I mean, Steve. I know we've just met and all," Edgar spoke as he grabbed his pack and his manuscript. "But," he finished, standing before his idol with the story outstretched to him. "It would be an honor for me if you would look through this."

Stephen Rice took the thick manuscript, flipping through it casually with that smile.

"I spent seven months on that story, and it got shot down in a second," said Edgar.

Stephen snickered to himself as he closed the story and handed it back to Edgar. "Son," he said. "It don't matter a hill o' beans if I like it or if some other guy don't. Ya see, I gotta feelin' you put seven months of your heart into this," he tapped the story lightly. "That's all that matters, son. Someday, some publisher'll read it with the same emotion you wrote it with, and then you'll see. I've a funny feelin' 'bout you; had it when I saw ya stranded here, flappin' your arms around. Boy's determined, I reckoned.

"Ya just gotta keep writin' with your heart, son, and you'll see, one day. I guarantee it."

At that, Stephen got back behind the wheel, leaving Edgar in deep thought about what his idol had just told him. A smile crossed his lips as Stephen hollered, "You comin'?"

"Yeah," Edgar replied, putting the manuscript back in his pack and heading toward the shiny vehicle. "Yeah, I do believe I'm coming. Just needed a tune-up, that's all." 🔲

A Petty Crime

by Peter Morgan

Who knows why I did it? I mean, it's not like I couldn't afford it. In fact, I had the money right in my pocket. It was more like I *had* to steal it. I had to satisfy that little part of me that had never done anything wrong.

I had never gotten into a fight, never cheated on a test, and certainly never stolen anything before. My classmates all thought I was a wimp. If I made a threat, everybody, including me, knew that it was meaningless. The girls all ignored me; they only liked those "dangerous" boys, the unpredictable ones. They wanted someone tall and strong, who could protect them and defend their honor. I could protect them, I knew I could. If I had ever got into a fight, I knew I could win. I had just never been given the chance, that was all. But I was just kidding myself. I was a wimp, a coward. I didn't play any sports, was never invited to any parties and was ignored by everybody.

I didn't go into the store knowing I was going to steal anything; it just sort of happened. At the front of the deli sat a large, marble counter with a glass window displaying the store's sandwiches and specialties. Behind the counter stood a short, fat man wearing a white, blood-smeared apron. He could just see over the top of the counter, but his eyes followed you wherever you went. On the wall across from the counter stood a long row of shelves stacked with newspapers, loaves of bread, paper goods, bags of potato chips and candy bars.

I was looking at these candy bars, trying to decide which to buy, when I started thinking. I thought about how easy it would be to pick one up, slip it into my pocket and walk out of the store. The man behind the counter had a customer and wouldn't notice me taking it. It would be so simple. Who cared if it was wrong? I had listened to my conscience for too long! But wait, what was I thinking? I couldn't do that. I couldn't just steal something.

Quickly, I left the candy bars and started reading the newspapers. "Man Brutally Killed," "Priceless Painting Stolen," "Baby Kidnapped," the headlines read. Was this the crowd I wanted to join? The life I wanted to lead? Of course not. It was just a stupid little candy bar. I wasn't going to hurt anyone. I went back to the candy bars and just sort of stared at them for a while. If I was going to take one, which would I take? I pondered this for a moment, then reached for the Snickers.

"Can I help you, son?" the storekeeper suddenly asked, peering over the counter.

"N-no, thanks, I'm just looking," I stuttered. Did he know? Did he know I was going to take the candy bar? How could he? I hadn't even touched it yet. Maybe he didn't know. Maybe he was just being helpful. But what if he did know? Should I risk taking it now, or should I just run?

Just then the little bell on the door rang, and a new customer stepped in. She walked up to the counter and started talking to him. It was the perfect chance; he was bent over looking at the meat. I grabbed the Snickers, turned to the door and ran. I didn't stop running until I was two blocks away. I sat on a bench and looked at the candy bar, the only evidence of my crime, held tightly in my sweaty fist. Slowly, I opened the wrapper and pulled it out. I held it there in my hand, staring at it, not even moving when the chocolate started melting and dripping over my hand. I just couldn't bring myself to eat it. There was a pain in my stomach, and all of a sudden I felt nauseous. I stood up and threw the candy bar away.

It was gone. The only proof of the only bad thing I had ever done was gone, sitting in the bottom of a trashcan. No one would ever know that I wasn't always a good boy. ▣

Photo by Amanda Beth Freedman

Mozart

by Lisa Schottenfeld

*I wear overpriced
flared jeans and
uncomfortable three-inch shoes while my
father closes his eyes
to mozart*

*and i wonder if there's a
prescribed age when you can
stop reading teen mags, like
shakespeare and learn to
close your eyes to mozart*

Rites of Passage

by Naomi Millan

The battered baseball trading card I'd stolen from my kid brother, Jon, rattled against the spokes of my ten-speed as I biked down Promise toward Ribit's house. It was the last week in August, the air warm against my face as it tangled my long hair that smelled of sunshine and chlorinated water. I couldn't believe I'd be going back to school in just five days.

Ribit's house was only three blocks from mine, so the ride took just a few minutes. I passed the Carusos' house with its huge in-ground swimming pool hidden by a screen of dark pines. Not many people in Lindie, Indiana, could afford the luxury of a pool. It wasn't so much the money but rather that the town seemed bent against things like pools, things that were not absolutely necessary. Every summer I'd burn with jealousy whenever I heard the high-pitched squeals and water splashing. It was always Melissa Caruso having pool parties for her snotty friends. The Filpes' green and white house flew by on my left. Ribit and I would play with their golden retriever, Dandelion, until the bus came. This would be the last year that would be my bus stop. After eighth grade I'd be starting high school, and then my bus stop would be on Mada, one street over, by the Carsoffs' ranch house. One left turn on Bearpaw, five houses down, and there was Ribit's to my right.

It was cream-colored with splashes of brick here and there and a small front yard that was a miniature prairie. One year Ribit's mother decided she was tired of mowing the lawn, so she went to Andy's Nursery downtown and got this thing called "Prairie in a Can." Following the instructions, she shook the seeds all over the lawn. Now every year the front yard was a tangled mess of wildflowers. My mother said it devalues their property and looks messy. It was neat to lie down in it, totally hidden except from the butterflies and Ribit's cat, Sir Whiskers. He was a marmalade tabby who liked to pounce on our stomachs when we weren't looking. The backyard was pretty normal, with lots of flowerbeds that spill outside of their borders, a gas grill and a tall swing attached to the branches of an oak. Ribit sometimes climbed up the rope like a monkey and threw acorns at me, laughing in her loud, abrasive laugh. I used to follow her up, but I didn't anymore.

I parked my bike next to her mother's green car and went through the gate into the backyard. I saw Ribit's mother bending over a small petunia in a teapot, examining the leaves. I had always thought that Ribit's mom looked . . . funny. Her body was shaped like a big carrot stick, and she had frizzy brown hair that poofed out from under the brim of a hat. She was always wearing hats. Today it was a huge straw hat with tomatoes painted on it. "Hi, Ms. Fendray!"

"Oh! Samantha, you just about scared the sanity right out of me! How are you?"

"Oh, I'm fine. Where's . . ."

"Will you just look at this poor baby?" She pointed at the wilting flower. "I've been nursing her for a week now, and she's still sick! Dear, dear . . ." She clucked softly to herself as she turned her attention back to her plant.

"I'm gonna go find Ribit, Ms. Fendray. See ya."

"Don't kill yourselves, now." She giggled and whispered something to the plant, but I couldn't understand anything except for the word "monkeys."

I always felt a little weird calling Ribit's mom Ms. Fendray instead of Mrs. Fendray, but she insisted.

"Just because I was foolish enough to marry that man doesn't mean I have to use his name!" she used to say. And besides, Ribit's parents had been divorced since she was five years old, so it shouldn't be that strange. But it was.

Out of the corner of my eyes, I saw Ribit's pale arms swinging violently back and forth. I turned, and when I saw her I could do nothing but laugh. She was sitting in her old wading pool in four inches of water. There were purple and green elephants dancing and doing cartwheels on the outside of the pool. Ribit was wearing jean shorts and the Barney shirt I had gotten her for her birthday. There was nothing in this world she hated more than that purple dinosaur, but she loved that shirt, especially after she took a red permanent marker and drew blood spewing from his smiling mouth and other body parts. On her head was a pale pink shower cap and a snorkeling mask.

In both hands she held water pistols. She grinned at me, her smile a perfect imitation of the Joker in *Batman*.

"Hi, Sam! Whatcha doin'?" she asked as she shot me with both guns, leaving parallel wet marks on my white tank top.

"Quit it!" I said, and she laughed as I stumbled backward, fleeing the streams of water. She thought I was joking, but I wasn't.

"Dude! Quit!" She looked at me with her head tilted sideways. My angry voice puzzled her.

"Why?! It's summer. You're supposed to get wet, dork. What's up with you?"

"I'm wearing a white shirt! If it gets wet, it'll get . . . see-through." Her eyes bugged out as she tried to stop from laughing.

"So?! You ain't got nothing to hide, Sam!" She beat her flat chest with both hands like Tarzan. Then she lay down in the water laughing. I could feel my face flushing and getting hot, but I didn't say anything. Instead I pulled over a lawn chair.

"Do so!" I whispered at her. She rolled her eyes and flicked some water at me. And then she said, "Why you got your face all painted up like a clown, Sam?"

"It's called makeup. And I do not look like a clown! I thought I'd learn how to use it so I could look more . . . grown-up. In just a few days we'll be the oldest kids at Mumford. Can you imagine? And then next year we'll be at Lindie Senior High . . ."

Ribit gave a little snort. "Oh please, Sam! The high school is just the same stupid old building we went to every week this summer for baseball practice."

"Nuh uh, there's sports teams and clubs and . . . guys. Those cute guys with cars that we've been watching all summer."

"Excuse me, but as I recall you're the only one here who has been drooling over those jerks. And so what? You're still only a little kid to them. Brian McDougall still doesn't know you exist. And if he ever did, you'd scare him off with that makeup!"

"Shut up!" I had been dreaming about Brian McDougall since the third grade. I had said hi to him one day in the hall, and he'd actually sort of smiled at me. Soon he would fall madly in love with me, I was sure. I watched Sir Whiskers stalking a blue jay that had alighted on one of the raspberry brambles. He was creeping forward, twitching the tip of his tail back and forth a few centimeters. I could almost see his muscles wound up like springs near his bones.

"Why are you acting so strange all of a sudden, Sam?"

"Hmmm?" I looked at Ribit. Little drips of water were running off her shower cap. Her eyes were all squinched up, like she was trying to see through me from behind the mask. Rebecca Elaine Fendray. The first time I'd met her was day one of kindergarten at Apple Grove Elementary. She was wearing a green dress with green socks, her spiraling hair trapped into two stubby braids.

"Hi! My name is Rebecca Elaine. Who are you?" she had said when we sat down at the same table. I remember being a little scared of her. I didn't remember her from nursery school, so I figured she was new.

"Um . . . My name is Samantha Lynn Wilcox. You look like a frog."

"Thank you. Ribit! Ribit!" The nickname had just stuck. Ribit hadn't changed much since then. She was just as silly as ever, just taller and skinnier.

"I'm not acting funny, Ribit." I crossed my eyes at her to see if I could get her to laugh. I felt uneasy when she got serious.

"Yes, you are! You're trying to act like you're so important now just 'cause you got that stupid white shirt on and you're wearing that retarded makeup. Last week we were running around my house in our pajamas throwing flour at each other." I remembered the sleep-over and how silly I had acted.

"That was different. It was just us . . ."

"What is up with you? Last week you wouldn't eat that gallon of chocolate-chip ice cream with me because it would supposedly make you fat. Then yesterday you stopped playing volleyball at the civic center because you said you hurt your hand, but then you went over to talk to Matt and Jimmy. And now this! Why . . ."

"I *do* have other friends, Ribit. It's not like I have to do everything you do."

"But we're best friends," she almost whispered the last word, and I suddenly felt very sorry for her, although I didn't know why.

"Besides, school starts soon. I can't act like a little kid forever, you know."

"No, I don't. I don't care about that stupid old school and those stupid guys. That's not supposed to change anything. It's nothing special! You're still thirteen, just like me. You're still just like me!"

"No, I'm not!" I hadn't meant to say it like that. But once I did, I couldn't take it back. I saw Ribit's eyes go flat behind the mask. Suddenly, I felt like I was really far away from her, like I didn't know her anymore. Out of the corner of my eye, I could see Ms. Fendray stop fussing over her plants and look over at us. I knew my face was red. It felt hot as a stove.

"I'll see you later, Ribit." She didn't answer me. She just stared at the air in front of her, as if I weren't even there. I turned and ran out of the backyard, past Ms. Fendray, her mouth open. Then I was past the gate and hopped on my bike. Only when I was far from their house did I let the tears come to my eyes, the mascara, I was certain, running in little black rivers down my face. At the corner of Bearpaw and Promise I stopped to wipe my face with a tissue. Before I got back on, I pulled the baseball card off the clip that held it to the spokes of my wheel. I let it fall from my hand and rode away, leaving it to rot face-down in the street. ▣

Soul Repair

by Tara Macolino

My soul drips with sorrow,
drenched in an ocean of tears.
I pick it up and ring out the sadness.
I hang it on a line and it dries in the setting sun.

The night fog settles in it,
dampening my emotions.
The moonlight dances with my disembodiment.
A gull snatches it, then sets it free.
It sails downward to the sand.

The next morning I walk on the beach,
two miles down and around the bend.
I find the ragged bits left of my soul.
I pick up the pieces and bring it to my best friend.
Together we patch and stitch,
glue and bond the fragments.

After we are done,
I leave her house with a renewed sensation.
I am ready to live again.

5 The Visitor: And More from Other Worlds

Photo by Flynn O'Brien

The Visitor

by Adam C. Benzing

His room is right this way, Mr. Perry. Are you sure you don't want anyone to accompany you? This guy's one of the looniest we've got here. An' that's sayin' a lot, considering we're an insane asylum. He's always talkin' 'bout some other dimension an' goin' fishin'. He's really whacked."

"No, I don't want anyone in with us. I should be all right. And as for him being 'whacked,' that's why I'm here. I figure I might take his so-called story down on paper and then sell it; that's what folks read nowadays," replied Perry.

"Well, I don't think I'd be willing to go in there alone. Ah, here it is," responded the guard, then added, "If he gives ya any trouble, just yell. I'll hear ya." Then the guard laboriously pushed open the heavy door, revealing a room about twelve feet long and nine feet wide. The room's ceiling, walls and floor were covered with a dirty yellowish-white padding.

Perry was about to ask when he saw the man he was looking for curled up in one of the corners. From what Perry could tell, the man was fairly tall, unshaven, smelled as though he hadn't bathed in weeks and wore a drab white straitjacket that matched the color of the padded room.

The man looked up and stared at the two men as though he hadn't seen anyone in months. It was quiet for a number of seconds until the guard broke the silence, saying, "If that's all, I'll be leaving you, Mr. Perry. Just holler if you need anything."

"No, no, that'll be all, thank you," said Perry while removing a notepad and pencil from his pocket and approaching the man in the corner. "That'll be all," he repeated, half to himself. The guard left, again breaking the silence with a clang of the metal door and the sound of a heavy bolt sliding into place.

"Ah, well, I'm Mr. Perry, the author they told you about. I'm here to write your story," Perry began awkwardly.

He extended his hand then retrieved it when he realized that the man he was talking to was wearing a straitjacket.

"I'm Benjamin Colt, at least I think I am. You can't be sure of anything anymore," the man said, struggling to sit up.

Perry approached the man and sat down next to him. "So, you're here to hear my story? It'll be nice talking to someone again. Where shall I begin?" asked Ben.

"At the beginning, if you don't mind," answered Perry.

"Ah, yes, the beginning," replied Benjamin, his eyes lost in thought.

After some time and thought, Benjamin began. "It was a Sunday. I had planned on going to a new creek that a friend had recommended."

Perry interrupted, asking, "Ah, creek? What do you mean?"

"I'm a fly fisherman, Mr. Perry; I love to be outdoors with the water swirling around me," replied Benjamin, seeming kind of annoyed at the interruption. "Anyway, I got my fishing gear and drove to the stream where I put on my gaiters and waded out to the middle where I tied my fly and began casting. Then, I saw it. A fish, at least I think it was a fish. Its scales were a color or colors that I had never seen before. The fish was about one and a half feet long and its body fluorescent as it swam. I was sure it could not have been from this world. The fish was so amazing that I became obsessed with catching it.

"And I did, after several weary and tiresome hours of chasing and casting. At last, almost reluctantly, I reeled it in. That's when it happened. As soon as I touched the slick and leathery scales, I felt a tingling all over my body. I dropped the fish, but it was too late. I felt as if I was being hurtled through random times and places. I could see whole solar systems, galaxies, even universes, and toward the end of my fascinating, but frightening journey, I saw something else that I couldn't identify."

There was a pause. Perry looked up from his notepad and said, "Please, go on."

Ben started again, almost reluctantly. "I now realize that what I was seeing were other dimensions. There are far more than any human has imagined. They go far beyond time, space, and the first, second and third. They are incredible. I stopped in one of these dimensions. The dimension of thought. In this dimension, thought is reality. I had been funneled through a transdimensional vortex, I didn't realize."

Perry interrupted, asking, "How do you know that? How do you know about that transdimensional stuff?"

"I'm not *just* a fly fisherman, Mr. Perry. I earned my living as a quantum physicist. I know, it's kind of ironic that something like that would happen to someone who has dedicated his life to studying it. Now, as I was saying, I didn't realize it at first because the scenery was the same, then reacting to my thoughts, everything changed. I saw equations. I thought of my lab, and when it appeared before me, I turned and ran up the path to my car. But when I got there, it turned into the fish.

"For about a day this went on. I thought I had gone crazy. But then I realized that everything was reacting to what I was thinking."

Then Perry spoke up, almost sarcastically. "What happened then? How did you get back?"

"You don't believe me, do you?" Benjamin was beginning to yell. "As far as I know I haven't gotten back! You're just a thought."

I haven't learned to control my subconscious thought yet, Benjamin said to himself while holding his head in his hands. He struggled to maintain the integrity of this thought. He was sick of jumping between realities. He could almost feel this reality slipping away.

Perry was now looking at him in total disbelief, realizing why this man was where he was.

"You don't believe me, do you?" Benjamin began yelling again. "That's why I could never go back, not to mention I can't. I've tried before. Do you think that if I had complete control of my thoughts, I would lock myself in an insane asylum?"

Just then the guards burst through the door. Benjamin smiled at himself while thinking how, in all the movies, the guards or police always showed up late. He then thought the guards gone and turned to Perry, who stared in bewilderment and fear at the place where the guards had been. Benjamin smiled at Perry and then disappeared. He was suddenly on a beach lined with palm trees, with a warm crisp sea breeze coming in over the ocean.

Benjamin smiled to himself again, finally gaining control of his subconscious thoughts and recognizing his newfound power. ▣

Photo by Halsey D. Smith

When Fall Does Come Throughout the Ancient Wood

by Seth H. Goldbarg

When fall does come throughout the ancient wood
And songbirds sing much less among the trees
The Reaper comes, unseen in his black hood
While fervent life is taken with an ease.

A wretched, unknown cold entwines the bones
Bright leaves that crunch beneath your very feet
Their color signifying fading moans
Of dead, unique, that you shall never meet.

When naked branches fail to mask the sky
The ground is frozen, tombs cannot be made
And the season of the living quickly dies
As winter takes the lives of those who strayed.

When fall arrives throughout the ancient wood,
Death abruptly comes, and come it should.

The House with a Lawn

by Sara Thoi

I'm late, I'm late . . . it's 8:31 A.M." Thomas Morris hastily climbed the last steps to his office; the elevator was broken. He was supposed to be in his office at 8:30. On his desk was a money-green frame with a picture of his royal blue Venux 4000 Transporter. Already, a pile of files was stacked painstakingly high. He was late.

He flipped open a manila folder, and a picture of an elderly woman slid into view. Her eyes gleamed with pride as she hugged a young man in a cap and gown. He was not smiling. Morris removed the picture with indifference. He had seen thousands of proud parents with frowning sons and daughters. From the crudely filled-out application in the folder, Morris learned that the woman was Cathy Nora, a widow, and her son was Damien. Under the section entitled "Reason for Legal Separation," Damien had written "Hindrance to development." *The good, old she-got-in-the-way excuse,* thought Morris, smiling.

All this was no surprise to the thirty-five-year-old. Over the years, he had received millions of applications from unhappy youths yearning for freedom from their legal guardians. He had the highest position in his firm and enough money to last him two lifetimes. His job was to inform parents when their child demanded a legal separation. He himself was an orphan and had been forced into the real world at the age of ten, oblivious to what family and love truly mean. His life was his job, and money was his goal.

Opening his drawer with a remote, Morris reached for his laser pen and notepad. His hand swept past an old pocket watch that seemed out of place in the modern room and stopped for a moment, as if he had made a connection with the inanimate object. The watch had been a gift from his father. Looking away, Morris quickly closed the drawer. As if programmed, Morris shuffled the paperwork into his lighter-than-air briefcase and began his routine trip to the defendant's home. He checked his watch and made a mental note to be back by nine o'clock.

Outside, the streets were empty except for some stray bots, rusty and tattered, clanking along. Apparently, their owners had gotten tired of the obsolete models, but had not disposed of them. And so they roamed the streets, looking for a home. Yet another sign of how society moves on—with or without you. Once settled in his transporter, Morris punched in the address code from the application, and the vehicle streaked forward. Within thirty seconds, he was looking at an old-fashioned home with brightly painted windows, wooden doors and a lawn. A flood of sweet, mouth-watering scents overwhelmed Morris. Was that grass he smelled? Carnations? Roses? Birds chirped joyously, while the wind gently brushed Morris teasingly. Unlike the rectangular steel complexes he was used to, the house seemed filled with coziness.

What surprised Morris the most was not that the lawn was green with flowers, but that there was a lawn. In awe, he followed the neatly paved walkway to the redwood door. Unable to locate an automated guest receiver, Morris struck an ancient doorknocker and heard a tiny, melodic voice from inside.

Slowly, the door opened and revealed a petite woman, smiling warmly.

"Good morning, ma'am. My name is Thomas Morris, and I am from the Legal 021 firm. Your son, Damien Nora, has filed for a legal separation from you and your property. I am here to inform you of your situation," Morris recited mechanically.

The smile disappeared from the woman's face. Obviously, she'd had no idea this was coming. For a brief moment, Morris felt a tug in his chest. He had done this too many times; why should this be any different? Was it the smile? No one had ever greeted him at the door, not even a hello! The woman moved aside for Morris to enter and directed him to a couch unconventionally decorated with flowers and birds as she disappeared behind a wooden counter.

The interior of the house was even stranger than its exterior. A wooden cabinet was filled with pictures of what appeared to be the Nora family. There were sinks and clocks with hands instead of air dish cleaners and fancy Teletheaters. No bots were sweeping the floor or cleaning the tubs. On top of an old 1980s television set were rows of trophies and medals, all glimmering in the sunlight.

Mrs. Nora reappeared and placed a batch of chocolate-chip cookies and milk in front of Morris. No one had ever brought him cookies before.

"Please, Mr. Morris, try some. They're freshly made. Damien used to love them."

At the mention of her son's name, Mrs. Nora burst into tears. Morris stared in disbelief. No one had ever cried. They all accepted it and moved on. Not knowing what to do, Morris shuffled around and spotted some tissue. Grateful, Mrs. Nora accepted one, but continued to weep uncontrollably.

Finally, her sobs subsided, and she was able to speak again. Morris checked his watch: 9:13! *I should leave and try to come back later,* he thought. *Why did I stay?* Quickly, Morris got down to business.

"Mrs. Nora, I know this is difficult for you, but I must be straightforward. Your son believes you are hindering his development. If you can sign here, I will be on my . . ."

"Look at these trophies. Damien is a wonderful boy. Very smart, too. He used to be so charming; everyone adored him. Once, when he was three, he soiled his pants and didn't tell anyone. When someone finally figured it out, he broke into a sheepish smile and obediently followed his uncle to the little potty room. Everyone used to love Damien, my sweet boy."

Unaccustomed to family stories, Morris was captivated. Mrs. Nora was different. She was not tainted by conformity. Her warmth could be felt, and her love was tangible. In a sense, she was purer than a child. Mrs. Nora continued her accounts of her once-adorable child as if they were an everlasting song. Her voice was far away, in her own world. Morris felt a tinge of sorrow.

"What happened? How did it come to this?" Morris heard himself ask.

"He started staying out late. He brought home machines I had never seen before. When he was home, he locked his door. He neglected his studies and played on stupid pieces of steel. He tried to use my money to redesign my living room with metal boxes and steel machines. When I refused, he turned his back and never talked to me again. Then one day, he was gone, without warning or notice. And now this." Tears revisited her eyes.

"I'm sure this is only a phase. I'll just put these papers away for now. Your boy sounds like a good fellow. He'll come around," Morris said, even though he knew it was not true. Something inside him tugged harder in his chest.

"Oh, he is, he is. Thank you, thank you. I'm sure he'll be back." Mrs. Nora glowed with a smile.

"And what about you, Mr. Morris? Where is your family?"

Where? My family . . .

Suddenly, the cork that had held in his entire life was removed. Thoughts he had buried flooded his mind. Perhaps it was the woman's kindness that dissolved this barrier, or maybe it was her warmth and cheerfulness. Morris took a deep breath and, for the first time, his life story spilled out.

When Morris checked his watch again, it was 4:53 P.M. Reluctantly, Morris said his farewells and promised to return the next day. He programmed his transporter to go to his house, but he did not get in. He wanted to walk.

Above him, the sky was purple with pollution, but it was beautiful. Morris had never noticed it. The air smelled like decaying sewage from countless factories and plants. On his street, not a living creature stirred. Suddenly, someone crashed into him with an intensity that almost knocked him down. Morris looked up into a familiar face. The expressionless man, barely past the age of a boy, was wearing a dirty T-shirt and ragged jeans. His every move appeared programmed, and he seemed not to notice he had collided with someone. In the man's left hand was a tattered briefcase. He quickly walked away with no apology.

Morris had seen that face before, but where? *In a picture,* his subconscious replied. *Damien!* Morris turned back, but Damien was gone, as if society had swept him up and carried him away. *The poor boy is not even human anymore,* Morris thought remorsefully. On the ground, he saw an airline advertisement that Damien had dropped with the flight package circled in red. Morris knew Damien would never be back.

* * *

At 8:35 A.M. Morris meandered into his office. New stacks of files had been placed next to yesterday's pile. He opened the drawer once again and took out the pocket watch. With the only legacy he'd ever had from his parents in one hand and a letter in the other, Morris sauntered to his transporter and punched in the familiar code. Seconds later, he was on the doorsteps of the house with a lawn.

"Good morning, Mr. Morris. Would you like some tea?"

"Please. I received a letter from your son last night. You should be very proud." Morris revealed the letter he had spent all night typing. He had written that Damien had been hired for an exploration he could not refuse. It was explained that the legal separation application had been filed only so his beloved mother would not have to be burdened with him. The counterfeit letter even said that though Mrs. Nora might never see Damien again, his love would always be there. Morris had not known he could write like this.

A tear slid down Mrs. Nora's face, but she smiled as she signed the application to fulfill her son's wish and handed it to Morris. Morris made a mental note to send it in before he went home. He did not know if lying was the best solution, but he could not bear to see her crumple before the truth.

"Mrs. Nora, this is a gift I want you to take in return for your hospitality. It's from my father and, maybe, if you don't mind, I could drop by once in a while . . . and . . ."

Mrs. Nora smiled, and Morris knew he'd be here more than once in a while. For he had typed two letters last night—the other one was sitting on his office desk right now, declaring his resignation. 🔲

Things Had Changed

by Tom Evans

It was a cold day, the kind of day when no one wants to go out. The snow fell in sheets. It had begun not much after five o'clock in the morning, and it showed no signs of letting up. Most of the men were still in their tents, trying to stay warm after the horribly cold night. Things had not looked so bleak in the last three years. They had always held the upper hand, rarely stumbling. Yet tonight it wasn't quite like that.

He had been on picket duty since four in the morning, and it was starting to take its toll. His hands had lost feeling, and his toes were long gone. He was tired and hungry. The hunger never ended; there was never enough food. *A country with an army should at least try to supply food,* he thought.

This war had gone on for too long. Things needed to change, starting with the rations. He couldn't remember the last time food had been passed out by the officers. The men were stealing from the land, their own land, just to eat. Things were changing.

His watch was almost over, and he looked forward to the short rest before he went on duty again. The lines were incredibly thin these days; once there had been enough men to space them every foot. Now, with the war taking its toll, it was every six feet.

He looked over at the other man in the pit. He could remember when his friends were there next to him. They would laugh and joke until the Blue men charged, with the shots going off and the thunder of the cannons.

Now the cannon crews seemed all but dead. On occasion a sickly sounding cannon would answer those of the Blue. They had been shelled all month, and snipers had been weakening the line more every day. Morale was still high, and thoughts of winning were in every man's mind, yet things would change.

It was enough to discourage even the strongest man. Some had been fighting since 1861. Those men were the ones who would not speak of bygone days, when the face of victory looked upon them with kindness. Some of the men from 1862 would talk on occasion, but most remained silent.

The world was a different place now. Some had thought that the British might help, but now that was not possible. Times had changed, and the world would not stop speeding ahead. How could so much happen in so little time? Where had the past three years gone? Would there ever be a time that he could sit down and think, and would the world wait for him?

A shell whistled overhead, and every man dove to the ground. It exploded some distance behind them. Things had begun to change.

Tomorrow might bring happiness or defeat. For now it was enough to see their flag still flying, like a buck who defies all of man's guns and shows himself in all his splendor. The buck had fought with a vigor that could not be tamed. Yet things had changed. He hoped tomorrow would be warmer; spring was coming, but he also remembered that with spring, the war would begin again in earnest.

He got out of the trench and went back to the tents. There he woke another man, who grumbled and got up. He fell down hard on the straw mats and was soon asleep. Things had changed, and new times were coming. As he dreamed, he saw himself and his wife and the children all out in the garden again. Yet he knew, even in his dream, things had changed. 回

Art by Cara Lorello

Future History

by Axel Arth

The TV blinked on, and the newscast began. The ancient anchorman began to speak, his tired voice solemn.

"Hello, America. This is Walter Cronkite, reporting on my one-hundredth birthday. Word has been leaked that the world's largest software company has offered to buy the government's national debt, and the government has accepted. This transaction has, in effect, sold the United States. More on this as the story develops. One thing may be said for sure: It is a dark day for the United States."

The picture froze, and a whirring sound came from the archaic VCR. A hand almost as old as the VCR reached down and pressed the eject button.

"Just as well it broke there. Anyway, the children will be home soon, and I need to fix this before they distract me," the old man mumbled to himself.

He let out a small sigh. He didn't know why he always liked watching that tape. It just felt good to see the old days before all the change. It made him feel good to remember a time when some were not a disgrace to the human race. "Well, at least it's not everyone," he mumbled as he walked slowly to his leather La-Z-Boy. With that, the three people with whom his faith in humanity still rested walked into his room.

"Tom, George, Ben! Welcome home," he said, a large smile on his face at the sight of the children.

"Grandpa!" they called in unison. The old man's smile grew even larger. He was in no way related to these children, but he'd been a family friend since before their father was born. He accepted the title with pride.

"And how was the first day of your Training Year Six? As good as your fifth grade?"

"Grandpa, why do you keep calling it that? Fifth grade? No one's used that phrase for a good forty years," Tom answered. Under his breath, he added, "No one who counts, anyway." That got laughs from George and Ben.

"And that's exactly why I use it," Grandpa said with a grin, not taking the jibe seriously. "Did you learn anything today?"

"Other than the required Business Skill classes, we started a unit on the government," Ben chimed in.

Grandpa's smile faded. "And what did you learn?"

All three boys let out deep sighs, a trait they had picked up from their grandfather. "We're getting that talk again, aren't we?" Ben asked.

"First, I need to hear what you learned, then we'll see," he said, his face still grim.

"We covered the basics. First, how the CEO gets appointed by the board of directors, and then how the board of directors gets appointed by local sponsorship of the community."

"You know what they mean by 'local sponsorship,' don't you?" their grandfather asked.

"Yes, Grandpa," Tom said, rolling his eyes. "It means

whoever has the most money gets to put in who they want. Even the kids in First Year know that."

"What else did you learn?"

"That the CEO has unlimited power as far as labor and pay are concerned, as far as the Working Class of the country is concerned."

"Let's see how well you remember your training. What exactly is the Working Class?" the grandfather asked.

"Everyone between the ages of twenty and seventy with no criminal record. With a criminal record, it's twenty years to start, with yearly check-ups on work status and social behavior. Fifteen to twenty are the years for the education specific for the job you've been selected to do. Lack of work means no income and no way to support yourself," Tom recited, struggling to remember everything he had worked so hard to memorize the year before. With a grin he added, "That puts you fifty years into paid retirement, Grandpa."

A grin finally cracked his old, wrinkled lips. "Looks like you finally figured out my age, you little rascal. Now, continue. What else?"

"The CEO can propose laws that need to be passed for the good of the company of the United States' continued profit." After a small pause, he conceded to his grandpa's stare and added, "Also financed by sponsorships."

"And what if the working man wants to change something? How does he get his say?"

All sat dumbfounded. Slowly, George answered. "They get enough money to get someone's attention?"

"That's it? That's the only way?"

"That's about the only way I see," George answered weakly.

"Do any of you remember John Kennedy?"

"I think so," Ben said, unsure. "He was one of the early capitalists of the country. He was a good president, when we still had those. I think he was good anyway . . ." he trailed off, unsure of how to finish the answer.

"Close enough," Grandpa responded. "But do you remember anything he said?"

There were several seconds of silence as the boys tried to remember anything they might have heard.

Grandpa continued. "He said, 'Those who make peaceful revolutions make violent revolutions inevitable.' What does this mean to you?"

Another few seconds of silence.

"I'll tell you," he continued. "Right now, we have no say unless we can buy our way in. This can't continue."

All three boys stared at him in awe. Their grandfather had been open about his feelings on the government before, but never like this.

"This government cannot stand. It is built on nothing more than greed and corruption. The only real power is the money in the hands of investors. This isn't the way our government was meant to be run."

"But what can we do? It's only four of us, even if we did try," George said, the confusion showing in his voice.

"You think I'm the only one who thinks this? One person is never alone in what they think, that much I know for sure. All you have to do is know where to look."

"And you honestly think it can get better than this?" Tom asked.

"Yes, if people take a stand against it. Corruption will always be here, but we don't have to accept it. If you care, you can challenge anything."

"But, four people can't make a difference," Ben said, sounding almost panicked.

"There's a reason why I convinced your parents to give you your names."

Confusion spread over the three boys' faces.

"Think of what this country was founded on. Think of who it was founded by: Thomas Jefferson, George Washington and Benjamin Franklin. They believed that if a government was flawed, it was the citizens' duty, their *duty*, to change it. By force, if necessary. You three have changed this country in the past. And I have all the faith that you can do it again."

He watched as determination filled their eyes. He knew there was hope for the future.

"What do we have to do?" George asked.

"First, I'll have to teach you the true meaning of a leader. And also the basic rights of every human. And then, you should be able to handle yourselves."

Grandpa cut off his sentence as he heard someone walking up the stairs. A voice called out. "Axel? Are you up there?"

Grandpa responded. "Yeah, I'm here. Just talking to the boys."

Their father's head popped up over the top of the stairs. "Oh, what about?"

"Just discussing what they learned in school today."

"Oh? And how are they doing?"

"Fine," he said slowly, with a small grin. "They're doing just fine." ▣

Shadows of the Past

by Allison Dziuba

She felt like a baked potato crisp as she bent over the site for what seemed like the hundredth time. She tossed aside a lock of red hair that had fallen into her perspiring face and then, grasping a trowel, began digging at the stubborn soil. Stabbing at the impenetrable dirt and rock for hours seemed a losing battle. Closing her eyes and releasing a moan, she gradually got to her feet. A cloud of dust formed around her.

"Having a little trouble, Gabby?" Squinting through the heat, the frustrated archaeologist tried to determine who had spoken.

"Oh, Josh. Yeah, I guess you could say that." The African dust finally settled enough to reveal two figures. One was a large, muscular man with a safari hat at a jaunty angle on his bleached hair. His jaw was strong, and his sharp green eyes seemed to smile. Beside him was a tall, slender woman with a long ponytail of carrot-colored hair under a straw hat. They were both tan, though the woman was covered with an extraordinary number of freckles.

"Well, I can relate to your frustration, but we haven't found so much as a bone fragment yet, so don't give up."

Josh Fields showed off his white teeth in a grin and chuckled, "Hey, you never know, you might even find the missing link."

"Very funny," Gabrielle O'Leary said, sarcastically. "If you're going to snicker, you can just leave—I'm very busy." The last was a lie, and Gabby knew it.

Since she had graduated from college and started field-work, Gabby had been unsuccessful. After four years of endless work, her sacrifice had not paid off. When she reflected on these years—the sweltering deserts of Africa, life in a tiny tent, the long nights of research on her laptop, visiting civilization once a year—she wondered whether it was worthwhile. Time and again she had gone to a potentially rich archaeological site only to be disappointed. This was her last try—in one week she would trade this career for law school, to the delight of her rigid, ex-attorney mother.

So, this is the last great adventure, Gabby thought, feeling both disappointed and relieved. She sighed and began again to scratch fruitlessly.

Crunch, crunch—the trowel continued to strike just earth. Crunch, crunch, clack! Eyes widening, Gabby pushed the trowel delicately. She had definitely hit something. Her heart racing, she carefully dug around the object. Sweat poured down her face from the strain of digging and excitement.

After an hour, Gabby had unearthed the mysterious item. She stood with difficulty and stepped back from the wide hole, panting and dropping the brush she had used. She observed her handiwork: a skeleton. This was not just any skeleton, but an almost complete one, missing only its left hand. It was lying relatively straight, and the skull was facing up. Gabby gasped in shock, and a smile of delight crept across her face.

"Wow, Gabby! You struck a gold mine!" said Dr. Robert Hansen, the site's head archaeologist and a specialist in evolutionary human fossils. He bent down to pick up the skull. The sun was setting, and Gabby was basking in the glow of the fading light and her colleague's compliment. Hansen identified the skeleton as a member of the human genus, *Homo,* an early human—the rarest of archaeological discoveries.

"As you can see," Dr. Hansen pointed out, using a caliper to measure the skull's dimensions, "the brain case is larger than those of *Australopithecines*—the apes of South Africa. And the mouth area is smaller, pointing to an evolutionary human with a roomier cranial capacity. Yet, I am puzzled because the skull is too small to have been *Homo habilis.*" Hansen furrowed his brow and took off his bifocals. "Therefore, it was either a less intelligent *Homo habilis,*" he paused again and inhaled softly, "or something else."

A murmur swept through the group of archaeologists who had gathered, and two words were apparent above all the rest: missing link.

Excavation intensified the next day around the skeleton's area. Gabby was elated—the bones were examined, and it was determined that the hominid had definitely walked upright. From the deep ruts in its molars, the team thought it had probably eaten nuts. This particular creature had been female, judging from the hip and pelvic structure. From her skeletal development, Dr.

Hansen estimated that she was in her late twenties—Gabby's age. What excited the archaeologists the most was that the skeleton appeared to be the link between ape-like and tool-using. Hansen dubbed it *Homo absentis,* meaning "missing human."

Gabby smiled as her brush moved methodically over where *Homo absentis* had been found, searching for the smallest fragment of bones—particularly the missing left hand. The sun had gone behind a black cloud that would possibly bring rain, and she wasn't sweating as much. Yet an ominous feeling permeated the site. Gabby tried to calm her nerves—after all, this was her fifteen minutes of fame. *By next week, my name will be in newspapers and magazines worldwide,* Gabby thought blissfully. *I can see it now — "Gabby O'Leary Finds Groundbreaking Missing Link!"*

A raindrop awakened Gabby from her daydreams.

"Okay, everyone, clean up the site and get to shelter," Josh called into a brisk wind. Lightning erupted, followed almost immediately by thunder.

Gabby and her fellow archaeologists deftly tied down the cloth around the find. Rain was a welcome occurrence in the Great Rift Valley. Gabby was refreshed as she stepped into her tent.

The day's work finally catching up to her, Gabby flopped down on her cot. She could hear rain on the canvas, and shadows wandered back and forth outside, large and dark one moment, then fading to gray and disappearing.

Her eyelids were closing as she surveyed her room. Clothes were packed, ready to go to the airport in a few days. A water purifier was at the other end, along with a water bottle. A sketch of the skeleton drawn by a colleague hung next to her cot. Under the detailed drawing were the artist's initials and the title, "Gabby's *Homo Absentis.*" The fatigued archaeologist grinned, and with a final yawn, her eyelids closed. She was instantly asleep.

That night, Gabby awakened abruptly. She felt she had just had a horrid dream; she was groggy and sweat dampened her face. She tried to shake off her anxiety by walking around the tent.

The gentle snore of her tent-mate and the drizzle formed a monotonous pattern of noise. Gabby turned toward her cot. Out of the corner of her eye, she caught movement. She rubbed her eyes and shook her head. *Too much time in the sun,* she thought. But wait, there it was again. Gabby turned.

A rush of wind blasted through the door flap. Gabby's hair flew off her face, and she squinted.

A high-pitched moan rent the air, sounding forlorn, yet enraged. The agonizing howl grew louder and closer, and a dark, hulking shadow was forming on the wall of the tent. The figure was next to the tent now, and its shape lengthened to reach the ceiling. It was human-like but cruder. It raised its long arms as the moan intensified as it mingled with Gabby's own petrified scream. The noise was piercing as the shadow's long fingers reached for the tent. Slowly, the hand ran down the canvas, making a jagged tear. As the figure pushed in, Gabby froze. The continuous shriek seemed to penetrate her soul.

It lurched toward Gabby. Out of the head appeared two gleaming eyes. They were blue, like Gabby's, yet primitive. But their look was far from primordial. They seemed fiery, and they stared unblinkingly into the archaeologist's face. For a moment, Gabby saw something familiar. There was a mystique that made her feel connected. They were simple and wise, beautiful and hideous. But this was short-lived. Gabby crumpled, unconscious before she hit the ground.

When she came to, she sputtered, her throat aching from screaming. It was still night, and oddly, her roommate appeared undisturbed. Panting, she reached for the clock. A shrill siren cut through the stillness. It was her alarm. A bolt of lightning abruptly interrupted it and illuminated the top of the crate.

The hand. The left hand of the skeleton. The bones on the crate shone in the lightning as Gabby's mouth opened to shout. But her voice seemed to have run away in terror. Her eyes rolled, her face blanched, and for the second time that night, she fainted.

The morning dawned bright as heat rose in waves from the ground. Gabby awakened with the sun, feeling panicky.

Gabrielle O'Leary might have cringed under the glare of the shadow the night before, but she knew how to react now. She hurried to the wall where the shadow had entered. With a wave of nausea, Gabby felt the rip in the canvas. It had most certainly not been a dream. Steadying her quivering body, she reached for her laptop. She hastily logged onto the Internet to check a hunch. Even though she was terrified of the answer, the hunger for knowledge that archaeology had instilled in her overruled this fear. Gabby searched archaeology Web sites, printed what she needed, then bolted out of the tent into the midst of the excavation.

There he was, Dr. Hansen. She stumbled to the scientist crouching beside another archaeologist, examining the ground.

"Dr. Hansen!" Gabby said. "Dr. Hansen, you have to see this . . . I need to talk to you."

"Gabby?" Dr. Hansen gave her a quizzical stare. She suddenly was aware of her disheveled clothing and matted hair.

"I need to speak with you—in private." Still giving Gabby a confused look, Hansen followed her into a tent.

"I'm sorry if I'm acting kind of, well, harried, Doctor, but something very strange happened last night." Her pupils dilated and she looked at him more closely.

"I think I was visited last night—I know this sounds weird—by *Homo absentis*. A real, live *Homo absentis*. I think it was trying to tell me something. It tried to get to me, but I fainted and then . . ." Hansen was walking away, back toward the excavation area.

"Dr. Hansen, I know you may not believe me, but please." Her tone was urgent, and the pleading was clear in her speech. Hansen stared back as though he did not understand a word. Annoyed, Gabby grabbed him by the collar.

"See," she held up her printed sheet. "This is a theory of *Homo absentis*. It was written by a French scientist. I came upon it weeks ago when searching for information on *Homo habilis*." She began to read the passage, her eyes moving from the paper to the protesting Hansen.

"'The Missing Link Theory' by Dr. Bernadette Aigner,"

she read. "'Many scientists have speculated about the supposed missing link of the human species. It is thought to have been in existence between *Australopithecines* and *Homo habilis,* two species who differed greatly. This missing link is thought to have some of the characteristics of both. The brain, theoretically, has a larger area than *Australopithecines*, and the posture is believed to be closer to an upright stance. On the other hand, it probably had not developed elaborate motor skills, so it most likely didn't use tools to the extent that *habilis* did. Therefore, we can conclude that the missing link's hands were in the process of adapting to using hand-held items.

"'But that is where scientific hypothesis ends, and possibility and guesswork steps in. Some archaeologists and others studying early humans have claimed that the main reason we evolved from ape-like hominids to intellectually complex beings who continue to hone our intelligence was because our early ancestors had a greater wisdom than we believe. The theory is that these missing-link humans had a larger, more general knowledge. They felt emotion. They certainly were not the brainless cavemen we think of today. They probably mourned their dead, but did not think to bury them. One can almost go so far as to compare these hominids with modern-day toddlers, except that their knowledge never became more specific. Perhaps they were the first to show definable emotions and distantly grasp the concept of life. But until we have hard evidence, we may never know. Perhaps we aren't meant to know after all.'" Beneath the text was an illustration of a missing-link human.

"Something very odd is going on . . ." Gabby trailed off

as Hansen finally pulled away from her and scrambled off toward the place where the guttural noise had come. She rounded the corner to see where the scientist had gone.

Her jaw dropped again as her eyes focused on the scene. Her colleagues were slumping around the site, no longer digging. They were either sitting on the ground gazing up at the sky or foraging for scrub brush. Some were munching on pieces of vegetation and small soil-colored nuts.

Gabby looked at the paper she had been reading and the illustration. She positioned the picture so it lined up with Josh. Sure enough, the body postures matched. Josh body-slammed another archaeologist to get to a particularly large, green section of shrub.

It was starting to come together. She was on the brink of excitement, yet exhilaration was the prize for stress and fear, and it had been nothing but that up until now.

She jogged back to her tent. Inside, almost nothing was left. The cots were gone, replaced by heaps of brush. Her trowels, paintbrushes, tape measures and caliper were gone, and in their place were crude stone hammers and arrows. And where had her bags gone? In their place were plants and vines. Horrified, Gabby grabbed one of the last remaining modern objects—the sketch of the *Homo absentis* skeleton.

"So, it's not just affecting the other archaeologists; it's also turning all our supplies into their stone-age counterparts," she said out loud. "And I'm the only one who is noticing."

She rushed outdoors, the words of the piece reverberating inside her: Perhaps the missing link is the key to our emotions and existence . . . *Perhaps we aren't meant to know about our origins after all.*

The cogs in Gabby's head were turning double time. Meanwhile, the tents themselves were disappearing, and she knew she didn't have much time to change everything back.

"Maybe if we had never found the skeleton, none of this would have happened. Maybe we're not supposed to know about *Homo absentis.* Maybe it doesn't want to be found. Maybe we are never supposed to find the answers to our past. Maybe life's meaning is one question that has no answer." Gabby suddenly felt philosophical, which made her a bit queasy.

Her tent, the one she had just run from, had evaporated.

"Maybe if none of this occurred, I could turn everything back. No one can reverse time, but I can try." She set to work.

First, she rolled up all the measuring tape that outlined the excavation site. She then retrieved the skeleton. She placed it back in the soil in the same position it had been. The left hand was missing once again, but this evaded Gabby's desperate mind.

As she packed the last shovel of dirt over the skeleton, gray clouds moved in, and a light rain trickled from the atmosphere. As though the rain had awakened the *Homo sapiens* in the others, they seemed to shake out of their primordial identities. Josh trotted up to Gabby, fixing his hat so it was again perched at that jaunty angle.

"Strange weather we're having, huh?" Josh asked nonchalantly.

Gabby tested her luck. "So what do you think of the

Photo by Erica J. Hodgkinson

artifacts we've found so far? Fascinating, don't you agree?"

"What are you talking about?" Josh grinned as though Gabby were crazy. "We haven't found anything. And this rain is a pain when it comes to getting work done. You'd better get to a tent." As he scrambled off, Gabby was glad to see a tent. She smiled and tilted her head back so that the precipitation splashed her face.

At the end of that week, Gabby caught a ride to the airport and flew home. Her last day on the site, the team of archaeologists had finally been successful: They discovered the remains of a stone shaped in a way that would have easily fit in a hominid hand and was thought to have been used by an early human. *Of course, the findings come the day I leave,* Gabby thought, as she boarded the plane. As she heaved her bag into the overhead bin, something fell out of her pocket: the drawing of the skeleton. She picked it up, eyes wide, and turned to her seat. There was a skeletal hand already there—a left hand. ▣

The Sneeze

by Alex Roan

I t started with a sneeze. It was actually a rather ordinary sneeze—not a long, drawn-out one that occurs when you inhale the six-year layer of dust that has settled on a couch in your grandmother's attic, but just a regular, early-morning, springtime allergy sneeze. In fact, the sneeze in itself was not particularly significant. It did, however, cause the jogger, the perpetrator of the sneeze, to blink, as sneezes often make one do. Right at that instant, a glimmering yellow spacecraft whizzed past the jogger's head, reflecting the sun's warm rays. Because the jogger was occupied with the process of blinking, he was not aware of the yellow blur that zoomed past and crashed in a nearby cornfield.

Meanwhile, Zyphlib4b Xebloom (the 4 is silent) was not happy. In fact, he was in a state of murderous, violent agitation, and he had just flung the remainder of his lunch against the metal floor of his spaceship. His mood did not improve as the ship ceased its tumbling, settling in an upside-down position and causing the floor to become the ceiling. This, of course, invited the discarded remains of his recently smashed lunch to plummet onto two of his three frowning heads. It was a bad start to an even worse day.

Zyphlib4b was a knight—a dark and stormy knight at that particular moment. He was a temporarily unemployed dark and stormy knight who desperately needed a job so that he could pay his long overdue gravity bill back home on Alpha Zipper 9. However, the service that Zyphlib4b offered, although important, was regarded by most as obsolete. He was in the business of saving galaxies. His problem was that in this day and age, most galaxies just didn't need saving. An even bigger problem for the moment was that Zyphlib4b was stuck on the third planet of an obscure star, lazily floating around in one of the duller parts of a dreary galaxy, without a gas station in sight. He sighed and stuck the head that wasn't covered with what looked like processed peas out of the hole that had recently materialized in the ship's wall. Zyphlib4b scanned the horizon and saw a scene common to that of a cornfield. He waited. Nothing happened. He waited. Nothing continued to happen. Finally, after realizing that nothing was not about to stop happening anytime soon, Zyphlib4b left his ship and accosted a stalk of corn.

"Er . . . excuse me," he interrupted the stalk politely.

After receiving the response that a cornstalk is likely to give a passing traveler, he took its advice, turned and stalked down the dirt path. Before long, he reached an old, beat-up gas station that looked like it hadn't been repainted since the first car had revved up and rolled squeakily down the street. In front of the station stood three anthropodular carbon-based creatures next to a four-wheeled vehicle marked "Unsolved Mysteries." One was looking at the other two through a black box of some sort, while another barked into a cylindrical wand, frequently holding it up to an orifice located in the center of the third creature's single head. These animals had obviously not yet discovered telepathy.

"Take six," barked the animal holding the box. "Action!"

"'Unsolved Mysteries' is broadcasting here today from Summerfield, Nebraska, where Mr. Joe-Bob Tucker has claimed to have seen a series of unexplainable crop circles, and . . ."

The yapping animal dropped his cylinder and stared blankly at Zyphlib4b.

"Well, um, hello there," Zyphlib4b began. "You see, I was wondering . . . well, that is . . ." he stopped as he realized that if he wanted a cornstalk-like response, he was probably better off talking to a cornstalk. The three one-headed animals gaped as Zyphlib4b filled up a container with gas and trudged back to his ship. After making a few repairs and exchanging good-byes with the cornstalk, he took off, resolving never again to become stranded on a provincial planet without intelligent life as the dominant life form, and never ever to engage in conversation with life forms who had not yet discovered telepathy. He zoomed off, seeking work in a more exciting and possibly more dangerous corner of the galaxy— a place where a gallant, dark and no-longer-so-stormy knight would be needed most.

As Zyphlib4b departed the atmosphere, the three anthropodular, one-headed animals stood speechless while they wondered which of two things had happened: Had a rival TV station sent a representative with three heads, two of which were covered with what appeared to be processed peas, to sabotage their television program? Or had the unthinkable—a real visit from another world—finally happened? After allowing a considerable amount of time for thought, they decided on the former. The tense silence was finally broken by a passing jogger. He sneezed. ▣

Lost Soul

by Meghan Keene

I t was a good day to cry. And I knew pairs of eyes that were not mine shed the grief that tormented me, too.

The sun was slowly setting over the skyline, a glowing amber melting into deep scarlet reds and rich oranges beyond the silhouette of dirty, ash-colored buildings. Another sunset ending another day, another day there. I was getting the feeling that many more sunsets would be seen through that simple, two-paned window.

The room was small, with a low ceiling, no doors, and the only light coming from the window. We could see all around the room, the azure blue background of the wallpaper, almost like the real sky we had left behind. We could see all the painted doves, the others, our brothers in this place. They lined the walls, looking just like I did and feeling the same way.

We were the same, down to every last detail. The long, luxurious feathers, the scaly little feet, tucked as if we were flying, but now suspended, trapped in this room with nowhere to go. We were the same in every aspect except our eyes. I know I saw them move and twinkle in the beam of moonlight flowing in through the window. Sometimes I would catch a glimpse of tears rolling down a dove's soft cheeks, falling to the floor, making a tiny sparkling pool of grief. And I saw this tonight. We were so real that, if someone did not know any better, he or she might expect us to pop right off the wall and fly away.

This concept is not totally absurd, of course, for most in the room. But it just barely pushed the barrier between what was real and what was fantasy for me. You must understand who I am, why I was there, and where "there" is.

My name is Catherine Bevel, and I was a lost soul. Trapped in the tiny room was I, the room with the simple purpose of being the Lost and Found for the human spirit. We have all been lost; admit it. And I'm not talking about losing sight of your mother in the supermarket when you were four. I mean truly lost. Even if only for a few seconds, we have all been to that room, that state of mind that allows us to lose touch with ourselves and everything wonderful in our lives.

It's interesting that lost souls, like I was, have only one hope of ever finding themselves, and that would be the truth. And, coincidentally, this room, where the walls sport souls disguised as doves, is the only place where we are completely sheltered from the truth. There exists nothing in that room. We don't see anything but the simple fact that we want to find ourselves, but we don't know how.

Usually most souls flew in that window fairly quickly, losing sight of what is true and popping on the wall into this place of darkness and uncertainty. Then, sometimes seconds, sometimes hours later, the person finds purpose, sees the light that means truth and stands for everything

Photo by Mary Amor

good, and he or she floats peacefully off the wallpaper and right out the window. Another lost dove always meanders in to take the empty space on the wall, taking its turn and leaving the same way. The same window that opened for him, however, somehow seemed locked tight for me, with no hope of me ever following the doves who "find" as easily as they "lose" themselves.

Once in a great while, a soul dies in the room. I saw it happen. The eyes would be aged, bluish and blind to everything—the room, and more important, the truth. They were blind beyond any hope of ever seeing anything that is true again. And they died lost, flickering and fading into the wall, another lost dove taking the empty space on the paper as usual after the last feather disappeared from view. I did not want to die lost.

The sunset I described was the last one I saw in the room. No one had been in the room as long as I had. I was truly lost in life for three full days. And nothing in that time opened my eyes; nothing pulled me from that mental place where people go to hide from themselves.

I was so lost. Looking back to my time spent in the room, it pains me to remember how long it took to be found. My mother had died, and everything in my life had died with her. Time stood still, and nothing was worth anything, not without her. All the hurtful things I had said to her, all the fights we had, came back to haunt me in dreams and thoughts. I loved her so much. Why hadn't I shown it? Why is it that I never told her that I loved her? Mom, I love you! Too late. She was gone, and life was no longer worth living. I was a zombie of grief and pain, trapped in the room.

Before she left me, I lived to play my flute, filling an entire room with its sweet, rich tones. It had been a year since I had picked it up. I left my other family and friends behind. No one knew how I felt. There was no one to find me but myself.

I lost sight of everything important, and that kept me from finding myself. I forgot the things that I lived for. I forgot about the people: my family, my friends, those more important than me. My flute. The simple things were not clear to me in the room: my pride, my dignity, my confidence, what I stood for. When those images came into my mind when I was in the room, my wings became real, and I could truly take flight. I looked at the world outside that window and wasn't afraid to reunite with it. Notes poured like water from my flute into the unsuspecting air, and both the flute and my heart sang.

Remember at all times that people, like doves, have wings to fly with. We should exercise those wings as much as possible. And even more important, never stay in that low-ceilinged, dark room, never stay lost for too long, because every second we spend trapped without sight of the truth is a moment we could have been living our lives, soaring high. 回

250 □ Teen Ink

The Righteous Wrangler

by David Steinhaus

"Oh, I love a rainy night, bum, bum, I just love a . . ." sang Artie as he rubbed Irish Spring over his stumpy body.

Suddenly, his doorbell announced the arrival of a visitor. He threw down the soap, gallantly leapt from the tub, slipped and fell onto the floor. Artie winced and rose from the tile, hopping into a suit of white spandex with a sparkly gold W emblazoned on his chest. The suit sagged around his waterbed paunch and was too long for the little man.

Artie, dressed but still dripping, raced to the door and opened it quickly. Standing on the stoop was a very professional-looking man. He looked about fifty and wore a dark green, four-piece suit. Artie gasped when he saw that the suit had four pieces. He knew this could only mean one thing.

"Are you Artie Abello?" The Austrian accent confirmed Artie's suspicions. Only Commission delegates wore four-piece suits and spoke with Austrian accents.

Artie was filled with excitement. "Why yes, sir, 'tis I." Artie pinched himself hard for using a word like 'tis.

The man in the suit raised an eyebrow and answered, "Mr. Abello, I have an official telegram for you from the

International Commission of Sidekicks. It is urgent that you read it now. I need to relay your response to the Commission by noon tomorrow." He handed Artie a gold envelope and winked.

Artie nervously opened the telegram. "Okay, sir, I'll read it right now." He unfolded the note and read, *The International Commission of Sidekicks has reviewed your recent work with Samurai Seth. We have decided to offer you a promotion to the position of ROOKIE SUPERHERO. You will receive a significant pay increase, an official patch for your uniform and funding for a secret lair. You will be responsible for the protection of Districts 11432 and 11433 on the south side of Municipal City. After 1,200 hours of service, you will again be reviewed for promotion to JOURNEYMAN SUPERHERO. Please respond immediately following your obtainment of this notice.* Artie sighed and suppressed a tear. The ingredients of his dreams were finally mixing into the pineapple upside-down cake he had always desired.

"Mr. Abello, it is imperative that I deliver your reply to the Commission as soon as possible," urged the Austrian envoy.

"Yes! My answer is yes! I accept the offer. Please, go and tell the Commission for me, sir. I really must go and distribute Wet-Naps to the unfortunate. Good-bye." As Artie closed his front door, he hoped he had impressed the man with his Wet-Nap comment. He sprang into the air with his super legs, clicked his super heels together and knocked over an antique lamp.

Two months later, Artie stood high atop the courthouse overlooking the territory under his protection. He now had an air of confidence about him. Artie's suit looked well-tailored and embraced every cresting muscle. The waterbed paunch had been replaced by a hard, rippling mattress. For the past sixty days he had looked after the people, buildings and vegetation of his two districts. Upon receiving his certificate, uniform patch and instructions, Artie had begun his reign as guardian of Municipal City. Now everyone knew his masked face, and his superhero name had become known in households and feared by criminals. As the Righteous Wrangler, Artie saved the innocent and defeated evil.

"Hey, Artie! What are you looking at?" asked a voice behind him.

"Just surveying, you know, looking for perps," replied Artie. He turned to view the table of veteran policemen playing cards.

"Well, why don't you give it a rest and let us handle something? It's been months since I've done anything more than hand out a jaywalking ticket. Old Snappy Stingray used to at least give us a car chase once in a while," shouted a skinny red-haired cop.

"I'm sorry, boys, but I have an evaluation in a week, and I have to perform at my best. That means not letting anything slide so you guys can pick it up." Just then a bright red boomerang cracked into Artie. Artie crumpled to the ground, and the policemen immediately drew their weapons. A red arm flopped onto the roof and pulled a stringy body over the edge. The droopy, enigmatic form stood, and the police force gasped.

"It's Snappy Stingray! Snappy, why did you hit the Righteous Wrangler with your Ballistic Boomerang? He's a good guy!" exclaimed the fat, bald sergeant.

"Why? You're asking me why? Isn't it obvious?" shrieked Snappy.

"Uh, not really," wavered the sergeant.

"Well, if I must really spell it out for you," sighed Snappy. "I'm not going to let it happen. I'm not going to let this Wrangler nitwit take my place. The Commission thinks they can force me into early retirement, but they can't! I'm only sixty-two! I can still fight crime, and I can do it better than this little white-clad punk! What kind of superhero wears white, anyway?"

"Well, The Gallant Ghost and Conundrum Charlie," said the sergeant.

"And Picket Pete," added a young officer.

"White's all the rage in Milan," chimed in a shorter cop.

Snappy clenched his arthritic fists and shouted, "Quiet! All of you! I don't care! The point is that I'm a better hero, and I won't stop till I have my job back!" Behind the Stingray, Artie was examining his torn costume. He stood and walked over to Snappy, saying, "Don't get worked up. You knew it would happen someday. I refuse to fight you. I mean, look at how you're gasping after just talking for a minute. Come on, even your costume needs retirement. It's really old and funky."

Snappy's eyes widened, and he spun to face the cops. "Did you hear that disrespectful fool? He just called me a golden monkey! What is that, some sort of young person slang?" A few officers giggled at the old man's mistake, but the sergeant kept his eyes on Snappy's boomerang. The Stingray began waving the Australian weapon in the air, "Why are you laughing? That whippersnapper insulted me. Show some respect!" Artie looked up from his bruised stomach and saw the boomerang accidentally slip from Snappy's arthritic fingers. It glided uselessly away, but the Righteous Wrangler dove forth with purpose. At the sight of Artie hurtling toward him, the Stingray shrieked and stumbled over the side of the building. When Artie reached the edge, Snappy Stingray was gone. He looked back to the policemen.

"Is everyone all right?" he asked.

"Yeah, we're just fine, Artie, but I don't think the Stingray is."

The following week, every time Artie went on a mission, Snappy Stingray would show up to try and reclaim his glory. The two heroes always ended up dueling while the criminal got away, then Snappy would totter back to his hideout in a mad rage. The last thing Artie wanted was to hurt the man who had been his idol for so many years, so he continued attempting to prevent crimes and fend off Snappy at the same time.

At the end of the week, Artie was relaxing in his newly finished Cabin of Justice when the intruder alarm screeched. He quickly changed into his white suit and dashed to the Observation Tower of Honor. He peered through his Periscope of Power and spotted the invader—the man in the four-piece suit. Artie jumped to the ground and extended a hand to him.

The man placidly turned to Artie and shook his outstretched appendage. "Good evening, Mr. Abello. I have another telegram from the Commission for you."

Artie stared at the paper, stunned. In all his dealings with Snappy, he had forgotten about the Commission's evaluation! Had this been Snappy's devious plan all along? *Probably not,* Artie thought. Snappy is pretty old for that kind of trickery. Artie opened the letter and read, *The International Commission of Superheroes has evaluated the recent conduct of Artie Abello and decided to refrain from granting the position of JOURNEYMAN. The progress was excellent until the conclusion of the period, when all competent crime-fighting halted. Mr. Abello will remain a ROOKIE SUPERHERO for one year until the next evaluation.* Artie fought back tides of anger and sadness as he read the names of those who had signed the letter.

The man cleared his Austrian throat. "My sentiments, Mr. Abello. Good-bye."

As the man walked away, Artie's eyes let forth a tsunami. He ran to his Futon of Friendship and buried his face in the covers.

When Artie woke, it was not with an air of irritation. His dreams had brought him the solution he needed. Artie ran to his typewriter. After a few minutes, the letter was complete. He dropped it in the mail on his way to work and anxiously commenced his day of crime-fighting.

For a month, Artie fought the forces of evil and warded off Snappy with an energy that could only be described as super. Then, one day while he was binding a couple of crooks together, the distinguished messenger of the Commission appeared. Artie finished his clovehitch and rushed to the delegate. Before the Austrian emissary could say anything, Artie snatched the letter and tore it open. After reading it, Artie jumped into the air and clicked his heels. The man in the four-piece suit smiled

knowingly and vanished. Artie suspended the two rob-
bers from a lamppost, then sat and waited.

Thirty minutes later, Snappy Stingray came puffing
around the corner, awkwardly brandishing his Ballistic
Boomerang. The Righteous Wrangler grinned and
walked over to him. Snappy looked terrified as Artie put
a hand on his drooping shoulder. "We can cease our
skirmishing. I have solved all our problems," Artie told
him.

"How did you do that, you little deadbeat? Did you use
your hippie sideburns?" replied Snappy as he pushed
Artie away and jumped flamboyantly onto the curb.
Artie stepped onto the sidewalk behind the hunched
man and knocked him down. "I wrote a letter to the
Commission . . ."

"You wrote a letter? Ha! I'll bet you couldn't even get
the cap off the ink to dip the quill into!" quipped Snappy
as he lurched to his feet with a groan. He caught his
breath and hobbled behind Artie.

Without turning around, Artie spoke, "Well, I did. They
promoted me to JOURNEYMAN SUPERHERO. Do you
know what that means?"

"Yeah, it means you're a runty little rutabaga due for a
pummeling!" shouted Snappy as he lunged toward Artie
and fell short.

Artie turned and looked at Snappy sprawled on the
sidewalk. He helped him up and explained, "No, it
means I can adopt a sidekick. I can choose anyone in the
world to help me safeguard Municipal City."

Snappy stopped struggling and looked into Artie's
eyes. "Anyone?"

"Anyone I want. It is my duty to elect the most powerful and able hero to stand by my side. I have chosen the valorous Snappy Stingray." Snappy's face became happy again. "If you accept, of course."

"It would be my honor, Righteous Wrangler," answered an overjoyed Snappy. He then straightened his tattered garment. "I am going to be more of a partner than a sidekick. I'm glad you finally admit to needing my help. I'll teach you everything about being a good superhero, Arnie."

"My name is Artie."

"That's what I said, Arnie. Lesson one: listen well," coached Snappy.

"Sure thing," Artie replied as he turned and led Snappy down the street.

As the two faded into the afternoon sun, Snappy could be heard saying, "Where's a hose? I need to take my pills."

The Righteous Wrangler and Snappy Stingray fought crime together for many years, except on Thursdays. Snappy had his cribbage tournament on Thursdays. □

Noctaphobia

by Zachary Handlen

I hate darkness.

I loathe the night, and shadows put me into such fits that it would take ten men to hold me down. I spend more than $200 each month on lightbulbs, and my neighbors hate me because I leave my lights on all the time, which keeps them awake. But they don't understand. All my closet doors are barricaded because I can't keep them lit, and I have over three hundred candles stuck around my house. I prefer to use the electric lights because they're brighter, but—but—what if the power goes out? So I keep candles everywhere, with matches next to them. And on stormy nights I light them all. Just in case.

There are reasons for this obsession. I am not completely mad, although I may sound it. This is not just some flighty fear without reason. Used to be, I was just like you—a fool, not knowing what lurked in black corners. But I learned, didn't I? The knowledge was forced upon me, a rape of the mind. And now my hair is white, I can't eat much, and breathing is difficult at times. And the dreams, oh, the dreams . . .

It started, as I suppose it generally does, with the occult. It always enticed me, ever since I was old enough to read and shudder. I began with horror stories by Lovecraft, Poe and less renowned authors. I started correspondence with one writer, Edward Derby. You most likely haven't heard of him. His stories are excellent, though; they chill in a way that subverts reality. A month after discovering his work, I decided to write him a letter expressing my admiration, not really expecting a response; imagine my surprise when I got one. After that, hardly a week went by when we didn't exchange messages—brief notes on the weather or full ten-page lectures on forbidden books. We became quite close in our letters. I put things down on paper I perhaps never would have told a friend in my "real" life, but we never met.

Edward steered me to more and more obscure texts, forcing me to hunt through the back rows of city libraries and mothball-smelling stacks in used bookstores. Each new author he told me about was more talented in his prose and more horrific in his images. I couldn't believe the vividness of some of what I read. Eventually, though, even these began to pale. I started to hunger for something that would truly terrify me. In my twenty-first year, I wrote Edward of my desires. He responded promptly.

Timothy (he wrote),

I hear you and can Empathize completely. I, too, experienced a sort of Disillusionment around my twenty-first year. Eventually, Everyday Fictions fail to excite Reaction in Educated men. They are, after all, only Made-Up tales, designed to spook the Naive. Those of a higher Intellect must seek Enlightenment in Other places. We must find the Truth where others

Dare not look. I have enclosed the title and location of a Certain Book that will hopefully help you conquer your Difficulties.

With fondest regards,
Edward

In the envelope, I found a scrap of yellowed, old paper. On it was written, in a strange script, a name that I dare not give here, as well as the name of an antique dealer in a nearby city. The paper stank of spice and felt oddly slick in my hands. I have since tried to find that paper, in order to destroy it, but have been unable to. That should set my heart at ease, but it does not.

I wasted no time in visiting the shop, eager to be inducted into this new level of thought. The place was rather nondescript and, had I not seen the name listed overhead, I would have doubted it was the object of my search. The front window was dark and dingy, and at first I suspected I had come during nonbusiness hours. But the door opened, and I slipped into its darkness.

The first thing I noticed was the sheer weight of the place. It felt like the atmosphere had been lifted from some alien planet where the pull of gravity was harsher. The scent of dust wafted through the air, and I could see its thick coats on everything—the tables filling the room, the piles of texts, the rows and shelves in the far back. A clerk looked sullen and bored as he taped torn book covers and checked for ripped pages. I could hear a radio playing softly somewhere above.

I spent three or four hours looking through the heaps and rows of old, dead things, trying to find the book that cannot be named. A few times I almost dared to question the clerk, but one look at his disgruntled expression told me there was no help there.

Then I found it, hidden underneath a few old children's books and a text on applied astrophysics. It was heavy, almost the weight of a small block of cement, but the reason seemed obvious—it was over 1,000 pages, bound in a thick, bunched-up material that was almost leather. It felt slick in my hands, almost as if it would fall if I did not grip it tightly. I bought the book, paying what seemed far too little, and left, excited, adrenaline making me giddy. I drove at least forty miles an hour over the speed limit, so great was my eagerness. I had to suppress the urge to pull over and at least flip through the tome. But no, that would have been cheating.

Despite my speed, it was after dark when I reached home. I ran inside, sat down in my favorite chair, turned on my reading light and, feeling a delicious shiver of anticipation run down my spine, opened the cover to find—nothing. Just a blank page, solid white from top to bottom, with a little yellow on the corners. I flipped it over and saw the same. I went through the book from cover to cover, and on each page was the exact same thing—no text, no diagrams, no horrors, just mile after mile of uniform emptiness.

To say I was upset would be like saying the Mona Lisa was a pretty picture. I wanted to hit something, to beat upon the very world with the agony of this defeat. So close—I'd felt so close—the thing started to vibrate in my hands, to hum with some sort of impossible power.

In a fury of fear and frustration, I flung the book, slamming it against the wall. It fell to the floor, opened near the front, and suddenly the pages began to turn—softly at first, then faster and faster, creating a whine like a mosquito. I stared, helpless, not wanting to get up, not wanting to move. And then, as quickly as it had started, the pages stopped, leaving the book spread to a section that seemed no different than any other. I almost went over. But then the page started to bulge and stretch like something was trying to pull itself up out of the white surface. I shrieked, pushing myself farther and farther back up into my chair.

The lights went out.

For a moment I couldn't breathe. So great was my fear that I could have sworn my heart stopped, and I thought, *So that's it. That's good. Because this—this is too much. Just too much for any sane man to deal with.* But my heart resumed its beating, and I started breathing again. For that one instant, I cursed my body for its strength.

Although I couldn't see in front of me, I could still hear. And smell. The sound was like flesh being ripped off a live body. And the smell—it was like castor oil and dead cats and something bad, something nasty, something fresh out of hell and rotten. I was frozen at first, but then I saw a dark shape move, and I bolted. I went for the kitchen closet, thinking I would make it easily, but a stool was right in front of me when I thought it was ten inches to the left. It hit me in the gut, and down we both went. I got up faster than the stool, my legs stinging, but not fast enough, because I could hear it lumbering behind me—no sound really, just the sense of moving air. I limped over to the wall and tried to find the door-knob. It wasn't there. I felt a little to the left, a little to the right—nothing.

I started to panic. What was this—had someone snuck into my house and moved everything? But there it was, less than an inch above where I'd been looking. I turned it, yanked it hard and, reaching up, felt around the top shelf for anything—a gun, a hunting knife, anything to save me. The creature was right behind me now. I could feel its furnace-hot breath on my neck and its cold, wet, sharp fingers stretch around my neck. My hand closed on a long piece of plastic, one of those lighters you can get for five bucks, and brought it out. I flicked it on, shoving it behind me.

And the touch vanished.

There was no scream of pain, no intake of breath. The lighter had met no obstruction. Just one minute ago I was being strangled, the next—nothing. I turned around, and in the dim light saw my kitchen floor, the bar and a few cabinets, no trace of anything else. I started to move forward, and an icy palm grabbed my neck. I twisted around.

And again—nothing.

Backing up slowly, I tried to get to my chair. But something got at my back and shoved me to the floor, hard. I almost landed on the lighter, but managed to raise it over my head, stretching my arm so hard I nearly sprained it. I lay down there for a while, panting, and from the living room I could hear sounds of movement, like a hundred thousand of those things were climbing out of the book, crawling across the carpet, coming forward. I wanted to moan, but didn't dare make any noise. The lighter was growing hot in my hand, so I let it go out.

Instantly, a dozen thick limbs were on me, pawing and groping and tearing. Yelling, I flipped over and turned on the lighter again. Whatever had been there vanished.

And I understood—whatever foul beasts were stalking me, they were the night. Whatever they were, wherever they came from, they ruled darkness, and the only way I could keep them off me was a small plastic lighter which might run out of fuel any second. Pushing myself over against a cabinet, I gathered my courage and let the flame die. Time passed. I waited for the paws to touch me again, but they didn't. So great was my anticipation that I'd feel them, try to strike away the touch and find nothing there. I waited. And waited. After what felt like hours, I felt myself drifting away, felt sleep having its way with me. I sank down, swimming through black seas.

A claw touched my wrist.

I jerked awake, screaming and, flicking it on, shoved the lighter out. My kitchen, outlined in shadow, confronted me.

That was the way I spent the rest of the night. I kept the lighter on as long as I could, but every so often it would grow too hot to hold in my hand, and I'd have to let it cool. Then there would be peace again, until I almost fell asleep, each time getting closer and closer to the bottom of that black sea. Then something would caress my leg, or my neck, or my chest, and I'd jump up, shoving out the flame that had become my only hope of salvation. Eventually, an hour before dawn, they got smarter and started grabbing for the lighter instead of me.

When the sun rose, I was half mad. I ran through the

house, screaming, turning on all the lights, opening all the doors. I tried to sleep, but all I could think about was that space under my bed. It was only about a half-foot high, but completely black.

So now I am afraid. Always and constantly afraid. You ask me for answers? I don't have any. I only wish I did. A month ago I sent a letter to Edward's address, asking, demanding, begging for an explanation. All I got back was my envelope, unopened, with "Return to Sender" stamped on the front. Every night now, no matter how many lights I leave on, there's always darkness. And noises.

I never leave the house anymore.

Too many shadows. 回

Photo by Jared Smith

The City Wept

by Allen Scaife

He was sitting in his cubicle, staring into the blank face of an iMAC while the sweet, crooning sound of some meaningless icon of society dripped from his headphones, when it happened . . . the City began weeping.

It was nearly silent in its mourning. Buildings did not shed water or shift in their foundations as the tears fell to the concrete below. There was only the softest sound, a sound he felt in his chest rather than heard in his ears. It was distant, muffled thunder.

The tears fell in the form of pigeons.

The birds fell stricken from the sky, a dark, dusty rain of beaks and glossy iridescent down. They all fell at once and made no attempt to flutter their wings, to rise from their doomed plummet and fly again into the fogged air. They made no attempt to land upon the benches of the park, the buildings or the street lamps that dotted the sidewalks, lamps that had once shed a yellow haze upon people, who now never seemed to sleep, never seemed to eat, never talked, never loved, never felt.

Some landed on the street, but no cars ground them into the road. No cars ever drove anymore . . . the people only walked. They walked without real destinations, stepping over the City's tears without anything more than dazed expressions.

He was the only one who still saw the real world when he opened his eyes. Had he known that existence would be like this, he would never have left the womb. Had he had the choice, he would never have been born, never conceived, never been a gleam in his father's eye.

But he was, and now he had no choice but to survive in a crying City whose denizens had been drugged into a state of senseless delusion. The only pleasure they took was in seeing one foot move in front of the other as they walked the City's streets, alleys and sidewalks. As far as he knew, they were down in the subway systems like rats, scrabbling along the cold steel, hissing and sniffling as their breath created momentary ghosts.

At first it had been fun. He could do whatever he wanted, any time. He traveled the City, walking into convenience stores and walking out hundreds of dollars richer. He walked into a Food Lion and came out pushing a shopping cart full of boxes of powdered and chocolate doughnuts. He was sick all night.

The man did not spend his time wondering what had happened. He never asked why he was the only person in the City, in the world, who seemed to maintain free will. He simply accepted the change in life and stepped over the growing drift of pigeons, as did all the zombies.

Now he stands outside a church.

Now he stands outside a bank.

Now he stands outside a massage parlor.

Everywhere, it was the same. Everywhere, people whom he had once known, who had once slept, once ate, once talked, once loved, once felt, just walked with vacant expressions.

Everywhere, but here. Here, there was nobody to see, nobody who looked through him as if it was he who was a ghost, as if it was he who had no depth behind his gaze.

Now he stands on top of a great building, perhaps the tallest in the City. It's still cold, and humidity clings to the air like an invisible leech, sucking both the heat and the life and leaving only a filmy residue that clings to his hair, his arms, his face. But he likes it up here. It is true. It is pure. It is what the City was like before the tears started falling. He doesn't mind the cold, and the moonlight is refreshing.

The moon looks so close. It is wreathed in rings of many colors, complete rainbows created by reflected sunlight bouncing off a silver, sterile world where no zombies pace dreamily across a frozen City.

The man shakes his head and shudders. A pigeon had gracefully given up its life at the top of this building and lies at his feet. He looks at the bird with pain in his eyes. The City had given tears for the people who made its survival possible, and now the man cries for the tears of the City.

He bends and picks up the pigeon and begins whispering to it. He describes his life, his fears and the depths of his mind. The dead pigeon's feathers stir in his warm breath until the small creature's body grows hot in his hands. Its wings stir, but he can't feel it; his soul is in his words, in every emotion that bleeds from his heart and every phrase that bursts from his mind. His own body, beginning with his legs and slowly moving up, begins to feel numb, as lifeless as the now-struggling form in his hands had been.

"The moon," he whispers, opening his hands, "take me to the moon."

The bird leaps from his hands, and suddenly he is flying in a cold world above a dead City, where the silver moon lights the lost souls with lifeless luminescence, where the pale rainbows dance in the air, where the warmest body is that of a man on the tallest building, that of a man who now paces across the City with a blank expression on his face. And even this warmth is cooling rapidly.

The bird has no interest in the freezing City and coos once before it flies straight into the sky. Ten thousand stirrings follow its call, and the rustling of twenty thousand wings waving in unison break the silence of the air as the pigeons waken from their cold sleep to follow him into the sky. 回

6 I'll Call You:
Love & Friends Explored

Art by Brandon Childers

I'll Call You

by Daron Christopher

Ever have one of those moments when you don't feel like you're watching the world through your own eyes, but rather through some strange television, as if you can observe yourself from an outside angle? I've been on Earth an eternity—sixteen years—but I've only had a few of those moments. One was when I fell during a track meet, and for a brief instant, it was as if I could see myself lying defeated in the mud as packs of runners swarmed past me. Another was when my father told me we were moving, and I felt as if I could somehow see the shocked expression on my face. A third was that day at the ice rink.

It was snowing—not one of those miserable little drizzles or one of those freezing blizzards, but that nice, pleasant way it always seems to snow in Norman Rockwell paintings. Down the block, someone was playing an oldies radio station way too loud. Next to me, a blond-haired boy in need of a shave grappled with the complexities of eating a hot dog without dousing himself in ketchup. The rink was too crowded, especially considering the number of people who didn't seem able to go more than a couple of feet without crashing to the ground. But none of that mattered. There was only one person I could see.

I'd seen her plenty of times before, don't get me wrong. I remembered how once when I was working at the drugstore on Third Street (before it was torn down), I had come outside to sweep and she was standing on the corner drinking a soda. I'd never really thought about her before. She was just another face filed away in the memory banks with those unruly neighborhood kids and that nice old lady who always tipped extra on Saturdays. But then I'd never seen her in the snow, seen her skate, seen her glow like an angel.

The obvious thing to do, you're saying, is get off your hide, skate over and start a conversation. Well, that's easy for you to say as you hide behind your defenses of retrospect and anonymous designation as reader. But if you were me, actually confronted with this situation, you'd be paralyzed, too.

Why was it so hard? In the movies, Cary Grant would always just whisk in, give Rita Hayworth some goofy line, and it was happily ever after. You never saw Cary Grant sit in the snow and mutter about how he didn't have any courage. No, sireee.

That's when I thought about some advice my Aunt Jude told me when I was nervous about trying out for the school play. "Child," she said, "ya can't go through life bein' scared to do thangs. If ya ever find yo'self in a situation like that, just think in twenty years, do you wanna remember that ya took action, or that ya sat like a frog on a stump cuz you were scared?" (Southern dialects always look horrible in print.)

I'd never really thought that was realistic, but I considered it then. Suddenly, I saw myself slide straight across the ice. I kept flinching, waiting for the inevitable vision of me flying into the wall, but I didn't. I watched in awe as I skated right up to that girl, wrapped my hand around her waist and asked, "Mind if I skate with you?" I didn't even spit as I spoke. Heck, I almost sounded as cool as Cary Grant.

But the really incredible thing is that she didn't laugh or make a face or break away. She just smiled and skated along with me.

I watched as she and whoever that person was in my body sailed around the rink, laughing, talking, falling.

Just as time stretches out like an accordion during a last period class or a visit to the dentist, the minutes flew by, and soon I followed behind as she and that mystery guy walked along the dim streets paved with newly fallen snow. I listened as they made small talk, and he cracked jokes far too witty for me to have thought of. I stayed in the shadows, *just another star in the sky.*

Finally, they reached what I presumed to be her home. I was oblivious to the cold as they made some final small talk. Only one thing the guy said stood out: "I'll call you."

I'll call you.

She went inside, and he walked into the night, probably gone forever. That was last Thursday. Tonight is Tuesday, and here I sit, in front of the telephone, quite aware that I'll never pick it up. I have no reason to call her. She's not expecting a call from me. ▣

A Lesson in Medicine

by Alison Nguyen

I could taste the Jell-O in his worried frown.
I swear I could see dandelions in his dejected eyes.
There must have been something that caused it—
I certainly didn't plan it the way sitcoms do.
Was it the way the sunlight teased his ears?
Or the way it made his watch skip about the wall
that made a string inside me unravel
with hilarious hiccups of laughter
bubbles of laughter
laughter that grabbed me by the throat
and threw me off the chair
summoning tears that tasted like fountain water?
I'm sure the other room could feel it
the vibration that overtook my stomach
performing Riverdance *on my ribs.*
Suddenly—
I heard it faintly at first
mezzo piano guffaws from the sunken corner
swelling into an orchestra of hilarity.
His eyes became twisted lamplights.
I could see the dark cave of his throat.
we gasped for air between hysterical chortles
doing nothing more than provoking more
splendid irrationality.
I looked outside.
Dandelions must have covered the porch.

Sauce

by Erin D. Galloway

T he smell of the spaghetti sauce I stir and the sound of neighborhood kids playing in the streets no longer seem familiar. I remember the girl who existed only a few months ago. It was her wide blue eyes that took in the stucco buildings lining the streets and the mopeds zooming past her. All the sights and sounds seemed intimidating when he was not with her. Even the smell of the freshly baked bread and chocolate-filled croissants did not calm her; it only made her stomach rumble.

* * *

Like a guardian angel, he came up behind her and pulled her into his strong arms. He hugged her, the hug of a lover. Surprised, she nearly stumbled to the pavement. He laughed, a rich baritone sound. Avoiding his eyes, she smiled sheepishly, uncertain of how to act.

"Tengo hambre," [I'm hungry] he told her. *"Quieres almuerzo?"*

She nodded, and they made their way down the crowded street to the apartment. Ripe peaches lay on the table along with a long loaf of fresh bread and a platter of aged manchego cheese. The freshly squeezed lemonade offered a succulent twist to the cheese.

He ripped off a hunk of bread and devoured it while she savored the flavor of the aged manchego. She eyed a particularly juicy-looking peach, but before she could claim it, he had scooped it up and taken a bite. Juice escaped down his chin, and he laughed.

"I was going to eat that," she scolded.

"I know," he said, with that sinfully unrepentant smile. She tried to frown, but only succeeded in laughing. He rose from the table and came back with a glass of ruby-colored wine.

"This is to go with the cheese," he told her.

She looked at him, unsure about accepting the potent elixir. "Okay," she capitulated. He was right; somehow the cheese did taste better with the wine, more flavorful and rich. Strangely, the wine did not have an intoxicating effect. Rather, she noticed a curious lethargic feeling steal over her.

"I think I'll go take my nap now," she told him.

* * *

The sauce churns like the waves of the ocean. At the beach, she frolicked freely in the water, feeling safe knowing he was nearby. Suddenly, she felt something on her foot, and she was yanked under. She came up sputtering, and as soon as he surfaced, she splashed him. With a wicked grin, he dove and took her under again. She shimmied away and swam to his left, hiding behind one of their friends. When he surfaced, facing away from her, she made her move, pouncing on him and pushing him into the cool water. He managed to turn and pull them both up out of the water to tickle her mercilessly.

* * *

Staring into the bubbling crimson, the memory of the scarlet red dress stirs. He couldn't take his eyes off that dress. She'd put it on knowing it would impress him, and she was not disappointed with his reaction. His eyes had lit up as she entered the kitchen in that dress with gold, glimmering heels.

Downtown, they hopped from club to club. She was euphoric, moving her body to the rhythmic beat. He took her hand, and she was spinning, turning under his arm, turning again, and she found herself back in his arms. Laughter bubbled through her like champagne. The night floated by like a dream: him laughing and smiling, him dancing with her, him walking her home, him kissing her.

* * *

I stare again at the sauce I stir. It reaches its peak, bubbling to life, signaling it is done; it no longer needs to be over the heat of the red-hot flame. I saw him a few weeks ago. He walked up to me, smiling, and pulled me into his arms. This time, it was only the hug of a friend. ▣

Art by Cory Zwerlein

All I Want for Christmas

by Sean Power

The doctors said it was painless.
"They died on impact."
I, somehow unscathed, walked away from
The accident, the hospital, and any chance I
Might have had at living the American Dream.
The one thing that mattered the most to me
Ripped from my clutches.

It's this very time of the year,
The time when everyone's together
With their families, the time where
Gifts are exchanged with one another
In hopes of bringing the recipient some sort of
Artificial happiness, that tears me up.
If they only knew what it was like not to have
The most important ingredient to happiness,
To know that all the gifts and other such
Superficial crap in the world doesn't mean a damn
When you don't have the one thing that truly makes
Life worth living. To know the feeling that you would
Trade every last one of your possessions to have it back
But also know at the same time that it is not possible
That you will never ever see them again in this lifetime.
But you live.
The only thing keeping you going is the thought that
Someday you will be reunited, but you will wait.

Balding Angels

by Devon Wallace

He met Lindy in night school. He noticed her not only because she wore bright sweaters and looked startlingly like a freckled girl he had kissed in high school who tasted like Gobstoppers, but also because of her hair.

Her hair made her an immediate seductress—long, lush and thick, like a jungle. When she flipped her bright red ringlets over her shoulder, he would breathe the apple cinnamon into his lungs with a full breath.

Once Lindy spoke, there was significant disappointment. He had outgrown his love for ditzy girls. Lindy's hair was much more enticing than her voice. He had fantasies about her, about grabbing fistfuls of that hair and pulling down viciously. Red curls did that to guys like him, drove him crazy and made him shy, although that wasn't hard to do. All girls turned him inside out, shrunk him with their downward glances.

Lindy liked him because he was "sooo cute." Most girls did. They all giggled at him like he was a little boy with a pink balloon.

Lindy turned to him five minutes before class started on Thursday.

"What are you doing Saturday?" she asked. He thought

of her curls, not his medical exam or his dead mother's birthday. He smiled and moved his sweating palms away from his mouth, wiping them on his khakis, and answered, "Nothing."

"Great!" she said. "I was wondering if you would like to meet my friend Annie."

His palms stopped. He looked down at his textbook, squinting at illustrations of bloodless organs and trying to concentrate.

"Sure," he said with a shrug, brushing thick red hair from his mind.

* * *

This is ridiculous, he thought. *One-fifteen in the afternoon is a ridiculous time for a date.* He didn't believe in blind dates, hated setups. He caught his breath, held it and knocked on the door. He was still angry at himself for accepting, for washing his favorite shirt the night before just to wear it now, for shaving twice for a girl who was not Lindy. He was weak, he told himself now and then during the in-between moments. He knew the girl behind the apartment door must be able to hear his heart throbbing. It was such a predictable organ.

The door opened, and he looked down.

A girl looked up at him with a big smile, one of those warm ones. Her whole face smiled. She was tiny, and her "hi" sounded like a mellow chipmunk, high and sincere.

"Come on in," she said.

He smiled dumbly, took two big steps into the living room and immediately tripped over something that crunched. He grabbed at an armchair to regain his balance while, pulse bouncing, he laughed self-consciously.

She smiled and shoved aside the cardboard box that had caused his stumble. He took a quick glance around the room, and his eyes widened. The room was small and lit only by the cloudy sky that drizzled through the open windows. Big, comfy chairs stood in random places.

But it was not just excessive furniture that cluttered the room; even if he had wanted to walk to the sofa, he would have been blocked by box after cardboard box. From a distance the walls looked like the crispy skin of a shedding snake, but, squinting, he realized every last inch from ceiling to floor was covered with yellow strips of lined paper taped to the paper. The room was infested with paper; every chair, the huge cardboard boxes and the windowsills were stacked with paper, in scraps, in booklets and tight little balls. He stood ankle deep in them. He looked back at her and immediately caught a smile.

"I don't really know much about you. I actually don't even like dates, but Lindy was so insistent," she said. He laughed a little. Annie didn't like dates. The fact stuck in his head.

"I'm so sorry," she said after a pause. "I didn't mean that I didn't want to meet you. I just don't do dates. The 'impress me' stage is such a pointless one," she said cheerfully.

Something in her tone made him want to shout "Hear, hear!" like old men in movies.

Instead, he said, "I'm not quite a blind dater either. In fact, I feel very lost right now. I just . . . well . . ." He felt his ego slip, then looked at her and changed his mind.

"Hey, I have an idea. This won't be a date; it'll be a visit."

"Wonderful," she said, as if sighing. "So, come in."

She walked in front of him over to the chairs, and he heard the *scrunch scrunch* of paper crumpling under her feet. She didn't even try to walk around them. He kicked off his shoes and followed her to the largest chair.

"Do you want some coffee?" she asked.

"Yes, that would be great," he answered.

"I don't make very good coffee," she warned.

"Don't worry. I've had the worst of the worst, and I still like it. There is no such thing as bad coffee," he said.

"It was just a warning," she replied, disappearing behind the door. He followed her with his eyes and realized he was still smiling. He shifted in his seat, which felt bumpy, then heard a familiar scrunch and pulled a yellow sheet of paper from under his leg.

The room was dim and chilly like outside. He unfolded the yellow paper in his hand and admired her chicken-scrawl handwriting, the letters large and green.

"The blue-eyed boy lived in a land of glass houses."

He reread it, then laid it flat on the coffee table. "A land of glass houses," he mouthed.

She was walking back into the room, trying to hold both mugs and the sugar bowl without spilling. He jogged in two crunchy steps to her rescue. She put their coffee on the table a little too swiftly. Her mug landed right on top of the house-of-glass paper.

He watched her scoop sugar into her mug and stir slowly while a wet circle formed and moved across the page around the spot where her mug rested.

"You're a writer?" he asked. *Glass houses.* He couldn't get the words out of his head.

"Sort of. I'm not very good. I'm more of a collector." She sipped her coffee, grimaced and said, "I told you I make bad coffee!"

He lifted his mug, which had a big clown face on it, and took a sip.

"Oooh . . . well, it's not so bad," he said smiling. *What had she done?* he wondered. *How could anyone make coffee taste so terrible?*

"So, you're a collector?" he asked, setting his mug back on the table with a little bang.

"Yes, an idea collector. Doesn't that sound deliciously romantic?" she asked, leaning back in her chair and crossing her legs. She was wearing loose blue jeans and a coral sweater.

"Yes, it does," he smiled at her, then stopped. He changed his face to neutral. She looked at him deeply and blinked slowly, as if taking a deep breath.

"You think I'm a little crazy?" she asked cheerfully. He looked in her eyes and knew they were reading his.

"Yes, you're a little crazy," he said, meaning it. "But I think it is wonderful. I wish everyone could be as crazy as you."

"Don't flatter me," she said.

"Okay, in that case, this coffee is terrible," he said, laughing. She laughed, grabbed both cups and headed for the kitchen.

"Come on, you can help wash the dishes," she said.

Thunder clapped.

He followed her into the kitchen, which was startlingly

bright after the dim living room. The room was painted white and had a yellow fruit border along the top of the high ceiling. There was a circular skylight, and tall windows on the back wall were covered by lacy curtains with clashing orange flowers that danced around the room like a running girl's skirt. The crisp air brought the room to life, although it had a funny smell, like spring and stale incense. There were yellow sheets of paper taped to these walls, too, but they were prettier than the others. These blew around with energy, flapping like trapped butterflies. He inhaled deeply. She stood by the sink, which was separate from the counter and looked like the one in his old high-school art room.

"I'll dry!" he said, grabbing a towel.

"Fine," she said, rolling up her sleeves. She turned the water on full blast, stuck her hand into the stream and pulled back immediately, flicking icy water at him.

"Hey," he said, smiling. He stuck a sponge under the cold water and held it above her head threateningly.

"Oh, no, you don't," she said, giggling and trying to bat the sponge away. He held it high and laughed to see such a tiny person try to match his height. He squeezed the sponge and down came the water in little squirts. She shrieked, icy water streaming down her back, then punched him pretty hard for a mock punch.

Over steaming dishes, they talked about their families.

"My mother was very Catholic," she explained. "All the girls in her family had names of virgin saints. I was named after my grandmother, Mary Anne. My dad hated the name and refused to call me anything but Annie. When my sister was born, Dad insisted she be named something a little more sacrilegious. He named her Aurora after no one. My father, you see, was very religious, too, but in a different way. His meditation was a little less formal, but Mother did all the religious training, and I think that because of my name, I got more than Aurora. You see, there was always hope that a girl named Mary Anne might feel the calling. I still think that when you're listening for it, you can't hear it."

She went on, and he listened more intently than he could remember listening to any teacher. Her voice was strong. Thunderclaps grew increasingly loud in the rapidly dimming kitchen.

He talked about his mom. He rarely did.

"It's her birthday today," he said, and she turned away from the suds to look at him questioningly.

"She died six years ago. I miss her a lot," he said in a relaxed tone.

She nodded, her lips tight. He was picturing his mother all dressed up before Easter Mass.

"I can't imagine that anyone ever stops needing a mother," she said. He looked at her in awe. She had spoken the exact thoughts in his head.

He couldn't remember later how it happened, but they started talking about the Yankees World Series game they had both been at in '96, the one where the kid caught the ball and the Yanks won. He thought the kid was a hero, and she thought he should have been kicked out for interference.

Her fingertips looked like peach-colored raisins by the time the dishes had been washed, dried and stacked. The orderly dishes looked strange in the room.

288 □ Teen Ink

"Oh, no!" she suddenly yelled and ran to the window. A gust of wind had shoved the drapes back, and a heavy draft had swept into the room like a wave. Yellow papers fluttered as if begging for freedom; one near the window was violently torn from its tape and flew out. She slammed the window and he rose, watching the paper escape into the outside world. He felt wild. It had been an amazing escape, magical. He felt as if he were harboring a secret.

"That was beautiful," he said.

"It was," she agreed.

He picked up one of the yellow sheets that had not made it to the window.

He read some words from a song aloud, then started humming the song under his breath. He remembered his uncle singing with his pretty mother harmonizing. "Angels watching over me."

"My mom used to sing that as a lullaby. She really believes in angels. Do you?" she asked seriously, almost too dramatically.

"I'm not sure. I'd like to," he admitted, then asked, "Do you?"

"Yes," she said. "Not as white winged things with pretty voices and blond hair. I'm not even sure if I believe in perfection at all. But I think I have an angel. A friendly, old, balding angel who knows me really well and gives me a little smack when I stop being me."

"Annie, I can't imagine you ever having trouble being you," he said, smiling and glancing around the room that was inside out and backward.

"Oh, maybe not anymore, but look at this."

She grabbed her wallet and sifted through credit cards to a photo of a girl with Lindy's hair. He took it from her and glanced at it, startlingly unimpressed.

"She's pretty. Is she your sister?" he asked.

"Oh, no. That's me."

"No way!"

"Hey, I'm pretty," she laughed.

"Oh, of course, but you look so different here."

"Yeah, I used to dress up. I had hair then, too."

"I didn't recognize you with that hair."

"I cut it all off and dyed it last year. It was a very dramatic action."

He shook his head in awe.

She went on. "I was just so sick of it all. Everything became this gigantic fugue, all repetitive with silly random details. Everything just seemed so petty! So I went all out, like a hippy. Chucked my heels, office job, skirts and hair."

"Really. That must have been something!" As he said this, he reached into her fridge without thinking and pulled out a carton of milk. Realizing his action, he blushed, but she didn't even seem to notice

"No, not really. It's not like it wasn't the same me under the hair and lipstick," she said, dipping her finger into a jar of peanut butter. She paused to swirl the peanut butter around with her tongue until it gathered at the roof of her mouth, her speech slurring. "It just felt really nice not to be painted. It was like a hot shower at the end of the day. I felt so clean. It was the same me, just less sticky."

She giggled at her own irony and offered him the

peanut butter. He poured some milk into one of the washed glasses, still warm from the steamy water, and took a big gulp. He cringed, tasting the sour milk.

He dipped his finger and got a dollop of goo. He decided her peanut butter must have more sugar than his mother's. It tasted so good. He wanted apple juice, but didn't want to waste a whole glass of milk, even though it didn't taste good.

She took a gulp of his milk, swallowed and made an expression that made her face look like stretched Fun Dough.

"Blech! Why didn't you tell me the milk was sour?" she asked, pouring it down the drain. He smiled, relieved and amused.

"Would you like some apple juice?" she asked.

His surprise came like an adrenaline rush, so strong that a laugh escaped him.

"What is it?" she asked.

"You can read my thoughts! I was just . . . Oh, never mind."

She turned away and smiled, grabbed two big plastic cups and filled them to the top. She gave him one and said, "Cheers," tapping them together with a clunk, not a clink.

The thunder roared. They both held their breaths, frozen in place, loving the dramatic danger. The sky had turned close to a maroon color. It was beautiful.

I love her, he suddenly thought, then dismissed it. *What a silly idea. That's not how it happens.* He didn't believe in all that soul-mate crap. ▣

34th Street Sunset Boulevard

by Sarah Aksoy

Once I went stumbling
Through the black pavement of night
And found solace
In the fluorescent glow outside the corner diner
On 34th Street Sunset Boulevard
I took a seat on the brown plastic plush
Listening to the hushed conversations
Watching the drowsy waitresses
Tripping over orders and waiting for
1:30 A.M. cigarette break to come
The pale blonde a booth over adjusting her stiff locks
Ignoring the pie on the table
Exchanging lovers' whispers with a man with glazed eyes
Thoughts seem to drift from the clattering that escapes
The kitchen's stainless-steel double doors
Smell of fresh grease and bacon envelops the room
The night owls await their breakfast biscuits
A little brown-haired girl no older than four
Is pulling out her pretty braids, trying to stare over the table
At parents whose eyes tell me they're not really here
I listen to the soft slush of the traffic

Against the puddles outside
And watch the rain beating down against
Fogged-over windowpanes
Swallow my decaf
Feel the rich heat coat over my chest
I soak up the hot steam that touches my face
And remind myself that he doesn't love me anymore

Photo by Caitlin Tumulty

The Same, Only Different

by Joanie Twersky

And do you know what I heard some guy say?" Michael's pupils shrank, or the whites of his eyes grew, the way they did when he was angry, as they did so often—too often. This time I was just happy his eyes weren't shrinking as a result of anything I had done. Unfortunately, the poor fool who had not known better than to spurt ignorant comments in the presence of this shrinky-eyed boy had not been so lucky.

"No, Mike," I answered robotically, so used to these stories that the stupidity of mankind was no longer as utterly shocking to me as it had once been.

"He said that Julie deserved it! The dumb little schmuck said that Julie was a little whore and deserved it!"

All right, so maybe I wasn't shocked by Michael's latest report of ignorance at our high school, but I still had to sympathize. As easily triggered as Mike was, it still couldn't have been easy to overhear someone bad-mouthing your almost dead friend. Julie had been hit by a car two days earlier while trying to cross the street and had been comatose ever since. It would figure that Michael's first day back to school in almost forever, someone would say something dumb. I just hoped Mike hadn't hurt them too badly.

"So what did you do?" I asked cautiously.

I knew better than to judge or accuse him. I had to say everything just so to get the response I was looking for. If he felt even the least bit attacked, he would quickly go on the defense, and that would be it for civilized conversation. Yes, just one wrong move and it would be exactly 10.5 seconds before he was gone (three seconds for his eyes to shrink completely, two for him to shout something obnoxious, three and a half for him to spin around and walk briskly down my driveway, and two for him to jump in the window that he has left down for such occasions, rev his engine and peel out leaving the faint smell of rubber—a souvenir of the day's soap opera).

"I can't tell you," he said, suddenly shy. "You'll be mad."

I had to laugh. He was worried about me being mad. Seeing as I was not the one with the slightly beat-up sports car, mad or not, there was little hope for an even slightly dramatic exit by me. The best I had ever mustered was a quick 180, a toss of my long hair, and a "well, forget you," secretly hoping he would shout, "Sweetie, wait!" and come after me. I sighed. I really needed a car.

"I won't get mad," I insisted, already beginning to get mad. "Just tell me what you did."

"Let's just say, never tell me someone I love deserves to get hurt."

"Michael!" I shouted, growing impatient. "Stop stalling and tell me what you did to the boy." I had a sudden realization of exactly how many questions I ask that I already know the answer to.

"Well, I walked up to him and said, 'Excuse me, did I just hear you say that Julie deserved to be hit?' And then he said, 'Yah, the girl was a dumb slut. She deserved every bit of it.'"

"And then?" I prompted.

"And now there's a huge dent in the locker we were standing next to."

"Made by what, Mike?"

"The guy's back."

I sighed. I hated when I was right.

"Man, I was so mad!" he continued. "I was gonna kill the little . . ."

"What stopped you?"

Michael's face suddenly softened, and his eyes returned to their normal size, which he promptly hid by staring at the floor. I had to admit, even with all the grief this boy had caused me, he did have beautiful eyes.

"I can't tell you. It's embarrassing."

I rolled my eyes. "Why, Mike? Did you have to stop attacking him to go to the bathroom or something?"

He looked up suddenly, his face serious. "No," he stated emotionlessly. "I had to stop because of you. You were in my head!" he blurted out, sounding utterly confused and amazed that anyone could have moved him enough to affect his actions.

"What was I doing in there?" I asked cautiously.

"What are you ever doing in there?" he answered with a sigh.

"Sitting there looking pretty?" I asked hopefully, a bad attempt at lightening the mood. He ignored me.

"Lecturing," he stated, annoyed. "I mean, there I was, all ready to beat up this guy, when there you were, clucking at me."

"Clucking?" I asked, trying to stop the smile that was rapidly forcing its way across my face.

"Clucking! Not chicken clucking, you know, but that *tsk tsk* that people do with their hands on their hips when they disapprove," he demonstrated.

"But, I don't cluck!" I protested, annoyed that I was now going to be in trouble for hypothetical clucking.

"Well, you sure as heck did today!" he blurted, eyes beginning to shrink again. "Right when I was all ready to finish this sucker off, and not just for Julie."

"It's the principle," I muttered under my breath.

"It's the whole principle! No one deserved that."

"Not even the guy who said that about her?"

"Not even him."

"And it was your job to teach him that?"

"Well, someone had to."

"And my clucking stopped you?"

"Yes—no! Not your clucking, you! I mean, there I am, and there he is, and I'm all ready to, well, you know, and then I hear this little voice in my head."

"You always hear voices in your head."

"Yes, but this time it was your voice! It was all, 'No, Michael. Put the boy down, Michael. You can be better than that, Michael.'"

Once again I tried to muffle laughter—unsuccessfully, I might add.

"I'm sorry?" I offered, before letting a sort of half-laugh, half-snort escape me.

"You and your damn moral high roads! Always telling me I can be better. "

"You *can* be better."

"Don't tell me that! Don't tell me I can be better when I like who I am."

"Who you are hurts people."

"Only people who . . ."

"Who ask for it? No one deserves or asks for it, Mike. You said so yourself."

"I can't just let people get away with that sort of thing!"

"It's not like you don't have to say anything. You just don't sink to their level."

"Explain."

My mind wandered back to the afternoon van ride home. I had drifted off and awoke to find Amanda and Robbie discussing Lex, a freshman I had formed an attachment to and taken on as sort of a little sister. Most people looked at Lex and saw a flashy little kid whose clothes and personality screamed, "Give me attention." I looked at her and saw the most talented, beautiful person I had ever met, one whose life had thrown her lemons out of which she had proceeded to make strawberry daiquiris.

Upon awakening, however, the first words out of Robbie's mouth had been, "The girl's dirty. You couldn't pay me to touch her."

I spun around in my seat, suddenly wide awake. "What makes you think she'd touch you?"

Robbie snickered. "That's a laugh. Who wouldn't she touch?"

Annoyed, I looked to Amanda for support, generally the more reasonable of the two. Amanda looked down at the ground and then back up at me, apologetically. "Trina, you know I love Lex. She's my friend, too. But you have to admit, she is sort of . . . dirty."

I glared at them both, disgusted, before stating flatly, "I wouldn't open my mouth about things neither of you knows about."

From the look on their faces, I could tell they knew better than to continue. Robbie had quickly changed the subject. Now, as I told Mike this story, his gaze softened.

"But, see, that's what I mean! Didn't that make you mad?"

I smiled sadly. "I was ready to throw them both out of the van."

"I would have."

"I'm sure you would have, but the point is that I didn't have to. They got the message anyway."

"No, they just humored you. They'll be talking about her again tomorrow."

"Yah, but tomorrow they'll feel guilty. And that other guy will still bad-mouth Julie; he'll just make sure you're not around next time."

"You'd just better not cluck at me anymore."

"I've never clucked in my life!"

"You did today."

"In your head!"

"Same difference."

"Is not."

Our eyes met, and we held each other's gaze for a good ten seconds. His eyes had returned to their normal size, so I knew he wasn't really mad. Suddenly, a smile broke out, coloring his face. He threw his arms around me and pulled me close in a bear hug. He then drew back, leaving his hands on my shoulders and catching my gaze again.

"Why you put up with me, Trina, I'm not sure I'll ever understand."

I cocked my head to one side, carefully contemplating my answer. This wasn't a matter of editing my thoughts for him, as were most of my delayed responses. It was more that this was a question I had been asking myself for a long time and was beginning to understand the answer. I just wanted to make sure it came out right.

"I guess . . ." I started cautiously, "I really don't view us as being that different."

He looked confused, but waited for me to continue.

"We're like opposite sides of the same coin. Think about it. We both grew up with a lot of—well, you know, we both went through more than we should have. Too much. And then we reacted to it. For whatever reasons, I became a pacifist, a vegetarian and a sickeningly good Samaritan, and you became—"

"A little overly aggressive?"

I smiled. "Just a tad. But I went left while you went right. I listen to Cat Stevens and Billy Joel; you like Nine Inch Nails."

"You fix things with your free time; I break them?"

"The point is, who knows which random event it was in either of our lives that provoked us to take the directions we took? One different turn and it could have been you calmly telling off Robbie and me making locker dents with that guy's back."

I saw a faint smile on Michael's face—the smile of someone who knows he's being understood.

I continued. "I guess what I'm trying to say is, even though I don't agree with how you react to everything, we really are coming from pretty much the same place. Not putting up with you because I don't agree, wouldn't that be like punishing you for not turning out exactly like me? It just doesn't seem fair. I mean, you really are like me, just a little different."

He scooped me up and spun me around. "You do know I love you?"

"You've mentioned it."

"You're the best."

"I try."

"You don't have to try too hard. You know, if I have to have a voice in my head, I really don't mind that it's yours. Just don't cluck anymore."

His hand gently covered my mouth, and his eyes, now big and bright, were smiling teasingly. Hot and cold didn't even describe him. It was fire and ice.

"So, can I kiss you good-bye?" he asked hopefully.

I sighed, "Don't ask me hard questions."

"That's a no?"

"It is what it is."

"It's a no."

"Fine, it's a no."

"This must be the different part."

"Explain."

"You said that we were the same but different. This must be where we differ."

"Among other things."

"Among other things."

"Mike?"

"Yes?"

"About today . . . I'm glad you stopped, even if it was because of me."

"I'm glad you're glad."

"Call me when you get home."

"I will. And about that kiss . . . maybe one day I won't ask."

"Maybe one day you won't have to."

I watched him turn slowly and walk down my driveway. He instinctively grabbed onto the roof of his car, the way he has to lever himself through the window. Then he thought better of it, opened his car door and slid in. I watched him drive down the block, radio blasting, and I shook my head in a desperate attempt to express something I didn't quite have words for.

I dropped to the ground slowly, propping myself up on both elbows so I could stare directly up at the sky. The moon was beautiful, and it seemed to be trying to express what I couldn't. Light radiated from it and bounced off everything that didn't know how to contain it. *It's like the sun,* I thought. *Only different.* Satisfied, I leapt to my feet and quickly made my way inside. I had a phone call to catch. 回

Purple Monkeys

by Sarah Donovan Donnelly

One, Stephanie, the answer is just . . . one.
Obviously, Sarah, like, duh.

She smiles and plays my game.
Maybe because she understands me . . .
But probably because she's used to me
I often wonder how we fit together, like
A puzzle
The two of us, connected somehow
United by a shadow

Funny how I can't shock her.

The purple monkeys were out last night, Steph.
Did they eat the stars?

Again, she smiles and plays my game.
I wonder if she always will.
For my sake, I hope so.
So many memories . . .
The years blend together like a water-color painting.
Distinctly perfect from a distance,
Yet far more complex as you study it.

Yes, Steph, and the plum pigs.
They ate the pigs!?
Yes, They were insanely jealous
Oh.
It's okay, though, the monkeys know.
That's good.
I thought so. Hey, Steph?
Ya?
Do you know?
What the monkeys know?
The meaning of Life?
Of course, Sarah.
It's friends, Steph. Friends and purple monkeys.

Photo by Erica J. Hodgkinson

Wash Her and Dry Her

by Emily K. Larned

5 months ago right now i would have been across the street at that little italian restaurant. my friend angelo works there because his parents own it. his mother sophia is the chef. angelo is a busboy because he's only 17 & therefore too young to be an actual waiter who serves chardonnay & budweiser. angelo always smiles. he has to wear a white dress shirt with a black bow tie but then he wears black jeans that are frayed at the crotch & this blue & red indian beaded belt. alice & i always found this incredibly funny. but i guess best friends always find everything incredibly funny, right?

yeah, well, that's 5 months ago or whatever. maybe alice is in there tonight with q & angelo hanging in the back room where the pasta-making machine is, but i wouldn't know. i'm here in the laundromat.

it is a little seedy in here. the lime green tile on the floor looks like it is about to vomit. i'm sitting on the 3rd washer from the door, exactly an 18-square-tile distance. i know because i just counted them. the room is set up like some sort of confrontation between the machines. there are 10 rusty white metal washers on the left and 10 smudgy faced dryers on the right, the 2 species facing

each other. the smell of tide & clorox permeates everything, drying out my nostrils. i can taste the tartness on
the red bumps of my tongue. it reminds me of a drug
education/AIDS class we had the week before spring
break. this woman with bloodshot eyes & 17 braids of
stringy orange hair came in to tell us how to clean hypo-
dermic needles. i think it's twice in bleach & once in
water but i don't remember. alice & q were doing something hysterical at the same time so i wasn't paying attention to the woman but i don't remember exactly what
they were doing either.

there is a tingling of rusty cow bells as a middle-aged
man stumbles in the door, precariously balancing a yellow plastic laundry basket on his beer belly. i wonder
what size his pants are because he is huge. his pants are
green, blue & yellow plaid, the same type of plaid that
the rich private school girls wear in kilts fastened with
giant silver safety pins. he is wearing a white v-neck
undershirt. i am wearing the same shirt. this strikes me
for some reason as being highly amusing. as he lumbers
past me i can see a little hole in the left arm's seam.

"you girlie, got any detergent?" he slurred the last word
to sound something like detrgn.

i shake my head, "sorry, mister."

i don't have detergent with me, or quarters, and i
didn't come here stumbling under plastic baskets of my
father's underwear & jeans & button-down shirts. i have
a washer & dryer at home. i came here alone & empty-
handed & that is how i will leave too but what else is
there to do at 1:14 sunday morning? i can't go home. dad
told me he didn't want me home.

it's not like we have a bad relationship at all. he's not taking home some woman named tami or bunni, the type of woman who hangs out in front of the tattoo parlor 6 hours after it has closed wearing a dress so tight she might as well have had it tattooed on. it's not like he's best friends with jack daniels & comes home raging drunk & raging mad & just, well, raging like q's dad did that time i spent the night with him. my dad just doesn't like to see his 17-year-old daughter sitting on the black & white striped sofa in front of the black & white t.v. on a saturday night.

i bet that if i go home in half an hour he'll believe that i went to the annex with alice & q.

i bet the annex & the laundromat are the only places open right now.

i bet my dad doesn't think i go to the laundromat.

i guess i never would have bet that i'd be at the laundromat. especially 5 months ago.

but i can't bring myself to go to the annex or to the back room of angelo's closed restaurant or wherever i should or could be. i can't be with them. i just can't.

i guess i can't really bring myself to do anything anymore. i can't do my trig homework or the laundry at home. i can't hang with alice, with q, but i didn't want to realize it. i think alice liked q, you know, really liked him, & that put a strain on things. it seems a lot of things are strained & artificial with them now. or maybe it's not them at all & i just don't want to think about what could really be wrong—with me—because then it might really become true. i know that can happen because it has happened before. i am trying very hard not to think.

i feel someone watching me. i turn to the fat man 2 washers down on my right but he is reading the black, rubbed-off instructions printed on the bottom of the washer lid.

i think it must be the dryers on the other side of the room watching me. all 10 of them have their impudent smudgy faces turned to me, except for the 8th one, which is masked by a handmade sign stating in purple marker "out of order."

i know i have a sketchbook in my backpack. i have a yellow double-ended highlighter too but only the wide end works. i tear a sheet out of the book & look to the fat man. he is trying to light his cigarette with a blue plastic lighter. i can smell the lighter fluid. it reminds me of q. i write "out of order" on the page from my sketch pad.

i fold the sign over the front v of my shirt like a bib, jump off the washer, & walk out the door, trying very hard to ignore the screams of the cow bells behind me. 回

We Sat

by Leigh A. Johnston

We sat outside your roof
Counting minutes, seconds and falling star bits
The sun set sweet over our heads
When I started to slip into sleep, you ran your fingers
* over my*
Rib cage till I was laughing so hard I couldn't breathe
When he and I fought and I came to you in tears
You sang in barely a whisper
"You're better off without him . . . don't call him
He's breaking your heart . . ."
And my breath fell away from my lungs
When I sent you my fears of being alone
You reminded me how much I was worth and worthy in
* your eyes*
You always greeted me with crushing hugs that pressed
* our heartbeats into one*
Now I am better off without him
And I'd rather be with you
But that's okay, we're "just friends"
I'll be content with your smile . . .

Suffocation

by Carmen Lau

Em felt as if her anger would break her mind, split it into little shards of chaos. There was violence brewing in her, scorching her heart. She wished it would drown her senses in its torrid waves.

Em stared at herself in the mirror. She had pretty features and an honest look. She refused to look in the mirror in the company of others, fearing they would deem her vain.

She felt a wave of shame when a blush invaded her cheeks. Em's mind had, against her will, conjured up an image of him gazing knowingly at her, his grin hidden by a bouquet of wildflowers.

She picked up a piece of harsh soap and scrubbed at her face vigorously in an inane attempt to wash off the blush. Her face changed from pink to an unhealthy red.

It won't leave. It wouldn't leave. It wouldn't leave.

Her agitation compelled her to dig her nails into her flesh and drag downward to the tip of her pretty chin. Four white streaks screamed against the red. Little dots of crimson, deeper in color than her flushed skin, rushed to the surface and dappled the purity. Em's muscles relaxed, and she sighed in contentment.

No one wanted a scratched-up girl.

Again an image of him snuck into her mind, holding the bouquet of wildflowers, bowing to her and winking.

Anger and disgust simmered in the pit of Em's stomach.

"She's in love," they had said, exchanging knowing looks. They hadn't dared say it directly to her, but Em overheard them as she paused in the middle of a song.

Her aunts always chattered by the doorway, spying on her and giggling like schoolgirls at the very mention of his name. It was rather amusing, actually.

Whenever she had free time, Em would pound on the piano, completely immersed in the music. In the very heat of the moment, she would halt. Her aunts would freeze. Aunt Mary would purse her lips and look about the room, commenting on how lucky they were to get such a large television set at such an incredibly low price. Aunt Lilian would simply stare abashed at her furry-slippered feet. It was this way that Em first discovered that his intentions weren't entirely innocent.

Em was twenty-four, single, and a teacher at the junior-high school. Her aunts craved the company of "young people," and since Em's social life had dwindled to the two of them, she saw no problem staying with them and helping to pay the bills. She was the perfect subject for a romance.

People soon forgot their caution and teased her openly about him, since word travels quickly in small towns. Em flushed whenever these circumstances choked her, strangled her in the pure claustrophobia they could induce. Em could not help but blush. Everyone expected her to, and the more she tried not to, the more her body disobeyed.

He must have often boasted to his friends about how he had captured her. He had chased after her relentlessly, and now conquest was clearly in sight.

"I love you," he always said, as if repeating it would make it true. "And I know you love me, too. Someday, you'll realize it."

It was inevitable. He was the protagonist in his own little story, and the protagonist always got the girl.

Em wanted to cry out in shame. Vulnerability she had never felt before shook her insides and made her sick. Voices from the back of her mind told her there was no escape.

You'll submit, the prophets said. *You know you will. You might even fall in love with him, eventually.*

Em couldn't help but listen to the voices. She had heard them many times, and the accuracy of their divinations was something she used to be proud of.

Em could feel it coming.

Maybe I do love him after all, she thought. *Everyone says so. Everyone can't be wrong.*

It wasn't fair. This was subtle, quiet rape.

Em hated him. Oh, if only she found out what he was doing to her, Em would no longer have to suffer the cage walls that were slowly closing in around her.

She'll save me. When she comes, she'll save me.

"Em! Someone's here to see you!" Aunt Mary's singsong voice scratched against the very core of Em's heart.

"I'm coming!" Em again checked herself in the mirror, wishing she hadn't scratched herself. They would ask questions. Pointless questions always annoyed her.

Em took her time traversing the hall and entering the living room.

He was there. Aunt Mary and Lilian stood giggling behind him. They hadn't noticed the scratches.

"Well, time to leave the two lovebirds alone!" Aunt Mary winked and pulled Aunt Lilian outside. Em blushed, and he grinned at her obvious surrender.

They stood in awkward silence for a while. Em realized that he was studying her. She met his eyes. He smiled, as if he had already won.

Em suddenly had an urge to bathe, to wash off the shame clinging to her like stubborn patches of dirt.

"What happened to your cheek, Em?"

"Oh, nothing. It was an accident."

"Oh." He smiled again. He stepped closer, framing her face with his warm, rough hands.

Em found herself running in her mind, running to the open arms of a blurry, uncertain figure she so often saw in her dreams. The figure held her, and it was so good to be held that way, without the need to cringe at the conqueror's touch.

Don't worry. I'll protect you. It was a soft, beautiful voice. Em looked up and looked at the slightly shrouded and smiling face. No eyes. No need for eyes; she could see everything.

I'll never leave you, the shrouded figure said. She began to hum. Em thanked her between sobs, thanked her for taking her away from that horrible place. Em thanked her for saving her from suffocation.

I was waiting for you to come, and now you're finally here. Thank you, thank you, thank you. I want to stay here forever. Don't let me go back. Please, please, please don't let me go back there.

"Em? Is something wrong?"

His voice shattered the darkness. Em recoiled in horror as her savior disappeared, and he took her place. There was no shrouded figure, no comforting voice. Em was torn from the embrace. She felt a tearing inside, something rending and breaking and being ripped off from her very skin.

Don't go, don't go, don't go, please don't go.

She was gone.

Em wanted to cry again, in shame, in disappointment, in shock.

Why can't I cry?

She was too tired to cry.

He smiled. "It's okay, Em. I'll be here for you."

Why can't I breathe?

She was too tired to breathe.

"I love you, Em." He leaned in, his lips brushing lightly against hers.

Why can't I breathe?

She was already dead. 回

Portrait of a Pal

by Caroline Marie Finnerty

Mr. Rogers
His neighborhood,
oh, so enchanting,
my forever pal.
When I,
a mere three,
would sit one half an hour,
my eyes glued to the TV.
My mind, though,
wouldn't stay there.
Yes, it left to go on
outings.
Post office, bank, town bakery
The renowned trolley forever
rattling on the tracks
bound for the world of
make-believe,
carrying with it my flight
of fantasy.
Oh, the way he tied his shoes,
fed his fish!
sang his song!
And at the end of each

adventure, a song
about tomorrow.
But did he know?
Tomorrows and tomorrows gone by,
I would desert him?
Mock his shoes, and his songs,
too-tight cardigans,
languid posture.
As I let go of my childhood,
he remains.
Still a perpetual kid in the world of
make-believe.
Protecting the preschoolers
of today from
the real world, for as long as he can,
only to be
deserted,
in years to come.

Photo by Elyse Montague

Don't Call Me Dearie

by Lesley MacGregor

Please call me Alexandra. It's funny how much you can change in a short period of time. A month ago, I would never have asked you to call me that.

The old lady's name was Carine Bates. When her husband died, she said a part of her had gone with him. She decided to drop Lanigan (her husband's name) and was now just Ms. Bates. She lived across the street in an old, wood house that looked like it was four centuries old. The reddish-brown paint was peeling, her garden needed weeding, her lawn needed mowing, and there must have been thousands of jobs to do inside. The truth was she could not keep up such a big house; she never admitted it, but we all secretly knew. My mother got the idea that I should be the one to help ol' Ms. Bates.

Before I continue, you must know my reputation would never have allowed such a thing and, if it weren't for my mother, I wouldn't even have come in contact with the old lady. I had a reputation for being the biggest, meanest, toughest kid in my entire school. I have always hated the name Alexandra, so I shortened it to Alexis—a much tougher name. My auburn hair was usually tied back with a bit of string, and kids said they would shudder when they looked into my intense green eyes. I have always been much taller than other kids, and I used my height to my advantage. I wanted to be cool and tough.

I remember the time I picked on Christopher Meeks. He was a short, overweight kid with bright red hair and freckles. I remember shouting across the playground, "Hey, Carrot Top, your fly's down!" Of course, his fly wasn't really down, but he bent over and inspected it. I started to laugh, and he got as red as his hair and slunk away. I felt badly for a few moments, but pushed my emotions aside when I heard others laugh. It was weak laughter at first but, as I smiled, the laughter became louder. Then, I felt powerful and told myself I didn't care what happened to him. If taunting Christopher made me cool, I would do it. I lived for my reputation at school.

So, you can understand how panic-stricken I was when I heard my mother had arranged for me to help Ms. Bates every weekend. I wanted to die for two reasons. What would the kids at school think if they found out I helped a little old lady? My reputation would just evaporate. All I had worked for would go down the drain. My other reason was that I was secretly scared of Ms. Bates. I thought she was a witch. She barely ever came out of her house and, when I went past it, I would hear her singing. She never did things all the other old ladies in our town did. She never sat in the park and fed the pigeons. She didn't invite women over to play cards or drink tea. She didn't even attend parties or go to plays. She talked to herself and had a black cat (well, not totally black, but black enough).

It was a Friday afternoon, and I was supposed to go tell Ms. Bates I would see her Saturday. I was a bit nervous, but not really. Okay, I was really scared. This would be my first encounter with her, and I was not looking forward to it. I knocked gingerly on her front door. I waited for ten seconds, decided she wasn't there and was about to go home when the door opened.

"Why, hello there, dearie!" she cried happily. "Please come in." She opened the door just wide enough for me to enter.

I stepped inside, not knowing what to expect. The first thing that struck me were the paintings. There were dozens hanging on her walls. I didn't know she collected art. I looked closely at a picture of a vase of flowers. They were pastel colors, pinks, blues and yellows. The vase was on a table, along with books and a pair of reading glasses. I had to admit it was pretty good. I looked in the lower right-hand corner and saw the initials C. B. L.— Carine Bates Lanigan. She didn't collect art; she painted it. I glanced around the hall and discovered all the paintings were by her.

"This way, dearie," she called. She ushered me into her spacious kitchen. The first thing I noticed was that this probably was the room where all the action happened. It was painted white with soft, lemony-colored flowers. From the ceiling hung flowers in wicker baskets. A round white table with two chairs stood in one corner; a stove and sink were crammed into the opposite corner. Cabinets that reached the ceiling were stacked with silverware, dishes and china. In the middle was space— nice, wide-open space. My tennis shoes squeaked on the wooden floor, and I shuffled after Ms. Bates with my eyes on the ground.

"Would you like a cup of tea, dearie?"

I nodded, still looking down. Ms. Bates was a small, round lady with more lipstick on her teeth than anywhere else and glasses that hung around her neck. She wore a brightly colored skirt that had a gypsy look to it. A gray, baggy sweater reached past her waist. The skirt and sweater didn't really go together, but they had a comfortable, relaxed look. When the kettle began to whistle, Ms. Bates poured our tea.

"Here you are, dearie. A nice cup of tea. Would you like milk or sugar?"

"My name is Alexis," I said, through clenched teeth. She kept talking to me as if I was three years old! I was the girl everyone admired for being big and tough. Why should this old lady treat me as if none of that mattered? If there was one thing I hated, it was being called "dearie."

"Why, of course it is, dearie," she responded. "Would you like sugar?" she asked again.

"I always have sugar in my tea," I mumbled.

"Very well," Ms. Bates replied. After our tea, Ms. Bates insisted that I have a tour of her house. The house wasn't very big, and the tour certainly shouldn't have taken as long as it did, but Ms. Bates was determined to show me every nook and cranny.

"This is the guest room," she said as we entered. "My father used to sleep here, but when he died, I turned it into the guest room. Now you see that chair over there?" she asked, pointing to a dusty chair in the corner. "That used to be my mother's. Her room is down the hall, but when she died . . ." I blocked out Ms. Bates's voice. I now knew more about her house than I cared to know. I didn't care that this chair used to be in that room and the dresser had been passed down by four generations. I rudely interrupted.

"I want to go home," I told her. She looked at me and sighed. She seemed disappointed that I wanted to leave.

"Well, I suppose we will just return to the tour tomorrow."

"Humph," was all I said.

"If you'll follow me, I will show you out."

"I don't need your help," I insisted as I barged past her and marched down the stairs. I didn't care that I really didn't know my way around. I got down the stairs and into her kitchen, but couldn't figure out where the front door was when Ms. Bates entered.

"How old are you, Alexandra?" she asked calmly.

"My name is Alexis, and I'm eleven years old," I mumbled to the floor.

"Well, the door is just down the hall, and you just give a holler if you need more directions," she said. I raced down the hall and slammed the front door. I didn't look back until I was far, far away. Something about that old lady unnerved me. The fact that I could scream, shout and make a fuss without her yelling back amazed me. I was as rude as could be, and she still remained her happy, cheerful self.

The next day, I was doomed to go to Ms. Bates's doorstep once again. I knocked twice, and Ms. Bates answered.

"Hello, dearie! It's so nice to see you!" she exclaimed with a smile on her face. *Wish I could say the same,* I thought. I suddenly became fascinated by my shoes.

"Hello," I muttered feebly as I stuck my hands deep in my pockets. We walked into the kitchen, and she poured me a cup of tea. All of a sudden, my curiosity got the better of my shyness and I asked, "Do you care if you're cool?"

She looked at me thoughtfully for a moment. "No, I don't. That's why I don't do the things everyone else does. As long as I'm happy doing what I do, I couldn't care less about what they think. Do you care, Alexis?"

"Well, no. Well, kinda yes," I admitted. This was the strangest person I had ever met. She was so unlike me. I stirred my tea and slurped loudly. But she didn't get mad and didn't care what others thought, so, from my standpoint, she wasn't human. She didn't utter a word—she only peacefully looked out the window. This day went by more quickly. We finished the tour of her house, and I was busy thinking about what she had said.

When it was time to go, I was looking at all the flowers when I noticed a vase that didn't have any blossoms. The buds were all wrapped up, as if trying to hide from the world. I studied them and Ms. Bates whispered, "Sometimes, the flower that blooms last will be the most brilliant." I left, eyes still glued to the floor and my hands still in my pockets.

On Sunday, I arrived at her house for the last time that week. I shuffled in and took my seat at her table in the kitchen. After tea, she asked if I would like to help her outside. I shrugged, which she took for a yes. Her lawn desperately needed help. I picked up her rake and began. We barely spoke, but I broke the silence.

"Why don't you care if you're cool or not?" I asked, not stopping my work or looking at her.

"Dearie, when you get to be my age, being cool just doesn't matter. You have so many other things that are important, that being cool is simply not an issue." She had stopped weeding her garden. "I like to garden and paint and do things around the house. Do you have anything special that you like to do?"

I cocked my head as I thought. "I used to collect stamps," I said wistfully.

"Then I think it's high time you got a hobby," she said and walked toward her house, forgetting all about the weeding. I dropped my rake and followed. We went upstairs into her father's room. She opened a drawer and brought out a cobwebby box. She blew dust softly in every direction. "This used to be my father's," she said. "He was a great collector of buttons." I leaned over her shoulder and positioned myself for a better look. I didn't know they made so many styles of buttons. There were big ones and little ones, square ones and round ones. The colors included black, red, blue, yellow, tan and white plus a few other colors, but I didn't know their names. Ms. Bates dumped them on the floor and began sorting them by color. I grabbed a handful and studied them closely before sorting them. Our conversation came quickly and easily.

"Would you please pass that blue one? Yah, the one by your foot."

"Are there any more red ones? Stand up so we can

check." We laughed at the button that looked the strangest and cried for the one that was alone.

Then, we were interrupted by someone knocking on the door. It was my mother. We had lost track of the time. I scooped up all the red square buttons and held them out to Ms. Bates. She put her hands over mine and said softly, "This is your hobby now." I smiled and gently placed the buttons back in their box. I walked slowly down the stairs with the box under my arm, not sure at all that I wanted to leave. I was on her doorstep and turned around to face Ms. Bates. "Good-bye, Ms. Bates. Thank you for having me," I said as I looked her in the eye for the first time. I extended my hand toward her. She looked at it for a moment, then embraced me. I held on tightly and buried my head in her shoulder.

Ms. Bates smiled and said, "You are welcome any time, Alexandra." Then, out of the corner of my eye, I noticed the vase of flowers, the one with all the buds. One had opened. 回

Art by Casey Fuller

Dragon

by Emily Tersoff

Jaina sat at a table in the adult section of the small Harperstown Public Library. A blank piece of paper, a soft pink eraser, a sharp pencil and a box of sixty-two colored pencils sat in front of her. Every librarian there knew her, and they smiled as they walked past her, returning books to the shelves.

When she was sure everything she needed lay on the table, she began to draw. At first there were just a few light marks for the outline, but those were soon darkened. Claws, scales and shadow were added, as well as the background. Then she began to color it in. Hours passed, and by the time she needed to go home, her drawing was complete.

Mrs. Jones, one of the librarians, asked softly, "May I see your drawing?"

Jaina nodded and handed her the paper. The silver-haired woman looked for a moment, examining every fine detail through her bifocals, then commented quietly, "I think this is the best one yet. You're quite a talented artist."

Jaina smiled. "It's a Great Blue," she explained. "Her name is Garowyn."

Jaina had a habit of naming her dragons. She had a

whole book of her drawings. Just then a young man came in asking where the science fiction books were. Mrs. Jones gave Jaina an apologetic look before leading the man to the other side of the room. She didn't mind. She needed to get home anyway.

She gathered her tools, put them in her backpack and turned to get her picture. When she looked over, however, she yanked her hand back in alarm. There, standing on the paper, was a dragon no larger than the white sheet it stood on. Its scales were a bright, deep blue with a sprinkling of violet, green and gold; its eyes were two oval pools of darkness, just like the dragon in her picture.

Hello, came a voice in her head. *What are you?* Jaina stared at the miniature Great Blue. The dragon gazed back. "Can you read my thoughts?" she asked softly.

Only if you let me, came the reply.

She nodded, then muttered, "Why do I have the feeling you're not just going to disappear when I turn around?"

You created me. When you drew me, you put a little of your soul into me, and I came to life. That's why I looked so much more real than your other dragon pictures. Now I must find a way to go home.

"Home?"

To the Dragonlands. Please help me find a way there.

Suddenly, Jaina was worried. She wasn't sure if she wanted Garowyn to leave. "If I help you get to your Dragonlands, can you ever come back?" she asked warily.

In a way. It's hard to explain.

Jaina sighed. "I guess you can stay in the weeping willow tree in our front yard."

A crying tree? Is it sad?

Jaina laughed. "They're called weeping willows because their branches hang down really low, at least that's what I think."

Then a strange thing happened. Jaina felt a weird sort of tingling, but then it was gone. She looked at Garowyn, surprised. "Did you just read my mind?"

The dragon nodded. *You love your crying tree, don't you? I will be careful there.*

Jaina smiled at her new friend.

* * *

The next morning Jaina went to the weeping willow in her front yard where Garowyn had spent the night. The tree's branches hung so low that their tips brushed the ground with the slightest breeze; the leaves rustled against one another and made a whispery kind of music.

She parted the branches and crawled in. There, on the soft, springy grass, was Garowyn. When Jaina asked her how she had slept, the small dragon replied, *I had a vision.*

"Of what?" she asked excitedly.

A Great Blue elder. He told me that to enter the Dragonlands, we must make a net of grass so finely woven it can hold liquid. When we fill it with water under a full moon, we shall see the Dragonlands reflected. Then I must go through the water, and I will be home.

"A net of grass that can hold water? How on Earth are we supposed to do that? And by tonight, too!"

Garowyn patted a mound of long grasses beside her. *The crying tree is magic, and anything within the circle of its branches is, too. We can use these grasses, and the tree's sap will hold together its edges so it doesn't unravel.* Jaina sighed and took some of the grasses. While Garowyn kept the pile growing, Jaina wove the strands together. At noon, Jaina's mother made her come in for lunch, saying, "I worry about you spending so much time out there in that tree."

Not wanting her mother to worry, Jaina spent a long time eating her ham and mustard sandwich, then tried to make her mother feel better by playing a game of Chinese checkers.

Later, when the net was finished, it was roughly four inches square. While the sap dried, they stuck sticks on the corners to hold it off the ground. It looked like a cross between a hammock and a table. That night, Jaina snuck downstairs and filled a pitcher with water, her heart pounding. She wasn't sure how much the net would hold, and she didn't want to take any chances on something this important.

Outside Garowyn was waiting. The net was directly under the moonlight and, when Jaina poured the water in, the net filled quickly and did not leak. The glowing full moon was still reflected in the water. Garowyn dipped her claw in, but the reflection didn't change. After what seemed like an eternity, the water rippled on its own and instead of the moon in the water, there were emerald forests, rocky mountains and sparkling blue water. Even though she had been warned, Jaina was still awed. Garowyn turned to her new friend. *I must go now, Friend Jaina. My home awaits. Promise me that you will not be too sad, for all shall soon be clear.*

With that, the small dragon flew up and spiraled down, slowly shrinking, so that by the time she touched the water she was two inches long—three including her tail.

"Good-bye," whispered Jaina, just as there was a flash of light. When she looked again, all that remained of the net was a clump of wet grass, four sticks and a piece of amber the shape of a dragon's claw.

She picked it up and closed her eyes. To her utter astonishment, she found herself riding Garowyn, now a full-sized Great Blue dragon, over the patches of shifting emerald, sparkling blue, and hard gray and brown. After a long while, Garowyn set her down in a cave and told her, *Wherever you are, simply hold the amber claw in your right hand. Close your eyes, and you shall be in this cave. Now, you must return home and go to sleep, for only your spirit is here, not your body.*

When Jaina opened her eyes, she realized the dew had soaked her clothes, so she went to bed. That night, Jaina slept with the claw under her pillow and dreamed of blue dragons with sprinklings of green, purple and gold scales who called her "Friend Jaina." ◙

Little Red Riding Hood: The True Story

by Brent Robitaille

I t was a beautiful spring day. The birds were singing, and the grass was green as could be. I, Cornelius Wolf, was going for a peaceful stroll along the path that led past my den. I make it a habit of doing this, especially since I have been gaining weight steadily in my old age.

So on I walked, enjoying the fresh air and peaceful woodland sounds. Suddenly, I heard something extremely strange—the voice of a little girl singing. I must admit that I was intrigued, since I had never met a human before. I simply had to investigate.

I followed the voice until I came to a clearing where the little girl was walking. She was quite young, probably only eight or nine years old. She was wearing a little satin dress, which was covered by a red hooded cloak. She was also carrying a basket that smelled of delicious baked goods. Slowly, I walked up to her.

"Hello, little girl. If you will excuse me, I really must introduce myself. My name is Cornelius Wolf. I was passing through this area on a stroll, and when I heard your singing, I was intrigued. I sincerely hope that you will not think me rude, but I was not aware that there were any little girls in these woods."

I think I really took her quite by surprise. She did not say anything for a full thirty seconds, but simply stood staring at me with her mouth hanging open. Remembering that a human was a rare thing in this area, I excused this moment of rudeness.

Finally, she overcame her shock and responded to my salutation. Her response, however, was certainly less than neighborly.

"Get away from me, you big dumb animal!" she screamed in a shrill voice that turned every eye in the woods toward us.

I looked slowly around, thoroughly embarrassed. Determined not to let her win, I softly returned, "I was simply trying to be friendly. You are, of course, welcome to go on your way. But, before you go, could you be so kind as to tell me where you are going?"

Reluctantly, she told me she was going to her grandmother's house to bring her some food to help her through her illness. Excited by the thought of actually meeting another human, I offered to go with her. When I put the question to her, it seemed as if I would get an instant refusal. At the last moment, however, I saw a vicious little light appear in her eyes.

"Well, sir," she said sweetly, "you are welcome to come, but it is a long trip."

Convinced that she had had a change of heart, I immediately accepted. And so we left.

The trip to grandmother's house was quite long indeed. As a matter of fact, we soon came to a part of the woods

I had never seen before. The girl's conduct was vastly improved from our initial moments. As soon as we were under way, she introduced herself as Red Riding Hood. As we walked, she chattered on happily about one thing and another—the blue sky, the green grass, the fresh air. She also apologized for her rude conduct earlier, saying that she was simply frightened.

"But we're friends now, aren't we, Mr. Wolf?" she asked sweetly. I heartily agreed, delighted to be in the presence of an actual human. When she thought I wasn't looking, however, that vicious look returned to her eyes. Puzzled, I assumed it was nothing.

After what seemed like a lifetime of walking, we came to a patch of berries. With a cry of dismay, she exclaimed, "Oh no! How I would love to pick those berries for my grandmother! My hands are full with this basket."

Only too glad to help, I offered my assistance. The girl readily accepted my offer and stood aside as I moved up to the bush. I picked thirty berries, but when I turned to hand them to my companion, she was gone!

I stood, bewildered, for a while. Why would she leave me here? I had no idea where I was or how to get home. Finally, I convinced myself that the girl had to leave, and, for some reason, could not tell me why.

The problem remained, however, that I did not know how to find my way home. I certainly could not stay here all day. So I decided to try and find my way.

I walked for what seemed like an eternity, but I did not see anything familiar. Finally, I came upon the semblance of a path. I followed it until I came to a clearing. In the center was a cottage.

Thinking that I could ask for help, I knocked on the door.

"Hello?" answered a feeble, quavering voice. I politely answered, "Hello. My name is Cornelius Wolf. I was wondering if you could help me find my way home."

"Come in, young man," answered the voice. I slowly entered the one-room house. Simply furnished, it was neat and orderly. In the bed was a little old lady. I approached and said: "Ma'am, I was wondering if you might tell me how I could get to Pinewood from here."

The lady responded, "Young man, I have no time for such things. Can't you see I'm dying?"

Shocked, I asked her, "Is there anything I might do to help?"

"I am afraid not. My time has come. I only wish that my granddaughter, Red Riding Hood, had been here to share my final moments with me. She will be devastated when she finds out I am gone."

"You are Red Riding Hood's grandmother? I met her when she was on her way here."

"You are a friend of hers? Please, do this for a dying lady: Do not let her know that I am gone. I simply can't bear to imagine her dismay when she finds out she just missed my passing. Please, promise that you will do that much for me."

"Of course, ma'am," I answered. And with that, she died.

I realized I had little time. Red Riding Hood would be here at any moment. Quickly thinking of what I could do to keep her from finding out, I came up with only one solution: I must pretend to be her grandmother.

I found a nightgown in the lady's trunk. I put it on and respectfully put the body of the lady into the box. Suddenly, I spotted the girl through the window, approaching the cottage. Realizing that I had little time left, I dove under the covers just as I heard a knock at the door.

Doing my best to emulate the voice of the lady, I responded with a feeble, "Come in." The girl entered and did not seem surprised that my face was almost completely buried under the covers.

"I brought you some food, Grandma."

"Why, that was very nice of you, dear."

"You look very different today, Grandma."

"Oh? It must be because of my illness."

"Yes, maybe. But what big eyes you have!"

"The better to see you with, my dear."

"And what a big nose you have!"

"The better to smell you with, my dear."

"And what big teeth you have, Grandma!"

"The better to eat with, my dear!"

"Wait a minute! Now I know! You aren't my grandmother! You're the mean old wolf that I saw in the woods! Help! Help!"

Realizing that my ruse had been discovered, I leapt out of the bed to comfort her and tell her the truth about what had happened. She was much too disturbed to listen, however, and kept crying for help. Unfortunately, a passing woodsman must have heard her, because he burst into the cottage, an ax in his hand. Seeing me with the crying girl, he must have misunderstood and thought I was attacking her. The next thing I knew, he had chased me out of the house, and I was fleeing into the safety of the woods.

I ran until I was tired, and by then he must have abandoned the chase. I learned a lot that day. I learned that I would never speak to strangers, human or not. I also learned never to interfere in the affairs of others, but simply to stay in my den and enjoy the peace and solitude of my home. And that is exactly what I have done, all these years.

That is the way it really happened. ▣

Art by Marcus Begay

Fairy Tale Monsters?

by Adam Masters

My legs danced upon the thin strands of my domain, each step carefully selected. I made my way toward the outer rim of the network. Something had rustled one of my supporting ferns; I went to survey the area. To my surprise, a human girl had sat down beside me—humans did not often venture this far into the undergrowth. I watched as she carefully spread out her blanket, smoothed it and began to set out a picnic lunch for herself.

I gazed skyward. The sun shone with a fierceness not often seen in these parts. As it permeated its surroundings, it seemed to lift the moisture right out of the ground, giving the air a soft, damp feel. Perfect fly weather. I might have been able to catch six, maybe seven of them that day, but something about the girl commanded my attention. I had to get closer. Hesitantly at first, and then with gusto, I began my way down the fern and onto her blanket. She had put down a bowl of curds and whey and was searching about for a spoon.

My body convulsed as she screamed; I quickly assessed the area for danger but found none. My head whipped around to look at her, and I discovered she was looking right at me! I had known humans were prone to fearful behavior, but I had no idea it was so pervasive in their attitudes. A quick side step was all that saved me from an untimely end—her hiking boot struck the ground I had been occupying. What a feisty girl! It was such a vicious, depraved attack on one so small as myself, and harmless as well. Her parents should be ashamed of such a whelp. I know it now—humans are not to be approached; they are just too treacherous. ▣

Bess and the Beanstalk

by Kyle Brenneman

My name is Bess, but you are more likely to know me as the bovine from Jack and the Beanstalk.

My life started peacefully enough. The proprietor of this establishment, Jack by name, seemed a reasonable fellow, if not terribly bright. We had a symbiotic relationship, wherein I provided dairy products and he provided room and sustenance.

Jack's mother, whose name was never revealed to me, was truly an arrogant shrew. The hell-spawned woman never missed an opportunity to berate the poor young man. She was also greedy beyond all reason. Now, I'll grant you that most humans are, but she surpassed any other creature I have had the misfortune of encountering.

One day, this woman commanded Jack to take me to the market and sell me. Knowing this woman's greed, I had expected this, although it still seemed a short-sighted decision. Milk production fluctuates based on many factors. By my own estimation, I would start producing "acceptable" amounts of milk in four to six days. Nevertheless, Jack, looking very apologetic, tied a rope around my neck and led me down the road to the marketplace. I followed, commencing the "big dumb animal" routine I had honed to near perfection.

In roughly three miles we came across an elderly human. He (or possibly she, I could not tell) was cloaked from head to toe in ragged textiles of every sort. The apparition hailed Jack, who approached. Disobeying orders, from a stranger or otherwise, was something of a foreign concept to Jack.

The apparition, a humanoid character hunched over as if fighting a cold wind, explained to Jack that, in exchange for me, he would bestow upon him a small handful of what appeared to be lima beans. He claimed they were somehow enchanted, although he would not state the exact nature of the enchantment, dodging the question quite skillfully. I knew that no such enchantment could exist, but Jack was not nearly as well versed in the biological and physical sciences because he had spent much of his life with his mother thinking for him.

Jack was both intellectually and psychologically ill-equipped to function outside of his agricultural milieu. Needless to say, Jack accepted the creature's offer and returned home. It would seem my story might end here, but the creature now resold me (at a considerable profit) to a farmer with a residence not far from my point of origin.

As it turned out, I received word of nearly every happening at my former home, and so discovered that Jack's mother had given him the shrieking of his life. The shrew had thrown the beans out her back door and sent Jack to his room without food. As I understand it, Jack was released from his confinement when an enormous plant sprouted from the earth and grew at an incredible rate. The plant grew straight up, and within minutes, its top was beyond sight.

Although this is difficult to believe, the plant managed to snare and even support an enormous structure that was, until then, in low orbit. The structure fell a fair distance until a small outcropping on the plant stopped the building's descent. Amazingly, the structure survived the impact with minimal damage.

Back on the ground, the roots of the plant dislodged a fair portion of the house's foundation, and its two occupants were barely able to escape before it collapsed. Jack's mother commanded Jack to climb the plant, apparently intending for him to check the area on top.

Jack did as he was told, climbing with surprising dexterity. What transpired in the orbital structure has been debated ever since, but after several hours, Jack came back down with a small harp in his pack and a bird cage housing a Canada goose clipped to his belt. He reached the ground and explained to his mother that the harp could make sounds without being played, and that the goose could lay eggs of solid gold.

Now, the harp story I might believe. One could construct such an instrument with a mechanism concealed in the frame that would make the strings vibrate. It would take precision, but it could be done.

A goose, on the other hand, could do no such thing. Genetics and evolution aside, the energy that would be required to deconstruct the atoms making up the bird's feed and rearrange the subatomic particles in the form of gold is beyond human capability. Needless to say, the goose never laid any golden eggs, although it did lay eggs of a light brown color.

Despite common beliefs to the contrary, Jack and his mother lived in poverty. Jack's mother continued to devise a multitude of "get-rich-quick" schemes, and Jack continued to carry them out. Eventually, the local home-owners' association got fed up with the enormous plant (still growing, albeit much slower), especially its roots, which had begun destroying buildings. I organized a group of other herbivorous creatures, mostly ungulates like myself, and we converged on the growth.

We realized that this plant could provide sustenance for all of us for quite some time. We began eating the lower areas, hoping to make the entire plant fall, thus providing a more convenient form. It did fall, although a very large human came down with it. This giant, possibly suffering from some sort of growth or malfunction of the pituitary gland, rose with an expression quite like Jack's and wandered off. Few claim to know his current whereabouts, and those who do continuously disagree.

Jack was later impaled on a coiled spring in the process of disassembling the harp to see how it worked. His mother, as loud as always, managed to ward off death for at least another forty years, when she was driven out of town by the neighbors. She may yet live, and if she does, you would be well advised to avoid her at all costs. ▣

Hansel and Gretel, Transformed

by Elayne Russell

Once upon a time
A lifetime, a millennium, a fortnight ago
In an age when life was simple
And stepmothers were invariably evil,
The business of living continued
With small pauses to fill in the
Oversimplified moral at
The end of an impossibly unreal story
That even a fairy would be loath to admit ownership of.

Such is the epic of Hansel and Gretel.
A terrible economic downturn had occurred in the forest,
(A mere depression, nothing a few tax cuts couldn't fix)
And there was not enough food to go around.
So Hansel and Gretel's stepmother convinced their
*   father—*
A loving, caring, hungry man—
To lead his offspring deep into the woods
And abandon them there.
It was a win-win situation for everyone
Except maybe Hansel and Gretel.

So the close family unit set off into the deep green yonder.
Scheming Hansel, however, had overheard his parents'
  diabolical plan
(Kids in those days were always eavesdropping)
And dropped bread crumbs along the path
(After all, he was only a child, not Einstein.)
That would lead them back home,
Unfortunately, after spending the night
Beside the fire their father had so benevolently built
Before leaving his two children all alone in the wild forest,
Hansel and Gretel discovered that the crumbs were gone.

After wandering through the woods
With no shoes and empty stomachs
Hansel and Gretel came across a
Quaint little house that smelled of good things to eat.
Ignoring the electric fences (a sure sign of trouble),
The children trespassed on the property,
Where they met the proprietor,
A little old lady, who seemed kindly
But had an evil core lurking beneath
Her wrinkled façade.

Hansel and Gretel should have heard
The sinister music in the background.
But they couldn't hear it over the Barney theme song
Running through their heads,
And besides, they smelled cookies and cakes.
They couldn't have known the senior citizen's
Evil plan.
So Hansel and Gretel followed her into the little house

Where they gorged themselves on treats
Like cows at a feed-lot.

After the old lady shoved Hansel into a stable
It suddenly became clear that Hansel and Gretel weren't
Out of the woods (literally or figuratively) yet.
The silver-haired criminal began to fatten Hansel up
To serve as a special meal at her bridge club meeting
*   next week.*
As Hansel's body-fat index continued to rise
The old lady became increasingly eager
To indulge herself in a sumptuous meal.
(Her measly Social Security check did not allow her to
*   do it often.)*

Finally, the day arrived.
The oven was pre-heated, the bridge tables were out, and
Hansel was sufficiently plump.
In a last act of revenge to all of the young people who had
Mocked her purple jogging suits and
Tailgated her Buick when she drove twenty in a thirty-
*   five miles-per-hour zone,*
The old lady told Gretel to get inside the oven.
Gretel was smarter than that, however, and
With the proper degree of humility and reverence that
*   should be adopted when speaking*
To one's elders,
She asked her captor to illustrate how exactly one steps
*   into an oven.*
(She should have read Sylvia Plath.)

The old lady's mind was not what it once was
And she fell for Gretel's trick.
Grandma Cannibal stepped into the oven,
And Gretel quickly shut the door,
Trapping the old woman within the flames.
Gretel rushed to free her brother from the stable,
Where he lay waiting for his execution.
The pair went to admire Gretel's handiwork in the house
And wonder of wonders,
They found a bag of jewels,
Allowing them to live a life of luxury together forever.

Fairy tales, like sitcoms
Always have a happy ending.
But what can be learned from Hansel and Gretel's tale
*   of woe?*
The answer is twofold:
Beware of old people
(They vote down school budgets and eat young people.)
And in the off chance you're in Gretel's situation
And have just shoved an old lady into an oven,
Check underneath the mattress.
That's where they hide the valuables.

Ebony Night

by Sheila Bailey

nce upon a time, not too long ago, in a place not too far away, a chick named Ebony Night lived with her stepmother, a rich and jealous socialite (an oppressor of the working class). The step-mother hated that Ebony's skin was so dark and finally banished her to work in the garden.

Ebony grew to feel at home with the plants and ani-mals (our true brothers and sisters with whom we must share the planet). Unfortunately, Ebony was not aware of the new civil-rights legislation that would have enabled her to get a better job.

Every night the stepmother looked into her mirror and asked, "Jackie Kennedy, Brigitte Bardot, who is the fairest woman you know?"

And the mirror would reply, "You are, Ma'am."

But one night the mirror answered, "Ebony Night is the fairest woman I know!" The evil stepmother was angry and ordered Ebony flown to Arizona and left there. But the tenderhearted pilot could not bear to leave her in the desert, so he gave her a bus ticket to Las Vegas. She never made it, however, because the bus broke down. Ebony was stranded in the middle of a desert thunderstorm.

She lay on the ground to sleep. The next morning, a miniature Airstream trailer was parked by the side of the highway. Ebony poked her head inside; it was empty. She saw seven tiny chairs, seven tiny foldout beds, seven tiny toothbrushes on the sink, seven bars of soap and seven tiny comb-and-brush sets. There were also seven tiny clown suits and seven tiny unicycles. The seven plates each had a name: Jack, Bobby, Malcolm, Martin, Caesar, Method Man and Big Dumb Roger. The place was a mess. "But hey!" said Ebony. "It is their prerogative." Then she lay down on the tiny couch and watched TV.

Hours later, she heard the trailer's tenants coming back. Seven little men (of various nationalities and ethnic origins) were singing a cheerful song. "Hi ho, hi ho, it's home from work we go."

"I am Ebony Night, and I'm hiding from my wicked and racist stepmother who is an oppressor of the little people," said Ebony.

"That's cool," said Caesar. "We can dig it."

"Right on, sista," said Bobby.

And so Ebony lived with the seven little men, traveling around the country, performing free concerts and spreading their message of peace and tolerance.

Back home, the wicked stepmother looked into her mirror. "Queen Elizabeth, Fidel Castro, who is the best-looking person you know?"

And the mirror answered, "Babe, two words—Ebony Night."

The wicked stepmother flew into a rage and immediately made flight reservations.

One afternoon the little men had gone into town to

buy more greasepaint and Ebony was alone in the trailer. Suddenly, she heard a knock on the door. Ebony looked through the peephole, and asked who it was and what they wanted.

"Avon calling," said an age-spotted, elderly woman who was not an Avon lady at all, but the wicked step-mother in a fun wig! "We have some lovely mint-scented body lotion samples."

"May I try some?" Ebony asked. She rubbed the lotion into her skin, but it was poison and she collapsed. When the little men returned, they called the poison control center (which you should always do). Then they took off after the evil stepmother, who had driven away. It was foggy and she could not see where she was going; she drove off a cliff in her rental car. Ebony was rushed to the hospital, where she was treated, even though she had no HMO. During her stay, she met a handsome young intern. They agreed to a committed, permanent relation-ship in which they were equal, yet separate. 回

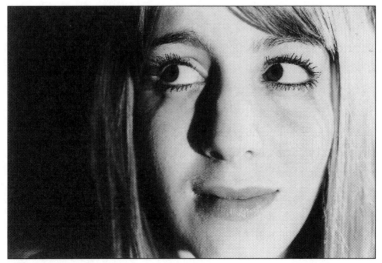

Photo by Mary Amor

Don't Bisect My Heart

by Jill E. Emerson

Once upon an undefined time, there was a beautiful young triangle named Isoscelisa Equius, whom many triangles (and some quadrilaterals) thought was the most beautiful polygon in the textbook. She was in love with the dashing Scaleonard Wright, who made many a female vertex angle flutter (he was tall, three-sided and handsome). Everyone in their chapter thought they made the best couple; they were both intelligent, honest and caring. The only ones who didn't want them together were their families.

Scaleonard's mother loved Isoscelisa. In fact, she couldn't think of any other multi-sided figure she'd rather have for a daughter-in-law, but her husband thought differently. He wanted his son to have a wife who would take him places, circumscribe him into the important circles. Isoscelisa couldn't do that. She was a sweet, young triangle who did handicrafts and taught the basic theorems to the trianglettes up at the Third Euclidian Church of Chapter Nine. No, what his son needed was someone like Octavia, the octagon from the other end of the chapter. She had a future in road signs, she'd go places, and besides, she had a figure that would stop traffic.

When it seemed that the two were getting serious, the two families tried to discourage them. The only member of Isoscelisa's family to object was her old maiden aunt Prunetta. She complained, "I've heard those Wrights (you're so fond of) don't have all 180 degrees," or "For the love of Euclid, he's a scalene! Never have I seen a scalene marry, and I hope to Euclid I never will! They're just not congruent!" Scaleonard's father took the more rational approach: "Have you any idea how much a plane for a growing family costs these days? They cost a hypotenuse and a leg!" Scaleonard's cousin Pontius didn't want the two together either. He was jealous of Scaleonard, and he, too, wanted to be with Isoscelisa. He tried to get Scaleonard to go along with his father's wishes to save the family unit, but in reality Pontius could not have cared less about family unity.

Scaleonard and Isoscelisa paid no attention to these objections. They spent more and more time together, until Octavia and Pontius really started competing for Scaleonard's and Isoscelisa's affections. Once this started, their mutual trust deteriorated.

Pontius and Octavia regularly made Isoscelisa and Scaleonard doubt their relationship until it seemed that all they did was argue with each other. Finally, they broke up after Isoscelisa saw Scaleonard and Octavia chatting rather romantically at the St. Pythagoras Day picnic.

They were both heart-bisected. They walked around in a pained stupor for days. The relatives who had been against their relationship thought they were acting foolishly. They felt very sententious, very "I-told-you-so-ish." Pontius and Octavia finally gave up when it became apparent that they couldn't replace their rivals. They told Scaleonard and Isoscelisa the truth—that they had lied, and Isoscelisa and Scaleonard deserved each other.

Isoscelisa and Scaleonard couldn't have been more thrilled. However, one more obstacle stood in their way: They weren't congruent. That didn't matter to Scaleonard. He didn't want triangles or any other polygons talking about them behind their backs, so he had angleplastic surgery performed to make him an isosceles right like Isoscelisa. Then he proposed to her.

Isoscelisa Equius became Mrs. Scaleonard Wright the next Gammaday in Isoscelisa's Aunt Prunetta's backyard. (Scaleonard won her over with his James Bond-like charm.) The wedding was as beautiful as the couple. Octavia caught the bride's transversal (which would come in handy as Octavia and Pontius were beginning to fall for each other). As Mr. and Mrs. Wright exited the church, well-wishers threw protractors at them (the symbol of many trianglettes to come). And they all lived congruently ever after. ▣

The Exceedingly Starving Caterpillar

by Julie Manheimer

On a beautiful, silvery moonlit night kissed by gentle, warm late-summer breezes, a little pink egg rested gracefully against the angry branch of a sycamore tree. For days, the penetrating summer sun had nourished its interior with red heat. The sun's throbbing power spilled into the tiny egg's hard exterior and threatened to shatter its delicate beauty, but the sleeping egg endured. Until that day. On that glorious Sunday, just as the brilliant blush of dawn embraced the sky, the little egg quivered with restlessness. Rocking back and forth within its green-leafed hammock, the excited ovum became electrically luminescent and then erupted, ejecting a new creature into the August day.

Announcing her arrival, birds sang a sweet and harmonious melody, while rainbow-dipped butterflies fluttered overhead to glimpse their newest member. She wiggled and stretched, dark and dizzy, while every muscle in her newborn body spasmed. She looked down at her fresh body and noticed it was muted, brown and emaciated. Panic-stricken, she looked up at the dazzling, opalescent nymphs who danced liquidly before her large, inexperienced eyes.

"I am not myself," she sobbed, unable to catch a breath. There was something plaintive in her protest; it was a child's wretched cry in the face of what she feared was true. She gazed at her physique, then observed the voluptuous, zesty prisms of the butterflies. She yearned for her shapeless carcass to transform into those aerodynamic goddesses of the forest. "I desire the libidinous, salacious form of those alluring butterflies!" she cried. "One day, my child, your body will ripen into a decorated prime. Eat. Let all savory edibles enter your lips, and one day, you will develop into the splendidness of the fluctuating butterflies," whispered the wind closely, dampening the skin of her ear with the moistness of its breath.

The little caterpillar refused to believe such lies, for she could not fathom that she could ever become one of these shimmering beauties. But deep in her trembling heart, she knew there lay a sleeping seductress on the verge of consciousness. So she vowed to devour every fruit that entered her vision. She was ready to indulge and quivered with excitement. She searched aimlessly for sweetness; her body palpitated when she discovered a strawberry, resting majestically, a vision of crimson eroticism. The swollen fruit resembled a naked woman with its shadowed curves and waxy surface. She sunk her teeth into the sugary treat. The very hungry caterpillar oscillated. She threw her head back, shivered, then let her body collapse with satisfaction. She devoured this heaven-sent gift, basking in its candied liquid.

She touched her body, running the tips of her fingers up, down and across her figure. She was changed! She stroked the rippling rolls of womanly flesh, hiding her nakedness. She glided back to her leaf; a half-grin glued to her face, eyes permanently open, dreaming of what she could now become. She sat upon her leaf and squirmed with comfort. She heard a voice.

"Build it, and you will become beautiful."

Her eager hands worked hard, although she was unaware of what they were creating. Her muscles throbbed; she was covered in perspiration as she exerted every ounce of her energy. Gasping for air, exhausted, she inserted herself into her new cocoon and closed her eyes, hibernating in peaceful silence for two weeks.

Reborn, she awoke, looked around and poked her head out of a tiny hole, wiggling, attempting to break free. Her delicate body squiggled and squirmed. She squeezed her way out of the opening, entering the world a new woman.

She looked down and noticed her vibrating wings. She could fly far, up and over the world to enthralling journeys of passion, anger and love. She could become one with the silvery moon and the fiery sun. She looked at her new body and shed a tear of joy, for she was the most voluptuous butterfly who ever lived. 回

The Jester

by Amanda Youmell

Next." It came as a shock. After fourteen years of entertaining the king and his family with thousands of jokes, hundreds of crazy stunts and numerous juggling acts, the royal jester could not make the king laugh. It's the day all jesters and jokers fear the most. For it is on that dark and dreary day that the end has inevitably come for the jester.

No one knows for sure where a jester is taken when the king utters that awful word "Next." The royal guards promptly drag the unwanted joker from the king's court and through a doorway that only unsuccessful jesters ever enter. Wherever that door leads, at the end, is almost certain doom for unlucky jesters.

There are rumors that just within the doorway is a bottomless pit, and the jesters are unmercifully tossed into its never-ending blackness. Others say they have seen the pit, but it is not bottomless. On the contrary, it is carpeted with sharp metal spikes that the jester can't avoid after his twenty-foot plunge. There are tales of torture of all measures—from solitary confinement to poisoning. Some believe that a jester will be taken to the gallows or possibly to the guillotine, depending on the king's mood. Servants of the king claim that from time to time they can hear the pleading cries of past jesters who are chained to the damp and mildewed walls of the castle basement. However, the maids swear that the jesters are cut up into tiny pieces by a demented butcher and fed to the king's ferocious hounds. There are some optimistic young jesters, though, who clutch onto the dream that beyond that door is simply the backyard of the castle.

At least this is what one particular young jester wanted to believe as he paced back and forth rehearsing his act in the dreary foyer of the king's mighty castle. For three and a half days, jesters from villages near and far had been coming to audition for the king with the hope that they would become the next royal jester. And for three and a half days, no ambitious jokers were accepted. It was rumored that the only word the king had spoken in three whole days was "Next."

This information was not very consoling for that certain young jester who was trying desperately to be optimistic. His nerves were getting the best of him. Beads of perspiration were forming on his brow, and his knees felt as though they would melt into the floor at any moment. Despite his attempts to remain positive, thoughts of where the unsuccessful jesters before him were taken by the guards cluttered his mind. What fate met them behind that door?

There were only a few jesters left to audition for the fickle king. All were dressed in traditional jesting attire: a colorful waistcoat, matching short pants and, of course, the obligatory silly three-pointed jester's hat. Each joker was rehearsing his routine over and over, attempting to increase the act's humorous appeal. Despite these attempts, the jesters seemed only mildly amusing in the extremely tense atmosphere.

The young jester stood near the entrance to the king's court, straining his ears to hear the king's reaction to the jester who was auditioning. The young jester had seen this act and thought it quite entertaining. He had even laughed uncontrollably at the punchline of a certain joke. Yet he hadn't heard the king laugh even once.

Suddenly, the doors to the king's court swung open, nearly knocking the young jester to the ground. A guard stood at the entrance, looking around at each of the auditioners. He had a strange expression on his face. It was almost fearful and at the same time sympathetic. He pointed to the young jester, who was positioning his hat, and with an emotionless voice said, "It's your turn; follow me."

With a slight hesitation, the jester followed the guard through the entrance. The doors closed behind him with a thud that echoed throughout the castle. He suddenly felt very small and completely alone. The guard silently led the young jester to the king's court. It was much brighter than the foyer and beautifully decorated with exotic tapestries, polished coats of armor and magnificent paintings of the royal family. The sheer brilliance of the room eased the jester's nerves.

Directly in front of the jester was the king, sitting high on his throne, looking down at the young joker who stood before him. The jester realized he was at the mercy of the king, but then he noticed the peculiar expression on the king's face. It seemed as though the king was pondering something amusing, and, as if he were a child who knew a secret, he wore a slight smirk. This eerie and calculating appearance sent a chill through the jester. He wondered what the deranged king was thinking. It was an intriguing and almost frightening look.

"Good day, Your Majesty," the young jester said in a voice that nearly trembled. The king simply nodded and, with a slight wave of his hand signaled for the jester to begin.

Make the king laugh, make him smile, was all he could think. It was his sole purpose as a jester, and all he had ever wanted to do. This was his chance, his only chance. He started with a simple joke, but it came out flat and boring. He quickly glanced at the guard standing next to the door, and a wave of fear swept over his entire body.

As the young jester went on, he began to loosen up, and everything started coming naturally. The joker was hilarious. Yet the king still had that peculiar look on his face. He had remained constant through every joke, and now as the young jester attempted to juggle seven raw eggs, his expression did not waiver.

At this point, the young jester began to wonder why the king had refused every joker who had attempted to coax a bit of laughter from him. What exactly was he looking for in a royal court comedian? Perhaps the king had no intention of choosing a new joker. The young jester even entertained the notion that the king had possibly become immune to typical jesting humor. Yet he quickly contradicted this thought with another, *Why would the king search for a new jester if they had become monotonous to him?*

The king watched unamused as the young jester juggled one egg, and he didn't so much as raise an eyebrow when he juggled two or even three. Then the jester juggled four eggs with no problem, then five, and six, and eventually seven with the same ease. Still, the king was unchanged, not even interested. It was as if he had already seen everything, and nothing would faze him. The young jester was starting to panic. He saw that mysterious door and the guard from the corner of his eye, and the king was staring right at him with that calculating expression and that evil smirk on his face.

Then came a revelation. The jester realized what he had to do: He had to make a complete and utter fool of himself. Still juggling the seven raw eggs with perfect form, he forced himself to interrupt the precise rhythm. One by one he threw each egg high into the air, then he waited. He looked directly at the king, and for a split second he recognized the peculiar expression on his face. It most closely resembled the playful yet dangerous look that a cat will sport when toying with its helpless prey.

One by one, each of the seven eggs landed with a crack right on top of the young jester's three-pointed hat. The yolks oozed down the sides of his head and trickled over his pale face. The young jester had done it spontaneously, as a last resort. Now he stood in the center of the king's mighty court, dripping with yellow goo, all of his dignity sacrificed, waiting apprehensively for a reaction.

Then, like the illuminating sun rising in the east bringing light to all the land, the king smiled. He even let out an eerie chuckle. The young jester had done it and, having completed his audition, he took a bow. As he bowed he thought of the king's previous expression, and now he wondered what he was thinking.

He pictured himself as the royal jester, roaming the castle, sitting next to the king, entertaining great nobles and knights. The young jester looked up just as the king was about to speak. The smile was gone. It had disappeared into oblivion, and the peculiar expression had returned. Then that devious smirk formed the awful word, "Next." 回

Art by Maggie Doben

How to submit writing, art and photos to the monthly *Teen Ink* magazine

We need:

1. Your name, year of birth, home address/city/state/zip, phone number, school name (and English teacher) and e-mail address.

   For art and photos, place the information on the back of each piece. Please don't fold art.

2. This statement must be written on each submission: "This will certify that the above work is completely original," and sign your name.

Send it:

By mail—Teen Ink

Box 30

Newton, MA 02461

On the Web—*www.TeenInk.com/Submissions*

By e-mail—*Submissions@TeenInk.com*

The fine print:

- Label all work fiction or nonfiction; include a title.
- Type or print carefully in ink. Keep a copy.
- Writing may be edited; we reserve the right to publish our version without your approval.
- If due to the personal nature of a piece you don't want your name published, we will respect your request, but you must include your name and address for our records.
- If published, you will receive a copy of *Teen Ink,* a

wooden pen and a special *Teen Ink* Post-it pad.

- All works submitted become the property of *Teen Ink* and all copyrights are assigned to *Teen Ink*. We retain the non-exclusive rights to publish all such works in any format. All material in *Teen Ink* is copyrighted to protect us and exclude others from republishing your work. All contributors retain the right and have our permission to submit work elsewhere.

To learn more about the magazine and to request a free sample copy, see our Web site: *www.TeenInk.com*. Our phone number is 617-964-6800.

All the royalties from the *Teen Ink* books are donated to The Young Authors Foundation

Established in 1989, The Young Authors Foundation, Inc. is the publisher of *Teen Ink* (formerly *The 21st Century*), a monthly magazine written entirely by teens for teens. This magazine has been embraced by schools and teenagers nationwide with more than 3.5 million students reading it every year.

The magazine empowers teenagers by publishing their words, giving them a voice and demonstrating that they can make a difference. *Teen Ink* is dedicated to improving reading, writing and critical-thinking skills while encouraging creativity and building self-esteem. The editors have read more than 350,000 submissions from students during the past fourteen years, and more than 25,000 of them have been published. There is no charge to submit work, and all published students receive a free copy of the magazine plus other items.

In keeping with its mission, the Foundation distributes thousands of class sets and individual copies free to schools and teachers every month. In addition, thousands of schools support the Foundation by paying a small fee for their monthly class sets.

From its beginnings as a small foundation with regional distribution of *Teen Ink,* The Young Authors Foundation has grown steadily and today is a national program funded through donations, sponsorships, grants and advertising from companies and individuals that support its goals. In addition to funding the magazine, the Foundation underwrites a number of educational programs:

- *Teen Ink Web Site (www.TeenInk.com)* includes over 13,000 pages of student writing, art, photos, resources, contests and more.

- *Teen Ink Poetry Journals* showcase more than one thousand young poets each year and are distributed free to subscribing schools.

- *Teen Ink Educator of the Year Awards Contest* welcomes nominating essays from students to honor outstanding teachers with cash prizes and publication of their essays in the magazine.

- *Teen Ink Book Awards* donates thousands of free books and award materials annually so schools can recognize students who have shown "improvement and individual growth in the field of English."

- *Teen Ink Interview Contest* encourages thousands of teens to interview family and friends, with the winners interviewing national celebrities including Hillary Clinton, John Glenn, Maya Angelou, George Lucas, Jesse Jackson, R. L. Stine, Whoopi Goldberg, Alicia Keys, Tony Hawk and Secretary of State Colin Powell.

The Young Authors Foundation, Inc. is a nonprofit 501(c)3 organization. See the next page for details on how you can become a member, support these programs and receive a monthly copy of the magazine.

Join The Young Authors Foundation and get a monthly subscription to *Teen Ink* magazine

Foundation Supporters Receive:

- Ten months of *Teen Ink* magazine
- Partner in Education Satisfaction – You help thousands of teens succeed

The magazine includes stories, poems and art plus music, book and movie reviews, college essays, sports and more

Only $25 per year

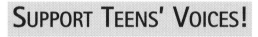

SUPPORT TEENS' VOICES!

Annual Dues $25*
I want to receive ten monthly issues of *Teen Ink* magazine and become a supporter of The Young Authors Foundation.
(Enclose your check or complete credit card information below.)

NAME_____ PHONE_____

STREET_____

CITY/TOWN _____ STATE _____ ZIP _____

PHONE_____ E-MAIL _____

M/C OR VISA (*CIRCLE ONE*)#_____ EXP. DATE _____/_____

Send a gift subscription to:

NAME _____

STREET_____

CITY/TOWN _____ STATE _____ ZIP _____

Mail coupon to: Teen Ink • Box 97 • Newton, MA 02461 – Or join online: *www.TeenInk.com*

* The Young Authors Foundation, publisher of *Teen Ink,* is a 501(c)3 nonprofit organization providing opportunities for the education and enrichment of young people nationwide. While all donations support the Foundation's mission, 75 percent is designated for the magazine subscription, and no portion should be considered as a charitable contribution.

Acknowledgments

irst, we must thank all the teenagers, past and present, responsible for making this book possible. We must also give our heartfelt thanks to those who have done so much to make the *Teen Ink* book series a reality. When we started publishing *Teen Ink* magazine in the late 1980s, we never imagined we would be working with so many talented and devoted people. Some have played an enormous role in the overall success of our nonprofit Young Authors Foundation (that helps fund all our projects). Others devote themselves tirelessly to our monthly magazine, which is the source for the *Teen Ink* books. Many more gave their time, skills and insight to make these books the best representation of teen writing possible. We are most fortunate to have all of these people in our lives:

Our Children:

Our son and daughter, Robert Meyer and Alison Meyer Hong, as well as Alison's husband, Michael, have been a never-ending source of support since our start when they were teenagers themselves. Their love, insight, encouragement and wisdom have helped guide us every step of the way.

Our Staff:

We couldn't have done it without our amazing staff. They are a constant source of help with words to advise and assist: Kate Dunlop Seamans, Karen Watts, Tony Abeln, Denise Peck and Paul Chase, as well as our long-time volunteer, Barbara Field, who has been a support for many years, and the many college and high-school interns who've been a tremendous help in so many ways.

Our Board and Other Important Supporters:

We always depend on our Foundation Board: J. Robert Casey, David Anable and Richard Freedberg, and our Advisory Board: Beverly Beckham, Michael Dukakis, Milton Lieberman and Harold Raynolds, who have served with us through the years. And to other very important sources of support: Alison Swap, Barbara Wand, Mollie and Steve Dunn, as well as our relatives.

Our Publishing Family at HCI:

We once again thank all the folks at HCI who have published, promoted and believed in our project: Peter Vegso and Tom Sand; Lisa Drucker and Susan Heim, our editors; Terry Burke and Lori Golden, whose skills keep the books out there; Kim Weiss and Paola Fernandez; Kelly Maragni and her staff; and Larissa Hise Henoch and her staff for their continued design creativity.

Contributors

Sarah Aksoy is working toward her degree in mass communication so she can write and get a paycheck. Although she's been published in a few other publications, she yearns to make it her career. In high school she was active in drama, choir and the environmental club. She remembers her eighth-grade teacher who encouraged her to write poetry. She found that her poems were created during random moments in her life.

Axel Arth is a junior in high school. In addition to acting, he enjoys playing football, writing, reading, video games and "any and all things nerdy." Some of his favorite authors include Harry Turledove and Matthew Woodring Stover. His future? He's considering either being a full-time writer or working for the FBI or CIA. He dedicates his two clever fiction pieces to Mrs. Mills because "without her, I would still be much less inspired."

Mary Amor wants to pursue a career in the photographic arts, and is currently studying at a local college with a phenomenal photo program where she's trying to shoot five rolls a week! Published often in *Teen Ink* magazine, three of her photos are featured in this book. She loves to shoot in the early morning and the last two hours before the sun sets when the light is gentle and warm. Mary hopes to become a photojournalist like Mary Ellen Mark or Margaret Bourke-White. She admires the way they capture the truth about people.

Katherine S. Assef has been writing since fourth grade as "a way to forget my ego and discover the world." Her favorite writers include Amy Tan, Raymond Carver, Margaret Atwood, Alice Munro and Toni Morrison. Now a junior in high school, she loves to sing, act, dance and draw. She also enjoys taking long walks by herself and spending time with her family and golden retriever, Duchess. Katie thanks Mr. Littell and Kelly, "two one-in-a-million teachers who helped me grow in so many ways."

Sheila Bailey wrote her fiction piece as a senior in high school. She is training to become a professional dancer and also runs a number of Web sites. She still loves to write and is involved in online fiction writing groups. Her favorite pastimes include doll collecting, drawing and cooking.

Valerie Bandura began writing because her biggest fear at five years old was growing up and not remembering what five felt like. She believes, "We write because we cannot imagine what it means not to write." A high-school senior when her piece appeared in *Teen Ink* magazine, Valerie echoes W. H. Auden: "As a rule, the sign that a beginner has a genuine original talent is that he is more interested in playing with words than in saying something original." Valerie is an MFA candidate in writing.

Amie V. Barbone wrote her poem as a senior in high school where she participated in the marching and concert bands, chorus and pit orchestra. She was first chair for her section (clarinet) and won two scholarships to college. She recently got her degree in elementary education. In college, she was very active in her sorority, worked in a nursing home and continued her interest in music as well as tutoring elementary schoolchildren.

Marcus Begay was president of the art club in his high school where he entered many of his pieces in gallery shows. He was published in *Teen Ink* magazine a number of times and was even honored as one of the artists of the year. He dedicates all of his art to his family who believed in him when he was very young. They taught him everything he knows. He feels honored to have one of his pieces in a book!

Ashley Belanger is a sophomore in college planning to major in journalism. Editor-in-chief and founder of her high-school literary magazine, Ashley says she writes constantly. The inspiration for this fun story came from a workshop at St. John's College in New Mexico. "Revision is the key to writing, and this piece has come a long way." Ashley dedicates it to her family and all the people of her hometown who provided a basis for its events.

Adam C. Benzing decided to take time off after high school to become bilingual, spending a year living and working in Mexico, an amazing experience that taught him invaluable lessons. He then went to college where he's majoring in philosophy and international relations. His creative piece was published in *Teen Ink* magazine when he was just a freshman in high school.

Torey Bocast is finishing her senior year in high school where she likes to write, study Japanese, draw, and, of course, do photography. In addition to having a number of her photos published in *Teen Ink,* she has also been published in *Peterson's Photographic Magazine.* Torey would especially like to thank her sister Brooke for indulging her and posing for this photograph that appears on the cover and opens the first chapter.

Kyle Brenneman completed his high-school education as a home-schooler. His biggest interests include fantasy, science-fiction stories and role-playing games. He also loves fencing, especially with a saber, as well as a foil and epee. Kyle is very into computers and even built a Web page for a music festival fundraiser. He received a clean bill of health recently from Hodgkin's lymphoma after a year of chemotherapy.

Anna W. Butterworth took her photo looking up at her grandmother's clothesline! She dedicates it to her best friend and inspiration in photography, Sara Booth [whose photo appeared in *Teen Ink: Love and Relationships*]. Anna is currently a sophomore in college majoring in art and theatre. She is into oil painting as well as photography and loves to quilt. One of Anna's interesting facets is that she loves to play college rugby, even though she is short, small and doesn't have a violent nature.

Timothy Cahill works as a paralegal in New York City and looks forward to attending law school. He was an English and history double-major in college, where he served as president of both the Mock Trial Society and the marching band. He was also an officer in his fraternity, participated in the film society and pursued his interest in creative writing. Tim wrote his fiction piece as a sophomore in high school. Two of his other short stories were featured in the first two *Teen Ink* books.

Maria Carboni is currently a senior in college and wants to become a lawyer. In addition to being editor of her newspaper in high school, she was active in student government and a service club. She also volunteered at a local hospital, which possibly helped with the focus of her piece. Maria claims she started writing because she lived for seven years without a television. She would like to thank her family for always supporting and inspiring her.

Olivia Cerrone is pursuing a degree in creative writing in college and says, "Writing is my utmost passion" ever since fourth grade. She also loves art, drama and music, including the piano, trombone and singing. Her favorite place is Florida, and her favorite artistic specialty is drawing caricatures. She also loves watching old black and white movies and reading, especially Stephen King. She sends a special thank-you to her father for supporting her love for writing.

Brandon Childers really only began drawing in high school. He says, "Before freshman year, I couldn't draw a face at all." Brandon is now majoring in art as a freshman in college. He created this face using an ebony pencil and thanks Mrs. Hardin for encouraging him to continue to draw!

Daron Christopher wrote his imaginative piece as a junior in high school. He's pursuing a film degree and his creativity spills into everything he does.

Jalina Colón is finishing her freshman year of college, where she is thinking about majoring in biology. In high school, she participated in cheerleading, gymnastics and art. She always enjoyed drawing and created this imaginative art as part of her senior project because she wanted to learn to play the violin. She also won the *Teen Ink* Art and Photography Contest with this piece.

Danny Crawford created his dragon that's featured on the cover during his sophomore year in high school when it appeared in *Teen Ink* magazine. Although he's not quite sure how he got into the arts, he loves drawing, painting and music. He plays the guitar and hopes to have a career in the arts. He thanks his parents and *Teen Ink* for their support.

Kristen Cupstid attends college where she has yet to decide on a major. She definitely loves to draw and created this drawing when she was a senior in high school, taking a picture of her jewelry in different positions and then choosing her favorite one to draw. She is a dancer through and through, having danced her whole life and is currently a member of her college dance company.

Lauren Daniels describes how she drew for hours while staring at herself, trying to capture every possible detail until she was satisfied with the outcome. This piece was part of her college-application portfolio. She is now finishing her freshman year, planning to major in biochemistry and molecular biology. She thanks her art teacher for encouraging her to take that extra step when creating, and also thanks her family for lending her the bathroom mirror for half a day!

Matt Davis is finishing his freshman year at college where he's planning to pursue his interest in physics and math as well as play football. In high school, he was quite the sports guy, playing baseball, basketball and track, in addition to being very active in student government. His piece gave him the opportunity to interview Red Sox pitcher, Pedro Martinez, as winner of a *Teen Ink* interview contest. His love of baseball continues!

Susan DeBiasio has fond memories of being published in *Teen Ink* back in high school, when she was a prolific writer. Unfortunately, she finds little time to write now that she is a full-time Web designer (which she loves, but has a long commute to work). She does enjoy painting, and has four ferrets for roommates: Cathy, Ralph, Daisy and Alice.

Thalia Demakes recently graduated from college designing her own major called Cultural Communications that combined art, music, literature, cultural studies and multimedia. She loves anything exotic and has spent time in Spain. She currently plans to write a book about her experiences listening to people's stories rowing them across a harbor. She thanks her parents, especially her mom for being such an inspiration. She took her photo when she was back in high school.

Matt Denno was published in *Teen Ink* magazine when he was a sophomore in high school. Now, many years later, he still loves to write and dreams of making it his career. In the meantime he lives in the Southwest, where he loves the climate after growing up in the Northeast.

Stephen D'Evelyn had his poem published in *Teen Ink* during the magazine's infancy when he was a freshman in high school. Now completing his Ph.D. in medieval Latin in England, Stephen still enjoys writing, as well as painting and playing guitar. As a proud expatriate, Stephen says jazz and pizza are the two best things about America! He hopes to teach Latin and medieval literature.

Susan Diehl wrote her piece as a senior in high school. Since then she has completed a degree in special education and teaches in a middle school. She really enjoyed speech team, participating on her high-school and college teams, and now coaching and judging middle-school children. Susan also enjoys open-mic nights and poetry slams, although she hasn't done much writing lately.

Maggie Doben created her linoleum cut during her freshman year in high school when it appeared in *Teen Ink* magazine. Since then she's graduated from college with a degree in studio art and education and received her master's in elementary education. After spending some time out West, she currently teaches first grade near where she grew up!

Sarah Donovan Donnelly wrote "Purple Monkeys" when she was thirteen. She's currently an eighth-grade English teacher. She has written a few songs and hopes to compose more. She spent a year after college on the road travelling from Boston to Key West to Colorado, creating and collecting stories from people that she wants to publish at some point. She'd love to dedicate her poem to an old elementary-school friend, Stephanie Salant, with whom she's lost touch.

Jason S. Drake will graduate from high school this year where he was active in the medieval recreational sport of Dagorhir. He loves loaves of French bread and the feeling he gets from putting Q-Tips in his ear. In addition to penning the preface, he dedicates his imaginative piece to his English teacher with much misplaced respect and admiration, his eternal friend and brother, Ian Llallendd, and in loving memory of his Laura.

Jessica Dudziak graduated from college a couple of years ago with a degree in communications and a minor in psychology. She saw her poem published in *Teen Ink* magazine as a senior in high school. Jessica gives special thanks to her parents, without whose support and love "I would not be the person I am."

Nick Duennes graduated from high school and is deciding what to do next. He is a "man of music," enjoying many styles, but relating most to punk and industrial. He claims he leans toward writing poetry, hoping to add musical accompaniment when he has the chance. He thanks his friends for offering him creativity and experiences to write about, and his family for being as understanding and accepting of him.

Kristopher Dukes is now a Los Angeles college student, and continues to freelance as a writer. Her piece appeared in *Teen Ink* magazine a few years ago, and that, along with her other works, is featured on *www.kristopherdukes.com*. Kristopher writes that there are so many folks to thank, but highlights in particular God, who blessed her with a loving family, beautiful friends and thousands of opportunities in life so that she might live and learn. And drink soy cappuccinos.

Allison Dziuba is a very busy eighth-grader. In addition to loving to write, she has been studying tae kwon do for six years, sings in the select school choir and is very active in theater, both at her school and her community. In ten years, her biggest goal is to be happy, but you'll probably find her performing!

Jill E. Emerson thanks all the great teachers who encouraged her to write. Her creative piece was published in *Teen Ink* magazine when she was a junior in high school. Since then, she's gotten her college degree and is working as a technical writer while she finishes up a master's in information science, and will be joining Columbia University's Teacher's College.

Tom Evans graduates from high school this spring. He loves science and is a very avid aquarist with five tanks that include many types of fish. His favorite by far is his "badis badis," which is also called a dwarf chameleon because of its ability to change color in a matter of seconds. Tom has been involved in both the chess and math clubs at his high school and penned his war piece when he was a sophomore.

Marcelino Farias created this multimedia painting on the cover with the idea that it should show many simple aspects of nature wrapped into a person, altering some of the ideas in their color and commingling it with other ideas. After high school, Marcelino spent time in the Navy and now is in college majoring in business management and minoring in art, while doing some freelance work. He sees his older work as a stepping stone to the caliber of his work today.

Leah Multer Filbrich is currently studying sociology near her home. She is quite involved in Students for a Free Tibet, the Sociology Club and Womyn's Action Coalition. She also coaches synchronized swimming for young girls. Leah wrote her poem as a senior in high school.

Caroline Marie Finnerty wrote her poem about Mr. Rogers as a freshman in high school. She works as a student prosecutor and hopes to practice family law when she finishes law school. Caroline loves skiing, tennis and traveling. (She lived in Italy and Australia during semesters abroad in college.) She still loves to write and thanks her family for their support.

Julsa Flum graduates from college this year after majoring in African Studies and Pre-Med. She spends her free time volunteering with the large Mexican population where she attends college. Since she speaks fluent Spanish, there is much work she can do to help with the transition to the United States—teaching ESL, organizing jobs, finding housing and medical care, as well as acting as a translator.

Amanda Beth Freedman is finishing her junior year in college pursuing a degree in apparel design. Her interests include ceramics, glass blowing and, of course, photography. She enjoys teaching gymnastics and claims her most memorable experience was participating in the Maccabi Youth games in high school. She gives a special thanks to all the counselors and staff at Buck's Rock camp and dedicates her photograph to its founder, Ernst Bulova.

Casey Fuller is a junior in high school where he is active in cross-country and track. In addition to running, he likes to lift and draw in his spare time. He created this dragon freehand over three years ago when he was thirteen. He still enjoys drawing dragons, especially since it is his school's mascot!

Dena Galie is finishing her freshman year of college. She has two younger siblings who have always been her photographic guinea pigs. She loves portraiture and as she learns more about photography, she become more sensitive to composition, although a lot of photography is luck. If she thanks anyone, it would be Krista and Marcus, her sister and brother, for letting her have a camera in their faces all the time.

Erin D. Galloway loves reading and writing, but dance is her passion. Her touching story was published during her senior year in high school. Now a junior in college, she's a member of several dance troupes. She continues to write as a member of the student newspaper staff. Erin counts her summer in Spain as her most memorable life experience. She'd like to thank her "amazing group of friends. You always inspire me."

Seth H. Goldbarg was involved with the fencing team, enjoyed sculpting and especially liked French in high school when his poem was first published in *Teen Ink* magazine. Poetry and writing were critical parts of his high-school life and continue as an important form of personal expression and self-questioning. Since then, he's written about his experiences in a refugee camp in Macedonia and several months spent in Ethiopia doing medical research. He's spent much of his writing energies on scientific papers and recently finished his internal-medicine residency.

Aditi Gupta has continued to excel in writing in college, where she is a sophomore. She was selected as a finalist by the National Foundation for Advancement in Arts, which entailed meeting many other talented artists. Her major passions are reading—anything from the classics to fantasy, with her favorite being fantasy, especially Patricia McKillip. She's also into crime and gardening, an interesting combination. She thanks her high school's English department who supported Aditi's budding skill, especially Ms. Potter, without whom she never would have discovered she loves to write.

Gabrielle Haber says that one of the best experiences of her high-school career was hiking thirteen miles overnight in the mountains of New Hampshire, "hands and face numbed with the cold, operating solely on the sugar from Mountain Dew, on a clear, moonless night with three people as tired and eager to reach the distant end as I was."

Patrick S. Hallock wrote his fun story during his senior year of high school. He has since graduated and is working full-time as a manager's assistant in a decorative soap factory. He still does a lot of writing in his spare time and is in a band where he plays drums and occasionally the guitar. He dedicates this story to the memory of his grandparents.

Zachary Handlen is an avid movie fan, which has clearly helped fuel his imagination! A voracious reader, his favorite authors include Stephen King, Kurt Vonnegut and Salman Rushdie. Published while a freshman in high school, Zack has since graduated from college and is currently editing and polishing a novel. He thanks his mother, father and sister, "without whom I wouldn't be where I am today."

Erica J. Hodgkinson was published in *Teen Ink* magazine many times during high school. Now a senior in college, she likes skiing, reading nonfiction and hanging around with her friends. She still enjoys photography of all kinds, although she shoots primarily in black and white. Her works were featured in two earlier *Teen Ink* books in addition to two appearing in this book.

Ed Jaffe has had many of his photographs published in *Teen Ink* during the last few years. He works for a commercial photographer, although he's not sure if this will be his life's work. He's into the jazz band, playing the tenor sax, and loves to act and direct. In addition he is a skier and a lifeguard; definitely one busy person.

Leslie D. Johnson is graduating from high school this spring and plans to go on to college after taking a year off. Her poem, "Hunger," shows the great sense of humor also evident in her high-school comic book,

Creature Feature, which even won an award! She has created a secret code/language with more than 200 symbols, known to only one other person in the world: her lovely boyfriend. She's working on a few 'zines right now and enjoys reading them immensely. She thanks her dad— authority figure, comic relief and astounding chef, all wrapped into one.

Leigh A. Johnston plans to attend her first-choice college after graduating from high school where she participated in the choral program and the literary magazine. Both won honors, with the choral group performing at the Kennedy Center in Washington, D.C., and the magazine being awarded ribbons from Columbia University. Leigh dedicates her poem to her English teacher, Ms. Renard, who helped her solve her writer's block with bubbles and always treated her as an equal.

Marnie Kaplan is active in college. Her poem was published in *Teen Ink* magazine during her senior year of high school, where she participated in her school's model congress during all four years and continues in college. Marnie says she loves spending time with her family, including her twin brother. "I revel in being a twin, yet also being my own person."

Meghan Keene was published in *Teen Ink* magazine as a sophomore in high school. A horse enthusiast, Meghan rides every day after school and competes on weekends. She's also active in her church and still finds time to play the saxophone. Meghan would like to thank her mom and dad ("I love you!"), and her English teacher, Mr. Hogue.

Eileen J. Kessler would love someday to be a writer, but her practical side says she better learn something else to do between books or before she gets famous! At college, Eileen plans to explore biology, English and Spanish. Eileen was involved in a Best Buddies program that matched high-schoolers and college students with mentally or physically handicapped people of the same age group in one-on-one friendships. Her fictional story, "Fireflies," is dedicated to her sister.

Adam Kirshner is completing his sophomore year of college where he's a business major with a very strong interest in television production. He loves creating and producing his own shows, and this year he came up with the idea of a blind-date show! Back in high school, he fell into a writing workshop and ended up being published many times in *Teen Ink* magazine, including this nostalgic poem that incorporated some of his "greatest memories of living in Illinois as a child, and one of my favorite times with my father."

Suzanne L. Kolpin is graduating from high school this year where she was involved in gymnastics, swimming and diving. She also volunteered as a gymnastics coach at a middle school. She is active in 4-H, and mentors and instructs youth in cattle judging and showing. Suzanne sends a huge thank-you to her writing teacher, Ms. Mac, "for teaching me that I really do know how to write, and I just needed the right opportunity to show it."

Alex Koplow is finishing his freshman year of college in the nation's capital. He took his photo of a guy looking down during his senior year in high school. He'd like to thank Mrs. Morse and Fred McGriff. Alex writes that he would like to be a writer or a zookeeper.

Juliet Lamb is completing her third year of college where she is majoring in environmental science, public policy and is a pre-veterinary student. One day she plans to work in Costa Rica as a zoo vet and naturalist. Until then she is doing research into the effects of CO_2 on plants and caring for rare-breed farm animals at a pilgrim village. She also keeps very busy playing the French horn, singing in a show-tune choir, teaching grade-school students in an after-school program and riding her bike. She wrote the thoughtful preface, in addition to her short story that was published in *Teen Ink*.

Emily K. Larned has graduated from college where she majored in art. She writes that she is the name behind Red Charming, independently producing books, clothing and 'zines for the pleasures of production and consumption. She penned these two creations back when she was a junior in high school.

Carmen Lau claims she is a rehabilitating Internet addict. Her piece appeared a few years ago in *Teen Ink* magazine when Carmen was a junior in high school where she was active in the newspaper and academic decathlon. She's finishing her freshman year of college not far from home and still loves writing short fiction and nonfiction. She's interested in tarot cards, feminism and anime, and thanks Mrs. Hickman, Mr. Hackett and her mom.

Cara Lorello most enjoys drawing in pencil, ink and charcoal, and painting watercolors in her free time. She also loves to ride her horse, Ko-pilot, and has been a member of 4-H for the last nine years. She received the "Class of 2000 Best in Fine Arts" award at her high school, and her artwork won a 4-H award and recently was displayed on a horse event T-shirt. Cara created her drawing during her senior year in high school. She is now a college senior studying journalism and studio art. She sends a special thanks to her grandma who was and to this day "continues to be a mentor in the world of art."

Diane Lowe is a total movie freak! She would adore travelling the world, but for now loves college. She is on the cheer squad and thanks her high-school English teacher for his support and friendship. Without him, many aspiring authors would never have taken the steps to get published. Her succinct poem appeared in *Teen Ink* magazine when she was a senior in high school.

Gretchen Loye loves taking photographs of "abstract things in different perspectives." In high school, she enjoyed playing the xylophone and drums, and playing with her guinea pig, Carmella. She also loves to travel and spending summers at her family's cabin, "four-wheeling in the woods, swimming, fishing and picking berries." She has even visited China and Singapore. Gretchen thanks "my photography teacher, Dalen Towne, for all the encouragement she gave me, and my brother, Jonathan, for inspiring me."

Lesley MacGregor started college this year where she hopes to study art history, especially Egyptian, Roman and Greek art. Not only did she write this long tale in high school, but she loved writing lyrics for the faculty-student band where she was lead vocalist. She is a huge fan of Motley Crue and Guns N Roses, even though she looks like she'd be more a fan of Britney. She adores music and plans to continue this in college.

Tara Macolino is in college to study illustrating, which is basically drawing and painting without using a computer. She loves to travel, but is busy with school and broke, like many students. Tara hasn't created many poems lately, having transferred her creative juices to art!

Julie Manheimer wrote this creative piece back in high school when it appeared in *Teen Ink* magazine. She really got into writing in high school, but now has found other outlets for her creativity in art. Finishing her junior year in college, she has settled on this as her major.

Brad Mann was born in Boston, a month late, on Labor Day weekend, during a nurses' strike. Since then, his life has had many ups and downs. Brad enjoys writing, reading, hiking, telemark skiing, road biking, watching thought-provoking films and TV shows, and making people laugh. He wants to thank his mother wholeheartedly, his mentor, Jamie Struck, and his beacons shining through the darkness: Walt Whitman and John Ashbery.

Arielle Mark saw her remarkable story published in *Teen Ink* magazine as a junior in high school where she worked on her school's literary magazine. She was also an active member of the poetry club and was president of the creative writing club. Now a sophomore in college, she is majoring in art history and creative writing. She plans to pursue a career in art curating, but writing "will always be my first true passion."

Adam Masters was published as a junior in high school in *Teen Ink* magazine. Adam loves driving his friend's old car with nowhere particular to go and nothing in mind. He has spent many summer months backpacking and traveling around Wyoming. At school, he's been a saxophone player for a few years. He thanks his parents for always supporting him, even when it was against his will!

Kathleen McCarney is studying journalism in college. She likes watching movies and reading books, magazines or anything that sparks her interest. She loves writing, learning and trying new things. Overall she is inspired by life in general, the good and the bad. Kathleen wrote her poem as a junior in high school. She explains, "I am grateful I found poetry and writing as an outlet, as the best listener ever. . . . I wish everyone could find such a meaningful way to vent, to cry, to live."

A. G. McDermott enjoys participating in local open-mic poetry nights as well as working on literary publications. Although she tends to write when frustrated or lovesick, she would like to expand her work to include more positive emotions. Her goals for college include completing a major in math and/or physics while maintaining her writing skills. While her favorite English poet is e. e. cummings, the best poem she has ever read is *"Me gustas cuando callas"* by Pablo Neruda.

Kerry E. McIntosh is finishing her freshman year at college where she hopes to major in international politics to fulfill her dream of being a true citizen of the world. She loves traveling any and everywhere after growing up on a farm. She loves writing, and most of her inspiration comes from the news or people she reads about. Her story can obviously be dedicated to the real Arien Ahmed and all those who regretfully find themselves in her place: "May peace prevail."

Jonah McKenna wrote "Mockingbird" while in high school. He thanks April for originally finding the bird who inspired his poem. He was published several times in *Teen Ink* magazine before moving on to college. Jonah is a writer and lives in New England.

Jennifer McMenemy finished her college degree in writing and theater. She spent a semester in London after receiving a grant to study children's literature there. She fondly remembers her high-school English teacher, Mrs. Krinsky, and thanks her parents for their support. Her piece appeared in *Teen Ink* when she was a junior in high school.

Terra J. McNary hopes to continue her interest in biology as a premed student in college. In high school, she jokes that her hobby was sleeping because she studied all the time. Terra did take time to help with many community-service projects. She always thought she was a terrible writer, but in her senior year she took a couple of writing classes and discovered she loved it! This tall tale (tail) is actually based somewhat on her dog, Frank, and his weird characteristics!

Naomi Millan went to a creative-arts high school where she specialized in creative writing. Her piece appeared in *Teen Ink* magazine during her senior year. Naomi loved theater, music and working on the newspaper as well. She especially enjoyed French, which became one of her majors in college. Now she's working toward her master's degree in creative writing. She'd love to work in journalism and dedicates her piece to her high-school teachers, Mr. Delp and Mr. Driscoll, for taking her seriously.

Rachel A. Miller wrote her narrative piece as a junior in high school when it was published in *Teen Ink* magazine. She currently enjoys reading, photography, psychology and philosophy. Rachel works full-time and loves animals, nature and observing people.

Elyse Montague thinks and expresses herself very visually. She writes, "I began video, film and photo in high school, but only just realized how important these mediums are in order for me to communicate. These visual languages encompass feeling, thought and senses. Thus they are able to allow the audience to feel what I feel." Now a college junior majoring in film studies, Elyse still enjoys photography and hopes to be a film director. She took her photograph during her senior year in high school.

Peter Morgan graduated from college, majoring in American literature. He served as a resident assistant and a member of the Community Judicial Board. He was also involved in the college's student newspaper and Ultimate Frisbee team. His creative piece first appeared in *Teen Ink* magazine when he was a sophomore in high school. More recently, Peter has traveled to Italy and Alaska (where he was a back-country trail ranger) and has fought forest fires in Montana. He is currently pursuing a law degree and a master's in environmental science, but still finds time to enjoy reading and creative writing.

Sarah Nerboso is a junior in college. Since she wrote "Click Three Times" in the ninth grade, Sarah has gone on an exchange program to China, worked as a teen health educator and taught drama at local schools. When not reading, she works in theater and writes strange stories. She is currently torn between majoring in East Asian history, philosophy and political science.

Alison Nguyen just graduated from high school. She would love to be a psychoanalyst or a published author. She enjoys soccer, archery, acting, mock trial, reading Allen Ginsberg, procrastinating and, of course, writing. Her favorite foods? Sushi and orange Pez! She sends many thanks and much love to her family.

Flynn O'Brien, in addition to photography, is into water polo at college where he is majoring in art. He lives on an Air Force base with a lot of abandoned buildings. While exploring one, Flynn saw this door with its unusual glass. He told his brother to put his arm on it and stepping back, was lucky enough to have the photo work out! Flynn thanks Mrs. Sig for mentoring him through high school.

Jenny Pirkle likes working with language. Now a junior in college, she is majoring in English with an emphasis on writing and a minor in French. In high school, she served as the French club secretary. This telling poem was published in *Teen Ink* magazine when she was a junior. Jenny also enjoys acting and performed in, or did technical work for, every play performed during her high-school career. She continues to work backstage for her college's theater.

Sean Power was very interested in sports in high school, mainly baseball, but he also played soccer. He also was involved in the Big Brother/Big Sister program as a junior and senior. Currently he doesn't do very much writing outside of classes in college, where he is finishing his sophomore year, but Sean hopes to start some short-story writing and also perhaps a novel.

Nicole K. Press has done gymnastics for as long as she can remember and currently teaches children. She also volunteers at the Special Olympics. Nicole enjoys reading, writing, photography and being a techie for theater productions. She would like to design sets professionally. A recent high-school graduate, her insightful poem was published in *Teen Ink* magazine last year.

Alex Roan graduated from college with a degree in East Asian Studies. He is now in the process of saving the world. In his spare time, he enjoys sculpting to-scale models of famous landmarks using Silly Putty. Alex can recite the fifty states alphabetically in less than twenty seconds. He lives in one of the M states, which is before Michigan and after Maryland.

Brent Robitaille loves to read and, obviously, to write. In college he worked for his college newspaper, but his true passion is teaching. He plans to zero in on teaching high-school English after graduation. His creative fairy tale was first published in *Teen Ink* magazine when he was a senior in high school. He thanks his high-school English teacher for giving him the encouragement and inspiration needed to write and, perhaps, to teach.

Elayne Russell is finishing her freshman year of college, where she is constantly constructing slingshots to defend herself against the insane squirrels on campus! She plans to major in international relations, and enjoys watching Pee-Wee Herman movies and *I Love the '80s* on VH-1.

Allen Scaife is finishing high school this year. He says, "I've been writing since I could hold a crayon." He even has a column in his city's newspaper. Allen reads anything, from Phillip Pullman to Kurt Vonnegut, and loves to protest civil injustices. He is also into hip hop and enjoys making digital music.

Lisa Schottenfeld graduated from high school, where she was editor of the newspaper and literary magazine, and was involved with chorus and the debate group. She performed in many school theater productions. Her greatest passion is Shakespeare. Lisa was published many times in *Teen Ink* magazine. She wrote this poem during junior year, and three of her other poems have appeared in other *Teen Ink* books.

Meredith Ann Shepard mentions that the most exciting thing that ever happened to her was a six-month trip around the world traveling with her family to Nepal, Thailand, Greece and other European countries. She loves to write, read, dance and play the piano and is studying French. Both her favorite book and movie is *Lord of the Rings,* and her favorite actor is Elijah Wood. She thanks all of the teachers she's ever had, especially her first ones, her parents.

Matthew Siegel enjoys playing guitar and singing with any band he ends up in. His most memorable experience includes the look on his mother's face when he dyed his hair blue and the band he was in was kicked out of the school show for being "too loud." He loves going to concerts and making noise with instruments. He plans to continue writing in college and beyond. Matt thanks everyone who likes poetry.

Renata Silberblatt has come a long way since her early days of hating polyester. She no longer needs writing, but she often thinks about it. Renata's poem was published when she was a junior in high school. She would like to thank her half-sister's pet hamster, Carolena the Fourth for, above all else, living so very long. She is currently studying English in college with a minor in history and environmental studies.

Stephen Siperstein was a frequent contributor to *Teen Ink* magazine during high school. He has had his photographs exhibited in a local arts festival where he also won an essay contest. In high school he was a musician "to the core." He has been playing the guitar and piano for years, and has even taught children how to play. Currently a sophomore in college, he shoots primarily black and white and was a finalist in a national photo contest for *Photographer's Forum Magazine.*

Halsey D. Smith recently graduated from high school where she enjoyed art and snowboarding. Now she is following in her mother's footsteps to become an artist and is studying at the same school. She loves animals and has quite a menagerie in her small apartment: a dog, ferret, fish, turtle and rats, but wants to add a skunk! She took her photo of the broken window as a junior in high school when it appeared in *Teen Ink* magazine.

Jared Smith is the youngest of four and loves football, wrestling and track in high school where he is finishing his sophomore year. He is also very active in the 4-H Club and is currently raising a puppy for the Seeing Eye organization. He works part-time at a garden center and loves spending time with his friends.

Rebecca Olsen Snyder is finishing her undergraduate degree and will soon be starting her master's in social work. An intern at the Department of Child and Family Services, Rebecca works with girls just like the main character of her story. Recently married, she thanks her husband who encourages her to write, and she dedicates her piece "to my dear husband and family."

Melissa Sowin does her writing in her spare time, mostly in a journal, and saw her poem published in *Teen Ink* magazine, when she was a high-school senior. Although she's not sure about her future, she's studying psychology in college and enjoys sports, especially soccer and being outside. She also loves children and is a counselor for seven-year-old girls at a summer day camp.

David Steinhaus will be graduating from college this year with a degree in creative writing and film. In high school he played hockey and made movies with friends. He enjoys writing stories with a humorous tone. "Everyone likes to laugh and if I can allow the reader to do that, then they are happy and I've done my job. The most important thing to me is creativity, whether it is in writing or not. It is easy to do what everyone else has already done, but it is a billion times more fulfilling to come up with something that is all your own." David thanks his English teachers, Mrs. Walsh and Mrs. Moelter. His future goals: pursuing writing and humor, crabwalking across Canada and visiting Branson, Missouri!

Katelyn Stoler is studying English and music in college. Her piece, which won *Teen Ink*'s fiction contest a few years ago, was actually the first she'd ever written. Now she enjoys creating poems and loves reading (especially Sylvia Plath) and playing the piano.

Katie Stuart plays both varsity and club volleyball. A high school junior, she plans to major in psychology in college because people intrigue her and she enjoys helping others. Drawing people she knows is a hobby. This drawing was a random girl "who looked like she had a lot on her mind" that Katie wanted to capture. She dedicates her work to Jenny "who saved me from myself."

Amanda Sullivan is a junior in college now, doing honors work in psychology and sociology. She created her amazing design that appears on the cover through a technique called encaustics which uses special irons and heating implements with waxes to create vibrant art. Amanda worked on several pieces at once, using techniques and designs until she gets the effect she wanted.

Joyce Sun enjoyed a random set of activities during high school: Quiz Bowl, Youth in Government, helping with theater productions and falling down a lot while trying to play soccer as a freshman. This poem was conceived from a combination of having to write a school report on e. e. cummings and thinking about Times Square at night. She's now a senior in college, double-majoring in philosophy and cell biology, where her hobbies include sleeping, Web design and writing short stories after encountering Rainer Maria Rilke, who accomplished everything that she's ever wanted to do in poetry—but infinitely better and deeper.

Amy Tangsuan, a "Thai-American," claims she is the weird one in her family because she is the first to be born in the United States and the first to speak English without an accent. She is immensely proud of being a published author. (Her amusing story appeared in *Teen Ink* magazine when she was a senior in high school.) Now in college, she's very busy with the Asian Studies Union Web site, being a teaching assistant, as well as working in a biology lab. She's studying hard so she can add another first to her list: graduating with honors with a degree in biology.

Tarilyn M. Tanice just graduated from high school where she had many pieces published in *Teen Ink* magazine as well as other publications. She loves acting, singing and played Hedy La Rue in her school's production of "How to Succeed in Business Without Really Trying." Tarilyn plans to major in psychology and minor in theater arts at college.

Emily Tersoff is currently a junior in high school where she plays the violin in her school orchestra and fences. She loves to read, and her favorite book is Tolkien's *The Lord of the Rings.* Emily penned her story as a sixth-grader when it first appeared in *Teen Ink* magazine. Emily continues to love writing and, this past summer, she attended a science fiction/fantasy/horror writing workshop. She dedicates her piece to all of her friends, teachers and especially fellow Alphans who have helped her grow as a writer and a person.

Sara Thoi graduates from high school this spring where she was very involved in speech and debate, spending many of her weekends at tournaments where she really enjoyed meeting new people. She also participated in a program called Project Bridge where she traveled to Korea and discovered what it was like to be a "foreigner." The trip really expanded her horizons. In her spare time, she enjoys going to the beach (even though she doesn't swim), plays basketball and watches movies.

Caitlin Tumulty is currently a freshman in college in London, majoring in development studies, African studies and Swahili. She took her amazing photo as a high-school senior, "during a frantic photography session the day before the first assignment was due, and I haven't stopped photographing since." Caitlin hopes to combine her passion for travel and photography in Europe and Africa—with her camera in tow, of course!

Joanie Twersky has been writing for quite some time and is now a senior in college. Aside from writing, she has been active in many community organizations, including soup kitchens, fundraisers, a crisis hotline and a shelter. She really enjoys meeting all kinds of people, anyone with a story to tell. She agrees with Gandhi, who said, "You must be the change that you wish to see in the world."

Kathryn Walat was a high-school senior when her poem was published in *Teen Ink* magazine. Since then, she's graduated from college as a creative-writing major, worked in New York as a theater journalist, and is currently a playwriting M.F.A. student at the Yale School of Drama. Even though she's concentrating on the theater now, she credits her high-school poems with starting her life as a writer.

Devon Wallace loves college. "It is a little utopia for me. I am surrounded by wonderful people." She is still writing and credits her experience of being published in *Teen Ink* magazine with giving her a lot of confidence. Her fiction piece was published when Devon was a senior in high school and resulted in the thrill of interviewing R. L. Stine as a winner of the *Teen Ink* interview contest.

Katie M. Weiss is majoring in nursing and Spanish as a junior in college. Her sweet poem about her brother was published in *Teen Ink* magazine when she was a sophomore in high school, where she was very active in soccer and lacrosse as well as being a member of the model congress and captain of the volunteer ambulance youth corps.

Brandon R. Wilke is studying mechanical engineering in college, although he still enjoys writing when he has the chance. He spends most of his time doing schoolwork, but is a huge sports buff following Major League Baseball religiously. One of his favorite pastimes is participating in fantasy sports leagues on the Internet. He's a normal guy who enjoys hanging out with his friends and family and watching movies. He dedicates his poem (which appeared in *Teen Ink* magazine when he was a high-school senior) to his grandfather, who made that trip possible. "We'll always remember the day you caught a tree."

Amanda Youmell is a very strong advocate of two goals: college and travelling. She believes that everyone should take advantage of college because it encourages taking risks and broadens one's horizons while providing an infrastructure. She writes, "There IS a way, and there IS funding." She also believes you should start saving now to buy a car and some money so you can travel! She thanks *Teen Ink* for creating a place where teens can see their work in print, and she encourages all writers who have not yet been published to keep writing.

Cory Zwerlein is finishing his freshman year studying architecture. A runner in high school, he has continued in college. His favorite place is

Ketchum, Idaho where he loves to ski. His staircase was inspired by one designed by Michelangelo. He thanks his talented and motivating high-school art teacher, who started him on this art-related career path. Cory also sends a special thanks to his family who always support him in his decisions and encourage him to give his best.